By Mike Mullin

Tanglewood • Terre Haute, IN

Cover photograph by Ana Correal
Design by Amy Alick Perich

Tanglewood Publishing
1060 North Capital Avenue, E395
Indianapolis, IN 46204
www.tanglewoodbooks.com

Printed by Maple-Vail Press, York, PA, USA
10 9 8 7 6 5

ISBN: 978-1-933718-98-9

Library of Congress Cataloging-in-Publication Data

Mullin, Mike.
   Ashen winter / Mike Mullin.
      p. cm.
   Summary: More than six months after the eruption of the Yellowstone supervolcano, Alex and Darla retrace their steps to Iowa hoping to find Alex's parents and bring them to the tenuous safety of Illinois, but the journey is ever more perilous as the remaining communities fight to the death for food and power.
   ISBN 978-1-933718-75-0 (hardback) -- ISBN 1-933718-75-7 ()
   [1. Volcanoes--Fiction. 2. Survival--Fiction. 3. Science fiction.] I. Title.
   PZ7.M9196Arm 2012
   [Fic]--dc23
                              2012010148

For Mom

Chapter 1

Ten months had passed since I'd last seen the sun. The rich blue of that final August sky was fading from my memory. Colors are slippery: If you cover your eyes and try to remember blue, you see black. Now we had a yellowish gray sky, dark as a heavily overcast day. Darla said Yellowstone's eruption had hurled billions of tons of fine ash and sulfur dioxide into the stratosphere, and it might be years before the sky returned to normal. I said the dim light was depressing.

In April, we prayed for a break in the winter, a warm spell to melt the four-foot blanket of snow smothering my uncle's farm. But April was colder than March, May colder still. In June, the mercury in the Farmall tractor thermometer hanging outside the kitchen window fell below zero and stayed there. Every day we watched the thin red line try to claw its way to zero. Every day it failed.

No more snow fell, but none melted, either. We'd run out of Chapstick months before. For a while we all wore my Aunt Caroline's lipstick, but now that was gone, too, and our lips were cracked and bloody from the dry winter air. The storms that had followed the eruption had spent their fury, and drought clutched us in its dry fist. My world was frozen, desiccated, and dead.

I was always cold. Cold as I worked during the day—cutting wood, hauling snow to melt for water, or digging for the corn buried under the snow and ash. Cold when I went to bed. Cold when I got up in the morning despite Darla snuggled against my side.

Before the volcano, if you'd told me that I'd be sleeping every night beside a girl I loved, I'd have said you were crazy. Mom would've filleted me and served the choice bits as hors d'oeuvres if I'd ever so much as closed the door with a girl in my room. Not that any girls would've wanted to be alone with me. Before I met Darla, I'd had a total of one real girlfriend, and she dumped me before we'd done much more than make out.

I still didn't think of myself as having a girlfriend. That word was too trivial for what Darla meant to me. When I met her on the road last year, I was bleeding, starving, and ready to give up. Ready to die. Without each other, we wouldn't have escaped from Iowa, from the devastation and chaos Yellowstone had caused. Now I wouldn't want to survive—to endure the desperate labor and daily frostbite—without Darla.

But if Mom showed up now, fillet knife in hand, to scold me for sleeping next to Darla, I'd hug her and savor every second of the scolding. She and Dad had left my uncle's farm near Warren, Illinois, leaving my younger sister Rebecca there with my aunt and uncle. Darla and I had arrived at the farm in early October, five weeks after my parents had left to look for me. No one had seen or heard from them since.

And Mom wouldn't find me sleeping *alone* with Darla, anyway. In April, the falling temperature had forced us to abandon the upstairs bedrooms at my uncle's. Now Darla and I slept in a clump with my aunt, uncle, two cousins, and sister on the living room floor near the fire. A night spent spooning with your girlfriend isn't nearly so exciting when your uncle is curled up against your other side.

We got the idea to sleep together from the ducks— they'd been doing it all winter. But a few days after we started imitating them, one of the ducks on the outside of their pile in the barn froze to death. So we cleared everything out of the main floor guest room, adjacent to the living room, and started keeping the ducks and goats inside at night. Our sleep was occasionally interrupted by quacks and bleats. And I never got used to the stench of the billies. Male goats stink worse than skunks.

"Earth to Alex," Darla said, drawing my attention back to the barn where we were working. "Would the former planet known as Alex please come in?"

"Former planet?" I asked.

"Yeah. I demoted you."

"Like Pluto? What am I now?"

"Um, a dwarf planet, I think?"

"Hey! I'm not that short."

"Whatever. Hold this wedge."

I took one of the wooden wedges we'd just cut and held it against the crack between the runner and bedstones of our grain mill. Darla softly tapped the wedge in my hand with a hammer, barely inserting its tip between the stones. I picked up another wedge, and we worked our way around the mill, trying to pry the runner stone free with careful, even pressure.

Darla had built this bicycle-powered gristmill not long after we arrived at the farm. In the bitter cold the night before, the stones had frozen together. Now we were trying to separate them without cracking the runner stone. Replacing it would take more than a week's labor.

Holding wedges for Darla left a lot of time to think. We were planning a birthday party for my cousin Max that night. He was turning thirteen. Everyone but Aunt Caroline and I had celebrated a birthday since I arrived on the farm. Darla had turned eighteen—two years older than I. Well, really just a year and a half.

While Darla and I worked on the gristmill, Max, Anna, and Rebecca were in the greenhouses caring for our crop of kale. It was worth its weight in gold now—more, actually, since gold was almost worthless. You couldn't eat gold or build anything useful with it, after all. Kale, by contrast, would grow even if the temperature in the greenhouses got close to freezing. And kale has tons of vitamin C, the only cure for scurvy, which had become an epidemic since the eruption.

When the weather had grown so cold that even the kale started to die, Darla designed a wood-fired heating system for the greenhouses. She found a description of a similar system, a hypocaust, in one of my cousin Anna's books, *Built to Last*. It had taken almost a month of back-breaking labor to build. A frozen dirt ramp led down to an enclosed oven-like space where we built a fire every night. A metal door with a small air intake covered the fire shelf. Smoke and hot air from the fire flowed up into a winding series of ducts buried under all three greenhouses, eventually escaping at the far side. That way, the fire heated the ground under our kale without filling the greenhouses with smoke. On the downside, we had to keep the fire outside the greenhouses burning every night.

So we had to cut more wood. Luckily, my uncle's farm backed up against Apple River Canyon State Park. We never would have cut its trees in normal times, but now we had no choice.

That's where Uncle Paul and Aunt Caroline had gone that day—to the edge of the leafless forest to cut firewood. Darla said they were going out there to get some "alone" time, but that didn't seem likely to me. It was way too cold to expose any more skin than you absolutely had to.

A crack of gunfire brought me crashing back to earth.

Darla froze and locked eyes with me. Then we heard Anna scream.

Darla dropped her hammer, and we dashed to the side door of the barn—the one that faced the greenhouses. I eased it ajar and peered out.

Four men wearing ski masks and ragged forest camouflage were clustered around the door to one of our greenhouses. Max lay face down, a wide arc of blood staining the snow beside him. One of the men was prodding Max with his toe, his handgun trained on Max's head. A man wearing a bright blue scarf had Anna on the ground, his knee in the small of her back. He was tying a gag around her head. The third seemed to be supervising everything—holding a shotgun at the ready. The last had a machine pistol trained on Rebecca. Even from a distance, I could see her shaking.

I held my clenched fists against my roiling stomach, as if to hold it in, to hold myself together. Max. Was he dead? He wasn't moving.

"I'm going for help," Darla said, and she was gone, racing for the main barn door, which faced away from the greenhouses.

Get it together, Alex, I told myself. Darla's getting help. Maybe there's something you can do in the meantime.

The bandits were preoccupied with their task—none of them were looking my way. I opened the side door wider, dropped to my belly, and slithered through. Immediately I wormed off the trodden path into the deep snow. The snow slowed me down, but it also hid me.

When I thought I was close, I cautiously raised my head above the level of the snow. The bandits had a homemade toboggan, laden with lumpy canvas bags. They'd gagged and bound Anna and Rebecca, stacking them on the toboggan like cordwood. Machine Pistol was leaving one of the greenhouses with a plastic sack overflowing with kale. He'd harvested it so fast that he'd pulled up the roots. Blue Scarf stepped over to Max's body, hefted it, and tossed it on top of the load. Blood pulsed from Max's temple.

I blinked repeatedly, but my eyelids couldn't clear the gruesome scene. My body was coiled tight, caught on a knife edge between two fears: I needed to help Max, to see if he was even alive, but I couldn't move, couldn't approach the sled without being seen.

The four bandits grabbed a knotted rope and started hauling the toboggan away. Max's blood drew an erratic pink streak in the snow. I couldn't let them abduct my sister and cousins. Rebecca was the only family I had left. I'd rather die than lie there in the snow and watch her being taken. I had a black belt in taekwondo. I'd been forced to use it during my flight from Iowa last year. But trying to fight four of them at once? Suicide.

Suddenly it struck me: All I had to do was slow them down until Darla came with help. If I could get them to talk . . . I stood up. "Stop!" I shouted.

All four of them turned. Three gun barrels swiveled toward me. I sent fruitless orders to my knees to be still.

"Leave the girls. Take me instead." I was relieved my voice didn't quaver. Much.

Handgun stalked toward me until he was less than
thirty feet away. His mouth twisted in a cruel leer, and he
raised his gun, aiming at my head.

Chapter 2

I was dead. He was too far away for me to rush him, too close for the bullet to miss. Trying to talk was a stupid idea—the last stupid decision I'd get to make.

A gun barked. Handgun was thrown sideways, arms splayed, as blood bloomed at the side of his chest. I glanced left. Darla was about 100 feet off, kneeling in the snow, her eye sighting down the length of Uncle Paul's hunting rifle.

Shotgun raised his weapon, business end pointed at me. Max, whom I'd feared was dead, punched at the bandit, aiming for his groin. He missed, hitting Shotgun in the hip. The gun wavered and boomed.

My side felt like it had been stung by a dozen angry hornets, though most of the pellets flew wide, peppering the snow beside me.

Another rifle shot rang out. The bullet caught Shotgun square in the chest and threw him backward against the toboggan.

I was running forward without ever having made a conscious decision to charge. I had to get to Machine Pistol before he started spraying bullets everywhere.

Blue Scarf turned and ran. Machine Pistol hesitated, then stepped backward and raised his gun at me. Darla shot again but missed. I put everything I had into my insane charge, screaming at the top of my lungs. Maybe he'd just shoot me instead of spraying Max and the girls.

Instead, he lowered his gun and fled.

Darla fired again. Machine Pistol stumbled, but collected himself and kept running.

I staggered to Max, my body trembling with fear and adrenaline. A bullet had carved a narrow trough along his temple. Blood soaked the side of his hat, scarves, and coat.

"Get the hell out of my field of fire!" Darla screamed.

I ducked, hoping she could fire past both of us. Bright red blood poured from Max's head, gushing in time with his heartbeat. I hesitated a moment, unsure what to do. A year ago I would have screamed for help and called 911. Now nobody but Darla would hear me scream. The phone wouldn't work, and even if it did, there was no one to answer it.

I knew how to stop the bleeding—put a clean cloth over

it and apply pressure. But what if his skull were cracked? Wouldn't pushing on it make it worse, maybe kill him?

I stripped off my gloves and started probing the wound as gently as I could with my fingertips. Max moaned. He was shaking and sweating despite the cold. My hands dripped blood.

Darla was alongside the sled now, kneeling in the snow and firing at the fleeing bandits.

Max's temple was firm under my fingertips—which I hoped meant his skull wasn't broken. I ripped off one of my scarves and pressed it against his head.

"They're in the south hollow, running like wild rabbits," Darla said as she lifted the rifle and stood. She took the knife off her belt and started cutting Rebecca and Anna free.

"This wound is going to have to be sewn up," I told her.

"I can do it," Darla said—she'd stitched up a vicious wound in my side last year.

"I think we should get Dr. McCarthy. What if he's got a concussion or a break I didn't find?"

"Okay," she replied.

"Rebecca?" I asked. "You okay?" She didn't look okay. She was trembling and rubbing her wrists.

"Not really," she said. "What should I do?"

"Can you run to the woods and get Aunt Caroline and Uncle Paul?"

She took a deep breath. "I'll be right back." She took two tentative steps toward the house, and then changed direction, sprinting for the woods.

Max's blood had already soaked through my scarf. Darla handed me one of hers, and I wrapped it around his head as tightly as I could.

Anna was crouched with her hands covering her inner thighs. I saw a spot of wetness around one of her hands.

"Anna," I said softly. "It's okay. I peed myself the first time I met bandits last year."

"You did?"

"Yeah, I did." It wasn't true. I'd thrown up. But I needed Anna's help. "Can you take care of your brother while Darla and I get Dr. McCarthy?"

Anna nodded.

"Your mom and dad will be back soon. Tell them we've gone to get the doctor, and we'll be right back, okay?"

She nodded again. I tied the second scarf around Max's head, and we carried him into the house and laid him on the floor by the living room fireplace. I grabbed a couple of spare scarves while Darla told Anna how to care for Max. As we ran toward the barn, I passed one scarf to Darla and wrapped the other one around my neck. It was one of Aunt Caroline's—bright orange-red and not particularly warm. Better than nothing. We threw open the barn doors and dragged out Bikezilla.

That's what I'd dubbed Darla's snowmobile. She'd built it not long after she finished the gristmill. The snowmobile was a tandem bike frame with a ski attached to the front fork where the tire had been. Darla had scavenged a track off a real snowmobile and installed it in place of the bicycle's rear wheel. Above that she built a small wooden load bed, almost like a pickup truck's.

A real snowmobile would have been a lot faster, but we couldn't get gas. The meager amount still stored in the tanks at Warren's only gas station was reserved for emergencies.

We'd been using Bikezilla for the last six months to haul kale to Warren to trade for pork. Warren had thousands of frozen hog carcasses stored, since there were several slaughterhouses nearby. Bikezilla wasn't as fast as a real bicycle, but it could handle deep snow okay, and the load bed could carry plenty of pork. On the icy road to Warren, it was at least twice as fast as running.

Darla and I stood up on the bike for the whole trip, kicking the pedals down. We had no extra breath for talking. My side hurt where the shotgun pellets had hit, and I felt a warm spot of blood soaking into my T-shirt. I gritted my teeth and ignored it.

Darla and I slid up to the clinic, beating our previous best time to Warren by five or six minutes. I could tell Dr. McCarthy was in because I saw his '41 Studebaker Champion parked around back.

We charged into the small, one-story clinic. Dr. McCarthy was in an exam room, chatting with a patient by the light of an oil lamp. When I told him what was wrong, he got his assistant to take over. "You want to ride along?" he asked.

"No," I said. "We'll ride back. I don't want to leave Bikezilla." I didn't think it would get stolen in Warren, but I didn't want to take that chance, either.

By the time we got back to the farm, Dr. McCarthy was almost done stitching up Max. Aunt Caroline was assisting him. The injured side of Max's head had been shaved. He was biting down on a leather-wrapped stick, since Dr. McCarthy had run out of painkillers months ago. I wondered if it was the same stick that Uncle Paul had bitten when Dr. McCarthy had set his broken leg the year before. The leather was scarred by dozens of bite marks.

"He okay?" I asked.

"Seems to be," Aunt Caroline answered. Dr. McCarthy was concentrating on his stitches. "He might be concussed. Although with Max, how would you know if his brains were scrambled?" She was smiling as she said it, but unbidden tears spilled from her eyes.

"Maybe instead of scrambling his brains the bullet knocked them back into working order," I said.

"I'm still here," Max grunted through clenched teeth.

"I know you are, honey." The gratitude in Aunt Caroline's voice was palpable.

"A leather-wrapped stick is a pretty crappy birthday present," I said.

Max grunted. I couldn't tell if he was agreeing or just annoyed at my lame joke.

Aunt Caroline broke the short silence. "Max said you just walked up to those bandits, Alex."

"Pretty much."

"That was stupid."

"Yeah. But I knew Darla was getting help. I'm just lucky she decided to get the rifle instead of going to get you guys."

Dr. McCarthy tied off the last stitch in Max's head.

"Hey, Doc, can you take a look at my side?" I asked.

"What's wrong with your side?" Darla said.

"Well, that shotgun—"

"You got hit? And you didn't tell me?" She was practically yelling.

"I thought you could tell from the holes in my coat."

"Shut up. Your clothing's so ragged nobody'd notice a few extra holes. And we rode all the way to—lie down on that couch right now, you jerk!"

I obeyed. When Darla was that angry, doing anything else was insane.

She started stripping my clothing, muttering all the while, "Stupid, pigheaded, obstinate, obnoxious, oviparous, egg-sucking boy." I both laid and sucked eggs? That didn't make sense. Whatever.

Most of the shotgun pellets hadn't penetrated my five layers of clothing. I had eight or nine purplish bruises and three blood-encrusted holes on the side of my belly. All three holes were below the huge, horseshoe-shaped scar where Darla had stitched up the hatchet wound a prison escapee named Target had inflicted on me the year before.

"What, are you collecting scars on that side of your body?" Darla said.

"I guess."

"Well, quit. The spot I stitched up is enough."

"That's a pretty rough-looking patch job," Dr. McCarthy commented.

Darla scowled. "Like to see you do better with an old sewing needle."

"I probably couldn't." Dr. McCarthy took the leather-

wrapped stick from Max, wiped it on a cloth, and gave it to
me to bite. He dropped a scalpel and scissor-like pair of
tongs he called a hemostat into a pan of water boiling over
the living room fire. While we waited for his tools to be
sterilized, he gently wiped away the dried blood on my side.

When he slit the side of the first wound, it didn't hurt
much. But then he started digging around in the hole.
Tears leaked from my eyes. When he got the hemostat
clamped on the pellet and pulled it free, I just about
launched off the couch to slug him. Darla grabbed my
hand, and I clung to her, trying not to move. Then we had
to repeat the whole procedure. Twice.

Dr. McCarthy didn't stitch up the holes. He just put a
bandage over them and taped it in place. "Guess you all get
a bulk discount today."

"I guess." Aunt Caroline sighed. "I'll get you some
supplies."

"Got any eggs?"

"A few. Some goat meat, too." Aunt Caroline stood up.

"Where's everybody else?" Darla asked.

"Out by the greenhouses," Aunt Caroline answered.

"I'll go see if Paul needs help," Darla said.

"Let me get dressed," I said. "I'll come, too."

"You need to rest," Darla said.

"If I can bike all the way to Warren with three shotgun pellets in my side, I can walk to the greenhouses
without them."

"Tell him to rest, would you please?" Darla begged Dr.
McCarthy.

"He won't listen to me, anyway. Just stay with him and don't let him do any heavy lifting for a couple days."

Darla scowled, but she got a clean T-shirt out of a basket in the corner of the room and tossed it at me.

As we approached the greenhouses, I saw Rebecca's and Anna's silhouettes moving around inside. Uncle Paul was bent over the toboggan, sorting through the bandits' supplies.

"Did you find the shotgun?" I asked.

"Shotgun?" Uncle Paul said. "One of them had a little .22 pistol in his hand."

I pointed at the other corpse lying in the snow. "He had a shotgun." I walked over to the body. A huge red stain had spread from the hole in the guy's chest to the surrounding snow, and the blood had already started to freeze. I looked around. Sure enough, there was a long depression in a snowdrift on the far side of the toboggan. The shotgun must have flown out of his hands and buried itself in the snow when Darla shot him.

I pulled the shotgun free and wiped the snow off it with my shirttail. Someone had painted four tiny blue flowers on the wooden stock. They seemed incongruous— too delicate to decorate a weapon of war. Amid the flowers, two words were drawn in fancy script: "Blue Betsy."

"Weird," I said to Darla. "Who decorates their shotgun with flowers?"

Darla shrugged.

"Decorates? With flowers?" Uncle Paul said. "Blue flowers? Let me see."

I passed the shotgun to him.

"How did—"

"What is it?"

"Remember I told you I traded a pair of goats for a shotgun and gave it to your dad? And he took it with him when he left here last year?"

"Yeah . . . ?" I said.

"This is it, Alex. The shotgun he took when he left for Iowa last fall. When he went to search for you."

Chapter 3

I collapsed into the snowbank. Not a good idea when it's below zero. But I didn't notice the cold—I was too numb.

"You okay?" Uncle Paul asked.

"I guess," I said.

"Give us a minute," Darla said as she sat down in the snow beside me.

Uncle Paul nodded. "I'm going to help Rebecca and Anna replant the kale those bastards pulled up," he mumbled as he shuffled off.

Darla turned to me. "You okay?"

"What does it mean? Is Dad dead? Why else would

this guy have his shotgun?" I punched at a clump of snow.

"I don't know."

"Maybe Dad sold it. Or traded it for something. He could be alive, right?"

"Yeah, he could."

We sat in silence.

After a while, Darla asked, "Why'd you stand up in front of those guys?"

"I was trying to talk to them. To delay them." In the rush to take care of Max and get Dr. McCarthy, I hadn't really thought about the fight. "You saved my life again."

"Yeah, what's that now, forty-seven times?" Darla shrugged.

"About."

"You have a serious talent for needing to be saved."

"I guess. Thanks."

"Trying to talk to those guys was stupid. I wasn't ready to shoot yet."

"I couldn't let them walk off with the kids. And you got ready in time."

Darla grabbed my collar, pulling me closer and yelling in my face. "Yeah, but Christ, you scared me! What if I'd missed? You do anything that idiotic again and I'll shoot you myself to save the heartache of watching someone else do it."

"Sorry." I really hadn't been thinking too clearly. Obviously. But still . . .

"And I still don't get why the guy with the machine pistol didn't perforate your sad hide."

"He was unnerved by my crazy taekwondo charge?" I forced a smile.

Darla glared. "You have a death wish or something?"

"No. Crappy as this world is, I don't want to leave it." I reached out and squeezed her hand. "Don't want to leave you."

Suddenly she rolled on top of me, yanking our scarves out of the way and kissing me. Darla pressed her body into mine, burying me in the snow. Her weight, slight though it was, hurt my side. I ignored the pain, wrapping my arms around her and trying to keep up. The kiss lasted for a dizzying minute. When she came up for air, she said, "Don't you ever do something like that again."

"If it means I get another kiss like that, I might."

Darla slugged my shoulder, hard enough to bruise.

"Got it," I said. "Shouldn't we be helping Uncle Paul?"

Darla stood, offered me her hand, and pulled me up. We made our way through the two plastic doors that formed an airlock for the greenhouse. It was relatively warm in there, which was good—I was freezing after being half-buried in snow by Darla.

Most of the kale had come out of the soft, moist greenhouse soil with its roots intact, so we could replant it. When we found a plant with badly damaged roots, we harvested the leaves, saving the stems and roots for the goats.

"Will the kale regrow?" I asked Uncle Paul as the five of us walked back toward the house.

"I think most of it will be okay." He laid a hand on my shoulder. "You sure you're okay?"

"Yeah." I thought for a moment, picking my next words carefully. "I'm going to leave. To look for Mom and Dad." I glanced at Darla and was relieved to see her nod.

"How will you find them?" Uncle Paul asked.

"I'll track down the two bandits who got away."

"They aren't going to volunteer the info you want just because you ask them to," Uncle Paul said.

"We'll bring guns," Darla replied dryly. "Those are pretty convincing."

There was a long pause in the conversation as we approached the house. Eventually Uncle Paul nodded. "I'll start sorting out supplies for you. You'll want to get moving at first light so they don't get too far ahead."

I held the storm door for my uncle and Darla. "Maybe we should leave now?"

"Better if you get a good night's sleep. They won't be traveling tonight either—their torches are still on the toboggan."

The scene inside the house was positively tranquil after all the craziness of that day. Dr. McCarthy was gone. Aunt Caroline was sitting on the floor beside Max, holding a cup of water to his lips while Rebecca stirred a bowl of corn porridge.

"What's this about traveling?" Aunt Caroline said to Uncle Paul.

"How's Max?" Uncle Paul asked.

"He's fine. Tell me what you're talking about."

"Alex and Darla are leaving in the morning." Uncle Paul frowned. "One of those bandits had Blue Betsy."

"What? No." Aunt Caroline sloshed water across

Max's face, and he spluttered. "There's no way we can keep up with all the work without Alex and Darla. And what if we get attacked again? What if they attack the house next time?"

"We'll have to manage," Uncle Paul replied. "We can board up all the windows on the ground floor, put bars on the doors, too."

"Your leg isn't completely healed from the fall and—"

"I've been off the crutches for more than a month, hon," Uncle Paul said, clearly exasperated.

"I know, but you're still limping."

"Not much. The muscles are weak, that's all. It's getting better."

"They're still kids. We can't let them go running around in this mess—they'll get killed."

"I'm eighteen." Darla folded her arms over her chest. "And Alex isn't a kid anymore, whatever his age."

"Why do you guys keep talking about Alex and Darla?" Rebecca said. "I'm going, too." She folded her arms, mimicking Darla so closely that it might have been funny except for her grim expression.

"Rebecca, no." I said, as gently as I could manage.

She turned on me. "You think it was fun, waiting for you last year? Thinking you were dead? And then Mom and Dad left, and I thought I'd lost everyone, my whole family, gone. I'm not going through that again."

"I know it's hard," I said, "but Aunt Caroline is right—she and Uncle Paul need help. Darla and I wouldn't be leaving now except for that shotgun."

"Darla can stay. They're not her parents."

"I'm going," Darla said flatly.

"Then I am, too," Rebecca said, although she sounded far less certain than Darla.

I shook my head, scowling. I understood how she felt—I didn't like being treated like a kid, and really, none of us were kids anymore. We spent our time struggling to survive, not going to school or playing games. But if she got hurt—or God forbid, killed—looking for our parents, I'd never forgive myself.

Rebecca looked down and whispered, "I . . . don't want to be alone again."

"I know." I pulled her into a hug. "But you won't be alone. You'll take care of Max and Anna. And help your aunt and uncle."

"Yeah," she murmured, holding onto me. "But you better come back."

"You and Darla had best get some sleep," Uncle Paul said. "Caroline and I will get your packs ready. I'll wake you before dawn."

I let go of Rebecca, and Darla took my hand, pulling me toward the kitchen. "Let's get washed up."

That night, I lay awake in bed for more than an hour. Darla was on one side of me; Rebecca, Max, and Anna on the other. My aunt and uncle still hadn't come to bed. The kids called out or moaned occasionally in their sleep— nightmares, I assumed.

From her breathing, I could tell Darla wasn't sleeping, either. I put an arm over her shoulder and hugged her closer. "You okay?" I whispered.

Her body heaved and she choked back a sob.

"It's okay," I whispered. "Shh. You don't have to be tough all the time."

"I . . . I never killed anyone before."

"I know." I stroked her back.

"It's not like killing a rabbit or pig."

"No."

"Does it get better?"

I thought about Ferret and Target—bandits I'd killed during our escape from Iowa last year. They still occasionally starred in my own nightmares. "No."

Darla snuggled against my shoulder. I couldn't hear her crying, but I felt the tears washing my neck. It was a long time before she fell asleep.

My side ached and my thoughts raced. I stared into the darkness, thinking about my trip from Cedar Falls last year, about all the people who'd helped me during my journey.

My thoughts turned to Mom and Dad. I couldn't call up a clear picture of either of them. I mean, I knew what they looked like, but the images were blurry. I lay awake, struggling to remember my parents' faces until Uncle Paul called to me in the grayness just before dawn.

Chapter 4

We ate a huge breakfast. Duck eggs scrambled with kale from our farm and ham we'd gotten in trade from Warren. Everyone was silent, like they had so much to say, they couldn't decide where to start. It made me uncomfortable, so I wolfed my food and excused myself.

Bikezilla's load bed was packed with bags and bundles. Darla untied the ropes holding down the load and started poking through it.

"I packed everything you'll need," Uncle Paul said.

"Doesn't hurt to check," Darla replied.

The pistol and the shotgun, Blue Betsy, were

there along with a box of shells. I was a little surprised. That gun, with the extra ammo, was worth a fortune. People everywhere were hoarding weapons, so their value had skyrocketed since the eruption. By now, the shotgun and shells were probably worth as much as a small herd of goats or a flock of egg-laying ducks.

The shotgun wasn't the most valuable thing Uncle Paul had given us, though. Twenty small envelopes made from pages of an old Dan Brown novel were tucked into a cloth pouch. Each envelope contained two hundred care-fully counted kale seeds. One packet like these had been enough to buy the snowmobile, tandem bike, *and* a weld-ing rig in Warren. If, before the eruption, someone had handed me a briefcase stuffed with hundred-dollar bills, it would have been about this valuable.

I stared at the bundle, shocked into silence.

Darla tilted her head toward Uncle Paul. "You sure?"

He nodded. "I saved enough for a safety margin. And we'll let a third of the next crop go to seed. We'll be okay."

"I don't know what to say," Darla said.

"You and Alex may not be married, and he may not be my son, but we're all family—you, too. We take care of our own."

Darla's eyes shone in the dawn light as she turned away.

Uncle Paul pulled her into a rough hug. "You come back. Find my brother and his wife, if they're alive. And bring that boy home, too."

"I will," she said. "I will."

"I'm right here," I said. "I'll bring myself home."

Darla and Uncle Paul looked at me in the exact same way. Yeah, right, their faces said.

I decided to change the subject. The pistol the bandit had used to shoot Max lay amid the bundles on Bikezilla's bed. I picked it up. "How's this work?"

"I'm amazed it works at all," Uncle Paul said. "I stripped it down and oiled it, but it's a piece of junk—a Saturday-night special."

"You test fire it?" Darla asked.

"Nope. There's only one magazine with four bullets. I could get more .22 pistol ammo in Warren, maybe, but I don't have any here."

"We should try it anyway," Darla said. "Better to have three bullets we know work than four we're not sure of."

"It worked on Max's head yesterday. Wish it hadn't. But go ahead if you want."

"I've never fired anything but a rifle or shotgun," Darla said as she took the pistol from me.

"It's a semi-automatic," Uncle Paul said. "Safety's on the side. Rack the slide to chamber a round."

Darla clicked the safety to "Fire," pulled the slide on top of the weapon toward her, and released it. She held the pistol in a two-handed grip and aimed at a patch of snow about ten yards off. She squeezed the trigger and I put my hands over my ears, expecting a bang. But the gun just clicked. Darla looked at Uncle Paul.

"Misfire," he said. "I was afraid of that. The ammo looked old."

Darla tried to squeeze the trigger again, but nothing happened.

"Rack the slide to eject the dud."

Darla ejected the bullet, aimed, and squeezed the trigger again. Pop! It wasn't much of a noise, even for such a small gun. A spray of snow kicked into the air where the bullet struck.

"Well, two bullets left. Which might or might not actually fire. You may as well keep it." She thumbed the safety on and handed it butt first to Uncle Paul.

"No, you keep it. Maybe you'll be able to trade it for something. Or buy some decent ammo."

Darla started repacking. In addition to the guns, Uncle Paul had given us a huge supply of cornmeal and dried pork, a tent, a large sleeping bag, extra blankets, extra clothing, a coil of rope, two pots, four water jugs, two spoons, a medical kit, old road maps of Illinois and Iowa, a small pair of binoculars, a lamp with an extra bottle of oil, a couple of homemade candles, and a fire-starting kit with a chunk of flint and a mess of dry, shredded oak bark.

I had a hatchet and a five-inch Bowie knife on my belt. I carried the *jahng bong*, or staff, I'd made not long after I'd reached the farm eight months ago. The staff had always been one of my favorite taekwondo weapons. I snagged the package of kale seeds and tucked it into the inside pocket of my coat, against my chest. Darla slid both guns and my staff under the ropes on top of the load so we could get at them in a hurry if we needed to.

Then we said our goodbyes. I hugged everyone in turn—my aunt, uncle, and sister. I'd said goodbye to my cousins Max and Anna earlier. Max was still too woozy to get up, and Anna was keeping an eye on him.

By this time, I was itching to get moving. I straddled the bike's back seat. I figured Darla should be in front, because she'd be better at spotting the trail than I would. Plus the view was better from the back seat of Bikezilla. Not that there was much to look at—Darla was wearing heavy winter coveralls, and her luscious dark hair was wrapped in hats and scarves. But still.

The biggest problem with Bikezilla was getting it started. Darla and I had to stand on the pedals, straining against our handlebars, just to get it inching forward. Once we got it going, though, we sailed across the snow.

I glanced back. My family had receded to tiny figures, indistinguishable from each other. They were already dispersing to start their morning chores. The land around us was low, rolling hills suffocated under the never-ending burden of ash and snow. Occasionally the sad remnant of a tree protruded from the snow, its branches broken and leafless.

Darla clicked into a higher gear and we sat down, settling into a ground-eating pace. My side hurt, but I ignored the pain as best I could, and soon it dwindled to a numb ache.

I thought we'd have to move slowly to track the bandits, but if anything, Darla was speeding up. I craned my neck to peer around her and figured out why. The bandits had left a trail of trampled snow heading roughly south across the fields. Every thirty or forty feet, a few drops of blood stained the snow—easy to see against the nearly featureless white expanse.

We raced along the trail for a half hour or so before it intersected a twelve-foot-high snowbank that ran north and south as far as I could see. Darla stopped Bikezilla beside it. Deep leg holes had been punched into the snow. Our two bandits had struggled across the bank directly in front of us. One of them had been leaking blood, staining the snow pink. I stood on the pedals, trying to get enough height to see over the berm. "Can't see over. Scout it on foot?"

"Yeah, guess so."

We dismounted Bikezilla and clambered over the snow berm.

On the other side there was a road, plowed but not salted. A fine dusting of snow blew over the icy surface the plow had left. It looked little-used, which wasn't surprising: Nobody but FEMA had much gas anymore. Keeping the roads clear was about the only useful thing FEMA, the Federal Emergency Management Agency, was doing—they were often more of a danger than a help to survivors.

"Well, they didn't cross here," Darla said as she inspected the far side of the road.

Between the packed surface and blowing snow, no footprints were visible anymore. Figuring they'd probably keep going in the same general direction, I wandered south. About 50 feet down the road, a drop of blood stained the snow. I turned and discovered that Darla had been following me.

"They're heading south, away from Warren. How are we going to get Bikezilla across that mountain of snow?" I asked as we walked back to the bike.

"Get up some speed and jump it, maybe?"

"Jump it?" It sounded more like a formula for a wreck than a plan.

"Yeah, sure. Didn't you ever watch snowmobile races on TV?

"Um, no."

"You're weird. Snowmobile races are the best. Were, anyway." Her voice sounded uncharacteristically nostalgic.

"If you say so." I climbed onto Bikezilla's back seat.

We strained to get the bike moving, and Darla steered us in a wide arc until we were lined up perpendicular to the snowbank. She shifted into a higher gear and stood up on the pedals. I stood, too, pounding my legs down, trying to put on as much speed as possible. As we flew up to the berm, Darla yelled, "Hold on!"

Bikezilla tilted backward and my stomach lurched as the front ski started to climb. Then it caught in a nearly vertical wall of snow, and the back end of the bike kicked up, throwing me over the handlebars and into Darla. We face-planted into the embankment in a jumble of arms and legs.

Chapter 5

Bikezilla fell sideways behind us and slid partway back down the slope. I lifted my head out of the snow and grabbed Darla's arm. "You okay?"

She looked dazed for a moment. Then she grinned. "Wicked. Let's do it again."

I vetoed that idea. But that meant I had to listen to Darla grumble for the next fifteen minutes while we struggled to drag Bikezilla across the berm. The snow was so deep that some of it got under my jacket and into the legs of my coveralls. I checked the load bed—everything was secure, but the guns were wet, so we spent some time cleaning them. By the time we started out again, I was chilled through.

We'd made good time across the fields, but on the packed snow of the road, we flew. Within moments I was shivering. The wind didn't help. I thought about stopping to change clothes but figured the exertion of pedaling would keep me warm enough until I dried.

Every few hundred feet, we passed another spot of blood. The bandits were moving faster, too.

We raced past two abandoned farmsteads. Plowed snow completely blocked both their driveways. Most of their outbuildings and barns had collapsed under the weight of the ash and snow.

The third farmstead we came to was different. Enough people had trudged across the berm to make a path where the driveway used to be. And someone had brushed against the snowbank, leaving a pink streak.

Darla pulled Bikezilla up beside the snowbank, where it would be hidden from the house. She slid the shotgun out from under the ropes and tried to pass it to me.

"No, you take it," I whispered. I took my staff and the pistol instead, tucking the gun into my belt. "You ready?"

Darla nodded.

I crawled into the driveway, moving slowly and dragging my staff along. As soon as I had a clear view of the house and yard, I stopped. The path continued to the front door of the small ranch-style home. Two grain silos, a barn, and two other outbuildings were arrayed in a rough semicircle behind the house. Except for the tracks leading to the front door, the farm looked abandoned.

I whispered to Darla. "Come up to the edge of the snowbank and cover me from there. I'll run to the house.

If I make it, you follow."

I waited until Darla squeezed in beside me with the shotgun. Then I took the pistol in one hand and my staff in the other and scuttled toward the house in a walking crouch.

The silence was eerie. My breath roared in my ears. I made it to the corner of the house and glanced around. Nothing moved. I waited . . . thirty seconds, a minute . . . then beckoned for Darla to follow.

We crept around the house, peeking in every window. Nothing stirred. The living room and kitchen were empty, but we couldn't see into the bedrooms—the windows were blocked by miniblinds and curtains. We stopped by the side door, where we had a clear view of the driveway.

Darla planted herself beside the door, the butt of the shotgun tucked against her side. I stood to one side, staying out of her field of fire. The door jamb was splintered. A smear of blood stained the knob. With one hand I gently pushed open the door. It groaned hideously, revealing a small mudroom attached to the kitchen.

I stepped through the doorway and pressed myself against the wall while Darla scouted the kitchen with the shotgun. The kitchen connected to the living room and a pitch-black interior hallway. The carpet was covered with clumps of snow and ash, some of which held crumbling boot prints. It smelled stale and musty, despite the frozen air.

"We aren't going to be able to see anything in that hall," I whispered.

"You think anyone is here?" Darla whispered.

"Might be asleep. They could have walked all night."

"Maybe. Get the lantern?"

"Yeah. Cover the door for me."

We left the house, and Darla stepped to one side of the door so she could shoot anyone coming out. I jogged back to Bikezilla to retrieve the lantern. Lighting it was a laborious and somewhat noisy process, so I did it beside the bike. I had to strike a spark into some of the oak bark using my knife and the flint, use that to light a candle, and then, finally, fire up the lantern with the candle. Before the volcano, I never would have guessed that matches and lighters would be among the things I'd miss the most if civilization collapsed.

With the pistol on my belt, lantern in one hand, and staff in the other, I jogged back, careful to zigzag, just in case. We stalked back into the house. The hallway was empty, and all three doors at the far end of it were closed. We moved as quietly as we could, but even the whisper of my feet against the carpet sounded loud in my ears.

I opened the first door, Darla beside me with the shotgun ready. The lamplight gleamed on porcelain. A bathroom. The toilet tank was broken, the water within frozen into a block of dirty ice. I stepped inside to peek behind the shower curtain. Empty.

The second door led to a bedroom. The bed was a rumpled mess. Filthy clothes were piled in one corner, next to scattered splinters that might have once been a dresser. The room was otherwise empty.

I opened the third and last door. The lantern revealed another unmade bed. The rest of the furniture had been reduced to broken scraps.

"Check the far side of the bed," Darla whispered.

I crept across the bedroom. Nobody was beside the bed. But as I turned to go, I noticed a bloodstain on the sheets. I swung the light in a big, slow circle, looking for more blood. And I found some: two droplets low on the closed closet door. I pointed at it.

Darla nodded, and we tiptoed to the closet. I grasped the knob, standing to one side, while Darla trained the shotgun on the center of the door. I yanked it open.

A blond man sat on the floor, his right side soaked in blood, wild blue eyes flicking up at us. The shelves and closet bar were empty. But I noticed all that in passing. What really caught my attention was the machine pistol he had trained on Darla.

Chapter 6

"Take it easy," I said, trying to pitch my voice low and calm. "No need for anyone to get hurt."

"You know," Darla said, "if I pull this trigger it'll turn you into bloody confetti."

I glared at her out of the corner of my eye. That wasn't exactly the calm, rational tone I'd been going for.

"Thish ish a MAC-10." The guy's words were slurred, as if he were drunk or something. "Put all 30 rounds into you in lesh than two sheconds. Back away!"

I held up my hands, clutching my staff in one and the lantern in the other. "It's okay. We're backing up." I took a slow step backward. "Chill."

Darla hadn't moved, and she was glaring sidelong back at me.

"Back up a step, Darla," I said, using as calm a voice as I could muster.

Her mouth hardened to a line, but she did it, moving back a pace with the shotgun still trained on the bandit.

He started to nod. His head drooped, and his eyes closed. The MAC-10's barrel fell. When it touched his knee, he gave a start and snapped awake, the gun barrel twitching from Darla to me and back to Darla. "Keep backing up," he growled.

I took another slow step backward, studying the guy. His right elbow was clamped against his side. His coat and pants shone with fresh blood in the lamplight. A small puddle had collected by his right hip. He could have shot me on the farm. But he hadn't—he'd run instead. Why? "What's your name?" I asked.

"Doesn't matter," he replied, almost whispering.

"Strange first name your parents gave you, Mr. Matter," Darla muttered.

"You had me dead to rights back on the farm. Why didn't you shoot?"

"Was a losht cause. Can't be washting ammo. Now git out of here!"

"We need to know where the shotgun Darla's holding came from. Maybe we could trade. We could patch you up if you tell us about that shotgun."

"I can see the flensing knife on your hip, boy. Don't take me for no fool." The gun sagged again, and he snapped it back to horizontal.

"You're bleeding out—we could help you if you tell us what we want to know. You even *know* where the shotgun came from?"

"Course I do. Was Bill's." His gun dipped again.

"Where'd Bill get it?"

He raised the gun again, training it on me. "Get on out of here," he whispered, "or I'll drill you both."

"Okay, okay. Take it easy." I backed out of the bedroom. Darla kept pace with me, the shotgun trained on the guy all the way.

Once we were in the hall, out of his line of sight, Darla hissed, "What now?"

"What was that?" I whispered back. "Last night you were crying about killing two of them. Today you're ready to blow one of them away?"

"Slumbitches had it coming. Just because I felt bad about shooting them doesn't mean it was wrong. They weren't taking Rebecca and Anna to the state fair, you know."

"Yeah. Maybe so."

"So what now?"

"Just wait and listen a sec."

Everything was still for a minute. It was so quiet in the hall that I could hear Darla's soft breathing. Strange, that such a quiet place was almost the scene of gunfire; that bullets could easily have shredded this silence—and Darla and me with it. I rested my hands on my knees, trying to stop their trembling. My side hurt, but I welcomed the pain. Welcomed the aliveness of it.

I heard a soft thump from the bedroom. I got down on my knees to peek around the doorjamb, figuring the guy would probably expect me to be standing.

I couldn't see anything in the darkness of the bedroom, so I thrust the lamp through the doorway. The guy had slumped sideways in the closet. The hand holding the MAC-10 was flung outward, resting on the carpet beside him. I stood and stepped quickly through the bedroom.

When I got to the guy, I stepped on his wrist so he couldn't raise the gun. He didn't even wake up.

Darla reached down and pried the MAC-10 from his fingers. She fiddled with it for a moment and pulled a rectangular piece off the bottom of the weapon. "Huh. Check this out." She held the block of metal out toward me.

I shrugged. "What am I looking at?"

"The magazine, dummy. It's empty. Guy was out of bullets. That's why he didn't shoot you at the farm."

"I can see why his buddy left him here. He was bleeding out, probably slowing his friend down. But why'd he leave him with the gun? It's valuable. And one without bullets? Useless for defense."

Darla shrugged.

I bent over the bandit. His skin was pale as snow, and his lips looked bruised. I put the back of my hand against his mouth—he was breathing. When I checked his pulse, though, I had trouble finding it. "He's alive, but barely."

"Let's melt some snow," Darla said. "Maybe if we splash water in his face, he'll wake up enough for us to ask him about the shotgun again."

"Should we try to stop the bleeding first? If he dies on us—"

"Then we won't find out anything. Yeah, I guess we should patch him up first." Darla scowled.

I didn't like the idea of helping this guy any more than she did. He and his buddies had shot Max, had tried to kidnap the girls for who-knew-what. But we had no good way to track the other guy—the one who'd worn a blue scarf, and I needed to know where the shotgun had come from. I yanked the guy out of the closet. Blood was still oozing from the wound at his side.

"Get the med kit off Bikezilla, would you?" I asked.

"Christ."

I stripped the bandit to the waist while I waited for Darla to return. She had shot him low on his right side. The wound on his back was just a small puncture that had mostly quit bleeding, but the bullet had left a crater the size of a child's fist as it exited the front.

"It's not like we have a lot of extra bandages to waste on this guy," Darla said when she returned with our first-aid kit.

I took a clean cloth out of the box, wadded it, and packed it into the wound as tightly as I could.

"He isn't going to make it," Darla said. "He's lost too much blood already."

I didn't reply, instead starting to wrap his torso with an Ace bandage. Darla shook her head in disgust but knelt to help.

When I pulled the Ace bandage tight, the guy woke up and started mumbling. Something about "Gun, gun, where's my gun?" His hands clenched and unclenched as he talked.

"Where'd Bill get the shotgun?" I asked him.

He kept mumbling, his voice dropping and his words becoming incoherent.

Darla slapped her palm over the wound and pushed down. "Where'd you get the shotgun!"

The guy moaned and batted at her hand, feebly trying to knock it away from the wound. Darla bore down harder, and suddenly his body went limp. "Is he dead?" she asked.

I checked his breathing and pulse again. "No."

We lit a fire in the living room hearth and melted snow. But no amount of water splashed on the guy's face would wake him. Darla went outside, scouting for signs of Blue Scarf. When she stomped back into the living room, she said, "That last guy with this loser isn't leaving a trail. He must have left here by the road. Maybe he kept going south, but as soon as he makes a turn, we'll lose him."

"He could have left hours ago."

"Yeah. I think it's a lost cause. Sorry, Alex."

"This guy's still alive. Maybe he'll recover."

"You want to hang around here and see if he wakes up?"

"No, that'll take too long. And he might die. Let's load him on Bikezilla and take him to a doctor." I lifted him by his shoulders and started jamming his arms into his shirt.

Darla sighed and helped me dress him. Then she lifted the guy's ankles while I grabbed his shoulders. We dragged him out of the house and laid him in the snow beside Bikezilla.

"We can tie him on the load bed, over the supplies," I said as I repacked the first-aid kit, lantern, and guns. "You know where we are?"

"I think so." Darla took the Illinois roadmap out of its protective, plastic folder and opened it. "I think we've been biking south on 78. We should be near Stockton." She pointed at a dot on the map south of Warren.

"You know anything about Stockton? Is there a doctor there?"

"I dunno. It looks bigger than Warren on this map. We could probably make it back to Warren in a couple hours—it's straight north on 78. Just take him to Doc McCarthy."

I looked over her shoulder at the map. "Let's try Stockton. It's a lot closer. And I don't really want to bring a bandit into Warren if we can help it."

Darla shrugged. We repacked all our gear and then laid the guy on his stomach over Bikezilla's load bed. Darla tied him down, leaving his arms and legs overhanging the sides.

We mounted Bikezilla and started pedaling south along Route 78. Less than ten minutes of travel brought us to a T in the road. We passed three metal sign supports that barely protruded from the snow, but someone had sawn the signs off them. I wasn't sure why anyone would bother to vandalize the signs—maybe they didn't want strangers to find Stockton. "Which way?" I asked Darla.

Darla looked over her shoulder at me. "Right, I think. This should be Highway 20. It'll take us straight into Stockton."

We rounded the corner and passed a burned-out building on our left. The sign in front read GALENA STATE BANK & TRUST. We raced on past a whole series of burnt buildings, but none of the rest of them had signs.

Peering around Darla, I saw something surreal. A few hundred yards ahead of us, a line of cars stood upright, resting on their front bumpers with their trunks in the air. They formed a wall that stretched as far as I could see to the left and curved away from us to the right. Where U.S. 20 passed through the car-wall someone had built a heavy timber gate across the road. Almost before I'd processed what I was seeing, church bells began ringing furiously. A line of men popped into view one by one, their heads and shoulders above the low log gate.

Every one of them was pointing a rifle at us.

Chapter 7

Darla must have seen the rifles, too, because she slammed on the brakes. I got off the bike and stepped up beside her.

"I doubt if any of them can hit us from this far off," she said.

"Yeah," I replied. "How about if I walk up there with my hands up and try to talk to them, and you turn Bikezilla around so that if they start shooting, we can ride out of here in a hurry."

Darla paused. "Okay." She pulled me close for a kiss. "I'll get out the binoculars and keep a lookout. If I yell, run back as fast as you can. And be careful."

"I will." I held up my hands with my palms open and started trudging down the road toward the guns.

The wind was in my face, blowing bits of ice that stung my skin. I had to squint, making everything look indistinct.

As I got closer, I could see the car-wall better. It was bizarre—made up of every conceivable make and model of automobile: from huge pickup trucks and SUVs to Priuses and mini Coopers. Their front bumpers were planted on the ground, hidden by the snow. The rear bumpers rose in the air at various heights, so that the arrangement looked like a monstrous row of multicolored teeth gnawing up from the ground. Each car touched its neighbor on both sides, forming an impassable wall. I couldn't tell what held them upright.

I got to within about a hundred feet of the gate and yelled, "Hello! Is this Stockton?"

Someone yelled back, "We're closed."

"You got a doctor here?"

"Yep. She's closed, too."

"I can trade."

"Trade what?"

"Guns, seeds, food . . ."

A lean man wearing a chocolate-brown coat and overalls set his rifle aside, climbed over the log gate, and started walking toward me. I noticed he was walking to one side of the road, carefully staying out of his buddies' line of fire. I briefly toyed with the idea of sidestepping to put him between me and the guns, but there was no point—he could easily sidestep, also.

He stopped about ten feet from me. "Who're you?"

"Alex Halprin."

"From?"

"Warren."

"No y'aint. Warren only sends four guys here to trade, and I know 'em all."

"I live on Paul Halprin's farm, near Warren."

"Don't know him. Said you got guns to trade? Any ammo?"

"No, just the guns. A MAC-10, maybe a pistol, too."

"Don't need 'em. Got plenty of guns, not enough ammo."

"What about seeds? I've got good, cold-weather kale seeds. Stuff's full of vitamin C."

The guy turned his head and spat sideways. "Like the last guy who sold us seeds? Claimed they were turnip seeds."

"Didn't sprout?"

"They sprouted all right. Grew spurry weed. Useless."

"This is kale. Same stuff Warren trades. It cures scurvy."

"Maybe. Maybe you're the King of England, too. Don't rightly know. What're you trying to trade for, anyway?"

"Medical care. The guy on the back of our bike's been shot. He's lost a lot of blood."

"Best you put him out of his misery and give him a proper burial, then." The guy shrugged. "Best hide the spot you bury him, too, 'less you want a flenser gang to dig him up."

Whatever a flenser gang was, I didn't think telling him that the guy was probably already in one would help my case at all.

"So what would it take to buy medical care for this guy?" I asked.

"How 'bout two hog carcasses?"

"I've got some pork, but not that much."

"I hear they got plenty up in Warren."

"Yeah, thousands. But they're not mine."

The guy spat again in the snow. "You're no use to me, then. So either go back where you came from or skirt around Stockton out of rifle range. You come within shooting range, we prolly won't waste a bullet on you, but you never know." He turned and strode back toward the gate.

I ground my foot into the snowy road. I knew they'd give me anything I wanted for a packet of kale seeds if I could prove they were good. I stomped back down the road to Darla.

"No luck?" she asked.

"Nope. They don't believe the kale seeds are real. I can't think of any way to prove it to them other than germinating a few, and by the time we do that, our bandit will be dead."

"Well, we can take him to Doc McCarthy in Warren. It looks like about twelve miles on the map. Take us an hour and a half, maybe two."

"Let's do that." I mounted Bikezilla's rear seat. "By the way, you know what a flenser gang is?"

"I've heard rumors. You don't want to know."

"If I didn't want to know, I wouldn't have asked."

"Okay. A flensing knife is used to strip skin or fat from an animal, originally a whale."

"So a flenser gang . . . ?"

"Well, if the rumors are true, it's a gang that's surviving by roaming around and butchering animals to eat."

"But almost all the wild animals around here died from the ash after the volcano—they got silicosis."

"Flensers butcher the animals that ventured outside but survived—the ones that were smart enough to cover their mouths and avoid breathing the ash."

I was silent for a moment, listening to the harsh noise made by the cold air rasping in and out of my lungs. "So we might have a cannibal strapped to the back of the bike?"

"Yeah."

"Great," I said in a voice as grim as my mood. "Let's go."

Chapter 8

An hour and a half later we were back in Warren. It was aggravating that more than halfway through the first day of our journey we were barely more than five miles from where we'd started.

Warren, unlike Stockton, had no wall. They hadn't had much problem with bandits so far, probably because Warren is a pimple on nowhere's butt, while Stockton sits astride Highway 20, which connects Dubuque and Galena with Chicago.

When we stopped at the clinic, Darla worked on untying our cannibal from the load bed while I squatted by his head, checking to see if he was still alive. When Darla rolled him over, he started thrashing and mumbling crazy stuff, which I figured counted as a sign of life.

We carried him inside. The waiting room was cold and dark, but light streamed from one of the exam rooms down the hall. When we'd first arrived in Warren last year, the doctor's office had always been packed with people suffering from scurvy. Now, with the steady supply of kale from our farm, we'd often find the place deserted.

Dr. McCarthy and his assistant, Belinda, were in one of the exam rooms working on patient files by the light of an oil lamp. Darla and I carried in our cannibal and heaved him on top of the examination table.

"Who's this?" Dr. McCarthy said. "I don't recognize him."

"One of the guys who attacked our farm yesterday."

The doctor picked up one of the bandit's hands and looked at it for a moment, then held his fingers to the guy's lips. "Lost a lot of blood. He needs a transfusion. We've got a donor system set up, but nobody's going to want to donate to a bandit."

"We need some information from him," I said.

"I'll do what I can, Hippocratic Oath and all, but—"

"I can pay. Two hundred kale seeds."

Darla shot me a glance so heated I felt my face scorch. "Couldn't you just wake him up? Give him some adrenaline or uppers or something?" she asked Dr. McCarthy.

"If I had any epinephrine or amphetamines, which I don't, they wouldn't work. He's unconscious from blood loss. The only way to wake him up is to give him a transfusion and fluids."

"So can we buy him a transfusion?" I asked.

"Yes. You don't happen to know this guy's blood type, do you?" Dr. McCarthy asked. "I'm out of test kits."

"No idea."

Dr. McCarthy turned to Belinda. "Who's next on the O-neg list?"

She had already retrieved a single sheet of paper from the desk drawer. "Nylce Myers. But she gave 38 days ago."

"And she can't weigh 110 pounds dripping wet. Who's after her?"

"Kyle Henthorn. He's at twenty-nine days, though."

"That's okay, he's a big guy. Will you go get him?" Dr. McCarthy held out a key ring. Belinda took the keys to his Studebaker, the only working car in Warren, and left.

Dr. McCarthy turned to me and Darla. "Help me move him onto the floor next to the exam table, would you?" As we lifted the bandit, I noticed his eyes were rolling around as if they were loose in his head. We put pillows under his feet to help treat him for shock and covered him with a blanket.

"You want me to take this bandage off?" I asked.

"No," Dr. McCarthy said. "He might bleed more, which he can't afford. Wait 'til after he's had a transfusion."

About twenty minutes later, a big, florid-faced guy burst into the exam room with Belinda trailing behind. "What's this Belinda tells me about donating again, Doc? My last one wasn't even a month ago." He stopped in the middle of the room and stared at our bandit. "Who is this guy? You know I'm happy to help out neighbors, but I've never seen him."

"This one pays, Kyle," Dr. McCarthy replied. "A hundred kale seeds."

"Damn. Bleed me 'til I faint." Henthorn hopped up onto the exam table and rolled up his sleeve.

"Why do I feel like I just failed Medical Ethics 101?" Dr. McCarthy said.

"Because you did." Belinda was glaring at him.

Dr. McCarthy shrugged and got to work. They set up a gravity-feed transfusion, straight from Henthorn's arm into the bandit's.

The transfusion had been going about five minutes when the bandit woke and started thrashing. I was pressed into service to keep him from ripping out the IV needle. Keeping his arms pinned to the floor was easy—he was feeble.

Dr. McCarthy cut off the transfusion after about ten minutes.

"You sure you don't need any more?" Kyle asked. "I feel fine."

"No, I don't want to take any chances—I feel bad enough about this already," Doc McCarthy replied. "I'll bring by your kale seeds later. Belinda, would you get him something to eat and then drive him home? Keep him in the waiting room about fifteen minutes—I don't want him to pass out."

Belinda and Kyle left the exam room. Dr. McCarthy started unwrapping the Ace bandage from the bandit's side. As the doctor gently pulled the packing out of the wound, the bandit screamed and started bucking.

"I wish I had some kind of sedative left," Dr. McCarthy said.

"I could put pressure on his jugular, try to knock him out," I offered.

"No, no. He's already suffering from anemic hypoxia, that'd only make it worse. Just hold him."

Dr. McCarthy cleaned and repacked the wound on the bandit's belly. He passed out again while the doctor stitched him up. Then I had to roll him over so Doc could work on the entrance wound at his back.

"How long will he be out?" I asked when Dr. McCarthy finished.

"Can't tell for sure. Could be an hour, could be he never wakes up. But he'll probably sleep for three or four days and heal okay."

"I want to go out to my uncle's farm," I said. "Can you keep him here until Darla and I get back?"

"You mean, restrain him?" Dr. McCarthy said. "No, I won't do that. You could talk to the sheriff about it, though."

"I guess we'll stay here until he wakes up then?" I looked at Darla.

She nodded. "Is there someplace to sleep around here?"

"We have a cot in the other exam room—one of you can use the exam table." Dr. McCarthy picked up the tray that held his instruments. "So long as you're waiting for him to wake up, would you take the night shift for us? Belinda and I have been trading off for six months now—a couple of nights off would be great."

"You sure?" I said. "What if a patient comes?"

"Yeah, you'll be fine. I'll show you where my house is. If you need me, one of you stay with the patients, the other run to get me."

Somehow I got stuck on the exam table that night while Darla got the cot. Well, I knew how it happened—I offered her the cot and she said, "Sure, thanks," when I was hoping she'd say, "No, you take it." Anyway, the metal table was uncomfortable despite the sleeping bag I spread over it.

So I was awake to hear the moans emanating from the room next door when the bandit woke up. I rolled off the table and padded over there in my socks, trying not to wake Darla. In the hall we'd left a lantern, turned to its lowest possible setting, in case the guy woke up. I turned the lantern a little higher and carried it into his room.

He was rolling around under his blankets, moaning "'a'er, 'a'er" in a breathy voice. I figured out what he wanted and poured some water from the jug on the counter into a plastic cup.

His hands were shaking so badly, he couldn't hold the cup. So I propped him up with one arm and poured the water slowly past his lips.

After he drank about half the cup, he started coughing. That went on for a while—a series of dry, rasping coughs that had to be painful with his fresh stitches. When his coughing subsided, he motioned at the water cup, and I helped him drink the rest of it.

As I turned to put the cup away, he said in a surprisingly clear voice, "Thank you."

I put the cup down and came back to his bedside. "What's your name?"

"Ralph."

"You know where Bill got that shotgun?"

He grabbed my arm, clutching it tightly enough to hurt. "The bones, they're burning. Burning. White ends turn brown and blacken in the fire." He levered himself partway upright and stared into my eyes. "The flame eats, but it's never satisfied. It eats all night, every night, but there aren't enough bones."

"What about the shotgun?" I pried his hand off my arm.

He moaned, then whispered, "There are too many bones." Then, abruptly, he fell back to sleep.

Chapter 9

Dr. McCarthy returned to the office early the next morning. He poked his head into the exam room, letting in a sliver of light. "You guys up?"

I groaned. I'd barely slept. "I am now."

"Bring your breakfast into the office so we don't have to light another lantern, would you?"

"Sure." I rolled out from under the blankets and groped for my coat. Darla was already up.

Dr. McCarthy stepped into the room and raised the lantern. Darla grabbed a couple packages of ham from our pack, and I picked up our toothbrushes and the pail of washwater. A crust of ice had formed on it overnight. All three of us trooped into the hall.

"I've got to check on the patient," Dr. McCarthy said.

Darla and I waited in the dark hallway while the doctor checked on Ralph. It took less than five minutes. "How is he?" I asked as Dr. McCarthy emerged.

"Unconscious. Pulse and breathing are okay, but he's running a fever."

"You think he'll wake up today?"

"No way to tell."

As we were eating breakfast, the mayor of Warren, Bob Petty, joined us. He was the only person I knew who'd retained his pre-volcano roundness—in his face, belly, and stentorian baritone voice. "Heard you've got a bandit here, Jim."

"They brought him in." Dr. McCarthy tilted his head at Darla and me.

"You catch him out at your uncle's farm?"

"Sort of," Darla said. "We killed two of them. One got away."

"We can't have his type here. I'll send the sheriff to escort him out."

"You will *not*," Dr. McCarthy said emphatically. "Bandit or not, he's a patient. And he's unconscious, hardly a threat."

"Folks are worried."

Dr. McCarthy stared at the mayor until the silence got uncomfortable.

The mayor cleared his throat. "Well, he wakes up, you fetch me or the sheriff. We'll talk about it then."

Dr. McCarthy changed the subject, asking about the latest news. The mayor had traded some pork for a hand-cranked battery charger and an emergency radio, which they were using to monitor the few shortwave stations still transmitting. Rumors and speculation abounded: The Chinese had annexed California, Oregon, and Washington, bringing in troops under the guise of humanitarian assistance. Mexico had closed its borders and started shooting American refugees. U.S. forces stationed in Afghanistan had left and were now occupying farmland in Argentina. Texas had seceded, and religious fanatics in Florida were agitating to follow suit. Half of Congress and four Supreme Court justices had resigned en masse and threatened to set up an alternate government. Some of them had been arrested. Black Lake, the huge military subcontractor that ran the camp where Darla and I had been imprisoned last year, had opened offices inside the Pentagon and White House.

There was no way to know if any of the rumors were true, and it didn't seem to matter much, anyway. The only news that mattered to me was news of my parents—and none of that came in over the shortwave.

Belinda came in just as the mayor was leaving. She smiled and shook his hand, but her eyes were wary. When we'd cleaned up from breakfast, Belinda put us to work organizing patient files. All the office staff had left, so the filing was way behind. Having us work with the records was a violation of HIPAA rules, Belinda said, but she didn't sound particularly worried, and I wasn't sure what

she meant by HIPAA, anyway. Each patient had a folder
with brightly colored tabs that slotted into one of the
open bookcases around the office. One entire bookcase,
packed with records, had been marked DECEASED.

After a while, I started looking inside the folders. I
knew I wasn't supposed to, but the work was tedious, and
I was curious. Every file ended with a sheet of copier
paper, neatly torn in half. They all had the same handwritten heading: CERTIFICATE OF DEATH. Under that in smaller
letters it read, "Prepared by James H. McCarthy, M.D."

Every sheet listed a time, date, and cause of death. The
causes varied wildly: stroke, exposure, heart attack, peri-
odontitis—whatever that was. Darla started looking in the
files, too, and we called out causes of death as we worked:
blunt trauma from a fall, chronic bronchitis aggravated by
silicosis, pneumonia, renal failure.

Then I heard a soft slap as the file Darla was holding
hit the counter. "Jesus H. Christ," she whispered.

"What is it?" I asked, turning toward her.

She didn't respond, just slid the file along the counter
to me.

There were two death certificates stapled to the file.
The top one was for Elsa Hayward. I'd never heard of her.
Cause of death: hemorrhage during childbirth. I lifted it to
read the second certificate. Jane Doe Hayward: suffocated
in childbirth. A full sheet of paper protruded below the
death certificates—Elsa had evidently been a patient of Dr.
McCarthy's for a long time and had a chart. The last entry
on the chart read, "If she'd been born six months ago, I
could have saved them both." The last phrase was repeated,

ground into the paper with such force that it had torn through twice. "I could have saved them both. My God, my God, why hast thou forsaken me?"

His scrawled signature was smeared, bleeding into the page. The paper rippled. I ran my finger across it, feeling it pop and crackle under my touch. Suddenly I realized what I was touching—dried tears. I pulled my hand away from the file and swallowed hard, deeply embarrassed, as if I'd opened a door and found Dr. McCarthy behind it, sobbing. I gently closed the file and set it in its place on the bookcase with the other records of the deceased. Darla hugged me, her eyes shining with unshed tears. After that, we quit opening the files.

After lunch we hauled water for the office on Bikezilla. Warren's water system had failed shortly after the volcano erupted. So we filled jugs and pails from the nearest working well, about two blocks away. Well water never freezes, even in the hardest winter, although the pipes and hand-pumps can.

As I set one of the jugs on the counter, I must have winced, because Darla said, "How's your side?"

"It's fine," I replied.

"Let me check it. I should change the bandage, anyway."

"I'm fine. Let's see what else Belinda wants us to do."

"After I check your bandage."

I sighed, sank into a chair, and started taking off clothing.

When Darla began removing the bandages from my side, I bit back a scream. I knew it would hurt—it had ever since I'd been shot, but not this badly. The three puncture

wounds were swollen and oozing puss. Red streaks radi-
ated from my side like cobwebs.

"Wait here," Darla said.

Dr. McCarthy took one look at it and said, "Cellulitis
manifesting as severe erythema."

"Ery-what?" I asked.

"The puncture wounds are infected."

"Can you treat it?" Darla asked.

"Yes . . ."

"But?" I asked.

Dr. McCarthy shook his head. "But nothing, just a
sec," he said and left the room. When he returned, he was
carrying seven large white pills and a cup of water. "Take
one now and one every day until they're gone. Should take
two a day, but I don't have enough for that."

There was writing on the pills, but I couldn't make it
out in the low light of the lantern. "What are they?"

"Cipro. Full-spectrum antibiotic."

"That must have been hard to come by." I took the
glass of water and swallowed a pill, feeling the lump it
made as it passed down my throat.

"There's a guy in Galena dealing in it. I don't know
where he gets it—I suspect he has access to the government stockpile."

"Why'd the government stockpile it?" Darla asked.

"It's one of the best treatments for anthrax. The
stockpile was a civil defense measure."

"How much do you have left?" I asked.

"Six tablets."

I picked up my jacket from the floor and pulled the bag of envelopes holding the kale seeds out of the inner pocket. I extracted two envelopes.

Darla glared at me.

"Use one of these to buy more Cipro," I told Dr. McCarthy as I handed them over. "I don't want anyone to go without because of me. I owe you one envelope for Ralph's medical care."

Dr. McCarthy carefully tucked the seeds into his coat, frowning. "Thank you. But I'm going to repay your generosity in about the worst way possible. I need to clean and debride those wounds."

"Debride?" I asked.

"Cut the dead flesh away."

"That's not going to feel particularly pleasant, is it?"

"Nope. Probably be the worst pain you've ever felt. I've been out of anesthetics for months, and buying more just isn't as important as antibiotics, fever-reducers, antiseptics, and the like."

I didn't trust my voice not to quaver, so I nodded.

"If you're lucky, you'll pass out. We can numb your side up a bit with snow."

"I'll get some," Darla offered.

"Get the cleanest snow you can find," Dr. McCarthy said. "Fill one of the small buckets from the supply room. I'll sterilize my scalpels."

While I waited for them to return, my mind wandered back to the last time I'd been in a hospital, before the volcano. I'd biked to taekwondo and forgotten my keys.

Nobody was home when I got back, so instead of waiting, I tried to break into my own house. I pushed the lower sash of one of our old-style storm windows inward, and the upper sash fell, snapping my arm at the wrist.

I called Mom, and she hurried home from a PTO board meeting to take me to the hospital. She prowled the waiting room like a caged animal, pacing until we were finally taken to an exam room. There she quizzed everyone who came near us about the best treatments for broken bones, the advantages of a sling versus a cast, and how to spot infection. Pretty soon, all the nurses were avoiding us.

When we finally got home, Dad glanced at my brand-new cast, said, "Looks good," and turned back to his movie. My parents. They drove me crazy, but I still missed them desperately.

Darla returned to the exam room. I lay on my side on the hard metal table and bit down on Dr. McCarthy's leather-wrapped stick. Darla packed snow over my wounds. She left the snow there until my side felt frozen and totally numb. But it wasn't. Darla sat on my legs to keep me steady, but when Dr. McCarthy started carving on my side, I bucked so hard she nearly fell off.

I hoped, wished—prayed, even—that I'd pass out. No luck. I heard a muffled trumpeting sound and was puzzled for a moment before I realized it was me, screaming around the stick clamped in my teeth. Some blood started to trickle from my side onto the table. I focused on the blood, watching it spread into a small, irregular pool.

"The bleeding's good," Dr. McCarthy said. "Helps clean out the wound."

"Uh," I moaned around the stick.

"Almost done . . . there."

Darla reached up and took hold of the stick. I couldn't unclamp my teeth from it.

"Leave it there for now," Dr. McCarthy said. "We'll let the punctures bleed for a bit, then I'll clean and bandage them. He'll need the stick for that. I'm going to get fresh water and antiseptic." He left the room.

"Can I let go of your legs for a minute?" Darla asked me. I nodded weakly.

Darla pulled her sleeve over her hand and used it to wipe the tears from my face. Until then, I hadn't even been aware I'd been crying. "You're a tough guy, you know?"

"Uh," I moaned.

Darla gently wrapped her arms around my shoulders and pressed herself against me. She softly kissed my eyelids, right then left. "Love you," she whispered.

"'Uv 'ou 'oo," I grunted back.

Dr. McCarthy came back into the room carrying a basin of water and two small bottles. "I leave for thirty seconds, and you're making out in my operating room? Teenagers."

Darla quit hugging me and glared at him, but he ignored her as he prepared to wash my wounds. I caught the hint of a smile peeking out of the corner of his mouth.

Washing and rebandaging the wounds didn't hurt as badly as the cutting had, but there were still fresh tears for

Darla to wipe away. It took a couple of minutes for me to relax enough to release the stick from between my teeth.

A wave of exhaustion washed over me. It was late afternoon, nowhere near bedtime, but I was suddenly so tired that I could barely sit upright. I stumbled to my feet. Darla grabbed my arm, concern plain on her face.

"I'm okay. Just tired." I didn't want her to worry.

She helped me down the hall to the exam room we'd slept in the night before, and I stretched out on the cot. My last thought before I drifted into unconsciousness: Why couldn't I have passed out half an hour earlier?

Chapter 10

Darla's snoring woke me. She didn't snore all the time, but when she did, she sounded like a hibernating grizzly.

She'd left an oil lamp burning as a nightlight. I watched her sleep for a while as she lay curled up on the exam table. Her face was gorgeous, golden in the lamplight, although the effect was ruined by the flutter her nostrils made with each rip-roaring snore.

I thought about waking her—sometimes a gentle shake would be enough to end her snoring. But we'd both had a long day yesterday. And my side hurt badly enough that I didn't think I could get back to sleep, anyway.

I rolled out of bed. I was dressed, but my boots were propped upright beside the cot. Darla must have taken them off me. I slipped on my boots, picked up the lantern, and went to peek out the back door of the clinic. It was pitch black and bitterly cold outside—still sometime in the middle of the night.

I closed the door and went back down the hall to the room the bandit occupied. He was curled on his left side under three blankets. Most of his face was hidden, covered by long hair and a scraggly beard. The one eye I could see was open, shining in the lamplight as he stared at me.

"You ready to talk?" I asked.

He tried to say something but started coughing instead. He hacked a huge wad of greenish phlegm onto the sheet. "Need to pee something fierce," he said finally.

I sighed. "Bathroom doesn't work. You want to go to the pit toilet outside or use a bedpan?"

"Try to get up, I guess."

"Okay." I grabbed a rag from the desk and tossed it at him. "Wipe up your mess first so you don't smear it everywhere."

He dabbed feebly at the phlegm, then dropped the rag on the floor. I scowled at him, picked up a clean corner of the rag with two fingers and tossed it into the laundry bin. He started to push himself upright, got to about forty-five degrees, and cried out. He grabbed his right side and collapsed back into the bed. When he regained his breath, he said, "Better use the bedpan."

"Tell me when you're done," I said when I returned

with it. "I'll wait in the hall." I left the door cracked so I'd hear if he tried to get out of the bed.

It seemed like a long wait. I remembered having to use a bedpan while I was staying at Darla's house after I'd been injured by Target the year before. Actually, what I used was her mother's second-best bread pan. We never did tell her mother about that. The memory of Mrs. Edmunds sat heavy in my chest. I'd known her for less than three weeks before she was murdered, but still, I missed her.

I'd be dead now if not for her. She'd shown me a kindness I could never repay—a kindness that moved her to welcome a bleeding stranger into her home.

"Done," I heard from the exam room.

I went inside and took the bedpan from the bandit. It sloshed with urine so dark it was almost orange. I carefully set the stinking pan on the desk and lowered myself into a chair. "So, Ralph, you got that—"

"Ralph? Who's Ralph?"

"You said your name is Ralph."

"I did? When?"

"Last night."

"Don't remember that. No, I'm Ed. My dog's name was Ralph."

"Huh, wonder why you told me your name was Ralph?"

He twisted his head and stared at the ceiling.

"I need to know where you got that shotgun," I said. "Blue Betsy, remember?"

"Why am I here?"

"Because I need to know where the shotgun came from." This was getting old. "Trust me, I'd have preferred to leave you where you were. You'd have bled out or frozen to death."

"Might've been better if you had."

"Yeah. But—"

"You want to know where we got that shotgun. You going to kill me after I tell you?"

"What? No."

"You're just going to let me go. Tell me another one, kid. How do they do it here? Hanging? Or a bullet in the brain?"

"Neither. You've just got to move on and never come back."

"Huh." Ed folded his arms and closed his eyes.

"Where'd that shotgun come from?"

Ed was silent.

I leaned forward and breathed out heavily, staring at him. I had to convince him to trust me, at least a little. "You hungry?"

"Yeah, but you ain't gonna feed me. Nobody's got enough food to waste it on half-dead strangers."

"Wait here."

He laughed a wheezy, halfhearted cackle. "I can't even sit up by myself."

He had a point. I returned to the room Darla and I shared. She was still loudly asleep. I dug through our supplies, pulling out packages of food. I thought about what would impress Ed, but while we had plenty of food, there wasn't much variety. I settled on a sandwich—two corn-meal pancakes for the bread with a slice of ham and a slab of goat cheese for the filling. Ice crystals shattered off the ham as I cut it, and the slice was hard as a board. We had no way to keep it warm. The cheese crumbled. As a finishing touch I peeled an icy kale leaf off the stack and added that to the sandwich.

Ed was staring at the door when I returned to his room. I put the sandwich in his hands.

"That's . . . for me?" he asked.

"Yeah," I replied, "Don't eat too fast. You'll barf."

"I know."

I sat him up, propped against the wall. He took a bite, chewing slowly. He held the sandwich in front of him as he ate, staring at it like a kid with a new iPhone on Christmas morning. Well, like a kid would have stared at an iPhone before the volcano. Now that kid would just toss the useless chunk of metal and glass aside and look for the good stuff: food, clothing, matches, or weapons.

I refilled his water cup.

Ed set the water beside him and said, "So this is corn, lettuce—"

"Kale," I said.

"Kale, okay. Cheese and a slab of?"

"Ham." I was quiet for a while as Ed ate. "Why'd your buddy leave you in that house, anyway?"

"I was slowing him down. I think he was going to put me out of my misery, but I got him to leave me there the same way I got you to back off. Pure D bluff. Told him I had one bullet left for the MAC-10. He didn't want to find out the hard way whether I was telling the truth or not."

"Took balls—so what did you do before the eruption?"

"Before the eruption?"

"Yeah, like, I went to high school. Cedar Falls High."

"I . . ." Ed lifted the sandwich, staring at it, not eating it. "Mandy used to love ham sandwiches."

"Mandy?"

"I haven't thought about her in months. She was my life—how could I forget?"

"What about—"

"I guess you just go along, don't you—"

"I don't—"

"Every day you do what it takes to survive. And every day what you're willing to do gets a little worse. Until you're—Jesus, we were shooting kids."

I tried to break in to ask about the shotgun again, but his voice dropped to a whisper and he kept talking. "Dear God, what have I done? What have I become?"

He buried his face in his hands and started crying huge, racking sobs that traveled in lurching waves down his belly. I was afraid he'd tear his wounds open, he was crying so hard. Tears leaked from between his fingers. I watched him, torn between disgust and an irrational desire to comfort the bandit who had attacked our farm, who would have killed Max and kidnapped Rebecca and Anna if he could have.

It took a while for Ed's sobbing to subside to sniffles. "I was a bookkeeper," he said at last. "I ran Peachtree for a machine shop in Ely. What happened to us? What happened to me?"

"What did happen to you?" I must have let some of the scorn I felt color my voice. He pulled his hands from his face and stared at me with an expression of such naked torment that I forgot to ask him again about the shotgun.

"It started with Ralph," Ed said. "He was our dog. We were starving to death, Mandy and me."

"I need—"

"Then a couple weeks later Mandy died anyway. Flu bug or maybe just the diarrhea. I should have just lain down to die next to her instead of burying her. A lot of people did, you know? I'd find them all over Ely, frozen together in their beds. The guys I ran with later laughed at them. But they did the right thing—instead of doing something just a little worse every day, all in the name of survival, shaving yourself away until the last sliver of who you were is gone."

I raised my voice, trying to break in. "Would you let me—"

"I still dream about him. Ralph. He was a good dog." Ed looked at me, his eyes stripped of color by the low light and his tears. "They say you are what you eat, you know? Sometimes in my dreams I'm Ralph, my tail thumping the floor, just happy to see Ed come home. Sometimes in my dreams I'm a pile of bones. Endless bones, burnt and cracked, feeding a greasy fire." He turned his head and started crying again, softly this time.

I watched him cry for a moment. "I need to know

where that shotgun came from," I said for the eight millionth time.

"How did I—"

"Goddamn it, Ed! Tell me where my parents are!" Without thinking about it I'd taken a step toward him and raised my fists to my chin, planting my feet at a forty-five-degree angle: a fighting stance.

"I want to stay. In Warren. Rejoin civilization. And I want a pardon."

"No freaking way am I letting a guy who tried to kidnap my sister and cousin stay within a hundred miles of Warren. The mayor was ready to throw you out while you were unconscious. Dr. McCarthy saved your ass. You tell me about that shotgun, and I'll try to convince them to let you stay until you're healthy enough to leave. Then you'll get the hell out. In fact, you'll get out of the whole state of Illinois."

"I'm not saying anything then."

"I could beat it out of you." I raised my fists again.

"Go ahead," Ed's voice sounded hollow. "I don't want to rejoin the gang, and if I leave on my own, I'm dead anyway. You may as well beat me to death. Wouldn't take much right now."

Ed's eyes were brimming with tears again. I let out the breath I'd been holding, and with it my whole body deflated. I couldn't beat on a defenseless man, no matter what he'd done. "You have to buy your way into Warren," I said. "They aren't taking just anybody—they don't have enough food to do that. You've got to bring skills or supplies they need. You've got nothing to offer—the only thing Warren needs even less than bookkeepers are lawyers."

"So you buy me a spot. Or convince your mayor to give me one."

"They don't want a bandit hanging around."

"That's your problem—if you still want to know about that shotgun."

Gah! It was frustrating to admit it to myself, but he was right—he was half-dead, but he still had the upper hand. And I didn't want to argue with him all night. I reached into my coat pocket and extracted an envelope. "There are 200 kale seeds in here. More than enough to buy you admission to Warren—if you can buy it at all. I'm not going to hang around here and try to convince the mayor and sheriff that you're an okay guy. *I'm* not even sure you are. So here's the deal—you tell me everything you know, and I give you the seeds. Trading them for admission to Warren is your problem, not mine."

"How do I know the seeds are any good?"

"Goddammit—!"

"Okay, okay. I'll take it."

I handed him the envelope. "Talk."

"Danny, he—"

"Who's Danny? You said the gun was Bill's."

"Danny's the leader of the gang I run with. Ran with, I mean. The Peckerwoods. Bill's just the guy Danny gave the shotgun to."

"Peckerwood? Isn't that some kind of insult?"

"Yeah, I guess. It's also the name of a racist gang in

Anamosa, in the state prison. I mean, I was never there, but that's where the leaders were when the volcano blew. Anyway, it started to get hard to find weapons and ammo. So Danny made a deal with some guards at one of the FEMA camps in Iowa. He got all kinds of weapons from them. Ammo, too. Most of the guns weren't military stuff, so I figure they were confiscated from refugees."

"So maybe my dad is at that FEMA camp? Where is it?"

"Might be, yeah. It's outside Maquoketa."

"Where's that?"

"About halfway between Dubuque and the Quad Cities."

That made it somewhere southwest of Warren. I wasn't sure exactly. "So Danny was trading for the guns? What was he trading?"

"I don't know for sure. Drugs, maybe. We had all the good stuff. Antibiotics, painkillers, aspirin. Danny had a source in Iowa City, but he never took me along when he cut deals." A pained look passed over Ed's face, and he moved his right hand to his side.

"What else do you know?"

"Nothing. That's it. I swear."

I shook my head. Two hundred more kale seeds gone. And for what?

Chapter 11

When Darla woke, we packed Bikezilla, said good-bye to Dr. McCarthy, and headed for my uncle's farm. We'd only been gone two days, but even so, the farm looked different. Rebecca and Uncle Paul were out front nailing boards over a window. Most of the ground-floor windows were already boarded over.

As we made the turn into the driveway, Max came out the front door, leading a string of four goats by a rope. I grinned and waved, thrilled to see him up and about. He waved back before continuing to the barn.

"Didn't expect to see you back so soon," Uncle Paul called as we pulled up.

"Didn't expect to be back," Darla said.

"Had to do a U-turn at Stockton," I said as I hugged him.

"Come into the kitchen," Uncle Paul said. "We've got fresh cornbread."

We sat around the kitchen table for a while catching up. Darla went out to Bikezilla and got our maps. She put the Iowa and Illinois maps on the table next to each other, and I traced a line from Warren to Maquoketa with my finger.

"So the biggest trick will be crossing the Mississippi River?" I said. "Looks like there are bridges in Dubuque or Savanna."

"It won't be a big deal," Darla said. "That river that flows through the park behind the farm is frozen solid. We can ride Bikezilla across the Mississippi anywhere."

Uncle Paul was shaking his head. "No way. That's Apple River. It freezes almost every year, but the Mississippi never freezes over in Iowa."

"It's never been below freezing for nine straight months either," Darla retorted.

"We could cross at the lock near Bellevue, like last year. It wasn't too hard to climb down onto the barge stuck in the lock and back up the other side." It hadn't been fun—I don't like heights—but I figured I could do it again.

"I'm telling you, it's not an issue. Look at these lakes." Darla pointed at a spot on the Mississippi just north of my finger. "I'll bet there's a bunch of boat ramps there—we can ride right down onto the lakes and across the river, which *will* be frozen over—and into Iowa."

"Falling through the ice on a river is no joke." Uncle Paul sounded concerned. "You can get swept downstream under the ice—"

"The Mississippi is frozen so solid you could drive a semi on it." Darla said mildly. "I'd bet my farm on it."

"We're not talking about betting farms—we're talking about betting your life—and Alex's. This isn't—"

"My farm was my life," Darla said.

"Guys, take it easy," I said. "We can go to the lock to cross."

"That's where you found the barge full of wheat last year?" Uncle Paul asked. "Stuck in the lock?"

"Yeah," I said.

"We could sure use some wheat," Uncle Paul said. "We've got to get some greenhouses going with something other than kale. A northern strain of wheat could work."

"I thought you couldn't plant just any old seeds," I said. "Didn't you tell me that's why we can't plant any of the corn we've been digging out of the ash and snow?"

"Corn hybridizes easily," Darla said. "Everything I planted at my farm was a sterile hybrid, kind of like mules are. Wheat's self-pollinating, so it's really hard to hybridize. Well, you can but—"

"Um," I had to interrupt Darla before she really got going. She'd babble on and on about hybro-pollinizing stuff until I got even more confused. "So what's all that mean?"

"Corn won't grow from seeds we dig up here. But if we get wheat kernels off that barge, they'll probably sprout."

"Yep," Uncle Paul said. "I was hoping you could stop at the barge and pick up some wheat. It could make a big difference—we're going to run out of stored corn, and we need some kind of grain."

"That a-hole at the FEMA camp near Galena, Captain Jameson, said Black Lake had a contract to guard the barges," Darla said. "Either the wheat's all gone by now, or those barges will be crawling with idiots in camouflage. They're not just going to let us ride up and help ourselves, you know."

"The lock is pretty much on the way, though," I said.

Uncle Paul fixed a stare on Darla. "Bringing back even a few pounds of wheat kernels would be a godsend if you can manage it. Might make the difference between surviving and starving if the winter weather doesn't break. I wouldn't ask if it weren't worth the risk."

"We'll take a look." I glanced at Darla. "Okay?"

Her lips tightened, but she didn't say anything, which I took as enthusiastic agreement. Right. So we spent some time mapping out a path to the lock that avoided Stockton and the FEMA camp near Galena.

"When do you plan to leave?" Uncle Paul asked.

"Tomorrow morning," I said.

"You sure you're up to it?" Darla took hold of my wrist. "Maybe we should wait and make sure your infection is under control."

"An infected wound is no joke," Uncle Paul said. "Kill you if you don't take care of it."

"No." I pulled my wrist free. "I want to get moving."

"How are you planning to break your parents out of the camp, anyway?"

I shrugged. "I don't know. But I don't want to wait."

"Be nice to have a bolt cutter and hacksaw for the camp fence," Darla said.

"Take them out of my shop," Uncle Paul replied. "I'll try to buy replacements in Warren."

We spent the rest of the day helping to fortify the house. Uncle Paul, Aunt Caroline, and Anna worked on boarding up windows. Max slept most of the day—his head was healing okay, but the wound had left him weak. Darla, Rebecca, and I built and installed pairs of brackets on the inside of all three exterior doors. Then we cut heavy logs to fit into the brackets, barring the doors from the inside.

It felt a little futile to me. Ed had started out as a normal guy, a bookkeeper. Would we all wind up like him; slowly forgetting our humanity in the daily struggle to survive? And when the world filled with people like Ed—bandits, murderers, rapists, arsonists—what good would a few bars on the doors do?

Chapter 12

By bedtime I was exhausted and sore. Everyone else
started to bed down on the living room floor, but
Darla grabbed my hand and pulled me toward the
stairs. "It's freezing up there," I complained.

"I'll make sure you're warm enough," Darla
whispered, grinning at me.

My resistance evaporated. I'm sure Uncle Paul
and Aunt Caroline noticed us leaving, but they
didn't say anything. Before we'd started all sleeping
in the same room for warmth in April, Darla and I
had shared the guest room. At first my aunt and
uncle had balked, but when they discovered we were

sneaking out of our separate rooms every night anyway, they relented.

We got extra blankets and comforters out of the linen closet and heaped them on Max's old bed. I took off my boots, coat, and coveralls. Even with three layers of shirts still on, I was freezing. I turned down the oil lamp to its lowest setting, and we dove under the covers, pulling them up over our heads.

Darla pushed her back up against me, spooning for warmth. I wrapped my right arm over her and cupped my hand over her left breast. She moved my hand down to her stomach and held it there—which sort of sucked—but holding hands was nice.

"I don't know how to say this right." Darla hesitated. "But you do realize that your parents might already be dead?"

I swallowed hard on the first reply that occurred to me: She was probably right.

She went on, "If they are dead, we're taking a big risk going into Iowa looking for them. We could get killed or trapped in another FEMA camp for nothing."

"Yeah." I fell silent for a moment. "But I've gotta know for sure."

"We might not be able to find out."

"What, you don't want to go? You volunteered—I didn't ask you. It's not like I'm dragging you."

"That's not it. You're not going anywhere without me, doof."

I squeezed my arm around her, hugging her tighter.

"All I was trying to say, trying to do, was to keep your expectations real. We might find them, sure. But they might be dead, or we might never even find out where they are or what happened to them."

"Never finding out what happened to them—that might suck worse than finding out they're dead."

"Yeah, it might." Darla let go of my hand and started stroking my arm, which seemed strange at first but was somehow comforting.

We lay together in silence. Talking about my parents hadn't been particularly arousing, but now, with her hair brushing my face, her hands on my arms, and her body stretched out against mine, pressing into, well, everything, I started to get uncomfortably cramped. So I began softly nibbling on her neck.

Darla closed her eyes and sighed. I moved up to kiss her ear.

She laughed and pulled her head away. "You know that tickles."

"Yeah, but you're so cute when you giggle."

"I do *not* giggle. Never have, never will."

"Whatever." I bent back toward her neck, but Darla fended me off with a hand.

"You've got to quit giving away kale seeds like a pedophile with lollipops."

"Huh?" I said. "Where'd that come from?"

"We need them to buy information—maybe to buy your parents' freedom."

"I know, but I've still got seventeen packets."

"We didn't need to give that bandit anything."

"I didn't exactly give him the seeds—I traded. For information. And look, if we repay brutality with more brutality, how does it end? We do something just a little bit worse every day, and soon enough we're just like him."

"We'll never be like him."

"Maybe not, but we need to cooperate, to rebuild. Someone's got to start. And why'd you bring it up now?"

"We could buy other stuff with those seeds, too, you know," she said in a husky voice.

"Other stuff?" I asked.

"Like more condoms, maybe."

"Oh," I said. "Good idea."

Darla spun in my arms. Her knee dug into my thigh as she turned, but I was so aware of, um, other parts of her that I barely noticed. She tipped up her head and kissed me.

When the kiss ended, I said, "I think generosity makes you horny."

"What do you mean?"

"Well, last year after we helped Katie and her mom, you pretty much attacked me. And today we helped Ed— saved his life even though we didn't really want to."

"No, it's stupidity that makes me horny."

"That's good then. I'm plenty stupid."

"Yes." Darla kissed me again. When she came up for air, she said, "You sure are."

I smiled and started undressing her. I usually thought the worst part of the winter was the frostbite or risk of starvation. At that moment, the endless layers of clothes seemed worse.

"So . . . no condoms," Darla said. "What do you want to do?"

"I'll show you."

Darla giggled and finished undressing me.

Chapter 13

Later, Darla lay on top of me, her head resting on my shoulder. Despite the cold, our skin was slick with sweat. I stroked her back slowly, feeling tired and more relaxed than I had since the bandits attacked. "I've got something for you," I said.

"What?" Darla murmured.

I pushed a corner of the covers aside and started groping for my pants.

"Quit letting the cold air in," Darla said.

I found what I was looking for in the pocket of my jeans. I pulled my hand into the tunnel of light the oil lamp cast into our cocoon and opened my palm, showing it to Darla. My face felt hot despite the cold air. I searched Darla's eyes—trying to see any sign that she liked my gift.

"It's . . . where'd you get it?" she asked.

"Belinda gave me the gold chain. I tried to buy it from her, but she said she had extras. I swiped the nut from Uncle Paul's toolbox. You like it?"

"I love it."

My face grew hotter yet, but now it was a happy warmth. Darla took the chain from me and clasped it around her neck. The nut slid down the chain until it lay on the sheet between us.

"Why'd you choose a 15/16ths? Nobody uses those."

"That's what I found. And anyway, I've always thought you were a sixteenth short of a full nut."

Darla groaned and slugged my shoulder, but she was smiling. "What do you want to do now?"

"Um, get some sleep?" I capped the lamp and pulled the covers back over our heads.

"No, I mean after."

"After what?"

"After we find your parents—or find out what happened to them."

"Maybe things will change if we find them. Get better."

"I don't know . . ." Darla said.

"I guess we'll come back here. Keep helping my uncle. As a family, we've got a shot at surviving the winter."

"Your uncle's okay, so don't take this the wrong way, but you're my family now."

I wasn't sure how to respond. I felt like I'd just shouldered a heavy backpack. Carrying that load was scary, but it felt good, too. Important. "The winter could last a decade."

"I'm not scared." Darla was whispering, but her voice sounded determined.

"I am," I said. "But if we have to die in an endless winter, I'm glad we're together. . . . I love you, you know."

"I love you, too. And if we don't have to die?"

"I used to think I'd finish high school, go to college."

"That's not gonna be an option," Darla said. "Things will never be like that again. If you're old enough to go to high school, then you're old enough to work."

"I thought I'd finish high school and go to college because my parents did. It wasn't something we discussed much—it was just assumed."

"You would've done great. You're a helluva smart guy."

"Am not," I protested.

"With no common sense whatsoever," Darla added. "Besides, I wasn't asking about that. I was asking about us."

"I don't know," I said. Darla tried to pull away from me, but I held her close. "My uncle said we might grow apart, and I know he was right—"

"We won't—"

"That's not what I mean. He was right that most relationships don't last long—my friends hardly ever dated anyone more than a month. The only other girlfriend I had, Selene, lasted two months. I've never had a girlfriend as long as you."

"Me, either. A boyfriend, I mean."

"And I think I love you more now than I did the first time I said it."

"Me, too."

We were quiet for a moment. I knew what I wanted to say, but it was bound to come out all wrong. Or hopelessly corny. Eventually, I gave up thinking about it. "If we're all going to die anyway, I want to die with you. And if we live, I want to live with you."

"Like, get married?"

I hadn't really thought about it that way. But wasn't that what I'd just said? That I wanted to live with Darla? Forever? The idea of it was thrilling. And terrifying. "I don't know. I'm only sixteen."

"It's hard to make plans." Darla wrapped one arm around her shoulder, hugging herself. "I mean, who knows if we have a future, if we'll survive that long."

"We will." I peeled her hand away from her shoulder and held it. "I mean, if there's no future, what's the point of trying? We'll find my parents. Things will get better."

"I used to love to daydream about growing up. About what my kids might look like," Darla said wistfully. "I always thought I'd have a farm. A big red barn, fields of corn and soybeans, maybe a few head of milk cows. Five or six kids running around."

"Five or six?"

"Yeah, being an only child sucked. So I always wanted to have lots of kids. Now . . . I don't know."

"Before, I never really thought about kids much," Well, to be honest, I'd thought about the process of making them a lot. But not the result. "Now I don't want any. Not unless things get a lot better."

"I've wanted a big family since I was a little girl."

"Well, if things do get better," I said, "you're going to need someone to take care of all those kids while you work on the farm. And to, um, help *make* all those kids."

"You don't get out of farmwork that easy, buster," Darla said. "You can watch the kids some days, but some days you're going to have to drive the tractor. You don't do your fair share, and I'll make those kids with a turkey baster, see if I don't."

"Do I even want to know how that works?"

"Duh, you—"

"No, I really don't want to know. It's just that the problem with me driving a tractor is, well . . ."

"You have no clue how to, right?"

"Yeah."

"I always imagined marrying someone who loved farming, not some city slicker."

I shrugged. "Well, you can't always get everything you want."

"If I can't have everything I want," Darla said, "then you can't, either."

"Huh?"

"Well, like getting married and having kids—we can do all that someday. But you remember what you said you wanted when we started this whole conversation?"

"Um, no."

"Good, 'cause you can't have it." Darla poked me hard in the shoulder with one finger. "You said you wanted to sleep!" She pushed herself up on her arms and kissed me. I decided sleep could wait—at least for a while.

Chapter 14

Early the next morning we set to work repacking Bikezilla. By the time we were ready to go, everyone else was up. So we had to say goodbye for the second time in three days. Coming back to the farm had its disadvantages, though when I thought about the night before, I decided the benefits outweighed them. Not just the making out, either, although that was fun. After our talk the night before, I felt closer than ever to Darla. Closer than I'd ever felt to anyone.

We finished our goodbyes and set out, staying on the route we'd mapped out with Uncle Paul. I'd fully expected to spend the day dodging bandits or

FEMA patrols out to catch us and stick us in a camp. They got paid by the government according to the number of refugees they housed, so they were always looking to put stray people in their camps. Thankfully though, the roads were deserted.

Early that afternoon, we turned off South River Road onto the access road that led to Mississippi Lock and Dam #12. We biked up onto a railroad embankment, and Darla slammed on the brakes, bringing Bikezilla to a sliding stop.

Across the road ahead, I saw the chain-link gate we'd climbed over during our trip last year. But behind it there was something new: a guard shack about eight feet square with light pouring from its windows. Black Lake's eagle logo was stenciled next to a window on the shack's side.

Darla whipped Bikezilla into a turn, and we took off again. We'd gone about a mile when Darla finally quit pedaling and craned her neck to peer behind us. I looked, too—the road was deserted.

"You think they saw us?" Darla asked.

"I dunno. Let's go check."

"Let's not and say we did. Just go around and avoid the lock."

"I want to know if they saw us—if they're going to be looking for us. And we promised Uncle Paul we'd try to get some wheat." I got off the bike.

"You promised, not me."

"Right." I got the bolt cutter off the load bed.

Darla scowled but helped me hide Bikezilla on the other side of the berm. We trudged back to the shack, taking cover behind the berms and railroad embankment. When we got close, Darla stopped to cover me with the shotgun, and I dropped to my hands and knees. I crawled up to the fence. If anyone came out of the shack, they'd see me for sure. But if they were just casually glancing out the windows, the corner of the shack would block me from their view. With the bolt cutters, I opened a hole in the fence just big enough to slither through on my belly. The snow rasped against my coveralls as I crawled to the building and hid beneath one of its windows.

Slowly I lifted my head to peek over the windowsill. Inside, two guys in camo sat at a small table playing cards. They'd slung their assault rifles over the backs of their chairs. Three piles of wheat kernels lay between them. I felt a stab of envy—the seeds they were pushing back and forth so casually across the table were worth a fortune. If we could grow them in the greenhouses, we could have real bread again instead of corn bread and corn pone.

A bottle of Grey Goose vodka sat on the table between them, about half empty. The guards were wholly absorbed in their game—not even glancing out the windows. I crawled back to Darla.

"Two guards," I whispered. "Playing cards. They're betting with piles of wheat. Might be drunk—we could take them easy."

"Let's see what's going on at the lock. Maybe we can get some wheat out of one of the barges without fighting."

"And we can make sure the river is frozen while we're there."

"It is."

We walked toward the river, keeping the snow berm between us and the road. It was exhausting to push through the deep snow, so I wasn't paying much attention to where we were going. We'd walked about fifteen minutes when I stepped out into thin air. I grabbed at Darla's hand, trying to regain my balance, but all I accomplished was pulling her with me over the drop-off in front of us.

We tumbled and slid down a steep slope. I lost hold of Darla somewhere along the way and slammed into a horizontal surface at the bottom, sliding a few feet before coming to rest. My shoulder and side hurt, but otherwise I thought I was okay.

"Darla?" I whispered.

"Yeah, over here."

I turned over and crawled toward her. The surface was hard and slick under my gloves—ice. "You all right?"

"Yeah, I think so."

We'd fallen down a steep embankment onto ice. I didn't think we were on the Mississippi itself—maybe one of the pools or inlets that I'd seen on the map, reaching out from the river's banks like pudgy fingers.

"Try to climb back up?" I asked.

"No, let's follow the embankment down here. We'll be invisible to anyone up on the road."

Darla took my hand and led the way, walking on the ice. After a few hundred feet the bank started to meander. Tree limbs jutted from it beside and above us. For a while we moved through some kind of narrow frozen channel—

in a few places it was tight enough that I could almost touch the trees on either side. I heard a faint roar of falling water growing steadily louder as we walked.

The channel we were following opened up suddenly, and I saw a small pool of open water, beyond which stretched the wide expanse of the frozen Mississippi. On the far side, trapped by the ice and the steel jaws of the lock, was the barge we'd visited the year before. Dozens of soldiers swarmed all over it.

Chapter 15

The soldiers were as busy as ants. Darla and I stood in plain sight, but a long way from them—maybe three or four miles across the river. I clambered up the snowy bank next to us. At the top, a grove of trees had caught the blowing snow, holding it in a deep drift. We dove in and hollowed out a foxhole, protected from the chill wind and suspicious eyes.

I raised my head above the lip of our foxhole. The river was mostly frozen. The noise of rushing water came from a pool just below us, where water cascaded over the roller dam and crashed into the river, keeping a small section of it from freezing.

Spray from the churning water had frozen around the pool, creating fantastical shapes that appeared to grow out of the ice.

A red dump truck was parked on the ice, backed up against the barge at the far side of the river. The soldiers were loading the truck, passing grain along a line in five-gallon buckets—like an old-time fire brigade. Another line of soldiers was moving the empty buckets from the truck back to the barge's hold. From our vantage point below the dam, we couldn't see the other two barges that had been here last year, stuck in the ash and muck above the dam.

"I told you the river would freeze hard," Darla said.

"I believed you. Well, until I heard the water. Then I wasn't so sure."

"Pretty efficient way to unload the barges, I guess."

"We're never going to get anywhere near that wheat with all those soldiers around."

"Forget about the stupid wheat already. Christ."

"We owe Uncle Paul. And besides, wheat might be good to trade—it's got to be almost as valuable as kale seeds."

"Whatever. I think we should just focus on finding your folks."

I nodded, frowning, and Darla led the way out of the foxhole. We kept to the woods until we were completely out of sight of the barge. The river ice was still and quiet. We neither saw nor heard a sign of anyone else, though occasionally we could see the scuff marks we'd left earlier. The embankment where we'd fallen was a challenge. It was covered with a crusted, icy snow—too slick to climb easily. I kept sliding backward until Darla took the lead and started kicking toe holds in the snow.

As we got closer to the guard shack, I heard a noise ahead—a low rumbling. "What's that?" I whispered.

"Engine. A big diesel." Darla replied. "Let's look."

We wormed our way to the top of the snow berm and poked up our heads. A Humvee painted in desert camo was parked next to the hut. As we watched, the two guards I'd seen earlier stumbled out and piled into the Humvee. The guy driving did a clumsy five-point turn, tapping the snow berm with his front bumper and the guard shack with his rear. Then he pulled through the gate, and the passenger jumped out to close and padlock it. I held my breath, hoping he wouldn't notice the hole I'd cut in the fence. But he was in a big hurry and didn't spend any time looking around. When they started out again, the Humvee lurched forward, almost stalled, and then bounced up over the railroad embankment out of our sight.

"Did they abandon the hut?" I whispered.

Darla frowned. "I doubt it. Let's get the bike and move on."

"I want to check the hut first. Maybe they left some wheat."

Darla shook her head but got the shotgun ready, anyway. I crawled along the snowbank toward the hut.

When I got there, I peeked over the windowsill. One guy in camo fatigues and a black watch cap was sitting at the table. A pile of wheat kernels was spread in front of him along with five or six purple cloth Crown Royal whisky bags. He was counting the wheat seeds and sorting them into bags. He sat facing the hut's door but was so absorbed in his task that he didn't see me.

I crawled back along the snow berm to Darla. "There's only one guy in there now, and he's got wheat."

"I can't shoot a guy just to get wheat."

"Who said anything about shooting him? Just hold the shotgun on him, and I'll tie him up or something."

"What if he goes for his gun? Then I'll have to shoot him."

I shrugged. "You ready?"

"I guess."

We crawled back to the guard shack together. Everything was still. We hid under the window. When I'd caught my breath, I peeked over the windowsill.

The guard was still messing around with his bags of wheat. We slithered around to the other side. A sliding-glass window faced the road, kind of like a fast-food drive-thru. Next to that was the door, a normal metal entry door with a lock on the handle and a deadbolt. I crawled up to it, reached up, and slowly, very slowly, tried turning the knob to see if it was locked. It was.

Darla pantomimed a kick. I shook my head. She had more confidence in my taekwondo skills than I did. Even with a perfect kick, I might not break the door, and then we'd completely lose the advantage of surprise.

I waved at Darla to follow and crawled around the shack to the opposite side. We peered through the window.

The guard's back was to us. His assault rifle dangled from his chair. He seemed to be completely absorbed in sorting the wheat. I raised my head to examine the window. It was an ordinary double hung, like the ones we'd had in my house in Cedar Falls. A brass latch at the top of the lower sash held it closed.

I ducked back below the windowsill and pantomimed my plan to Darla. She nodded after I went through it once, but I did the whole thing again just to make sure. By the time I finished, she was scowling and rolling her hand as if to say get on with it.

I held up three fingers . . . two . . . one.

Chapter 16

We stood simultaneously, and Darla rammed the barrel of the shotgun through the window. The clash of breaking glass shattered the stillness. The guard swiveled in his chair and yelled, "What the—"

"Hands in the air!" I bellowed.

His face tightened as he took in the broken window and shotgun.

"Get your hands up! Now!" Darla yelled.

The guard raised his hands slowly, muttering all the while, "For shit's sake, how many times do I have to tell the captain it's not safe to have one guy here."

"Guess he'll believe the next guy," Darla said. She bashed out more of the window glass using the barrel of the shotgun. I reached through, careful to keep my arm away from the business end of the gun, and unlatched the window. Darla backed up a step so I could push open the sash.

"You gonna flense me?" the guard asked.

"Might not. You look stringy to me," Darla said. "Hardly worth the trouble."

"Maybe you don't have any shells for that shotgun."

"You can test that theory. You'll find out the truth a millisecond before you die." Darla moved to the side as I crawled through the window.

I stood up behind and to one side of the guard, trying to stay out of Darla's line of fire. I took the assault rifle off the back of the chair and slung it over my shoulder.

"Hand over the wheat," I ordered.

"Well why don't you ram a barrel brush up my ass while you're at it! That's a whole week's pay."

"Black Lake pays you in wheat?" Darla asked.

"Only idiots take cash. There's nowhere to spend it."

He had a radio on his belt and a couple of leather pouches. The first one I unsnapped had an extra magazine for the rifle, which I took. In the second, I found what I really wanted: three sets of plastic zip-tie cuffs. "I'd buy the wheat from you if you promised not to report us."

"Alex," Darla said, complaint clear in her voice.

"Buy it with what?"

"Kale seeds. You could say you broke the window leaning back in your chair too far or something."

"I wouldn't know kale seeds from bird droppings. How would I know you weren't cheating me?"

"It's not like you have a choice," Darla snapped.

"Hands behind your back," I ordered. He lowered his hands behind the chair back, and I slipped the plastic cuffs over his wrists, cinching them tight. Then I used the other two sets of cuffs to affix his legs to the chair.

"I broke the window by accident and cuffed myself to the chair by accident, too?" The guard snorted.

I checked his belt and found the knife I expected on the other side. I pulled it off his belt and tossed it into the corner. I threw his radio into the corner, too. "Cut yourself free after we're gone."

I reached into my jacket, carefully extracting one envelope of seeds from the cloth bag. I laid it on the table in front of the guard.

"Christ," Darla said. "Those things don't grow on trees."

"Sure they do." I grinned at her. "Haven't you ever heard of a kale tree?"

She shook her head and glared at me, but I saw a hint of a smile at the corner of her mouth. Then she tensed up. "Shit! Somebody's coming." She glanced around wildly. Then she dove through the open window into the shack with me. I heard the rumble of a diesel engine and a grinding noise as the driver shifted gears.

"It's a dump truck," Darla said, popping up once to glance out the window. "Tall one."

The truck pulled up alongside the guard shack. The driver's window was so high off the ground that there was no way he could see us. An arm reached down from the truck holding a clipboard and tapped it against the glass four times.

The guard we'd cuffed started to yell, "Hey—"

Darla wrapped her hand around his mouth. "Shut. Up." she whispered.

I took a step toward the window. But Darla had just come in through there to avoid being seen. I froze, unsure what to do.

The radio in the corner crackled to life. "Hey, Benson, quit foolin' around. We've got a schedule to keep. D.C. ain't getting any closer while you jack off."

I had to do something. Now. I ripped the watch cap off the guard's head and jammed it on my own. I stepped up to the window, looking down so that only the top of my head would be visible to the driver—hopefully. I slid the window open and took the clipboard. I cleared my throat and grunted, "Sorry," like I had a cold or something.

The clipboard held a manifest for a truckload of grain—600 bushels—to go to someplace called the Interim Quartermaster and Food Services Authority in Washington, D.C. There was a space for a signature marked GATE CHECKPOINT—ORIGINATING STATION, so I grabbed the pen dangling on a string by the window and scrawled an unreadable signature and date.

I passed the clipboard to the driver, praying I'd get away with it, praying he wouldn't notice my shaking hands—or the sweat dripping from my wrist.

He took the clipboard, and there was a long pause. I balanced on the balls of my feet, ready to run.

"Benson, you dickwad! How long are you going to make me wait to countersign, anyway? It's already gonna be after dark when I make Atterbury."

I glanced around in a panic. Countersign . . . countersign what? A clipboard rested on a little table near the
window. I grabbed it. A whole stack of papers was clamped
in its jaw. I flipped through them—there were two types,
one labeled PERSONNEL TRANSIT RECORD, the other labeled
FREIGHT TRANSIT RECORD. I moved a blank copy of each to
the top of the stack and passed the clipboard to the driver,
keeping my head low and my face out of sight.

"You couldn't even fill out the basic shit for me? Well,
get the gate open while I do your damn job for you."

I took a step toward the door. Then things started to
happen way too fast. Darla screamed, an involuntary yell
that she cut off in an eye blink. I looked—she had pulled
her hand away from Benson's mouth. Both her hand and
his mouth dripped blood. He started shouting, "Security
breach! Security breach!" over and over again at the top of
his lungs.

I heard a clatter and turned my head back toward the
truck. The driver had whacked his gun on the truck's window frame in his haste to shoot me.

Darla screamed, "Down!" and her shotgun went
crunch-crunch as she chambered a shell. Benson threw
himself sideways, chair and all, hitting the floor with a
crash. I dove the other way.

I heard a pop-pop-pop and then a deafening boom followed by the crash of breaking glass. Darla screamed,
"Go!" The driver was holding his gun out the truck's window. His arm was a dripping mess of raw meat and
blood—Darla's shotgun blast and the resulting flying

glass had shredded it. The gun slipped from his fingers and fell between the truck and hut.

Darla hurled herself through the window on the other side of the shack. I scrambled to my feet, swept the bags of wheat and the kale packet off the table, and jammed it all into my coat. I stepped over Benson and launched myself through the window, following Darla.

We slithered through the hole I'd cut in the fence and sprinted along the snow berm toward Bikezilla. It was either eerily silent, or the shotgun blast had deafened me. Given how my ears were ringing, maybe some of both. I risked a look back. The dump truck was still parked beside the guard shack. I couldn't see anything moving, but you could have hidden a platoon behind the hill of snow between us and them.

Just that quick look had given Darla time to get about twenty feet ahead of me. By the time I caught up to her, she was struggling over the snow berm to where we'd hidden Bikezilla. "You get the wheat?" she huffed.

"Yeah. And the kale seeds. How's your hand?" I gasped.

"Hurts. I'll live."

We pushed the bike upright, stowed the pistol, shotgun, and assault rifle, and took off. We both stood on the pedals, straining to get the beast moving. In a few seconds we were flying away from the snow berm on virgin snow.

I wasn't sure why we were going deeper into the area Black Lake was guarding instead of trying to get out. Maybe Darla figured they wouldn't expect us to double back. I didn't know exactly how we'd get past the fence or down the embankment on Bikezilla, either. But I didn't have the lung capacity to ask while we were pedaling like maniacs. I hoped she knew what she was doing.

We bounced up the railroad embankment and braked hard, skidding down the back side. We came to a complete stop by crashing into the chain-link fence. "Hurry! Cut the fence!" Darla ordered.

I grabbed the bolt cutters and started chopping chain-link as fast as I could. We needed a huge hole to accommodate Bikezilla. Luckily we were far enough south of the guard shack that we couldn't see it and, presumably, couldn't be seen. I finished up the hole, stomping flat the huge piece of chain-link I'd cut out. Darla nearly ran me down in her haste to push Bikezilla through. She didn't stop, either—I had to stow the bolt cutter and remount the bike while it accelerated away from the fence.

As we approached the steep slope down to the river, Darla didn't slow down. If anything she was speeding up. I yelled and tried to back off my pedaling, but the pedals on Bikezilla were ganged together—I had no choice but to keep up with Darla's frenetic pace. And all the brake controls were at the front of the bike.

"Hold on!" Darla screamed, and we were airborne. The back end of the bike hit the slope with a thump. Then the front end slapped down, and I was pitched forward, my head thudding into Darla's back.

We careened down the slope, totally out of control. When we hit the ice at the bottom, the front ski flexed almost forty-five degrees, but nothing broke.

And just like that, we were out on the river ice. We still both stood to pedal, but slightly slower than before.

"I'm going to head south," Darla grunted. "Cross the open part of the river somewhere out of sight from the lock."

"Sounds good," I yelled.

"You think we're in the clear?"

"Yeah."

Then I heard an engine rumble behind us.

Chapter 17

I glanced back. A Humvee was rolling down the embankment we'd just flown down. The slope was so steep it looked like the truck would tip forward and tumble down end over end, but it didn't—unfortunately.

I redoubled my efforts at the pedals. Darla veered left. The ice was slick and fast, dusted here and there with a little snow. We were moving quicker than we ever had on Bikezilla. Still, I didn't think we'd be a match for the truck.

We pedaled south on one of the dozens of frozen lakes that lined the Mississippi. As we raced for the far bank, I looked back. The Humvee was down the embankment, accelerating toward us across the ice. It veered slightly, so I could see the passenger window roll down and a rifle barrel emerge. Chips flew from the ice around us as bullets struck, and I heard the rattle of automatic gunfire.

I screamed, "Darla!"

"Shoot back!"

I twisted and tugged at the shotgun. Freeing it or the assault rifle from the ropes one-handed was hopeless. I couldn't quit pedaling and I couldn't twist back far enough to reach both hands into the load bed. I snatched the pistol instead.

I aimed at the Humvee closing fast behind us. The passenger's head, covered by a black ski mask, was out the window now. He withdrew into the vehicle as I pointed the pistol at him. Two bullets. I waited. We were less than halfway across the lake, and the Humvee was closing in fast, seeming to swell in size even as I watched it approach.

The rifle barrel appeared again in the window. I pulled the pistol trigger. Nothing happened. It wouldn't even depress. The safety—I'd forgotten the safety. I poked it with my thumb, trying to snick it off without dropping the pistol as a new fusillade tore up the ice around us.

I pulled the trigger again. Click. Nothing happened. I'd forgotten to rack the slide. I brought the pistol back in front of me, took both hands off the handlebars for a second, and jerked back the slide.

The truck was right behind us and a little to our left now, still accelerating—preparing to turn us into a hood ornament. The passenger was hanging his head out the window again. I took aim and fired.

My shot whanged off metal. The passenger and rifle withdrew. The truck was almost on top of us. "Darla!" I screamed.

She cranked Bikezilla into such a tight right turn that half of the rear track lifted off the ice. I leaned into it, hoping to keep us upright. Our pursuers tried to mimic our turn but spun out, quickly turning three full circles as they slid south, away from us.

Darla straightened the bike and the back end thumped onto the ice. Now we were headed roughly northwest, in the middle of the lake, and the closest bank was probably ahead of us.

We flew several hundred yards before the Humvee came out of its spin and started accelerating toward us again. My neck worked overtime twisting backward every few seconds. I couldn't figure out what they were doing— they were way out to our left and behind us, not on a direct route to intercept us.

When the Humvee pulled even with us, about one hundred yards to our left, it became clear what the driver was doing. He drifted into a long turn designed to intersect our course and splatter us all over the ice. There was no way we'd make it to the trees at the edge of the lake. The passenger leaned out his window and started firing at us again.

"Darla!" I yelled again.

"I'm on it!" she gasped, but she kept us on the same course, still pedaling like mad.

I aimed the pistol again. Click. Nothing happened when I pulled the trigger. I pulled it again, but the trigger wouldn't even depress. Did I need to rack the slide again? I tried it, and a bullet flew out—a dud, I guessed.

We raced toward a deadly crash. Sixty yards . . . forty yards. The passenger aimed his rifle at me. I was out of bullets. I pointed the pistol at him anyway, and he flinched. Twenty yards . . . ten. I threw the pistol at him, catching him right in the eye. His shots flew wild. Every one of my muscles tensed for the impact.

"Darlaaaa!"

"Stop! Now!" She slammed on the brakes and jammed the pedals to a stop so abruptly that it hurt my ankles and knees. We skidded along the ice. The Humvee shot by in front of us. Our front ski missed their rear tire by inches.

"Go! Go!" Darla yelled as she turned Bikezilla directly toward the Humvee. It was braking—the tires carving two shallow troughs in the ice. We picked up speed, heading directly toward the truck's back bumper.

I thought I understood what Darla was doing. The Humvee would have to turn in a wide arc to get lined up to try to run us down again. By then, maybe we could make it into the woods.

But the driver wasn't cooperating. He skidded to a complete stop, almost putting the nose of the Humvee into the woods. But instead of turning around, he started backing up. Straight toward us.

"Christ!" Darla screamed. "Male drivers!" She kept accelerating directly toward the Humvee as it raced backward toward us. Playing chicken with a truck fifty times our size didn't seem like a great idea to me, but I wasn't in the driver's seat. And Darla had dodged the truck twice now—one more time and we'd make it to the woods.

"Yeeaaah," Darla screeched a banshee wail. "Faster!"

I was already white-knuckling the handlebars, pumping for all I was worth. A drop of blood oozed out between Darla's right hand and her handlebars and was whipped past me by the wind.

The back of the Humvee loomed. I wanted to close my eyes. I couldn't close my eyes. At the last second, Darla swerved left. The driver of the Humvee swerved, too. The truck's front quarterpanel sideswiped Bikezilla's load bed just behind my right leg.

We were thrown into a spin. I was sure we'd roll, but Darla steered into the skid, pedaling like mad, and somehow kept us upright. She shot between a pair of trees that were too close together to admit the Humvee.

We were racing along a tiny frozen creek, forest lining either side. I looked back and almost got knocked off the bike when an overhanging branch smacked me in the side of the head. I didn't see any sign of the Humvee.

Both banks of the creek were overgrown with leafless bushes and trees. I had to watch Darla carefully; when she ducked, I had a split second to follow or get whacked by a branch. Several times Darla threw an arm up to block them instead. The branches were dead and shattered easily, bits of dry wood spinning away as we whizzed past.

Drifts of snow had covered the ice here and there. I felt these as much as saw them—it got much harder to pedal, and Bikezilla rose and fell slightly, following the contours of the blown snow.

Suddenly we burst out of the narrow confines of the creek onto another lake. Darla steered the bike in a broad left turn. We'd been following this new course less than a minute when I started to hear a faint new sound under the chatter of our rear track: the roar of falling water.

I yelled, "Is that—"

"The roller dam, yeah," Darla yelled back. "We're headed right toward the barge and all those soldiers. Look for a place to turn left."

"Up there?" I pointed.

Darla was already steering toward the break in the trees I'd seen. We turned into the new channel, a broad, straight stretch of river. It would have been easy to pedal down it except for one thing: The Humvee was again accelerating across the ice, directly toward us.

Chapter 18

The Humvee was about a mile south of us but racing north fast. Both banks of this stretch of river were densely forested—I didn't see any place we could get off the river ice. Darla braked hard and spun us into a tight turn, and we stood on the pedals, accelerating north away from the Humvee.

"Darla, look!" I yelled and pointed.

"I see it."

To the north, there was a break in the trees: a path barely big enough for Bikezilla, its opening flanked by two huge cottonwoods that would prevent the Humvee from following us. Darla steered straight toward it.

My legs burned. We'd been pedaling flat out since we left the guard shack more than a half hour ago. My body was coated in cold sweat—from exertion or terror, I wasn't sure which. I tried to coax one more burst of speed from my body, but I could barely maintain our current pace.

Darla was exhausted, too. I could hear her gasping for air even over the clatter of Bikezilla. If anything, we were slowing down. But then I heard the Humvee's engine revving behind us and discovered I did have some hidden reserve left.

I bore down on the pedals and we shot forward, a missile homing in on the safety of the trees ahead. There were no tricks left, no fancy maneuvers. If we kept playing chicken with the Humvee, eventually we'd lose.

There was no gunfire. Maybe I'd actually done some damage by throwing the pistol. The rumble of the engine behind us crescendoed. I looked back—we weren't going to make it.

I braced myself uselessly, thinking a collision was inevitable. But suddenly the gap between us and the Humvee widened. The truck braked, sliding toward us across the ice. We shot between the cottonwoods and up a snowy slope. The Humvee slammed into one of the trees with a shriek of tortured steel.

We reached the top of the ridge we'd been climbing, and the trail leveled out, leading into a large clearing with a huge oak. Its branches spread so low we had to duck to pass beneath it. At the far side of the meadow the trail dove back into the woods, down the other side of the ridge toward the river.

Blood rushed in my ears, and my breath came in gasps. But even over the noises of my body, I heard a roar ahead—water rushing over the roller dam.

We came around a bend and the woods opened up, the trail suddenly ending at the frothing pool at the base of the dam. Darla slammed on the brakes, but Bikezilla slid inexorably toward the pool.

"Darla!" I screamed.

"Jump!" She swerved, trying to miss the open water. I jumped and landed with a thud in the snow on the hillside. The bike fell sideways, trapping Darla's leg and dragging her in a rush toward the deadly, roiling water at the base of the dam.

Chapter 19

Without hesitation or forethought, I jumped. I stretched out in a flying leap, Superman-style, hurling myself down the hill toward Darla. I landed half on top of her, our arms entangled, both of us sliding toward the frothing water.

Darla was digging her fingers into the snow, desperately trying to stop her slide. But the weight of Bikezilla, trapping her leg, dragged us toward the edge. I dug my toes into the hillside, groaning with effort.

We slid to a stop. Bikezilla's rear track hung out over the water. Ice from the spray was already freezing on our gear.

"I've. Got. You!" I whispered through clenched teeth.

Darla wrapped one arm around my shoulder. "Maybe you could pull me away from the water now, numbnuts?"

I heaved a huge sigh of thanks and started tugging Darla back toward the bank. A sound like a gunshot rent the air, and the ice under Bikezilla broke. I watched in horror as the whole sheet was instantly sucked under by the vicious undertow.

Darla's legs fell into the pool. She twisted, clinging desperately to me. I scrabbled backward, trying to stay on the unbroken ice. Bikezilla slid off her, sucked down into the gray, foaming water.

The undertow pulled at Darla. It was surprisingly strong—I felt like I was playing tug-of-war with the river, with Darla as the rope and both of our lives hanging in the balance. I couldn't get enough leverage on the icy bank to drag her out of the river. I tightened my grip on her. I would *not* let go. If Darla got dragged into the river, I'd go with her.

Darla heaved her right knee up, trying to get it up over the ice shelf, but she bashed it instead against the edge of the ice. I plunged my left hand into the icy water and got a grip on the back of her knee. I howled and dragged her leg up onto the bank, and she rolled toward me, heaving her other leg free of the pool in a splash of freezing water.

She lay on her back, gasping. I looked across the water and ice of the Mississippi—I didn't see anyone at the barge. Maybe they'd left for the evening.

Bikezilla was thrown to the surface. It slammed into the concrete base of the dam and was sucked back under. The churning water coming over the dam was tossing it around like a tennis shoe in a washing machine. I shuddered—if we'd fallen in there, neither of us would have survived.

"S-s-so c-c-cold," Darla said.

She was sopping wet to her waist. The water was already starting to freeze in little icy patches on her coveralls. I moved my wet left arm experimentally—I could barely feel it. Flakes of ice fell off my sleeve. "We've got to get out of the open."

"All our s-s-supplies." Darla stretched one arm toward the roller dam.

"It's hopeless. They're gone." I stood and helped Darla up. She was shivering violently. We had to hide. Had to get warm—and do it in a way that Black Lake couldn't track us. "Come on. Try to stay in the tracks." I pulled her back up the hill, trudging along the path Bikezilla's rear track had made.

Darla stumbled and fell. She lay shivering in the snow. I hauled her to her feet. "Can you jog?" I asked. "You've got to warm up."

"I'll t-t-try." Darla stumbled up the hill in a shambling half-jog. We were moving a lot slower than I would have liked, but at least we were out of sight of the barge.

Darla started to fall, and I caught her again. I looked down and saw I'd stepped outside of Bikezilla's track. We were leaving a clear trail despite our efforts to stay in the path.

Darla fell once more before we made it to the top of the ridge. The woods were silent and still. On the mostly level ground at the top of the hill, Darla stretched out her pace, and we made better time. Maybe the jogging was warming her up, though she was still shivering. I rubbed my wet arm as we ran. I still couldn't feel it.

I stopped when we got to the massive, spreading oak in the clearing. "We can get off the path without leaving a trail here."

"How?" Darla asked.

"That branch." I pointed above our heads. "I'll boost you up. We'll crawl along it to the trunk, climb around, and crawl out another branch on the far side."

"G-g-good idea."

I wasn't so sure it was a good idea. If Darla fell and hurt herself, it would be a disastrously bad idea. And I'd never been much of a tree climber—I don't like heights. "Can you do it?"

Darla just nodded, shivering.

I squatted and grabbed Darla by her thighs. Water squished out of her coveralls onto my coat. I lifted her high enough that all she had to do was flop her arms over the branch to hang by her armpits. She kicked out—I had to duck to save my head—and got one leg up over the branch. Then she swung herself up on top of it and started dragging herself toward the trunk, inchworm-style.

I jumped and grabbed the branch in both hands, facing away from Darla. I swung my legs back and forth a few times, working up momentum, and threw them up and around the branch. Then I just had to roll over, pulling myself to the top of the tree limb. Darla was already about halfway to the trunk. I dragged myself along behind her.

"There's a great view from back here," I said.

"Q-quit looking!" Darla snapped, but I could hear a hint of a smile in her voice. Maybe my stupid joke had worked. I needed something, anything, to distract from the desperation building in my gut.

Darla stopped at the oak's huge trunk. "There's no way to climb around."

"What about up to that fork in the tree?" I asked.

"Maybe. I might need a boost."

Darla wasn't stuttering or shivering as much. I hoped that was a good sign. I let my legs dangle over either side of the icy branch and scooched over to help. She sat up and threw one knee up on the branch and reached to try to get a handhold in the fork of the tree. I held her waist, trying to keep her steady. Darla stood up on the branch so she could reach farther into the fork. "Push me up."

I put my palms under her butt and shoved. She pulled herself upward until her chest was wedged into the split in the tree. She rested there for a moment and then pulled herself the rest of the way up.

"There's a branch here that goes the right way," Darla said. "We can get at least another thirty feet from the path."

"Okay, good. I'm coming up." I pulled my knees onto the branch. Standing was tricky. I got one foot flat on the ice-coated branch, but I felt wobbly. I stood, trying to keep the unsteadiness in my knees under control and clinging to the trunk. I wasn't that far off the ground—maybe ten or twelve feet. There was no real reason to be scared. I focused on the tree trunk and tried to get my breathing under control. In through the nose, out through the mouth—like I'd use for a sparring match in taekwondo.

I reached and got a grip on the fork in the tree. I bent my knees to jump and give myself a head start on pulling myself up, but I slipped—and suddenly I was dangling, my feet clawing futilely at the air.

Chapter 20

I kicked out, bashing my toes against the tree trunk. Feet scrabbling against the trunk, I tried to pull myself onto the branch. I didn't have a solid grip on the fork in the tree; my fingers were slipping on the icy bark. Darla's hands wrapped around my left wrist and hauled upward. I strained, pulling myself up until my chest was wedged in the fork. Darla was sitting on a slightly higher branch, reaching down to help me.

"Thanks," I grunted.

Darla turned and started inching away from the trunk on the new branch, saying, "I think this branch will work best." I scrambled to follow her.

The end of the new branch looked none too safe. It was more than fifteen feet above the ground, and we couldn't afford to fall and sprain an ankle or worse. But as we inched outward, the branch sagged until it was only ten or twelve feet over the snow.

Darla reached a spot where the branch forked into two smaller limbs that probably wouldn't support both our weight. She grabbed the branch and swung off it, dangling for a moment. "Hold on tight," she said. Then she let go, dropping into the snow below.

Before I had a chance to adjust my grip, the branch sprang upward, trying to buck me off. I clung like a squirrel in a thunderstorm. When the motion calmed, I called down to Darla, "You okay?"

"Yeah, fine."

I inched out to the fork in the limb and slid off, dangling by my hands. I bent my knees a little and let go. When I hit the snow, I let my legs crumple so I wouldn't jam my ankles or knees. Practicing falls at the dojang, we used to roll or slap the floor to break our momentum, but the snow was so deep there was really no surface to slap. Still, for once I was glad for that deep snow—it cushioned my fall.

Darla grabbed my hand and hauled me to my feet. "Are *you* okay?"

"Yeah." I looked around—we were at least sixty feet from the path. I hoped that would be enough of a break in the trail that nobody would notice our new track. With any luck, they'd assume we went into the river with Bikezilla and drowned at the base of the roller dam.

I struck out on a course perpendicular to our old path. Pushing through the deep snow was hard, cold work. Soon both of us were shivering again.

We left the clearing and entered a dense wood. The trees were all dead and leafless, so it didn't offer much cover. I pushed onward for twenty or thirty minutes, breaking the trail for Darla.

I heard a clicking sound behind me and turned. Darla was shivering violently.

"Crap, I've got frozen peas rattling around where my brains should be. We've got to get you out of the wind."

"I'm 'k-k-kay," Darla said around the rattle of her teeth. Her lips were turning blue, and the legs of her coveralls were crusted in ice and snow. She was definitely not okay. But even if our fire-starting kit hadn't gone down with Bikezilla, we couldn't afford a fire now—we were still too close to the barges and the Black Lake guards.

"Crap, crap, crap," I whispered. First things first—I could take care of the wind and wet clothes—maybe. I looked around for the deepest drift, a spot where a cluster of trees had captured and held the blowing snow. "Come on." I took Darla's hand and led her toward the drift, using my body as a plow.

When we got well into the drift, I dug a foxhole, shoveling away the snow with my hands and arms. Darla tried to help, but her arms were shaking so badly she could barely control them. My wet arm in particular was freezing, and I was shivering, but Darla had nearly been dunked. I had to get her dry somehow. Now.

As I finished digging, I hit the ash layer under the

snow—a grim reminder of the cause of this abominable winter, of the volcano's eruption ten months ago. Some of the ash came up with the last few armloads of snow and left dirty gray blotches on the white ramparts of my foxhole.

We squatted in the foxhole for a few minutes. I wrapped my arms around Darla, hugging her from behind and rubbing her arms. The foxhole kept us out of the wind, but it wasn't warming up Darla—if anything, she was shivering more.

"Stand up," I said. "Let's get these wet clothes off." I unlaced her boots and gave one a tug. It came off with a crackle of breaking ice and squelch of wet sock. When I finished with both boots, I reached up, unzipped her coverall, and started pulling it down off her torso.

"I'm n-n-not really in the mood," she said.

"Yeah, me either," I said as I pulled the coverall down over her legs.

"That's a f-f-first."

I forced myself to smile. I was terrified she'd freeze to death as I watched, helpless. I started stripping off her jeans. Water had gotten through her coverall at the waist and ankles, so only the knees of her jeans and long johns were dry. When I got her long underwear off, I put my hands on her hips against her pink panties. They were sopping wet with river water.

With both my hands against her icy skin, I realized she wasn't shivering as hard. I took that as the worst kind of sign: When the body quits shivering, it's preparing to die.

Chapter 21

I stripped off Darla's panties and socks, so she stood bottomless in the frozen air. Her bare feet were porcelain white, streaked with blue. She set them in the snow without protest—obviously she couldn't feel her feet at all. I had maybe a minute before she started to get frostbite, and not much longer than that before the hypothermia would kill her.

I stripped off my boots as fast as I could and squatted on them to keep my socks dry while I pulled off my coveralls.

I jammed Darla's feet into my coverall. She was so far gone now I had to lift each foot and put it in the pant leg for her. I had two pairs of socks on, a wool outer pair and some nylon liners. I stripped off my wool stocks and forced them over Darla's feet. My boots didn't fit right without the thick wool socks and my toes hurt terribly, but I figured that was a good sign. If they quit hurting, I'd know I was in trouble.

I thought about what to do with Darla's feet. If I left her in socks, her feet would get wet from the snow. But her boots were sopping. I wrapped my hand in the dry part of her long johns and pushed it up into her boots to try to dry them. I don't know if it helped much, but it was the best I could do. I put the wet boots back on her feet and tied the laces.

"Come on, Darla," I said. "You've got to run now."

She started to shamble into the snow at the edge of the foxhole. I threw an arm around her waist to stop her.

"No, just run in place. We've got to stay hidden until dark." It wouldn't be long. The day was already fading.

Darla lifted one foot and set it back down.

"Faster." I wanted to yell, but I knew I shouldn't. Black Lake might have people out looking for us.

Darla started stepping desultorily in place. She lurched from side to side as if drunk, her balance so bad that I kept both hands on her waist, ready to catch her if she started to fall over.

"That's it. Faster, Darla, faster."

She started moving more quickly. I concentrated on holding her upright and trying to jog in place without kicking her. When she started shivering again, I breathed a sigh of pure relief.

"W-w-what now?" she asked.

"It's maybe an hour 'til full dark. We can sneak out of here then and head back to Uncle Paul's farm."

"N-n-no."

"What do you mean, no? We just lost all our supplies. It's going to get even colder after dark. I don't even know if we can survive tonight. We might have to turn ourselves in to Black Lake. Better to wind up in a FEMA camp than frozen to death."

Darla didn't reply. Instead, she started running in place faster. She was shivering hard—her arms made unpredictable spastic movements. I backed off a little so I wouldn't get brained.

We ran for fifteen or twenty minutes. Darla steadily picked up her pace, while I stuck with a comfortable, warming jog. Her shivering gradually subsided. She started pumping her arms instead of waving them around, and her teeth quit clattering.

Without any warning, she spun back toward me and quit running. "We are not going back, Alex. We're going forward."

"Bikezilla's at the bottom of the Mississippi with all our supplies."

"I know. You still have the kale seeds?"

"Yeah, and the wheat, but even if we ate all of them, they'd only last a few days."

"Not to eat, to trade."

"Yeah, that's what I'm trying to say. We hoof it back to Warren, trade the seeds, and get outfitted for another expedition."

"No—we go forward to Worthington and resupply there."

"How do you know anyone's still in Worthington? They might all be dead—or locked in FEMA camps."

"They might be." Darla's shoulders hinted at a shrug. "But they're my people—I know them. They're farmers, used to coming through hard knocks and bad weather. They were already well organized last year. They had water and were digging corn. If anyone's still alive and free in Iowa, it's the folks in Worthington."

"And the bandit gangs, and Black Lake—"

"I never thought this trip would be easy."

"Look, I don't even know how we're going to survive *tonight*, let alone get to Worthington."

"You still have a hatchet and knife?"

"Yeah, on my belt. But we need a fire, and the flint went down with Bikezilla."

"We're okay then. With a knife and hatchet, we've got fire."

"How?"

"Easier to show you. And we should wait for dark and get someplace farther away from the lock, so Black Lake won't spot the fire." Darla started jogging in place again as if the conversation were over.

I stayed still. "I don't want to get us—get you—killed, Darla."

"We're only in this situation because *you* insisted on going after that wheat."

Much as I hated to admit it, she was right. "I know. . . . I'm sorry."

Darla shrugged. "It's okay. We're tougher to kill than you give us credit for. We've got money—kale seeds and wheat kernels—we've got a knife, a hatchet, and some clothes. We'll get to Worthington, buy supplies, and then go break your mom and dad out of the FEMA camp in Maquoketa. We'll be okay."

Half an hour ago Darla had nearly frozen to death, and now she was trying to talk me into continuing our trek. She was certifiably grade-A, prime-cut crazy. "I love you."

"Love you, too. Now get your ass jogging so you don't freeze."

"I've got to figure out something to do with these clothes." I picked up Darla's coveralls, thinking I'd wring the water out of them, but they were frozen solid. They crackled, and ice flaked off the legs.

I beat the coveralls on a nearby tree trunk to loosen them up and knock off more ice. I thought for a moment about how best to carry them. I could stuff the coveralls into my coat, but they'd melt and get my chest wet. We needed to keep the coveralls and dry them out, but I couldn't afford to get hypothermic.

Finally I loosened my belt and tucked the coveralls through the back, so they dangled along the back of my legs. I repeated the process with Darla's pants and long johns, beating them against a tree and tucking them into my belt.

Darla was still jogging in place, but now she had a silly grin on her face.

"What?" I said.

"You should see yourself—you look ridiculous."

For a second I was annoyed, but then I realized that, yeah, I probably did. "What, you don't appreciate my super-powers? I'm Clothesline Man! Faster than a tumbling dryer, stronger than the scorching sun, saving the day by flying across the snow to dry all your clothes." I rotated my hips, making the clothing swing around me in an arc.

Darla was laughing now. The joke seemed pretty lame to me, but probably anything would have been funny after the past few hours.

"I can even dry these!" I picked her pink panties up out of the snow.

Her mouth curled at one side. "Usually you have the opposite effect."

I thought about that for a moment and then felt my face heat despite the frigid temperature.

"Actually, forget about those. I'll just go commando for a while."

"Okay." I pushed the panties into the snowbank to hide them, although I couldn't have said why I bothered. Then I resumed jogging; I needed to warm up.

Despite our jogging, we both started shivering again as night fell and the temperature dropped. It got so dark I could barely see the piles of snow around our foxhole.

"How are we going to figure out which way to go?" I asked.

"Shh. Listen."

I stood still, suppressing my shivering for a moment. I heard the susurration of rushing water very faintly in the distance.

"Which way is it coming from?" Darla whispered.

I pointed.

"Yeah, that's about what I thought, too. We can use the noise to figure out what direction we're going."

"Lead on."

Darla pushed her way out of the foxhole into the deep snow. I followed, watching the snow, trying to place my feet in her footsteps. After a few minutes of that, I looked up and felt a surge of panic when I couldn't see her.

Our chances were bad enough together. If we got separated, I didn't see how we'd survive. Well, Darla might, she knew how to make a fire. I fought down my fear—all I had to do was follow her trail.

I ran for twenty or twenty-five feet, high-stepping through the snow. I almost bowled into Darla's back. She was trudging along, oblivious to my panic.

Another half hour or so brought us to a break in the trees. A steep slope led down to the frozen river. I heard the roller dam faintly to my right. I could see a little farther here without the trees overhead, but the other side of the river was completely shrouded in darkness.

Darla got down to the river by sitting down and sliding on her butt. I waited a moment for her to move out of the way, then slid to join her.

Walking across the Mississippi felt like exploring an alien planet. The darkness hid everything but the tiny circles of ice on which we planted our feet. Our boots made weird squeaks and crunching sounds. I feared we might walk through this dark limbo forever, slowing gradually until we froze in place, statues lost from their museum, admired by no one.

Chapter 22

I saw Darla's shoulders trembling and said, "Let's pick up the pace."

"Yeah. C-c-christ, I'm cold."

"And hungry," I added.

"Thirsty, too. I'd even eat some s-s-snow, but that'd just make me c-c-colder."

We started jogging across the ice. Darla fell twice. Both times she took my hand, levered herself up, and kept going without comment. Wiping out had to hurt, but she ignored the pain, determined to keep us moving forward.

It seemed like it was taking way too long to

cross the river. I mean, yeah, the Mississippi is huge, but
we'd been jogging twenty or thirty minutes.

"How much farther?" I asked.

"How should I know? Keep moving." Her voice was
huffy from exertion—or annoyance.

Not five minutes later we finally reached the bank.

"Head downstream following the bank?" Darla said.
"That'll take us farther away from the barge."

"Yeah."

We jogged south, away from the lock and barges,
skirting around big snowdrifts. After a while, the bank
started to curve to the right. As we followed it, I noticed
the trees were bigger here—their branches hung far out
over the river ice. When I caught a glimpse of a tree to
our left, I figured out where we were: traveling into an
inlet, a frozen tributary of the Mississippi.

Darla stopped. "Let's make a camp here. That bend
should shield us from anyone at the lock."

"Okay. So how are we going to build a fire?"

"Rubbing sticks together."

My chest sank. "Um, that's going to take for-freaking-
ever."

"Not the way we're going to do it." Darla explained
what she wanted me to do.

I had to do most of the work. Darla was still shivering
badly and spent a lot of time running in place or slapping
her legs, trying to stay warm. I split a small cottonwood
log twice, forming a roughly flat plank that Darla called a
fireboard. Another piece of the log became a small round-

ed grip—a thunderhead, again according to Darla. I whittled an eight-sided spindle out of a cottonwood branch. A long, curved oak branch became a bow, and one of my bootlaces served as a bowstring. I discovered that the inner bark of cottonwood trees would shred nicely to form a fine, dry firestarter or bird's nest. It took more than an hour to gather and make everything we needed.

Then we put it together and tested it. I wrapped the bowstring around the spindle, which I placed vertically between the fireboard and thunderhead. The idea was that I'd use one hand to hold the thunderhead in place and the other to pump the bow back and forth, to rotate the spindle. In turn, that'd generate friction between the spindle and fireboard and, hopefully, create a spark.

Of course it didn't work. The bootlace slipped on the spindle, and we had to tighten it. Then the spindle kept flying off the fireboard, and we had to cut a deeper dimple to keep the spindle in place.

While we worked on fixing our makeshift fire-by-friction set, I asked Darla where she'd learned how to build it.

"From Max's *Boy Scout Handbook*," she replied.

"I thought he quit scouts after a month?"

She shrugged. "I didn't know that. I just thought the book looked interesting. And it was."

Finally we got it all working. I sawed back and forth on the bow, holding the thunderhead with my other hand, trying to keep even pressure on it. Both ends of the spindle started smoking in surprisingly little time, just a minute or two. About thirty seconds after the spindle started smoking, a spark fell out of the thunderhead onto my glove. I froze, trying to avoid any sudden move that might extinguish the spark, not caring if it burned my hand.

It winked out.

"Well, at least we know it works," Darla said. "The spark is supposed to come from the fireboard, not the thunderhead. I wonder what we're doing wrong?"

We set it up again. I was surprised by the spindle—it was noticeably shorter. Deep black holes had been drilled in both the fireboard and thunderhead. Darla put one hand over mine on the thunderhead and grabbed the other end of the bow. Working together we could pump the bow much faster and more smoothly. Less than 30 seconds had passed before smoke was pouring from both ends of the spindle.

I heard a cracking noise and the thunderhead broke. The end of the spindle hit my palm, twisting the nylon and burning my hand through my glove. I snatched my hand back and the spindle went flying. It had drilled clear through both the thunderhead and fireboard.

I shook my hand and looked down. The hole in the bottom of the fireboard was nearly filled by a huge spark glowing atop the ash.

"Now I know what we were doing wrong," Darla said. "We were supposed to put a notch in the fireboard to let out the spark. Probably supposed to lubricate the thunderhead somehow, too."

I gently lifted the fireboard. There were bits of snow and ice around the spark on the floor of our foxhole. If any of those melted, our spark would be extinguished. I picked up my knife and slid the blade under the spark.

Slowly, very slowly, I lifted the spark while groping around for the bird's nest. Darla placed it in my hand. I gently slid the spark off my knife and into the nest, cupped in my left palm.

The spark was growing, igniting some of the black dust I'd scooped up along with it. I scooped some more of the dust from the fireboard with the blade of my knife and gently fed it to the spark. It grew larger still, a glowing coal nestled in the shredded bark on my palm.

I whispered to my spark, letting my breath coax it, "Burn. Burn, damn it, burn." And with a pop and whoosh, it obeyed. The bird's nest flared to life. I set it down slowly, not caring if it singed my fingers. We had made fire—created life!

We fed the fire together, starting with slivers of left-over wood and quickly moving on to twigs and branches. Darla's hands shook so badly that the twigs she dropped occasionally missed the fire altogether. I shuddered to think what might've happened if the fire-by-friction set hadn't worked.

I took the hatchet and cut three long limbs with forks on their ends. By jamming each branch into the snow and interweaving the forked ends, I created a rough tripod next to our fire. I took Darla's frozen clothing off my belt and draped it over the tripod to dry.

Darla was huddled right up against the fire, getting warm. I squatted next to her. "Let me see your hand," I said.

She held out her right hand, and I pulled off her glove. She had two roughly parallel crescent-shaped wounds between her palm and the base of her middle finger. Benson had bitten her so hard he'd drawn blood. The bite was scabbed over, but the flesh around it was red and swollen. I got some clean snow to scrub her wound.

When I started washing it, Darla screamed. I found a mostly clean leftover piece of cottonwood and gave it to her to bite. "Sorry," I said. "I gotta clean it."

Darla nodded, tears rolling down her face. I kissed her cheek, tasting salt. She laid her hand back in my lap, and I resumed scrubbing while she cried.

"I think it's getting infected," I said as I finished.

Darla just moaned.

I put her glove back on and rooted around in my jacket for a minute. I'd kept the Cipro tablets zipped into my inner pocket with the kale seeds. I took out a tablet and handed it to Darla. "Take this."

She spit the piece of wood out from between her teeth. "They're for you."

"I'll take a half."

"How many do you have left?"

"Five, counting that one."

"Aren't you supposed to take antibiotics for, like, ten days or something?"

"Doc said seven. I'll take a half. If you take full ones today and tomorrow and then go to halves like me, we can make five tablets last three more days. By then maybe we'll be in Worthington. Maybe we'll be able to buy some more."

"My mouth is too dry to swallow this damn horse pill."

"I'll get some clean snow."

We had no pan to melt the snow in, so we put little balls of it in our mouths to melt. That was tolerable with the fire roaring beside us. Darla swallowed her Cipro, and I cut a tablet in half with my knife. The rough edge of the tablet caught in my throat. I had to eat a bunch more snow to choke it down and wash away the nasty taste it left in my mouth.

Then we cleared off snow from a larger area to sleep in. By the time we'd done that, we needed more firewood. So we spent at least a half hour chopping enough wood to last through the night.

I felt woolly, like I'd been awake for three days straight. My eyelids drooped, and I had to force myself to concentrate as I chopped wood lest the hatchet miss and add to our growing inventory of injuries.

But Darla looked even worse. Her eyes made a pair of black holes in her face. She was yawning almost nonstop.

"Go to sleep," I said. "I'll take first watch."

"We can both sleep if we build up the fire first."

"What if Black Lake finds us? We'd better take turns."

Darla used a couple of small logs and one of her scarves to make a crude pillow, and then she lay down beside the fire. Within seconds her breathing slowed as sleep claimed her.

I wanted nothing more than to curl up around her and sleep, too. But I knew it wasn't safe. I sat in the volcanic ash beside Darla and watched her chest slowly rise and fall. The firelight played in her hair. I reached out to stroke it but thought better of it and pulled my hand away—I didn't want to wake her.

I felt suddenly morose. What was I doing, dragging Darla back into Iowa? Her parents were dead—she had no particular reason to want to find mine. Already she'd been injured. If I got Darla killed on this insane trip, I wouldn't be able to live with myself.

Chapter

23

I struggled to stay alert, trudging back and forth beside the fire. When I saw the first hint of dawn in the east, I shook Darla awake. "I gotta sleep," I said. She mumbled something and pushed herself upright. I was fast asleep before my head fully settled on the log.

It seemed like no time at all had passed when Darla pushed on my shoulder, saying, "Alex, wake up."

I startled fully awake, sat up, and looked around. "Something wrong?"

"No, everything's okay. But we should get going."

"What time is it?"

"I don't know. Around noon, maybe."

Darla was dressed in her own clothes, and my coveralls were laid out on the tripod by the fire. I slipped my
toasty warm coveralls on, struggling to pull the legs over
my boots.

Darla fiddled with a bundle of wood. "What's that?" I
asked.

"I worked on the fire-by-friction set while you were
asleep. Made a new thunderhead out of oak, so it won't
burn through. We've got two extra spindles now, too.
Here's your shoelace."

I started relacing my boot while Darla tied all the fire-
by-friction stuff into a neat bundle using a drawstring
she'd cannibalized from her jacket. We kicked snow over
the fire, tore down the tripod, and set out.

"Which way?" I asked.

"Maybe follow this creek upstream? Easier to walk on
the ice. Hopefully we'll hit a road."

"How far is it to Worthington?"

"I don't know, exactly. We're near Bellevue. It's about
thirty miles from Worthington to Dubuque, but I think
Bellevue is farther. Maybe forty or forty-five miles?"

"That's going to take forever if we have to walk
through deep snow. And I'm already famished."

"Let's see what the roads are like. If they're bad,
maybe I can improvise some snowshoes."

We'd walked along the creek until we reached a railroad trestle that passed about twenty feet above the ice.
Beyond that, I saw the concrete pylons and steel girders
of a highway bridge.

We walked under the railroad trestle and turned to fight our way up the bank between the two bridges. The bank wasn't steep, but the snow was so deep that it was difficult to force our way upward. For every step we managed, we slid back a half step.

Finally we got to the top, only to confront an enormous berm of plowed snow alongside the road. I led the way up the berm, thrusting my hands into the snow to make tenuous grips and kicking footholds into the side of the pile. The snow here was a filthy blend of volcanic ash and ice plowed off the road.

We hid near the top of the berm, watching the road for more than an hour. Nothing moved. There was no sound but the chattering of our teeth. I was worried about patrols, but it would take too long to get to Worthington traveling cross-country.

I got down the far side of the berm to the road by sliding on my butt. We were on a two-lane plowed highway.

"You think all the roads are this good?" I said.

"I hope so." Darla stood and dusted the snow off herself. "We'll make good time on this. Maybe get to Worthington in two, two-and-a-half days. Before we starve, anyway."

"I guess there is one advantage to FEMA being in Iowa now." Last year none of the roads on this side of the river had been plowed.

"That's the only good those ass-puppets do."

"Yeah." I looked up and down the highway. "Which way?"

"Right. North. Worthington is northwest of us somewhere."

"Won't that take us closer to the lock and Black Lake?"

"Yeah. We'll turn west as soon as we can."

We made great time on the packed snow of the road. We didn't talk—I was listening for engine noises and continually glancing behind us. I hoped there wouldn't be any Black Lake trucks, but if any trucks did come, I wanted time to try to get away, although that might be impossible—the piles of snow and ash alongside the road were so high that we were essentially trapped.

We got off the highway onto a back road at the first opportunity. Darla led us through a dizzying succession of turns, heading north and west, she said. The roads were all deserted, which was a relief but also a bit puzzling. Why bother plowing roads nobody was going to use?

We passed six or seven farmsteads. All of them were clearly abandoned. About half the houses had burned. "Why do you think so many houses are burned?" I asked.

"Probably people took shelter in them and lit fires in places they shouldn't have," she replied. "You build a wood fire in a hearth that's only designed for a gas log, you'll burn the house down quick-like."

As twilight set in, we stopped at a farmstead. It consisted of two cylindrical concrete grain silos and a one-story farmhouse. There were three hillocks of snow that might have been collapsed barns or sheds—I couldn't tell. The front door and door trim of the farmhouse were missing—a drift of snow more than two feet deep graced the entryway. It was too dark inside to see much, but what I could see wasn't pretty. The house had been thoroughly

looted—furniture, doors, door trim, baseboards, and cabinets were all missing, probably burned as firewood. The
mantle around the living room fireplace was gone, leaving
an ugly hole in the wall, but there was a tiled area around
the fireplace where we could safely build a fire. A big sooty
stain proved we weren't the first people to build a fire
there, although there were no other signs of past occu-
pants.

Darla started setting up the fire-by-friction set while I
looked for wood. Everything burnable inside the house
was gone. There were a bunch of trees outside, but all the
lower limbs and smaller trees had been cut. I picked out
the smallest of the remaining trees and started the long
process of felling it with my hatchet—a job that really
required a chainsaw or at least a full-size ax.

It was almost an hour later and fully dark by the time
I returned to the living room with an armload of wood. I
could barely make out Darla's form hunched over a tiny,
glowing spark.

"This is so cool—this black dust the set makes will
keep a spark alive, like forever. We've got to find some way
to store this stuff."

"Sorry I took so long. Had to cut a tree down to get at
the branches."

"It's okay. Make me a bird's nest, would you?"

It was so dark, I could barely see anything. I stripped
the bark from a couple of branches, working by feel. I took
off my gloves to make it easier to shred the bark, and soon
my hands were freezing. Darla stayed hunched over her

spark, feeding it with black powder from the fire-by-friction set and fanning it gently with her knife blade.

"I think this thing is ready," I said, holding the bird's nest out to Darla.

"Just hold it next to the spark." Darla cut the spark in two with her knife and lifted half of it into the bird's nest.

I slowly lifted the bird's nest to my lips. I whispered to it, "Burn, baby, burn," letting the gentle breath of my whisper fan the spark. Darla was feeding the other half of the spark more black powder, building it up in case mine died.

A strand of bark flared orange, looking like the filament in an old incandescent lightbulb. A tiny flame followed, and in seconds the whole bird's nest was engulfed in fire. I laid it down in the middle of the tiled area. It threw off just enough light that I could find pieces of kindling to feed it.

Darla abandoned the rest of the spark and helped me feed the fire. I offered to get more wood, but it was so dark out that I wasn't sure I could find the tree I'd felled again. I took a flaming stick out of the fire, hoping to use it as a torch. It went out before I even reached the front doorway.

I bent low, using the faint glow of the embers still clinging to my stick to follow my footprints back to the tree. I worried that I wouldn't be able to find my way back to the house, but the glow of the fire was clearly visible through the open maw left by the missing front door.

That aroused a new worry: What if someone came by? It would be obvious from the light that we were camping in the abandoned house. But we hadn't seen anyone on the roads all day, and it would be even harder to travel by night.

I broke more small branches and carried them back to the house. "We're going to need some bigger logs to keep the fire going all night," Darla said as I dropped the wood.

"I can't see well enough to use the hatchet," I replied.

"Hmm." Darla gathered up several long, slender branches, arranging them in a bunch. She thrust one end into the fire. When she pulled it out, the tip of the bundle was engulfed in a steady flame that survived movement, unlike the single branch I'd used. "Come on. I'll hold the light for you."

With Darla clutching her makeshift torch and me chopping, we got enough wood to last the night. By the time we finished, I was hungry and thirsty. I'd been hungry all day—there was nothing I could do about that. But the thirst I could deal with. "I'm going to get some snow," I said.

I didn't bother taking a torch. Snow was easy to find—it was everywhere. I molded two cantaloupe-sized snowballs and carried them inside. Darla took one, broke off a piece, and put it in her mouth to melt. "Just when I get warm, I've got to eat this damn snow," she said.

"Beats going without water."

"I guess. Let me see the hatchet."

I passed the hatchet to her. She wandered around the bare living room for a minute, staring at the ceiling and floor and holding the hatchet by her side. Just as I was getting ready to ask her what in the world she was doing,

she gripped the hatchet firmly in two hands and buried it
with a thunk in the floor.

She swung the hatchet like a madwoman, chopping at
the floor. Tufts of ash-filled, mildewed carpet flew everywhere. Darla was quickly coated in ash and dirt. She
looked like a chimney sweep turned ax murderer: completely insane.

Chapter 24

"What are you doing?" I yelled.

"I am sick . . ." The hatchet thunked back into the carpet. "Of eating . . ." A chunk of wood from the subfloor flew up. "Snow!" Darla slammed the hatchet back into the floor.

"Take it easy. How's killing the floor going to help?"

Darla didn't answer, just kept destroying the floor. I saw wood joists and a rectangular metal heating duct through the ragged hole she'd opened. Darla turned her attention to the heating duct, slamming the hatchet into it with a clang and screech of tearing metal.

I heard another noise when Darla hit the duct, an almost musical tinkling, kind of like a bottle rolling on the sidewalk. It seemed to be coming from the far side of the room beneath one of the windows. I followed the path of the duct with my eye—it led straight to a grate in the floor.

I stepped over to the grate, giving Darla and the wildly swinging hatchet a wide berth. She was still whaling on the ductwork, trying to cut it or rip it up out of the floor. Had the cold and hunger tipped her over the edge?

I couldn't see what was holding the grate in place, so I got my fingernails under its edges and pulled it up. It came free fairly easily. The duct behind it jerked and shivered as Darla whacked the other end of it. I clearly heard something rolling around. I reached down into the duct and withdrew a half-full bottle of Canadian Mist.

"Hey," I yelled, "check this out."

"Just a sec." Darla was totally focused on butchering the heating duct. A big chunk of it came free with a metallic shriek. She set aside the chunk of metal and let the arm holding the hatchet fall. "That was in the duct?"

"Yeah, someone must have hidden it down there. You think we should drink it?"

"I dunno. Alcohol has calories. Maybe it would help."

I unscrewed the cap and sniffed the bottle. Even the smell of alcohol made my empty stomach turn and clench. "I'd probably barf."

"Yeah. Let me finish, and then we'll put that whisky to good use." Darla started hacking at the piece of ductwork with the hatchet and knife. The sheet metal was thin and soft enough that our knife would cut it—although Darla was straining at it, holding the duct in one hand and sawing the knife back and forth with the other.

I groaned, thinking about what she was doing to the edge of the knife. We didn't have a sharpening stone. But saying anything was useless—getting between Darla and a project was as futile as standing on a railroad track hoping to stop a train with an upraised palm.

So I watched while Darla shaped the sheet metal into a rough, square pan. Each corner had a triangular fold, and the top was sharp and ragged, but it looked like it would hold water. "Tada," she said. "No more eating snow."

"That's great. But will the hatchet still cut wood?"

Darla picked it up and looked at the edge. Even by firelight, the nicks and dull spots were obvious. "We'll look for a stone to sharpen it on tomorrow."

I shrugged and loaded the balls of snow into the pan. Darla set the pan at the edge of the fire. Then she plucked the bottle of whisky from the floor.

Darla sniffed the whisky and wrinkled her nose. She lifted the bottle to her lips and took a huge swig.

"Ugh, that's disgusting," she said, coughing as she passed the bottle to me.

Disgusting or not, I couldn't let Darla show me up. I raised the bottle to my mouth and knocked back as much as I could swallow at one gulp. It was horrid—a smell like paint thinner and a sharp taste so strong it burned my throat. I bent double, gasping and coughing, trying to clear the alcohol sear from my nostrils. Once that passed, though, it tasted kind of good for a few seconds, sort of like smoke from a campfire. But the pleasant taste passed, too, and then I was left with nothing but the chemical aftertaste of the cheap whisky.

"Maybe this stuff does have calories, but I don't think I want to drink any more," I said.

"Me, either," Darla replied. "Maybe we can find some real food tomorrow. Save the rest of the alcohol to use as an antiseptic."

"Makes sense. Let me see your hand." I gently stripped off the makeshift bandage from Darla's palm. The wound looked better—a little puffy and swollen, but there were no red streaks, and it didn't smell bad. I washed it as best I could with whisky, then rebandaged it, using more cloth torn from my undershirt.

"Your turn." Darla took the whisky bottle and went to work on my side. It looked a lot better, the red streaks had mostly faded, and it didn't smell like roadkill anymore. By the time Darla finished washing and bandaging me, we'd torn up more than half my T-shirt. All that remained were the shoulders, neck, and a ragged fringe of cloth hanging partway down my chest.

"If you keep using my clothes for bandages at this rate, I'll be naked in a few days," I said.

Darla laughed. "Fine by me. I'll enjoy the naked boy-friend show. Might be a bit cold for you, though." She pulled the makeshift pan away from the fire. All the snow had melted.

"Yeah, maybe I'll wait until we get somewhere warmer before I let you rip all my clothing to rags."

"Deal."

We waited a bit for the pan to cool, then carefully sipped warm water from its sharp edges. "We've got six bags of wheat. Maybe we should cook one?"

"We don't need to," Darla said. "We should make it to Worthington the day after tomorrow."

"Better to keep up our strength. How do you cook wheat, anyway?"

Darla shrugged. "Boil it like corn? I don't know."

I refilled the pan with snow. When that melted, I dumped a bag of wheat in. While I waited for that to boil, I whittled flat spots on a couple of sticks—improvised spoons.

I had no idea how long to cook it. After about fifteen minutes of boiling, I scooped out a few kernels with my stick. They were so hard that they were difficult to chew, and they had an unpleasant, hairy texture.

"How is it?" Darla asked.

"Not good."

She frowned. "Let's get some sleep. Figure it out in the morning."

I pulled the pan off the fire and started getting ready for bed. We hadn't had any Cipro yet that day, so I split a tablet and handed half of it to Darla. She choked it down with a grimace.

The floor beside the fire was hard, but we were so tired it didn't matter. I wrapped Darla up in a hug and kissed her goodnight. We slept like that, our limbs entangled, warmed by each other and the comfort of our hard-won fire.

Chapter 25

The next morning I tried the wheat again. The pan was warm from sitting by the fire all night. Soaking overnight had transformed the kernels—they were soft and delicious. Darla and I quickly ate them all.

When we'd finished breakfast, I packed the makeshift pan, the bottle of whisky, and the remaining bags of wheat under my coat. I cinched the drawstring around my waist extra-tight so everything would stay put. Darla carried the fire-by-friction set under her jacket, the bow sticking out at her collar. We looked lumpy and awkward, strange aliens trudging across the snowscape. The pan rubbed uncomfortably as I moved, its edges digging into my chest through the coveralls and overshirt.

The countryside reinforced my feeling of strangeness. Last year, more than half of the Iowa farmsteads had been occupied. Many of the unoccupied ones had collapsed under the weight of the ash and snow, but very few had burned. Now all of them were abandoned and more than half had burned. Often all that marked a former farm was a grain silo and some charred rubble. Where had all the people gone?

A faint stench of charcoal, melted plastic, and sulfur followed us along the road. The burnt-out buildings made the countryside seem more desolate. The only break in the solitude came late that morning. We heard an engine in the distance and rushed to the side of the road, thinking we'd hide. But the noise faded, and we never saw the vehicle that made it.

Iowa had been a vibrant place just ten months ago. Even on the back roads, you could always see signs of civilization, of people. Now . . . nothing. What kind of life could Darla and I hope for in this desolation? I took her hand and held it for a while as we walked.

I was hungry despite the half-pan of boiled wheat I'd eaten that morning. The hunger made us tired. Our steps slowed as the day wore on, and we barely talked.

About an hour before nightfall, we passed a whole series of burnt houses. All that remained were a few scarred and blackened brick walls and chimneys. We trudged up a slight rise. At the top perched a dark-blue, cylindrical water tower overlooking the town. CASCADE, it read in huge white block letters. Below the town's name, someone had spray-painted a crude drawing of a woodpecker in garish red and neon blue. The woodpecker stood on its hind feet, wings thrust into the air some twenty feet above his head. Fat red boxing gloves capped each of the woodpecker's upraised wings.

"Excellent," Darla said. "Cascade is only ten miles from Worthington. But what is that drawing on the water tower?"

"Woody Woodpecker," I said.

"Woody what?"

"You know. The cartoon." I tried to make the Woody Woodpecker sound, but it didn't come out too well.

She looked at me like I'd lost my mind.

"You've never heard of Woody Woodpecker?" I asked.

"No."

"Country people." I shook my head in mock seriousness. "They lack cultural awareness."

Darla slugged my shoulder. "Well, if that's a woodpecker, it's got a huge evolutionary advantage."

"What's that?"

"It's so ugly, trees will die at the sight of it."

"Yeah, it is ugly. I wonder why someone bothered painting it up there. Must have taken a lot of spray paint to make it that big."

As we got closer, we could see beyond the water tower. There was an open snowfield boxed in by two small apartment buildings and a massive metal shed. The shed's sliding door was open, and we could see a fire flickering within.

"I think I see people moving by that fire," Darla whispered.

"Check it out?" I asked. "See if they look friendly?"

"Yeah. But stay hidden 'til we're sure."

We crept closer, keeping below the level of the wall of plowed snow that lined the road. Once we were within a few hundred feet, Darla and I slowly raised our heads.

Inside the shed, four men clustered around a small, bright-yellow machine. They were big guys, heavily muscled and tattooed. They looked like they'd been eating well. Three women sat by the fire. Two of them had their backs to us. They were working on something in their laps. The other woman was hunched over the fire, cooking.

"What's that machine they're working on?" I whispered. "A jet ski?"

Darla shook her head. "A jet ski? What would they do with that? It's a snowmobile," she hissed.

One of the women stood up. She carried a crude mortar and pestle. She dumped ground meal out of her mortar into a paper bag and scooped something from a feed sack. Behind her, I saw something roasting on a spit over the fire: a leg.

Chapter 26

"Is that . . . ?" I asked.

"It's too thin to be a cow's leg," Darla whispered. "Too long to be a pig's."

"Let's get out of here."

"We need to find a place to spend the night."

"Not in this town."

Darla started crawling beside the snow berm. I followed on my hands and knees. We didn't stand up until we'd left the metal building far behind.

Cascade was wrecked. We moved slowly and silently, sticking to the shadowed area alongside the road. Burnt, partially collapsed buildings flanked us, leaning in like gravestones in an unkempt cemetery.

We reached a major intersection. On the far side a mostly collapsed building still sported its bright red CONOCO sign. The area in front of the building, where the gas pumps used to be, was now nothing but a fire-seared crater. A sign clung to a fallen light pole: HIGHWAY 136.

"Right turn here." Darla's voice was so soft I could barely make out her words.

The building on the corner to our right had burnt, too. Only its brick walls still stood. A half-melted plastic sign read TRI-COUNTY BANK. Below that, someone had spray-painted a crude drawing of a woodpecker similar to the much-larger one on the water tower. I shuddered, and we hurried past the bank's abandoned shell.

As we reached the outskirts of Cascade, total darkness fell. Darla and I held hands and stumbled along more by feel than by sight.

After about twenty minutes, I felt a break in the berm at the road's edge. I groped around, trying to figure out if we'd come to a crossroads. To my right, there was a steep uphill slope. It was strange—the slope was concrete, not snow or ice. I struggled partway up it, trying to figure out what it was—it was far too steep to be a road. The underside of a girder loomed in the darkness. We were under a highway overpass.

There was a low, flat shelf at the top of the slope. The girders were at least five feet high—I could stand upright in between them. "Let's stop here for the night," I said.

"We're still too close to Cascade," Darla whispered.

"It's sheltered here and hidden. We're going to freeze if we keep going."

I lay down on the concrete floor of our hidey hole. It was intensely cold, chilling my side almost immediately. I wanted a fire for warmth and to cook more wheat, but the flames would have stood out like a beacon. Darla lay next to me, and I wrapped an arm around her, pulling her close. We were both shivering. Darla pushed back against me until we were sandwiched together as close as any two people who still have all their clothes on can be. Eventually our shivers subsided, and I fell into a fitful sleep.

In the morning, I woke to the rattle of gunfire.

Chapter 27

I elbowed Darla, but she was already awake. The pop-pop of gunfire was faint, coming from our north, the direction of Worthington, but drawing steadily closer. I could barely make out the muted roar of distant engines, but that noise wasn't tied to a direction; it seemed to be coming from all around us.

I peered to the north. The light was good—we'd slept at least an hour past dawn, but I couldn't yet locate the source of the noises. "Let's move," I whispered.

"Yeah." Darla rolled over and started crawling to the north, away from Cascade and toward the gunfire.

"The other way," I hissed.

Darla kept going. "We need to know what's happening."

The gunfire grew louder as we reached the edge of the overpass. A few miles off, a line of trucks raced directly toward us.

"They're going to pass right through here," I whispered. "Let's get on top of the overpass and hide."

We turned around and crawled as quickly as we could toward the other side of the overpass. There were two bridges above us—both sides of a divided highway with a gap in between. I forced my way through the snow that had fallen between the bridges and wormed to the south side of the overpass. Peeking out, I discovered why the engine sounds seemed to be coming from all around us. Another line of four vehicles was barreling toward us from Cascade to our south. They were small and low, each one kicking up a plume of snow into the air behind it.

"Snowmobiles," Darla said. "Christ."

As we watched, the snowmobiles spread out to surround the south side of the overpass in a rough semicircle. The one closest to us stopped, and the two men riding it dismounted and pulled long guns from a saddlebag. They wore military-style fatigues and camo jackets.

"Let's go!" I tugged on Darla's jacket. We crawled as quickly as we could back to the center of the overpass. When I reached the break between the bridges, I darted out from under the ledge and started clawing my way upward through the deep snow on the embankment.

I scrabbled with my arms and pumped my legs in and

out of the snow, high-stepping, thrusting with panic-fueled urgency. It probably only took us ten seconds to race up the slope, but it seemed like forever. I hurled myself over the snowbank that edged the road atop the overpass. Darla crashed into me a second later.

"What the hell is going on?" Darla asked.

"No idea." I dashed onto the bridge and peered over the snow berm to the north. The gunfire had gotten louder. Four trucks raced along the road in a column, only a few hundred yards from us and approaching fast. The closest was a modern pickup, followed immediately by a cloth-topped, army-style deuce-and-a-half. After the cloth-topped truck there was a gap, then came two ancient pickups—the type with big rounded fenders and small wooden load beds.

Both the antique trucks were packed with men wearing a ragged array of clothing—five or six squeezed into the back of each truck. Two guys on the closer of the old pickups were leaning over the top of the cab, firing rifles at the deuce in front of them. I thought I saw the muzzle flash of returned fire but couldn't be sure.

"Oh my God," I said. "It's an ambush. The first two trucks are luring the old pickups through the overpass. On the other side all those guys on snowmobiles are perfectly set up to massacre them."

"Great," Darla replied. "We'd better hide and sneak out of here when it's all over."

The guys on the old pickups looked like farmers to me, and they were driving into a bandit ambush. I clenched my fists. "We've got to stop it."

"Alex, wait—"

I scrambled to the top of the snow berm and stood up. It was a long drop in front of me down the far side of the berm and off the edge of the bridge. I wavered a moment, then started yelling and waving my arms.

"Get down, you idiot!" Darla screamed. She started scrambling up the snow berm toward me.

All four trucks roared toward us. I pointed at the first old pickup and held my arms out, palms forward, in a gesture to stop.

A spray of snow kicked up beside my feet and the pop of a gunshot sounded from my left. The first pickup roared under the bridge directly below me. I glanced to my left. I could barely see one of the guys from the snowmobiles lying atop the snow berm a couple hundred yards off, pointing a rifle at me.

I felt Darla's hands grab my right arm. She wrenched me around, throwing me down. I heard another gunshot. Darla exhaled heavily—a quiet "oof." A red stain bloomed on her right shoulder and everything slowed around me. Her knees crumpled, and she slid down the outside of the snow berm. I lunged toward her. Snow plumed into the air beside me, and another gunshot sounded. I grabbed for her. My hand caught in her hair. It tore from her scalp, and Darla slipped away.

Chapter 28

Darla fell from the overpass and landed on her back with a whump of compressed fabric on the roof of the cloth-top deuce passing underneath us. My scarf followed her, twisting in the wind. I teetered on top of the snow berm for a split second, afraid to jump after her, a hesitation I would regret for the rest of my life. I was left holding a clump of her hair and the necklace I'd given her, now broken. The truck passed under the bridge. And she was gone.

I ran for the south side of the overpass, hoping to catch the truck there. As I ran, I jammed the broken necklace into the pocket of my coveralls. The situation seemed impossible. I couldn't run as fast as the truck was moving, let alone cross the gap between the lanes of the highway in time.

Something punched my right arm, and I heard another gunshot. The impact spun me partway around and knocked me off balance. To my west, the guy with the rifle was aiming, lining up yet another shot at me. Running across the road in full view of him was suicide. I turned away from him, sprinting east and dodging back and forth, hoping to make him miss. I felt the wet heat of blood flowing down my right arm.

I heard another gunshot, but didn't feel or see anything. A miss. When I reached the northern edge of the overpass, I scrambled up the snow berm and threw myself over the other side. I slid face first down the snow berm and then down the long embankment to the base of the overpass. Flecks of snow flew into my eyes and ice abraded my cheek.

The two old pickups had pulled up and stopped north of the overpass. A guy jumped out of the lead truck's load bed and ran up to me. I pushed to my feet and turned to run to follow the cloth-topped truck with its precious cargo under the bridge. My red scarf was pooled on the icy road. The guy grabbed me. Pain so intense that my fingertips tingled shot through me when his fingers closed around my right arm. I fought down dizziness and tried to pull away.

"Why were you trying to signal us?" the man demanded.

"Let go!" I tried to punch, aiming for his radial nerve. He caught my other arm before my punch could connect. I was weak, slowed by hunger and shock.

"You signaled to stop," the guy shouted. "Why? What's on the other side of the overpass?"

"Let go!" I yelled again. "Darla, I've got to get to Darla!" The words didn't come out clearly. I realized I was sobbing.

The man let go of my right arm and slapped me. The blow rocked my head sideways, brought fire to my face, and stopped my sobbing. "What's on the other side of the overpass?" he yelled.

I sucked in a deep breath. "It's an ambush. There are eight guys on snowmobiles set up on the far side in a semi-circle. If you go under that bridge, it'll be a massacre."

The guy turned toward his buddies in the truck, still holding one of my arms. "Ambush! Eight snowmobiles. Far side of the overpass." They all readied their rifles. Four guys jumped down from the truck to take up flanking positions on either side of the road.

"Four snowmobiles. Eight guys," I said. "Now let me go—I've got to go after Darla!" I thrashed, trying to break the guy's grip. I reached across my body with my left hand and dug my fingers under his pinky. That put more pressure on my wound, and pain spiked up my arm so intensely I saw colored lights. I ignored it as best I could, concentrating on bending his pinky backward.

The biggest guy in the world can be holding you, but if it's your whole hand against his pinky, you can break his grip—or his finger—either of which should do the trick. The guy holding me let go rather than allowing me to break his pinky, and I cranked his hand around, twisting him into an arm bar.

I could have broken his elbow or kicked him in the nuts, but I was just trying to get away. I settled for a round kick to the back of his legs, forcing him to his knees in the icy road. Then I turned to run.

Another guy had jumped down from the back of the pickup and planted himself squarely in my path. He looked familiar.

"You run under that bridge, you're dead for sure," he said. He grabbed the collar of my coveralls as I tried to dodge around him.

The driver's window was down. The guy at the wheel said, "Just let him go. What do we care if he gets his fool head shot off?"

"He saved us from a serious ass-kicking," the guy holding me said.

"This is how you show your gratitude?" I tried to snake my right arm through his arms, preparing to throw him off, but a burst of pain so intense that it left me gasping stopped me.

"I've seen you before," he said. "In Worthington with Darla Edmunds."

Suddenly I placed the guy. The sheriff who'd met us outside Worthington last year. He was thinner now and had a nasty puckered scar running along his left cheek. "I remember you. I'm Alex. I've got to get out of here. Now."

"Earl. How—"

"They've got Darla. She fell onto the roof of that army truck. She's been shot. I've got to go after her."

"Thought you said there was an ambush over there?"

"There is! But that's the way Darla went."

"Guys on snowmobiles are probably part of that bandit gang we were chasing. You go through there alone, you're dead," Earl said.

"Well, come with me, then!"

"We drive into that ambush, we all might die. Wouldn't do us or Darla any good. And these pickups are no good in deep snow—we can't get around and flank them."

"But they can flank you pretty easy on their snowmobiles. They had a scout up on the overpass. Guy who shot Darla," I glanced at my arm, "and me." The outside of my coat dripped blood.

"We should see to that arm," Earl said. "Looks like it needs stitching."

I scanned the top of the overpass. My eye caught on a flash of gold—blond hair peeking out from under a watch cap. "Up there, peeking over the snow berm." I pointed with my left arm.

One of the guys still on the truck lifted his rifle, took aim, and fired. The scout on the overpass ducked below the snow berm. "Damn, you missed him," Earl said.

"What are we going to do about Darla?" I said.

"We should bandage your arm," Earl replied.

"Hell with my arm!" I yelled. "How are we going to get Darla back?"

"You aren't any use to her at all if you bleed out," Earl replied mildly.

One of the other guys in the pickup bed turned toward us. He had a pair of binoculars dangling from his neck.

"Earl, snowmobile to our west. About a half mile."

"They're flanking us!" Earl yelled. "Pull out! Back to Worthington."

Earl pulled me toward the truck. I whipped my left through his arms and spun, using my forearm like a crowbar to wrench myself free. The guy who'd grabbed me the first time was standing behind me now, trying to nab me again. I kicked his legs out from under him and turned back toward the overpass in time to see Earl's fist just before it crashed into my temple. Everything went black.

Chapter 29

I saw Darla's face, hair streaming past, as she fell away from me. But now she was falling upward, into the yellow-gray post-volcanic sky. I reached for her, but she faded, and my hand passed through her insubstantial form, stirring it like smoke until it dissipated.

The ground under me bucked and my shoulder blade hit it hard enough to bruise. I realized I was on my back in the pickup as it raced along the road.

I sat up far too fast. Pain and nausea mounted a twin assault on my head and stomach. I twisted and vomited bile onto the wooden floorboards of the truck bed.

"Y'okay?" Earl laid his hand against my back.

"No." I shoved myself onto my feet, ignoring the pro-testations of my head and stomach.

I stumbled, and Earl grabbed my left arm, holding me up. "Worthington's a bit different from when you were here before," he said.

I held onto the back of the cab for support and looked around. A gleaming wall stretched away from the road, curving out of sight in both directions. It was a solid, vertical wall of ice about sixteen feet high. A heavy wooden gate had been built across the road. Three guards struggled with each half of the gate, wrenching it open so the trucks could pass through.

"Impressive, ain't it?" Earl said.

"Yeah." It was amazing. I might have been awestruck if Darla had been there to see it with me.

"We built it with two bulldozers and a sprayer truck. Bulldozed huge piles of snow, carved a vertical face, and then sprayed it down with water to freeze it solid."

I grunted.

"Keeps us safe, anyway. And it'll last exactly as long as we need it—'til this cussed winter is over."

"I gotta get going." I took a step toward the back of the truck, wobbled, and would have fallen except for Earl's grip on my arm.

"You need to get that arm patched up," Earl said.

I glanced at it—he'd tied a rag around my right bicep. It was already blood-soaked. "I don't care. I'm going back to the bridge." I tried to twist free, but Earl held on.

"There's some hard facts to this situation," Earl said, talking in a low voice directly into my ear. "You said Darla got shot. That might have killed her. If that didn't kill her, they might have flensed her by now. Easier to carry meat than a person."

That couldn't be true. Darla was alive. She had to be. "Let go!" I shouted. I threw a punch at him, but my right arm was weak. He caught it and wrapped me in a bear hug.

"Don't make me hit you again, son. Hurt my dang knuckles. You come into town, get patched up. If the mayor gives the say-so, I'll take you back to the bridge and help you look for Darla."

We pulled through the gate and the guards strained to close it behind us. As it crashed shut, Earl released me. On the inside, the wall was just an enormous pile of packed snow. Steps had been carved into it here and there so defenders against a siege could easily reach the makeshift battlement at the top.

The pickups rolled slowly through town. Nobody was outside, but that wasn't surprising; it was too cold to be outdoors without a good reason. We pulled up at the low metal building that housed the library, city hall, and fire station—the same building where Darla and I had met the town's librarian, Rita Mae, the year before. The fire truck that had been stuck outside was gone. Other than that and the deep snow, it looked about the same.

"C'mon," Earl said. It was an order, not a suggestion.

I leaned against the roof of the cab, ignoring him. My mind whirled around the idea Earl had planted, that Darla was dead. I kept approaching the concept in my thoughts and then skittering away from it, like trying to catch a porcupine bare-handed.

"Let's go see the mayor," Earl said.

I didn't respond.

Earl's hand pressed against my back between my shoulder blades. "Look, son. I'm sorry 'bout what I said to you, 'bout Darla being dead and all. I know it wasn't Christian of me to put it that blunt. But lyin' to you wouldn't be doing you no kindness, neither."

I whirled and whipped my left hand toward his neck. I grabbed the collar of his coat and shook him so hard his head nodded involuntarily. "Darla is alive," I growled.

"Okay, okay. Let go of me."

I released my grip on his collar.

Earl said, "If she's alive—"

"She is—"

"Let me finish," Earl said. "If she's alive, how are you going to find her? You've got no pack, no food, no weapons—nothing. You leave the city walls like that, *you're* going to die."

"So help me. Gather up some men, and let's go get her."

"I can't. Not without the mayor's say-so. I can't even let you stay inside the city walls unless she okays it. Things are tough. We're not taking in refugees, much as some might want to."

"Fine," I said. "Let's go see your mayor."

"That's all I was trying to do in the first place," Earl grumbled.

He led me through the middle door of the building labeled CITY HALL. My gut clenched with a fear as visceral as any I'd ever felt. I had to convince these people to help me. To find Darla. My Darla.

Chapter 30

Inside City Hall there was a reception room with a desk. One wall was completely covered in a mismatched patchwork of every imaginable type of bulletin board: cork, cloth, framed, unframed, tan, white, red, and black. A crowd of people pressed around the boards, reading the hundreds of handwritten notices posted on them.

Earl led me deeper into the building past a row of office cubicles. One of them was occupied by an elderly woman doing some sort of paperwork. Three others contained people listening to radios through headsets. They had sheets of copy paper beside them, which they were filling with tiny, neatly handwritten notes.

We stopped at a door at the back of the room of cubicles. Earl knocked once and, without waiting for an answer, opened the door to usher me through.

We interrupted a discussion so heated it seemed likely to ignite. A tiny, elderly woman with a huge flare of crazed white hair stood with her back to us. She was gesturing forcefully at a much taller, regal-looking woman, her steel-and-salt hair tied up in a bun.

". . . have to supply more lamp oil, Kenda," the shorter woman said.

"We don't have any to spare," the taller woman said.

"Then at least cut some more windows in the walls."

"I already told you, Rita Mae. All the window glass is allocated to build cold frames. You'll just have to read your precious books outside."

"It's not good for the—"

Earl cleared his throat. "Excuse me."

Rita Mae spun and glared at Earl. Then her gaze skipped to me. I recognized her—she was the librarian who'd helped me and Darla last year. "You," she said, leveling a finger at me. "I've met you. Alex, right?"

"Yeah. Alex Halprin," I said. "How'd you remember?"

"I never forget a patron. Or their questions. You asked about rabbit diseases."

"I found him on the road," Earl said, addressing Kenda. "Or he found us. Couple a' bandit trucks took a potshot at us as we were getting set up to dig corn. We chased 'em, but they were trying to lure us into an ambush. He," Earl nodded my direction, "saved us."

"Hmm," Kenda said, "guess we owe him, then."

"Owe him a place in town, you ask me," Earl replied. "Would've lost a lot of men without his warning."

"Why not?" Kenda frowned. Then her words turned bitter. "What's one more soul to starve to death with the rest of us?"

"I'm not staying," I said. "I need help to rescue Darla."

"I was about to ask if she was with you," Rita Mae said.

"She was . . . she fell. Got shot, I mean, then fell on the roof of a truck." I bit the inside of my cheek hard enough to taste blood. Rita Mae looked away.

"She fell on one of the bandits' trucks," Earl said. "If the bullet didn't kill her, they probably have."

I turned to glare at Earl, fists balled. He held out his hands in a gesture meant to be placating and said, "I'm sorry to keep offending you, son. But it's nothing but the unvarnished truth."

"Much as we'd all like to," Kenda said, "we can't spare anyone to go chasing after Darla."

"But—"

"We're having a hard enough time keeping everyone safe and fed without risking a rescue mission for a girl who might already be dead."

"Darla is not dead!" I let my voice get louder than I'd intended. But I was sick and tired of everyone assuming she was dead. They couldn't know that. They were just guessing. She was alive. She had to be.

Kenda stared at me—the turn of her mouth and droop of her eyes made her look tired. "I'm sorry."

I swayed, sidestepping to stay on my feet. "Maybe the mayor will have a different opinion. Can't I at least ask him?"

Kenda's frown turned to a scowl and her eyes narrowed. "You just did."

"Oh, you're . . . sorry. I mean, sorry Mrs. Mayor. Um, I mean Madame Mayor? Um—"

"Just Kenda will be fine."

I jammed my hand into my pocket and ran my fingers over the broken necklace I'd stowed there. "Please help," I whispered. "I know Darla's alive. We can save her. Please?"

"I'm sorry," Kenda said, her own voice low. "We're barely digging enough corn to fend off starvation. I need everyone we have to defend the town and the corn-digging expeditions. We can't afford to risk anyone in a rescue attempt."

My legs felt weak. I fell, my butt thumping onto the hard floor. Something trickled along my cheeks.

"You need anything else from me, Kenda?"

"No, Earl, thank you."

"I'll go see about putting another corn-digging expedition on the road, then." Earl left the office.

Kenda knelt and laid her hand on my arm. "I wish we could help. But it's impossible. No matter how much you love her. I couldn't send a rescue mission after my own daughter."

"I can pay," I said through my tears. "Seventeen packets of kale seeds—3,400 good seeds. Grows even in cold greenhouses, and it cures scurvy." I reached into my jacket pocket and pulled out the pouch holding the seed envelopes.

Kenda looked at Rita Mae. "Would that work? Is kale better than dandelion greens?"

"Let me check." Rita Mae left the office.

"Dandelion greens?" I said.

"Yes," Kenda replied. "When the first cases of scurvy hit, we built greenhouses and planted every kind of seed we could lay our hands on. Nothing survived but weeds. So now we cultivate dandelions. They're the only source of vitamin C we have."

"I didn't even know you could eat those."

"Sure. They don't taste bad. Bitter sometimes if you don't pick the leaves young enough."

"Where do you grow them?"

"Cold frames on the roof of the school."

"What's a—"

"A cold frame is sort of a really small greenhouse. We heat ours using power we're generating with old windmills."

"And grow dandelions."

"Yes. But if kale has a higher vitamin C content than dandelion, those seeds could be a huge help."

Rita Mae walked back into the room, carrying a fat, well-used paperback: *The Nutribase Nutrition Facts Desk Reference*. She was flipping through it as she walked. "Kale . . . kale . . . here. Well, break my bindings—80.4 milligrams per cup. That's, um . . ." she flipped through the book, "more than four times as much vitamin C as dandelion greens! Probably tastes better, too."

"So you'll do it?" I said, holding out the pouch toward Kenda. "You'll help me save Darla?"

"I can't. I wish I could. But we need your kale seeds, so I can give you a place in Worthington, a house if you want it, any supplies you need. I'd do more if I could. But we just can't risk any of our people."

"What do I need with a house? Or a place in Worthington?" I hurled the pouch across the room. It thumped against the wall and fell intact to the floor. Not that I cared if it had burst and spread kale seeds everywhere. If the seeds couldn't buy Darla's return, then they were worthless to me.

"Are you crazy?" Rita Mae grabbed the bundle of envelopes off the floor.

"We need those seeds," Kenda said.

"I need help going after Darla."

"It's impossible."

"Then sell me a snowmobile, guns, and supplies."

"We don't have any working snowmobiles. And I can't let you leave."

"You can't let me—?"

"What?" Rita Mae said. "We're not letting most refugees stay, and you're telling this young man he can't leave?"

"He's just a boy!" Kenda said.

"That doesn't make it right to hold him against his will," Rita Mae replied.

"He'll get killed wandering around out there on his own."

"That's his choice to make."

"I'm going after Darla. Unless you throw me in jail, I'm leaving now."

"We don't even have a jail," Rita Mae said. "And you need supplies."

"And you need my kale seeds. Sell me one of those pickups. And some gas."

"We've only got two that work," Kenda said. "We can't spare one. Or any gas. We're running out."

"You won't help me go after Darla, don't have any snowmobiles, won't sell me a truck—why shouldn't I take my kale seeds and leave?"

Kenda started, "Because you'll get killed out—"

"Because we need them," Rita Mae interrupted. "And you need supplies. Guns, ammo, food—"

"I can't just let him wander out—"

"You can't stop him." Rita Mae turned to me. "Here's what you need: a blanket requisition for personal items."

"I'm not giving him carte blanche to take anything!" Kenda yelled, exasperation plain in her voice.

"It's a fair deal," Rita Mae said. "Just what supplies he can carry—plus ten gallons of lamp oil for my library."

Mayor Kenda shot Rita Mae a look sour enough to spoil milk.

"I'll need guns," I said. "A rifle and a pistol, at least."

"A blanket requisition from the mayor will let you pick out whatever you need from the town's stores."

"Fine," I said, staring down the mayor until she broke the standoff, averting her eyes.

"Fine," Mayor Kenda said. "A blanket requisition for personal items in return for all your kale seeds."

"And the lamp oil for the library. In return for a thousand kale seeds. Five packets." I didn't need the lamp oil, but I figured insisting on it would piss off Mayor Kenda. And she deserved it for threatening to keep me from leaving. It was the least I could do to repay Rita Mae for her support.

"Five packets? You offered seventeen packets not ten minutes ago."

"Sure, for mounting a rescue," I said. "That deal's still on the table."

"I can't." Kenda pulled at her ear.

"Then you only get five packets." I took the bundle from Rita Mae, counted out five envelopes, and held them out to Mayor Kenda. "Take it or leave it. Darla doesn't have time for me to waste arguing."

Mayor Kenda took the packets. She scrawled something on a scrap of paper from her desk and signed it. When she held the paper toward me, Rita Mae grabbed it.

"My lamp oil," Rita Mae said. She handed the paper back to Kenda.

Kenda wrote something else on the paper and thrust it at Rita Mae. "Satisfied?"

"Yep. I'll see that he gets everything he wants." Rita Mae ushered me out of the office. As we left, she gestured at the bloody cloth tied around my right arm. "Should check on your wound."

"I guess. Earl said it needed stitches."

"We'd best visit the fire station, then. Paramedic there, Floyd, has a better hand for stitching up flesh than I do."

Floyd did prove to have a deft hand with his needle. He worked fast, too, which was a blessing—getting stitched up without anesthetic isn't much fun. The needle itself wasn't all that bad, but the pressure it put on the gouge in my flesh sent flashes of pain up and down my arm and even into my teeth.

While Floyd worked on my arm, I tried to distract myself by thinking about the supplies I'd need. Skis, guns, a tent, a pack—the list seemed endless. "Can you write a supply list for me?" I asked Rita Mae.

"Paper's dear. Just tell me; we'll remember it."

"Okay. Ow!"

"Sorry," Floyd said, "almost done. Maybe just two more stitches will do it."

Rita Mae and I talked through the supply list while Floyd finished up. He got the wound closed with just four stitches—one for the entrance wound at the back of my arm and three for the exit wound at the front.

Then Rita Mae led me around the town—starting from the fire station, we went back to City Hall and then to the small downtown business district. The piece of paper signed by Mayor Kenda magically produced whatever we asked for. At our last stop, St. Paul's School, we picked up two five-gallon gasoline cans full of lamp oil. Mrs. Nance, the principal, was none too happy about giving it up. We were taking more than half her supply. But when she complained, Rita Mae shook the paper with the

mayor's signature under her nose. By the time we finished
our tour of Worthington, I was equipped better than
Darla and I had been when we left Warren on Bikezilla.

I had a big, internal frame Kelty backpack; set of
Saloman XADV backcountry skis; boots and poles; a Big
Agnes tent; an REI down sleeping bag; a plastic tarp; a
coil of nylon rope; a working butane lighter (an amazing
luxury compared to a flint and steel or the fire-by-friction
set); three candles; a set of aluminum pans; a small first-
aid kit; a needle and thread; enough cornmeal, dried meat,
and dandelion greens to last for weeks; two changes of
insulated winter clothes; a Bushmaster .308 hunting rifle
similar to Uncle Paul's; a Browning Hi-Power pistol I had
no idea how to use; and a box of extra ammo for each of
the guns. The weight of the backpack on my hips and
shoulders amazed me. A handful of minuscule seeds had
turned into this? It wasn't too different from before the
volcano, when wealth could be carried on a tiny plastic
card. But the best part about the supplies—the only part
that mattered—maybe they'd give me the chance to reach
Darla.

Chapter 31

As we trudged away from the school, I heard a burst of far-off gunfire. I dropped both cans of oil, ducked, and swiveled. All I could see was the back side of the town wall. I looked at Rita Mae; she hadn't even flinched.

"Who's shooting?" I asked.

"Blasted bandits taking potshots at someone," Rita Mae replied. "Happens almost every day. They never hit anyone; they're just reminding us they're still out there, waiting."

"Waiting for what?"

"Waiting for us to let down our guard, maybe.

Waiting for a chance to get inside the city walls. Waiting to butcher us all, no doubt."

"And FEMA does nothing." I heard another shot from closer by. Looking toward the wall, I pinpointed the source of the sound—a guy I hadn't seen before on his belly atop the wall, returning fire with a rifle.

"Worse than nothing. Jumped-up peacock that runs that camp in Maquoketa came up here and offered to protect us. All we had to do was abandon Worthington and move into his camp. Mayor Kenda said anyone who wanted to leave with him could. No one left."

Four guys carrying rifles ran past us on their way to the wall. "Should we do anything?" I asked.

"I'm certainly not about to go climbing up the steps in that ice wall. Now if the bandits made it to the door of my library, that'd be a different matter. Then they'd have me and a 20-gauge deer slug to deal with. You do what you think best, son."

"You think the guys on the wall need help?"

"Doesn't sound like much of a firefight."

The shooting died down to an occasional pop. I picked up the gas cans and trudged along the road beside Rita Mae. The weight of the can tugged at the stitches in my right arm. I bit my lip and ignored the pain—the least I could do in return for Rita Mae's help was carry the oil to the library.

The roads had all been bulldozed clear, although icy patches of packed snow and frozen ash clung to them here and there. I had to move slowly and watch my step. "You were smart not to let FEMA put you in a camp. Darla and I got locked in the camp outside Galena for a couple of weeks last year. It was hell."

"The colonel who runs the Maquoketa FEMA camp came back a few weeks after his first visit. Had a bunch more men with him. Said we had to relocate to the camp for protection whether we wanted to or not."

"What'd you do?"

"Showed him the business end of our rifles. The people still here who've survived—they're tough. Rather be killed than locked up in some camp or made slaves, I reckon."

"Yeah. Me, too."

"So how did you and Darla wind up in a FEMA camp?" Rita Mae asked.

"We were trying to get to my uncle's farm near Warren, Illinois."

"You got picked up by FEMA on your way there?"

"Yeah."

"So what happened? Tell me about your trip."

I didn't want to talk about it. The trip itself had been bad enough—we had encountered humanity at its sublime best and its savage worst. I would excise parts of that trip from my mind forever if I could. But the worst part was thinking about Darla. That she might be—I didn't even want to think the word. I wanted to curl up in the icy road and cry until my tears froze me to the pavement. But that wouldn't help Darla. And she was alive. She had to be alive.

"Are you all right?" Rita Mae asked. "You look like you just heard your best friend died."

"Darla," I choked on her name.

"Oh. Of course. I shouldn't have brought it up. Forgive me."

I put down the gas cans and adjusted my grip.

"You don't have to talk about it."

"No, it's okay." And for some reason, it was. I told her about our trip. About how Darla had saved my life, first in the icy stream and again at the FEMA camp. I told Rita Mae about our life at Uncle Paul's farm: how we'd managed to survive so far, about our plans to build more greenhouses to raise wheat and outlast the volcanic winter.

By the time I finished, we were at the library. Rita Mae unlocked the door and showed me where to stow the cans of lamp oil. "What I don't understand," she said, "is why you came back. Why didn't you stay in Warren? Sounds like you had a decent chance of surviving."

"We were looking for my parents. A bandit gang attacked my uncle's farm. We beat them off, killed two. One of them was carrying my dad's shotgun. Darla and I tracked down another member of the gang and found out that the shotgun probably came from the Maquoketa FEMA camp." I lapsed into silence for a moment. The enormity of what I'd done—dragging Darla back into this mess—fell over me like smoke, choking me.

Rita Mae broke the silence, "I can—"

"I'm too stupid to live. I should never have dragged Darla back out here, not for anything."

"Bad things are happening everywhere. You weren't safe on your uncle's farm, either—you just said a bandit gang attacked it. Darla could have gotten hurt anywhere, anytime."

"Yes, but—"

"But what I was trying to say was that maybe I can help, at least where your parents are concerned."

"How? What do you mean, help?"

"Just because a supervolcano erupts, it doesn't mean the library's business stops. I'm still developing 'my collection,' like those modern librarians say."

"What does that have to do with my parents?"

"I'm getting to that, keep your horses reined. Ever since FEMA opened the camp in Maquoketa, Kenda and I have been trying to get a copy of their roster. Folks want to know if their missing friends and relatives are locked up in there."

"You got one? A roster?"

"Yep." Rita Mae pulled a huge stack of worn and dog-eared copy paper off the bookcase behind her desk. "We bought it off a gleaner, Grant Clark, two months ago."

"A gleaner?"

"Yep. Gleaners are groups of people who roam around scavenging and trading. At least they used to be—we haven't seen any of them in five or six weeks. Gangs might have gotten them all."

"How do you know it's real?"

"We don't. Not for certain. But Grant said he got it from a guard at the Maquoketa camp. And he's always been reliable before."

My hands shook. A memory flashed through my head: Mom scolding me for leaving my bike in the middle of the

garage; Dad's distracted half-smile as he listened. I'd
mostly tuned Mom out then, but now I desperately wanted to hear her again, regardless of how much we had
fought. My brain was alight with hope—I felt dizzy and
realized I'd forgotten to breathe. After ten months of
searching for them, news of my mother and father might
be only an arm's length away.

Chapter 32

Rita Mae was already flipping through the papers. "Goodwin . . . Hailey . . . Halprin . . . Doug?"

"Dad," I whispered.

"Janice?"

"Mom." I planted my hands on the table, holding myself up. I had to remind myself to breathe again—they were alive!

"They were alive two months ago, anyway."

"And they're in Maquoketa."

"They were when this list was printed—that's all we can say for certain."

I collapsed onto a bench. My backpack jammed

against the wall behind me. I scooted forward and put my head between my knees, trying to think.

My parents might be alive . . . and close by. Darla might be . . . dead. Dad. Darla. Mom. Darla. I couldn't think, couldn't focus. I had to try to rescue my parents; I had to go after Darla. And I had no idea how to accomplish either of those things. A shiver passed down my spine, making me sway involuntarily.

I felt an arm across my shoulders. Rita Mae had sat down beside me on the bench and pulled me toward her. I flopped right over, my head cradled in her lap. She smelled of book dust and mildew—not entirely pleasant, but somehow comforting.

"I can't do this," I moaned. "I can't handle it. Everything's gone to ash. I don't know how to make it right again."

"None of us can handle it, sweetie. We just do the best we can." Rita Mae gently stroked my hair.

"Earl says Darla's dead. She can't be dead. Earl's got to be wrong." I rubbed my fists against my eyes. "What do you think?"

"Are you asking me for reassurance or for the truth, Alex?"

I thought for a moment. My mother used to say never to ask for the truth unless you were prepared to handle it. I swallowed hard and said, "The truth."

"She's probably dead. Either the bullet killed her or the Peckerwoods did."

I choked back a sob.

"If she is alive, that might be worse," Rita Mae said.

"What do you mean?"

"Grant told us the gangs are trading in slaves. Young girls, mostly."

"So Darla could be alive."

"Not a life such as I'd want to live—a slave to bandits and rapists."

"But—" I pushed myself out of Rita Mae's lap. "I'm going after her."

"Your parents—"

"Have been in that camp for months and have each other. They can wait. Darla can't. I'm leaving now."

"There can't be much more than four or five hours of light left in the day. Won't do her any good if you get killed. Best you go at first light, rested and with a full stomach."

Every muscle in my body was tensed, as if screaming at me to get moving—now! But Rita Mae was right. I was sleepwalking through the day in a fugue state, dead to the world, dead even to my body's needs. At least I could force down some food before I left. I breathed in. "Okay," I muttered.

Rita Mae closed up the library and took me to her home. It looked different than it had the year before. Back then, the front porch had been a collapsed wreck. Someone had cleaned up the mess, removing the jumble of joists, rafters, and shingles. They hadn't rebuilt the porch, though; long scars marked where it had been attached to the house. The front door was about three feet off the

ground. I saw a new structure behind the house: a small
outhouse built of unpainted gray boards.

"We'll go around back," Rita Mae said. "The first
step's not such a doozy."

Rita Mae fed me a huge meal. A dandelion-green salad
drizzled with a bit of soybean oil. Then hasty pudding—
her version turned out to be cornmeal mush flavored with
dandelion flowers and tiny bits of beef. It tasted a little
odd but was filling, so I ate three servings. She did all the
cooking at the hearth in the living room over a small fire
she fed with scraps of two-by-four. My offer to help was
met with a dismissive wave. For dessert, she fried a hamburger only a little bigger than a quarter.

"Where'd you get the meat?" I asked.

"Some of the cows survived the ashfall. We slaughtered almost all of them not long after winter set in. We
ran out of hay, and we can't afford to feed them on corn.
That's most of my meat ration for the week."

"Here." I pushed my plate toward her. "You eat it."

"Now what kind of hostess would that make me?"

"An alive one?" I shrugged and cut the burger in half
with the edge of my fork. "Halvsies. Or I'm not eating it,
either."

"Okay." Rita Mae speared her half of the hamburger
with her fork and lifted it to her mouth. The beef was delicious—hot and crispy and juicy.

When we finished cleaning up from our huge late
lunch, I picked up my backpack and struggled to force my
aching right arm through the straps.

"You leaving already?" Rita Mae asked.

I nodded.

"Won't make it to Cascade before dark."

I shrugged.

"Going to stick out like a sore thumb with that bright blue backpack."

I thought about it a moment. The insulated coveralls Rita Mae had helped me procure were light brown—not too bad. But the backpack would be painfully obvious against the snow.

"I guess you're right. I need some kind of camouflage," I told Rita Mae. "Something that won't stand out against the snow."

"A ghillie suit," Rita Mae said.

"A what?"

"It's a suit with lots of cloth strips hanging off it made to blend in with underbrush. Snipers use them. I read about them in *Rainbow Six* by Tom Clancy. Good book."

"Can we trade for one?"

"They're usually made in brown-and-green camouflage. What we want is a white-and-gray version to blend in with the snow."

"Yeah. That'd be perfect." I put down my backpack.

"I'll see if we can't make something that'll work." Rita Mae dug through some cabinets, coming back with two old white bedsheets, a fat black Sharpie, and her sewing kit. We spent the rest of the evening tearing strips from the bedsheets, streaking them with the marker, and sewing them onto my coveralls, backpack, and ski mask.

I tried on everything when we were done, posing in
front of a full-length mirror in Rita Mae's bedroom. I
looked completely ridiculous, like a survivor of an explosion at a sheet-making factory. Still, the strips of fabric hid
most of the bright colors of my clothing and pack. It
wasn't like I was a contestant in some postapocalyptic
fashion show. It'd do.

By the time we finished, we were working by lamplight. I still wanted to leave but knew Rita Mae was right
about waiting for daylight. I might get lost wandering
around in the black, postvolcanic night and never get close
to wherever Darla was.

We put away the sewing supplies and started dinner. I
tore up dandelion leaves for a salad, while Rita Mae fried
cornpone pancakes in soybean oil. The aroma of cooking
brought my hunger back powerfully, despite the huge
lunch I'd eaten. I ate everything, fueling my body for the
coming fight. After dinner, Rita Mae made up a bed for me
in the living room near the fire and said goodnight. I lay
awake for a while, knowing I needed to sleep but unable to
shut off my mind. Unable to stop thinking about Darla.

• • •

When I awoke, Rita Mae was already up. The dim yellow-
gray light in the eastern windows told me it wasn't much
past dawn. We had leftover corn pone pancakes for breakfast—Rita Mae ate just one, but I wolfed six of them. I
would need the energy.

I double-checked my gear and finished packing. "You sure you want to head out there?" Rita Mae asked as I worked. "Seems like a good way to get killed."

"Yes," I said and then hesitated. Was I answering yes, I wanted to go, or yes, it was a good way to get killed? Both, I decided. "If Darla's alive, she needs me. If she's dead, I need to know."

Rita Mae nodded and gently took hold of my left arm.

"And if I get killed . . ." I shrugged, "at least I'll have died trying to help the girl I love."

Rita Mae pulled me into a hug. "Guess I'll see you as far as the gate."

I had to keep my pace slow to match Rita Mae's, but I didn't mind. I'd spent enough time with her last year and again over the last twenty-four hours that she was familiar and comfortable. I didn't even feel the need to speak as we walked toward the south gate.

Walking with Rita Mae brought my mother back to mind. I couldn't remember ever just walking with Mom in comfortable silence like this. Sure, I usually hadn't said much when we were together. But Mom always kept up a steady stream of chatter: plans, information, and admonitions that I got remarkably good at tuning out. I took Rita Mae's hand and squeezed it once before letting it drop. She looked at me and smiled, maintaining the easy and precious silence between us.

Perhaps I thought of my mom because it was too terrifying to think about Darla—that she might be dead or worse. Still, I had to focus. Darla first. If I survived looking for her, then I'd resume the search for my parents.

We reached Worthington's south gate, the one I'd entered through the day before. Two guards sat on stools beside it, four more arrayed at the top of the nearby walls. All of them were armed with rifles.

"Open up," Rita Mae called. "Crazy boy wants to leave our fine upstanding town."

One of the guards stood up. "No can do, Miz Rita."

Chapter 33

"What do you mean?" Rita Mae said. "Lift the bar and pull that gate open. That's what you're here for, isn't it?"

"Can't do that. Mayor says he's got to stay inside the city walls."

I strode toward the gate, figuring I'd just climb over it. One of the guards sidestepped, putting himself in my path. I butted chests with him—the top of my head barely reached his neck.

"What right do you have to keep him here? Get out of his way and open the gate this instant, Roger Thornton!"

"Orders are orders," he replied. "I can open the gate and let you out, Miz Rita. Heck, with how much you fuss with the mayor, I might not be allowed to let you back in. But if he tries to leave, I've got to stop him."

"We'll just see about that," Rita Mae muttered. She yanked on my right arm, clearly forgetting about the gunshot wound.

"Easy. That hurts," I hissed under my breath.

"Sorry. Let's go talk some sense into Kenda."

The leisurely pace Rita Mae had set in reaching the gate was now replaced with a walk so brisk I had to jog to keep up, the pack thumping rhythmically against my back. We crashed through the reception room at City Hall and barged into the mayor's office without knocking.

"What is this nonsense about imprisoning this young fellow who's done us no harm?" Rita Mae yelled. "In fact, he's done us considerable good by bringing those kale seeds."

"Rita Mae, he's just a kid," Mayor Kenda replied.

"I'm sixteen," I said.

"Exactly. How can I in good conscience let you go wandering around in that mess outside? You're going to get killed."

"How can you in good conscience keep him locked inside the city?" Rita Mae retorted. "How are we any better than those FEMA goons locking people into their refugee camps, if we do the same thing?"

"He's a child, Rita Mae," Kenda yelled. "Without children we don't have any future."

"Without freedom," Rita Mae yelled back, "why would we want a future?"

"Look," I said, trying to alleviate the shouting match, "can we—"

"Come on." Rita Mae grabbed my arm and towed me out of the mayor's office. She slammed the door so hard the whole wall shook.

She led me back to her house, muttering all the way about "damn bureaucrats" and "interfering do-gooders."

"I've got to get out of here."

"I know. I'm making a plan."

"What?" I asked as we stepped into her living room. I hoped it was a good plan—I didn't really relish a sixteen-foot drop off the outside of the icy wall.

"Never mind that. Help me untie this clothesline."

A nylon rope was tied just above head height in Rita Mae's living room, zigzagging five or six times in front of the fire. Rita Mae started taking clothespins off the line while I struggled with the knots. "You know, I have rope in my pack."

"You might need that later. Best we use mine for this."

"Won't the guards see us? I don't want to wait 'til dark."

"You let me worry about that."

I shrugged and got back to work on the knots. When we finished, we had a coil of good nylon rope about fifty feet long. Rita Mae led me out of the house and to the southeast corner of town, out of sight of the south gate.

The ice wall ran right through the backyard of a one-story house. A path led to a staircase carved on the inside of the wall. Not far from the staircase a man lay atop the wall, scanning the horizon through his rifle sight.

Rita Mae pushed through the deep snow near the base of the staircase, whispering, "It was here somewhere. I know it was." After a minute or two of that, she gestured for me to join her and started digging in the snow. I helped her uncover a hidden tree stump. Rita Mae tied one end of her rope around the stump and tugged hard on it, making sure it was secure.

"Now, when the time is right," she whispered, "you run up those steps and use the rope to lower yourself down the far side of the ice wall."

"But the guard—"

"I'll handle him. Now get your skis and poles secure in one arm so you can manage the rope with the other. And Alex . . ."

I paused in my preparations. "Yeah?"

"Take care of yourself." Rita Mae pulled me into a hug.

I nodded, but the lump in my throat prevented me from saying anything. I fought down sudden tears.

The guard still hadn't noticed us—his attention was focused completely on the world outside the ice wall. Rita Mae released me and tiptoed up the steps. When she reached the top of the wall, she took a step toward him, and he startled, swinging toward her, his rifle at the ready.

"Rita Mae! Don't go sneaking up on me like that. I could have shot you!"

"You're more of a danger to yourself than to me with that rifle. Now Mr. Chapman, I have important business to take up with you." Rita Mae's voice was laden with disapprobation.

"Well then, get your fool head down while you conduct whatever your business is," Chapman said. "You're liable to get shot standing up here like that."

Rita Mae stepped over Chapman and crouched on his far side, so to face her he was forced to roll over and put his back toward the staircase.

I took that as my cue. Paying out rope from one hand, I crept to the base of the ice stairs.

"Mr. Chapman, you checked out a copy of *Gone* eighteen days ago. As you are no doubt well aware, checkout periods for fiction have been reduced to two weeks for the duration of the emergency."

"Jesus, is that what you came all the way up here for? I'm on duty! Besides, I returned that book last week."

I moved up the steps as fast and quietly as I could. They were slick, and my hands were fully occupied.

"My records clearly indicate that *Gone* has not been returned to the collection."

"Well your records are wrong, Rita Mae."

"Librarians never make mistakes, Mr. Chapman. Now I must insist that you—"

While they argued, I reached the top of the wall. It was at least eight feet wide and sloped slightly back toward the town. I stood at the outer edge and stared over the brink. Sixteen feet doesn't sound like much, but from where I stood it seemed like a long drop. I dropped the rest of the rope over the side. The slap of the rope hitting the ground drew Chapman's attention. He rolled back toward me. "Hey, you! Stop!"

It was now or never. I grabbed the rope, scrunched my eyes closed, and stepped off the edge. I fell sickeningly at first, but then the rope went taut and caught me with a jerk that threatened to tear my left arm out of its socket. I eased my grip on the rope and let it slide slowly through my glove. In seconds, I felt snow under my feet.

When I opened my eyes and looked up, Chapman was standing atop the wall, aiming his rifle at me. Rita Mae grabbed the barrel of the rifle and pushed it upward, so it aimed at the horizon instead of my head.

"What are you thinking, aiming a rifle at that boy? We can't go shooting our friends."

Chapman sighed so heavily I could hear it at the base of the wall. "There never was any problem with any over-due library book, was there?"

"Of course not. Although I do have the sequel for you. We can stop at the library and get it on our way to the mayor's office. You do want to turn me in to Kenda for insubordination or some such, don't you?"

"Not really. But I have to."

I'd gotten snapped into my skis while they talked. Now I looked up and called, "Thanks, Rita Mae."

"You're welcome," she replied. "You be careful, you hear? I'd like to see you again—to know you made it."

"I'll be careful. And I'll visit again if I can." I turned my skis south toward Cascade and pushed off, sliding away from the safety and confinement of Worthington's wall.

Chapter 34

The only way I knew to get to Cascade, where Darla had been shot, was by following Highway 136. But on skis I could stay off the roads, and traveling cross-country seemed safer. So I veered left until I could just make out the snow berm alongside Highway 136 and followed that south.

I needn't have been so cautious. The road and surrounding countryside were deserted all morning. I reached Cascade in about three hours and slid between the close-set brick walls of two burnt houses to rest and have a quick lunch.

After lunch I clambered up a fallen and charred beam inside one of the houses until I could poke my head above the exterior wall and look out over the town. The blue steel water tower that marked the Peckerwoods' base was barely visible in the distance. Between me and the water tower there was a downtown with a lot of fire-gutted brick buildings. To my left, the land fell away into a valley with a small frozen stream well below the level of the town itself. That appeared to be the best route. The buildings and slope would shield me from anyone who might be looking. On the other hand, if anyone did get close enough to see me, I would get barely any warning.

I inched carefully back down to ground level, sliding along the beam on my butt. I snapped into my skis and set out, heading toward the valley. To get there, I had to cross the highway I'd been following all morning. I stopped alongside a shell of a convenience store and looked both ways, waiting and listening for anyone who might be in a position to spot me as I crossed the open road. After five minutes or so, I decided it was safe and darted across.

On the far side a steep slope led down to the valley. I dropped into a tuck and whooshed silently down the hill.

I skied through the valley until I'd left the downtown behind. A small, frozen creek with steep banks cut across my path. I slid down onto the ice and sidestepped labori-ously up the far bank. I emerged from the gully onto a football field. The turf wasn't visible, of course, but the yellow goal posts still stood, shockingly bright against the snow. The blackened and broken windows of a low brick building looked out over the field—the local high school, I figured. Past the school there were several large metal commercial buildings, mostly crushed by the ash and snow. Everything was quiet, dead.

Finally I reached the base of the hill that supported the water tower, where I'd seen what I figured was part of the Peckerwood gang hanging out. The huge Woody Woodpecker graffito mocked me. I ducked behind a wrecked building, hiding myself from Woody and any other observers who might be keeping watch.

I worked my way slowly up the hill, moving from building to building, trying to stay under cover. Each time I left the shelter of a building, I stopped to listen for a minute or two first. I still heard nothing, but the silence felt ominous.

I reached the back of one of the twin apartment buildings at the top of the hill. Attached garages jutted off the rear of the building at regular intervals. Beyond this point, I remembered, there was a large open field flanked by the huge maintenance shed where I'd seen the Peckerwoods working on their snowmobiles and cooking. If I went any farther, I'd be seen.

I hid in the corner between the apartment building and one of its attached garages and tried to think through my next move. I needed to spy on the Peckerwoods to see if they had Darla. I had to find an unexpected vantage point—someplace they'd be unlikely to notice me.

An idea occurred to me. I unsnapped my skis and hid them in the snow beside the garage. The snow was mounded so high that the gutter was in easy reach. I took hold of it, tugging experimentally. It seemed solid. I swung my legs and did a chin-up, trying to clamber onto the roof. Under normal circumstances, it would have been easy, but the wounds on my arm and side hurt, and I was weighed down by my backpack. The gutter bent in my hands, and I heard the screech of a nail starting to pull free. I threw myself onto the roof and released the gutter. It was badly bent—I did my best to straighten it to hide any sign of my passage.

I crawled slowly up the icy garage roof. From the peak, the roof of the two-story apartment building was within easy reach. I took hold of the edge and swung myself up.

The ridge at the top of the apartment roof would give me perfect cover to scout the maintenance shed. Unless someone looked directly at the roofline, I'd be safe. I fought down my fear and started crawling toward the top. At least it wasn't very steep, though the ice and snow made it tricky.

I poked my head up over the ridgeline. The door of the maintenance shed was open. A group of people were clustered around a roaring fire just inside.

I observed for a while, motionless, stomach pressed into the shingles. Three men were working on a truck—it looked like the same pickup I'd seen the bandits driving yesterday. I watched intently, hoping for any sign they might be holding Darla captive. Maybe someone would take food or water to her, and I'd learn where they were keeping her. I was so focused that I lost track of time and was jolted out of my observational trance when my body started shivering. If I waited much longer, I'd freeze to the roof.

I low-crawled backward until I was completely hidden from the Peckerwoods by the ridgeline. I needed to warm up, but a fire was out of the question—far too dangerous. The apartment roof was too steep to jog on. I scuttled over to a standpipe that jutted from the roof. By clinging to it with my hands, I could safely do leg lifts and side kicks. I worked on those until my leg muscles were burning and my whole body started to warm up. Then I turned around, hooked my ankles around a standpipe, and did push-ups for a while, ignoring the pain of my wounds. By the time I finished, my arms were sore, but I was toasty warm. I slithered back up to the top of the roof and peeked out.

Nothing had changed. I stayed on the roof most of the rest of the day, growing more and more uneasy as I watched the Peckerwoods. There was no sign of Darla. I tried to get into the apartment building, but there was no way to break in that wouldn't make my presence obvious. Finally, at dusk, they abandoned the garage, trooping back into the apartment building beneath me.

I crawled off the roof and stalked across the field between the apartment building and maintenance shed. The snow here had all been packed down by something— I couldn't see well enough to tell what had done it—boots, truck tires, or snowmobile tracks, most likely. The surface was slippery, but at least my footprints wouldn't show.

When I got closer to the shed, I could see part of the reason the fire looked smaller than it had during the day-time—the big sliding doors were mostly closed. I crept toward the opening. I could faintly hear the crackle of the fire and something else underneath that sound: a low, regular rumbling I couldn't quite identify. It sounded a bit like the purr of a well-tuned engine. I was so close that the heat of the fire warmed my side, but I still couldn't figure out exactly what I was hearing.

After about five minutes of this, I decided that whatever was making the noise probably wasn't a threat and leaned sideways to peer into the shed.

A snoring man in a filthy orange sleeping bag lay on the far side of the fire, facing directly toward me.

Chapter 35

Most of the guy's body was hidden by the sleeping bag, but judging by the way it bulged, he was huge—fat, heavily muscled, or both. His eyes were closed, and he was snoring gently. Why couldn't Darla snore like that instead of her grizzly bear roar?

Thinking about Darla brought a wave of sadness so intense I had to bite my lower lip to hold in a sob. I pulled my head back, trying to get my feelings under control. If I found Darla, I'd gladly stay up all night just to listen to her beautiful garbage-disposal snore.

When I'd calmed down a bit, I thought about the guy by the fire. There had to be a reason he was

there. He was guarding something. The snowmobiles and
the trucks maybe. Maybe something else. Maybe Darla.

I looked back through the opening. The guard was still
snoring rhythmically. I measured the space between the
sliding doors with my eyes. I'd fit sideways, but not with my
pack on, and I didn't want to go anywhere without my pack.

I slipped it off my shoulders and held it out to my side.
Slowly I took a step sideways, sliding my pack through the
opening, careful not to touch the metal doors lest they
make noise. I stared at the guard, looking for any sign of
wakefulness. The fire was so close to the doors, I was
almost standing in it when I got inside. I held my pack as
high as I could, but my arm was still hot from the flames.
If the nylon on my pack melted, the smell alone might
wake him. I stepped to the side, pulling my arm and backpack away from the fire.

The pickup truck was parked to one side of the fire.
On the other side was an open space big enough for another truck. Beyond that I saw a row of snowmobiles—four
intact and one in pieces. I didn't see any sign of the cloth-
topped deuce that had carried Darla away from me. I
slipped behind the pickup truck, out of sight of the sleeping guard, and crouched to catch my breath.

It took a minute for my eyes to adjust to the dim light
on the shadowed side of the pickup. When they did, I saw
a workbench loaded with tools. Next to it stood a dozen or
more tall cylindrical tanks. Beyond that, in one corner there
was an old minivan resting on blocks. The other corner had
been walled off. Corrugated steel formed an interior room
of some kind, its metal door directly ahead of me.

Judging by the snoring, the guard was still sleeping soundly. I slipped my pack back over my shoulders and slunk toward the door.

There were two handles—one affixed to the door and another to the frame. Someone had jammed the broken arm of a large ratchet through both of them, holding the door closed. Why would they bar the door from the outside? To keep someone in?

Trembling with excitement, I slipped the ratchet out of the handles. It made a scraping sound that seemed impossibly loud in my ears. I turned to look toward the fire, but the pickup blocked my view of the guard, so I couldn't tell if I'd woken him. A creaking noise sounded behind me. I spun back; the door was slowly opening inward of its own accord.

I looked inside, half expecting to see Darla in the dim light. But nobody was there—the door was falling open because of some quirk in the building. When it swung fully open, I saw something else hanging from a meat hook, pink and streaked with frozen, red-black rivulets: half of a human ribcage.

I let out a short, involuntary yelp.

Chapter 36

"Hey, who's there?" a voice yelled from the direction of the fire.

I stepped inside the abattoir to hide. Bits and pieces of people hung everywhere. The stomach-turning stink of blood that I'd barely noticed as the door opened now overpowered me. I turned my face toward the wall, trying to hide from the room's gruesome contents.

"Guuuys. It ain't funny punking Brick again."

His voice had a weird singsong quality—like what I imagined a preschooler might sound like with the vocal chords of a grown man. I slid the glove off my right hand, drew the pistol from my belt, and tried to thumb off the safety. My hands were shaking and slick with sweat. My thumb kept missing the safety, sliding just over the top of it.

"I ain't going to jump and scream like last time, so you can come on out now." The voice sounded closer.

I tucked the pistol under my arm, pulled off my other glove, and used my left hand to snick off the safety.

"I know you're in there," the voice was very close now. "You think Brick's a dump truck, but I'm not that dumb. That ratchet didn't fall out on its own."

I held my breath. The guy stepped through the doorway. Half of him was in shadow, the other half lit by firelight. He looked like something an amateur sculptor had attempted to chisel out of an enormous block of granite before giving up the job as hopeless. Then an equally inept painter had come along and covered the sculptor's work with crude blue tattoos of Woody Woodpecker. He turned away from me, checking behind the door.

I took one step toward him and jammed my pistol against the back of his head. "Down! On the floor! Now!" I used the most commanding tone of voice I could manage while whispering.

"Oh-uh?" He sounded like a mooing cow.

"Down!" I repeated.

He turned toward me slowly. I pressed the pistol harder against his head, but he kept turning, so that by the time he could look at me, my pistol was against his right temple rather than the back of his head. "Who are you?"

"Nobody! Now get down, or I'll shoot you."

"Oh. You're a bad guy."

I had to stifle a panicky laugh. I was holding a gun on a cannibal named Brick, standing in a room full of frozen human flesh, and *I* was the bad guy? "On. The. Floor."

"You won't shoot me."

"I will."

"You won't."

"What? Do you want me to shoot you?" It was like arguing with a two-year-old.

"No. But if you shoot, my brothers will hear it."

The apartment building was about one hundred yards off. A pistol shot might not wake them. But if they had posted guards . . .

Brick started turning again, slowly reaching for the gun in my right hand. I quickly sidestepped to stay behind him and snapped a front kick toward him.

My kick connected perfectly, catching him right between his legs. The hours of farm work, pedaling Bikezilla, and skiing had paid off—my kick was so powerful it lifted him onto his toes. Then he crumpled, collapsing and clutching his crotch.

When he could breathe again, he moaned, a sound that started as a low, monotonic "Oooh" and grew into a high-pitched screetch: "Eeee!" I quickly shrugged out of my pack and grabbed the first thing that came to hand from the top—a dirty T-shirt. I tied the T-shirt around Brick's head, forcing it between his teeth to muffle him. Then I cut a hank of rope from my coil and used it to tie his hands behind his back. He didn't resist at all—just rocked back and forth on his knees, moaning through the gag.

"Get up," I said.

"Uh-uh," he moaned, shaking his head.

I moved around to his front and cocked my leg behind me. Which was sort of silly—no martial artist would telegraph their moves like that—but I figured it might scare him. "If you don't get up, I'm going to kick you again."

He moaned and struggled to his feet.

I retrieved my gloves, safetied the pistol, and put my pack back on. "Come on," I said. I led him out of the meat locker into the main part of the shed and shut the door behind us, sliding the broken ratchet back into place. Closing the door on that grisly morgue brought a sigh of relief to my lips. I hoped I'd never have to open it again.

Threatening him with further violations to his family jewels, I forced Brick to hide with me behind the dilapidated minivan. Then I made him sit down so I could tie his ankles together.

"I'm going to take my T-shirt out of your mouth." I lifted my foot, letting it hover over his groin. "You know what happens if you yell, right?"

He nodded. His gaze was affixed on my foot. I knelt beside him and untied the T-shirt. He'd drooled all over it. I tossed it aside—no way was I going to put that thing back in my pack.

"Listen up," I said. "Darla . . . the girl you caught—is she in there?" I gestured toward the meat locker.

"Girl?"

"Yeah, a little shorter than me, long dark hair, cute?"

Brick shook his head.

"She was shot. She fell on one of your trucks."

"Sky Girl?"

"Sky Girl?" I repeated, confused.

"She fell out of the sky. Whumped on the roof of the cage. Made Brick jump."

"Cage?"

"The truck."

"Yes, that's right. Sky Girl." I swallowed hard. I didn't want to ask the next question. But I had to know. "Is she alive?"

"I dunno."

"What do you mean, you don't know? Was she alive when you found her? Did you kill her?" I balled my fists and lifted my elbow, thinking about smashing his nose.

"She wasn't hurt too bad. Ace said she was a hardbelly. Hot enough to trade."

"Trade? Where is she?"

"Ace took her. To trade for bullets."

"Took her where? When?"

"To Danny. Yesterday."

"Who's Danny? Where did he take her?" I had to stifle the urge to yell.

"He's the Big Willy. At Grandma's."

"You're not making sense."

"Danny's boss of all the Peckerwoods in Iowa. At the big house in Anamosa—Grandma's. Ace went to see him yesterday."

"And he traded Darla to Danny? At Anamosa?"

"That's what I just told you. He ain't back yet." Brick
had an expression on his face like he thought I was stupid
for even asking. "You gonna eat me?"

"How far is it to Anamosa from here?"

"'Bout an hour in the cage. Maybe two on a sled."

"Sled?"

"Yeah, sled . . . snowmobile, you know."

I thought about the row of snowmobiles parked at the
far side of the shed. They'd be perfect for traveling: I
could stay off the roads and go cross-country, which
would probably be a lot safer. An hour by truck might be
forty or fifty miles, two or three days on foot—maybe longer. Darla might not have that long. I had to steal a snowmobile. The only problem was how would I find Anamosa?
I vaguely remembered it was somewhere southeast of
Cedar Falls.

I stepped around the minivan to the closest snowmobile.
I'd never driven one before or even ridden on one. The
steering seemed obvious—it had handlebars like a bicycle's.
I found the ignition, but its key was nowhere in sight.

I went back to the corner where I'd left Brick. "Where
are the keys to the snowmobiles?"

"Anybody's got their own sled, they keep the key.
Posers ain't allowed to touch the sleds or the keys."

"Where's your key?"

"I just told you, posers ain't allowed to touch the keys."

"What's a poser?"

"Guy who ain't got a sled."

"Like you."

He glared. "Yeah."

Great. How was I going to get a key? I started searching Brick's pockets.

"What you doing?" he asked.

"Looking for a key."

"I already told you, I ain't got a sled."

"Whatever."

"You going to let me go?"

"Not right now."

"Let me go!" Brick was yelling now. I grabbed my T-shirt from the ground and gagged him again.

I searched his pockets, finding a billfold with a bunch of worn photos of guys on motorcycles, a handful of heads for socket wrenches, and a rock with eyes and a mouth painted on it.

I kept searching, starting with the minivan. It was hard to see—the fire had almost burnt out. I went back to the front of the shed and peeked out the door—everything outside was dark and still. There was a small pile of wood near the fire, so I threw two logs on. As it flared back to life, I saw a bundle of crude torches beside Brick's filthy sleeping bag.

I lit a torch and resumed my search. Besides the keys, I needed a map—or some way to figure out how to get from Cascade, where I was, to Anamosa, where they'd sent Darla.

A quick pass through the maintenance shed didn't reveal anything useful, so I settled in for a serious search. I probably spent a half hour just on the minivan. I

searched the glove compartment, under the hood, under
the seats, in the compartment where the spare tire used to
be, inside all the cup holders—everywhere I could think
of. I found three water-stained salt packets, a fossilized
French fry, and an old maintenance log.

I moved on, searching each of the five snowmobiles,
the pickup truck, and the tool bench. My torch burned
down, and I had to swap it for a new one. It seemed like I'd
been searching for hours.

The only place I hadn't looked was the meat locker. It
didn't seem a likely place to hide anything. And I would
have preferred a hatchet wound in my side to spending
more time in that horrific abattoir. But I had little choice.
I turned toward it, torch in hand.

A woman's gravelly voice boomed from outside the
shed. "Brick, you lazy sonofabitch! Why ain't you built up
the fire for breakfast?"

I dropped my torch, stamped out its flames, and threw
myself to the ground. A heavy woman wrapped in a huge,
shapeless gray coat stepped into the shed. She kicked
Brick's sleeping bag and harrumphed. Then she turned
and started feeding the fire.

While her attention was on the fire, I belly-crawled
behind the minivan. Brick was making a low trumpeting
sound, trying to shout around his gag. I put my elbow on
his throat and leaned down until he got the message.

Another woman trudged through the shed's doors.
"What, Brick ain't built the fire up?"

"He ain't even here, lazy sonofabitch."

"Well, where'd he get to?"

"The hell should I know? Guy's so dumb he probably went out to piss and forgot where his own pecker was."

Brick moaned around the gag. I jabbed my elbow against his throat again, and he shut up even before I had to press down.

The first woman said, "Fetch some belly meat, would ya?"

"Mmm, bacon." The second woman left the fire, heading toward the door of the meat locker. I pulled my head behind the minivan.

I heard a clatter as the door to the meat locker opened. There was a long silence. I crouched behind the minivan on my hands and knees, ready to spring up to run or fight.

The door clattered again as the woman shut it and jammed the ratchet back in place. I let out the breath I'd been holding and relaxed—the fire was a lot farther from my hiding place than the door to the meat locker.

As the women cooked, more people started to straggle into the shed. They all stayed near the fire, which made sense—it was freezing in my hiding place at the far corner of the shed. But how was I going to get out of here? The only exit was through the big sliding doors—right where the fire was. I peeked out. There were now ten guys and five women clustered around the fire.

I was trapped.

Chapter 37

I thought through my options. That didn't take long—I could sit, wait, and hope not to be discovered, or try to make a break for it, in which case I'd almost certainly be caught and killed. I could get caught immediately or later. I sat tight, choosing later, although waiting made my stomach clench with fear. What was happening to Darla?

The meat sizzled over the fire. It smelled like bacon—if I hadn't known what it was, the smell might have made me hungry. As it was, I wondered if I'd ever be able to eat meat again.

I tried to listen in on their conversation as they

ate, but with all of them talking at once, it was hard to make out what they were saying. Someone mentioned Brick's absence. The cook repeated her joke—that he'd wandered off to pee and forgotten where his thing was— and everyone laughed and dropped the subject. I also gathered that Ace, the boss of this group, was gone but expected back today.

After breakfast, four of the guys mounted two of the snowmobiles and roared out of the shed. That still left six guys and five women. The guys dragged a rickety table and some folding chairs near the fire and sat around playing cards.

The women put a huge steel tub on a metal rack at one side of the fire. Then they all trooped in and out of the shed, carrying bucket loads of snow to fill the tub. The men didn't help at all—just kept playing cards. That seemed awfully sexist to me, but I guessed they weren't the enlightened kind of cannibals.

After a while, I figured out what the tub was for: washing clothes. The women put another tub over the fire next to the first one and filled it with snow, as well. One of them dumped some Tide—where they'd found laundry soap was beyond me—and a load of clothing in the first tub and started scrubbing. The second tub was the rinse water. They were scrubbing the clothing with a serrated wooden stick, wringing it out by hand, and hanging it on a line strung near the fire to dry. It reminded me of how back at Uncle Paul's farm, we'd found an old-time washboard someone had been using as a percussion instrument before the volcano. And we wrung out our clothes with a machine Darla built—you pushed down on a lever, and it used a series of gears to amplify the force—clothes came out of that wringer almost dry.

My hand was in my pocket—I realized I'd been running my fingers over the chain I'd given Darla. I looked around again, desperate for a way out. There were no windows, but high on each gable a big metal fan was set into the wall. Maybe I could pry the cover off one of the fans and slide through the unmoving blades. But to do that, I'd have to climb up into the network of metal trusses that supported the roof. I might be able to get up there by standing on the roof of the minivan and jumping, but I'd be completely exposed.

I checked on Brick. He looked asleep—or maybe dead. But when I put my hand against his nose, I could feel him breathing. I'd kept him awake most of the night—hopefully he'd sleep quietly for a while.

The card game got boisterous. The women were yelling back and forth to each other, too, so I couldn't make out what any of them were saying in the general hubbub. But at least the din would cover any noise Brick or I made.

The women had just started their fourth tub of laundry when one of the men facing the shed's door shouted, "Ace's back." They laid down their cards and jumped up to heave on the sliding metal doors, opening them wider. A blast of frigid air blew in, shuffling up some of the cards and eliciting howls of protest from the men.

The cloth-topped truck started backing into the shed alongside the fire. The women rushed to move their clotheslines.

When the truck was fully inside, two men hopped out of the cab. The guys instantly crowded around the driver, clasping his forearm and bumping his shoulder in greeting. When the clamor of hellos died down, I heard one of them say, "Yo, Ace, what'd Danny give you for them skanks?"

"You won't believe me unless I show you." Ace strutted to the back of the truck, untied the canvas flap, and pulled it away with a theatrical flourish. "Reinforcements!"

Burly guys in heavy camo jackets and balaclavas started pouring out of the back of the truck—twelve of them in all.

"We're going to *own* Worthington now!" Ace shouted. Raucous cheers echoed through the shed in response. It was getting crowded. If one of them moved a few more feet in my direction, I'd be spotted for sure. I ducked into the deeper darkness behind the minivan.

Would twelve more men be enough to overwhelm Worthington's icy walls? I wasn't sure. But I needed to warn them. I wasn't too happy with Mayor Kenda, but I owed Rita Mae big time. A warning was the least I could do to repay them. But I had to find Darla—fast. And reach my parents at the refugee camp in Maquoketa. It all seemed so overwhelming; I swallowed hard, gritting my teeth. First things first: Focus on getting out of this shed alive.

I thought about what one of the gang members had said. They'd traded "skanks" to Danny for reinforcements. Hearing them refer to Darla as a skank was infuriating, but it also brought hope. I'd rather hear them calling her a skank than a carcass.

A clunk of wood striking wood interrupted my thoughts. It was followed by a steady stream of sliding noises, more clunks, and the hard exhalations of men at work. When those noises ended, there was a squeal—nails ripping free of wood. Someone yelled, "That's what I'm talkin' about!" and I risked a glance around the minivan's bumper.

A huge pile of crude wooden crates had sprouted by the back of the truck. The lid had been pried off the top crate, and Ace stood beside it, his arms upraised as if in victory. One hand held a crowbar, the other an assault rifle.

"No peckin' way Danny gave you all those for a little vee jay," someone said.

"Course not," Ace replied. "They're short on supplies at Grandma's. I'm headed back now to take them our meat and some truck parts."

"What the—"

"Just shut up right there. We'll be in Worthington by this time tomorrow. Dining at the all-you-can-eat long pork buffet. So load it up!"

Most of the group turned toward the meat locker door on my side of the shed. I ducked behind the minivan again and checked to make sure Brick and I were out of sight.

The ratchet clanked as someone pulled it free of the door. I realized this could be the perfect opportunity to escape and slithered around the minivan on my belly. The gang members' feet were silhouetted by the fire as they tromped back and forth from the meat locker to the truck.

There was an open area between the minivan and the closest snowmobile—ten feet or so. I waited, ready to rush across the gap. All my muscles were tensed; my breath came in short, fast gasps. Everyone seemed to be focused on their work. I hurled myself across the gap.

A voice boomed, "Hey, there's someone back there!"

"Uhh," I groaned softly. I'd *almost* made it.

Chapter 38

The shed was suddenly silent. I heard footsteps coming closer. "Who's there?" a voice barked, so close it felt like he was on top of me. I scuttled around the snowmobile, keeping it between me and the voice.

Someone else said, "It's just Brick."

"That you, Brick?" the voice said. I prayed Brick was still asleep.

"Dumbass is probably planning to jump out and scare us." The same voice continued, yelling now. "It don't work like that, Brick. It's not scary when you hide and jump out—only when we all do it to you."

Everything paused for a second, as if they were expecting a response. I held my breath and scrunched as tightly into the darkness as I could.

"Back to work," Ace yelled. "I want to make Anamosa, deliver this meat to Danny, and get back while there's still daylight."

"But Brick oughta be helping—"

"You can deal with him after I'm on the road. Now finish loading, or I'll be bringing Danny more carcasses than I promised." I heard a door slam—Ace getting into the truck, maybe.

I heard footsteps moving away from my hiding place, and the general racket resumed. I slowly let out the breath I'd been holding. My hands were trembling; I closed my eyes briefly and tried to relax my muscles.

I was still at least twenty feet from the back of the truck and even farther from the shed's doors—plus the open area between me and the truck was close to the fire and well-illuminated. I'd never make it across without being seen. I needed some kind of distraction.

I wormed toward one of the workbenches against the shed wall, being careful to keep the snowmobile between me and the Peckerwoods. I reached up with one arm and blindly groped around the surface of the workbench. I felt something cylindrical and grabbed it.

It was a heavy flathead screwdriver. That would work. I crawled back to my hiding place alongside the snowmobile. Ready as I'll ever be, I thought.

I reached over the snowmobile and hurled the screwdriver at the opposite wall of the shed. It clanged against the metal wall so loudly that the sound reverberated through the building. I peeked over the top of the snowmobile. Everyone was looking in the direction of the noise, and about half of them were moving that way. Now or never. I thrust myself upright and ran behind them, moving fast but running on my toes, trying to keep my boots from making too much noise.

I reached the back end of the truck and ran alongside it, so it was between me and the gang investigating the noise at the other side of the shed. The cab of the truck was sitting just inside the open doors of the maintenance shed. A beautiful rectangle of light beckoned: freedom. I ran for it, sprinting alongside the truck.

Just then, a leather-jacketed arm pushed the cab door open, blocking my escape.

Chapter 39

I skidded to a stop. I was less than ten feet from the door. When the driver got out, I'd be dead meat. A boot appeared. I dropped to my belly and tried to worm under the truck, alongside the double set of rear wheels. My backpack caught on something. Another boot joined the first under the cab door. I scrabbled against the concrete floor, forcing myself forward. Something ripped as I popped under the truck's dark, oily underbelly.

I heard Ace yelling from the direction of the cab. "If the rest of that meat isn't loaded in five minutes flat, I'm adding one of you to the load."

"But there's someone in here, Ace!" one of the gang yelled back.

"Forget that! It's just Brick messin' with you. Fix his hash after I'm on the road."

The boots disappeared, and I heard the cab door slam. A moment later thumping sounds started coming through the floor of the truck—the Peckerwoods had started loading meat again.

I had five minutes to get out of here before the truck pulled out. It seemed hopeless. If I crawled out the back or side of the truck, the guys loading meat would spot me. If I crawled out the front, Ace, in the driver's seat, would see me.

I crawled forward. My backpack caught again. I backed up and rolled, trying to see if I could escape on the far side of the truck, but I wound up on my back with my pack holding me off the ground like a turtle upside down on its shell. I struggled, trying to turn over in the tight space under the truck without making any noise. I could smell my own sweat over the stink of grease and tire rubber—it smelled like fear.

Then the truck roared to life.

The noise of the engine was deafening. I craned my neck to look toward the back end of the truck. I was clear of the wheels. If it pulled out, I wouldn't get crushed. Instead I'd be left lying in the middle of the shed, completely exposed to the not-so-tender mercies of the Peckerwoods. Being crushed would be preferable.

Out of desperation, I did the only thing I could think of. I groped around above me and found a greasy strut. I pulled on it experimentally—it would support my weight. Then I kicked out with my feet. My boots thumped against the spare tire stored horizontally underneath the truck. I forced my boots into the space between the undercarriage and the spare tire. My head was perilously close to the front wheel.

I heard a clang of metal on metal coming from the back of the truck, and then someone slapped the truck twice. It ground into gear and pulled out of the shed— with me clinging to the bottom like a doomed barnacle.

Chapter 40

My backpack rubbed on the packed snow rushing by beneath me. I clung desperately to the strut as the truck dragged me down the road. The straps on my pack bit into my shoulders, and the nylon made a noise like tearing paper as it dragged, almost as loud as the truck's engine. I straightened and arched my back, pushing harder on the spare tire with my legs, trying to lift myself off the road to spare my pack from destruction.

The noise and the pressure eased instantly. As long as I kept my back arched and my hips up, thrust against the filthy underbelly of the truck, I could ride underneath without dragging.

The truck lumbered through two slow turns. Its gears ground again, and as we picked up speed the wind bit cruelly at the exposed skin around my eyes and wrists. The whine of the engine was overwhelming.

My back and legs ached. The bullet wound drew a line of fire across my arm. Clinging to the truck was like holding a push-up at the halfway point—I could do it for a while, but soon it was going to start to really hurt. Eventually I'd collapse.

Would falling off be such a bad thing, I wondered? We hadn't gone far—I was probably still in Cascade. From there, I could hike to Worthington in three or four hours. I'd probably get there in plenty of time to warn them about the reinforcements. Surely the Peckerwoods wouldn't launch their attack until their leader had returned from his errand?

But any move toward Worthington would take me farther from the Peckerwood base in Anamosa—farther from Darla. And Mayor Kenda had tried to imprison me in Worthington—tried to prevent me from going in search of Darla. I knew Mayor Kenda meant well. She thought I'd get myself killed, and right now that seemed pretty likely. But I still had to try. Even with so little cause for hope, the thought of Darla kept me going. Worthington would have to do their best without any warning. I tightened my grip on the strut.

My hands joined the chorus of pain coming from my back and legs. My ears ached and pulsated from the chill and the roar of the engine mere feet from my head. There was nothing to do but hold on for dear life. How long would it take to get to Anamosa? An hour, like Brick said? I didn't know for sure—didn't know how long it would take, nor how long I could realistically hold on.

The truck was rolling down a long straight highway. We seemed to have left Cascade, although I couldn't really tell. All I could see was the grimy underside of the truck, and out of the corners of my eyes, the snow berms on either side of the highway flying past.

I tried to shift my position, to take my weight on my right arm and let my left relax for a moment. But I sagged into the road. The ice tore at my backpack, jerking it so hard that something ripped and my fingers were pulled from the strut. In less time than it took to blink, I twisted through a 180-degree turn. My right leg bent at an impossible angle, and the spike of pain forced a moan from my lips. My left boot dragged against the ground. I strained to raise it. I craned my neck as my back dragged, trying to keep my head off the road. The truck pulled me along by my right ankle, which was still jammed between the spare and the undercarriage. Something fell out of my backpack, and I snapped my head back just in time to see the twin rear wheels of the truck bump over my sleeping bag and rifle. Not good.

I froze, despite the bone-jarring ride. The huge wheels that had just flattened my gear were less than a foot from my head.

Chapter 41

I moaned, not knowing or caring if the Peckerwoods in the cab could hear. My right knee was twisted at a terrible angle. I strained to keep my leg bent—if I relaxed it, I was afraid my leg would be wrenched apart at the knee.

The wheels crunched through the snow inches from my face. Pellets of ice peppered my neck. The engine's roar was all-consuming, inevitable in its bass growl. I groped frantically, trying to grab something, anything.

I got my fingers hooked around the other side of the spare tire and pulled. The instant my body was off the road, the bone-rattling shaking eased. I planted my left foot against the strut and tried to straighten my right leg. I was finally able to straighten my ankle, easing the pressure on my knee.

I was still terrifyingly close to the deuce's rear wheels, clinging to the spare tire like a spider. I had to move—if I slipped, I'd be crushed.

I groped blindly to my right, toward the center of the truck. My glove touched a spinning shaft. It threw my hand down against the road, wrenching my arm. I snatched my arm back and flexed my fingers experimentally. My whole arm hurt, but everything seemed to work.

When I reached out again, I moved more slowly, trying to see what I was grabbing. The underside of the truck was a chaotic mess of parts spinning furiously in the dimness. I reached up past a U-beam, my right hand inches from the whirling driveshaft, and grabbed some kind of strut. Slowly I inched sideways, sliding my left hand to join the right. That moved my head out from the path of the rear tires, although now I was perilously close to the driveshaft.

I didn't think I could hold on to the bottom of the truck much longer. I needed to get inside the truck, where I could rest. I worked my way toward the back, moving only one hand or foot at a time. The pain of my tortured muscles was excruciating—it felt like they were burning up under my skin. Tears leaked from my eyes, dried instantly by the whipping wind. I longed to let go. But every time my fingers slipped, I thought of Darla. This truck would take me to her, but only if I held on.

I slid under the first rear axle, clinging to it with my hands and dropping a few crucial inches closer to the road. My pack dragged, and more of my supplies flew out the top. Moving one hand or foot at a time, I slowly pulled myself under the second rear axle to the back of the truck. My muscles had become ribbons of fire, scarcely holding my battered skeleton together. My butt had been dragging—it felt like everyone at my dojang had practiced round kicks on it for an hour instead of using the punching bags.

I got a grip on the truck's tiny rear bumper and tried to pull myself up. My feet fell and were whipped from under me. Now I was hanging from the back of the truck, my body dragging behind it. I bent my arms, pulling myself upward, groaning through clenched teeth with the effort.

I couldn't climb into the load bed. The canvas cover was tied too tightly. I groped for my knife, breathing a sigh of relief when I found it still on my belt. Clutching the knife, I stabbed upward, cutting a slit about two feet wide in the canvas. I heaved myself over the gate, sliding through the hole I'd made.

I collapsed into the darkness inside the truck. My arms trembled spastically. Something sharp dug into my side— one of the spare truck parts the Cascade Peckerwoods had loaded into the truck, maybe. I tried to breathe deeply, gulping air, but that didn't help—there was a vague rotted scent in the air that nauseated me. I jammed my head through the slit in the tarp. Clean outdoor air poured over me, and gradually the trembling in my limbs subsided.

Chapter 42

Something shifted in my backpack, and I heard a clunk behind me. I pulled my head back into the truck. One of my pans had fallen out of the backpack, thunking into a metal truck part I couldn't identify. I shrugged out of my pack to check it— that pan had been packed securely when I left Worthington.

Dragging the pack along the road had torn the top flap off and shredded much of its body. I'd packed or tied the most important and useful things at the top, where they would be easy to get at. My rifle and sleeping bag were gone. I'd lost a lot of my food, water, and extra clothing. Three bags of wheat were gone, too. Only the stuff packed at the bottom had stayed put. I inventoried what was left by touch. I had plenty of food, four or five days of drinking water in a wide assortment of old plastic bottles, some extra ammo, a change of clean clothes, a lamp, and a plastic bottle of low-quality lamp oil. I checked my belt—I'd lost the pistol at some point and not even noticed. I was relieved to find that the kale seeds and two bags of wheat I'd packed inside my coat were still there.

I'd packed a needle and thread in the first-aid kit at the bottom of the backpack. I dug it out and set to work trying to repair my pack. I sat on one of the truck parts and lifted my leg, forcing my boot into the slit in the canvas. That pose was supremely uncomfortable, but it let enough light into the truck to see and kept my hands free for sewing. My hands shook—my muscles were still a limp, noodly mess from being dragged under the truck. Forcing the needle through the nylon with shaking hands was tough, and the thread I had wasn't really heavy enough, but I managed a crude repair. It would be good enough—I hoped.

That done, I put my pack back on and started exploring, hoping the truck might contain something useful—maybe even a gun or two. A mountain of frozen flesh filled the front of the load bed, and the truck parts were at the back with me—luckily not the other way around. I navigated here and there by feel. I went all the way around the perimeter of the load bed, winding up back by the tailgate. If there was anything useful in the truck, I hadn't found it.

The truck slowed and tilted through a series of turns. Had we been on the road long enough to reach Anamosa? The truck swung through a final, wide arc and stopped. I held my breath, reserving every ounce of energy for listening and trying to figure out what was happening. I heard a gear grind, and the truck lurched into reverse.

I thought about looking out the back. But if anyone was standing there waiting to unload, I'd be seen for sure. Of course, when they opened the tailgate, it was going to be pretty obvious that some of their meat was still alive and kicking. I started scrambling around the pile, thinking I'd hide behind it.

The truck stopped again and the engine sputtered off. I froze, only halfway around the pile. I was afraid to move without the engine's growl to cover any sound I might make. I heard the cab door slam, and a moment later a banging noise like someone beating on a door.

Everything was quiet for a moment. Ace's voice broke the silence. "Get some men out here to help me unload the meat," he yelled. "I need to gas up and get back to Cascade."

"Yeah, yeah, hold your pecker a minute," an unfamiliar voice replied. "Everybody on kitchen duty's busy making lunch."

"Screw that, I've got all our meat here, just like Danny wants. I gotta get back and catch some fresh."

"Whatever," the other voice replied.

"Len!" Ace roared, "Sons of bitches are making us wait. May as well get out and stretch your legs."

I heard the truck's passenger door creak open and then

slam. A few moments later, there was a distant scream, abruptly cut short. Who was Len? I'd had no idea there was anyone else in the truck, although I guessed it made sense—nobody with any instinct for self-preservation would travel through this failed and frozen world alone. And what was that scream? More importantly, how was I going to get out of this truck? I could try to get out through the back or sides of the truck by cutting more holes in the canvas. But I wasn't sure exactly where Len and Ace were, and I was certainly better off avoiding a face-to-face meeting with them.

I resumed moving around the perimeter, trying to get to the front of the truck. I could hide behind the pile, but that wasn't going to be a viable plan for long.

Something slipped beneath my feet. It rolled down the pile and hit the side of the truck, making a loud clunk. I froze.

"Something's moving in there, Ace!" The voice sounded like it was right on the other side of the canvas wall of the truck.

"There's something moving in a truck of meat? You been listening to zombie stories again?" Ace yelled back.

Someone pulled up the canvas at the side of the truck an inch or two, letting in a wedge of light. I quit breathing, closed my eyes, and prayed that the darkness would hide me—prayed that nobody would notice the slit I'd cut at the back. The moment stretched as I waited for Len to give the alarm, to shout the words that would inevitably end with me—or parts of me—joining the pile of meat I was leaning against.

The moment finally passed, and I heard the slap of canvas against steel. I let the breath I'd been holding escape my lips and opened my eyes. The inside of the truck was as black as an ashfall again. I remained motionless, afraid to move.

A few minutes passed before the silence was interrupted again. The same voice I'd heard talking to Ace earlier yelled, "Long pork's on the fire—at least enough for lunch. We'll get you—"

The voice was drowned out by a babble of men joking with each other and laughing in rough tones. Their noise was drawing steadily closer.

A memory of Darla came to me: her body hitting the roof of this truck, compressing the canvas around her. There was one direction I'd forgotten that might prove accessible. I ran up the meat pile, heedless of the noise. I hoped the talk of the approaching men would cover it.

I whipped my knife off my belt and stabbed it into the canvas roof. The noise it made as I cut the tough fabric seemed loud, but it was probably no worse than a piece of paper tearing.

The canvas at the back of the truck flapped as the men started to untie it. I thrust my knife back into its sheath and reached through the slit, grabbing one of the bows that supported the roof. The weakness and pain washed from my muscles in a flood of adrenaline. I heaved myself up through the slit, out of the darkness and rancid stink and into the light and the clean, cold air above.

I heard a heavy metallic clunk: the Peckerwoods were

opening the tailgate. I reached back to make sure the slit in the canvas was closed, but I needn't have bothered. The canvas was stretched so tightly over the bows that formed the roof of the truck that it had sealed itself behind me.

I lay on the roof, panting and trying to hold myself motionless. The bows supporting the canvas held me up— one of them dug into my thighs. My body was probably making a bulge in the truck's ceiling, but I figured if I didn't move, the Peckerwoods might not notice.

I rotated my head slowly left and right. I couldn't see anyone around the truck—I was on my back, roughly in the center of the roof, so my view was blocked. Which was a good thing: If I couldn't see them, they couldn't see me.

Boots clanged against the truck floor beneath me. The Peckerwoods' boisterous chatter was so close, it felt as though I were standing in their midst. I could even hear their grunts and heavy breathing as they unloaded the truck's horrid cargo.

I twisted my neck, trying to see a way off the truck's roof. Perhaps I could slide over the front windshield while the Peckerwoods were occupied, but to do that I'd have to turn around. A lump in the canvas ceiling of the truck might not be noticed, but one turning and crawling toward the front surely would be.

I looked up—the prison's wall loomed above me. It was built of white limestone, carved and ornamented in a gothic style. I'd always assumed a prison would be spare and utilitarian, but Anamosa was fancy—more like a castle than a penitentiary. Tall, narrow windows stretched from the ground floor to the battlements, four or five stories above me. The barred windows were opaque, which was fortunate because no one inside could spot me through the frosted glass.

I could do nothing except wait and pray that I would remain unnoticed. I felt like a mouse hiding in a cat shelter. Each minute crawled past like an hour.

The truck growled back to life. The Peckerwoods withdrew from the load bed beneath me, and the tailgate clanged shut. I drew in a huge lungful of air. The truck lurched forward, and I clung to one of the bows.

The truck turned twice, circling the prison. I thought about jumping off—I sure didn't want to go back to Cascade. Before I could do anything, we pulled into a huge metal garage.

In the sparse light admitted by the doors, I could see that the building was packed with vehicles. There was a windowed office just inside, but otherwise the garage was one big open space. I scooted to the side of the truck's roof for a better view.

We pulled up alongside a huge stack of gas cans. Hundreds of red, plastic five-gallon cans were arrayed in layers—each layer separated from the one above with a sheet of plywood.

The truck's engine cut out, and Ace slid out the driver's door, slamming it behind him. Someone else was approaching from the direction of the office. I scooted backward on the roof, out of their view.

"Fill 'er up!" Ace roared.

"Five gallons should be plenty to get you back to Cascade," another voice said.

"Screw that! You wouldn't be eating tomorrow 'cept for me. Fill it the peck up. All fifty gallons."

"Can't spare that much juice."

"Whaddya mean? You've got a few thousand gallons here."

"I gotta conserve it—there's no new supply coming in. Every tank in Iowa's empty now."

As they continued to bicker, I looked around for a way down. I belly-crawled to the far side of the truck. From there I could see a large work area. A pickup sat in the middle, its hood off and engine suspended on a chain hoist beside it. Two guys were working on the engine. I pushed myself slowly backward, out of their line of sight.

To my right—two guys and the engine. To my left— Ace and the argument over gas. To my rear—a large open space with no cover. To my front—Len, probably still sitting in the passenger seat.

Apparently, I had an unfortunate talent for getting trapped inside cannibals' garages.

Chapter 43

The two mechanics walked over and started unloading the truck parts. They were carrying everything to their work area to my right, so I couldn't slip off the truck on that side. The bickering about gas ended. Ace and the guy from the office had agreed on twenty gallons and were pouring the first five into the tank.

It occurred to me suddenly that I was making the same mistake I'd made just a few minutes ago. I was forgetting about one direction—up. The roof of the garage was held up by a latticework of steel trusses, like the ones that support the roofs above gas pumps. The closest truss was nine or ten feet from the roof of the truck and made up of a triangular network of steel tubes.

Best of all, it was dark up there. Very little light from the open doors reached that high. I'd be visible from the floor, of course, but difficult to spot. And none of the Peckerwoods had a reason to look up, anyway.

I waited until the mechanics had finished unloading. They stood over the pile of truck parts, checking them over and planning. I stood slowly, balancing on one of the bows, watching and waiting for a moment when no one was looking my way. When the moment came, I jumped. I caught the bottom strut and dangled, checking to see if I'd been spotted. The metal bars of the truss were so cold I could feel it even through my gloves. The mechanics were still absorbed in their work. I couldn't see Ace or the guy gassing up the deuce—they must have been right up against the side of the truck.

I slowly curled up, flexing my arms and raising my legs until I could hook my ankles over the lowest strut. One of my boots bumped it, making a resonant clunk that sounded as loud as a car crash to me. My heart leapt into my throat. I froze, dangling by my hands and ankles. They must have heard me. My mind raced. What would I do if they raised an alarm? I'd drop back onto the roof of the truck and try to fight, I decided. It would be hopeless but better than getting shot while clinging to a girder.

But no alarm came. I slowly swiveled my head. The mechanics were sorting the truck parts. In the other direction, I still couldn't see Ace or the other guy.

My head swam. The room made little quarter-turns around me, spinning and then lurching suddenly back to its starting place, making me nauseated. I could hear the blood rushing to my ears. Maybe the dizziness was caused by my position, hanging with my head lower than my feet. Maybe it was the height, the risk of being noticed, or perhaps the beating my body had taken under the truck. I had to get to a more secure perch or I'd fall.

I seized two of the crossbars connecting the struts. Using them for leverage, I strained, trying to twist my body onto my stomach. No way could I push straight back into the truss—my backpack would have gotten caught. I would have grunted with the effort, but with the Peckerwoods so close, I had to keep my mouth clamped shut.

As soon as I got twisted all the way onto my stomach, I could push farther back into the triangular space within the truss. When I'd shoved myself completely inside, I collapsed, panting quietly and resting from the exertion of forcing my way into this tiny perch. The crosspieces that made up the truss held my body and legs securely. I closed my eyes and waited for the room to stop spinning around me.

A few minutes later, I heard the truck roar to life. I opened my eyes just in time to see it pull away. Without the truck, it was a long fall to the garage's cement floor—twenty feet or more. My relief at not having been seen balanced almost perfectly with my fear of heights. The guy who'd been gassing up the deuce sauntered to the office. The other two guys had resumed working on the pickup's engine.

I waited for nightfall, afraid if I continued to move around in the rafters, I'd be spotted. I watched the mechanics, my hand thrust into my pocket, fingering Darla's broken chain. When the wan light outside started to fade, two new guards entered the garage, and the mechanics and day shift guard left. The night shift closed, chained, and padlocked the big entrance doors and retired to the office.

I pushed myself up off the girder I'd been resting on. Painful welts crisscrossed my side and legs where the struts had dug in. I worked my way backward within the truss, away from the office, and then dropped down onto the roof of a parked pickup with a heavy crunch. No one heard the noise—or at least nobody came to check on it.

I explored the garage, looking for a way out, working more by touch than sight. It was packed with vehicles parked in ranks so close that I often had to turn sideways to pass between them. In the darkest parts of the garage, the back corners most distant from the door and guardroom, the trucks were dusty and partially disassembled. Some were missing wheels or body panels. All of them had their hoods propped open. I didn't know enough about trucks to tell for sure by touch, but I guessed these vehicles were being cannibalized for parts.

Darla would've been able to figure out what they were doing with the trucks, even without being able to see clearly. That thought gave me hope. Maybe the Peckerwoods would put her to work when they discovered her genius for machines. Maybe she would walk into this very garage in the morning.

Then I remembered the crack of the gunshot and the red bloom spreading across her shoulder. I crouched and put my head between my knees, trying to catch my breath and waiting for the trembling in my limbs to subside.

I couldn't find any exit except the big vehicle doors. The key to the padlock holding the garage doors shut would probably be in the office, but there was no way to get close without being seen by the guards. I retreated to the darkness of the far corner of the garage to think.

I climbed into the bed of a deuce and curled up, holding my head in my hands. But my thoughts just ratcheted over and over the same territory, like a slipping gearshift. The longer I sat there, the more futile my situation seemed, and the more despondent I got. I was aware of being hungry but couldn't summon the energy to take off the pack and get food. Soon I was yawning. I curled up on the floor of the truck and slept.

In the morning, I woke to shouted curses and the clang of metal on metal.

Chapter 44

The clanging noise was so close it sounded as if it were coming from within my skull. I curled up more tightly. The blackness within the truck bed turned oppressive—before it had hidden me, now it presaged the moment when the cloth flap at the back of the truck would be lifted, a light would pierce my shelter, and I'd be discovered.

When . . . if I was found, I didn't want it to be like this. Curled in a ball on the truck floor, helpless. I stretched out and rolled silently, fighting the stiffness of my battered limbs. I balanced on my hands and feet like a tiger, poised to spring. If anyone came through the flap at the back of the truck, I would attack. A futile, hopeless gesture—like flying a flag on a sinking ship. I drew in a deep breath, filling my lungs with stale, oily air and my heart with renewed determination. So long as any light remained, I would struggle to survive and to find Darla.

The clanging crescendoed, like a series of hammer blows, and there was a sharp crack.

"Throw my ever-lovin' tie rods!" someone yelled, almost in my ear.

"What's wrong now?" The other voice was as rough as a dry, gravel-filled creek bed.

"Blasted bolt sheared. I cain't work in these conditions." He'd switched to a fake Cajun accent—*zhees condishawns.*

"If I had a gallon of gas for every time you said that—"

"Yeah, yeah, you'd be the richest punk in Iowa. Come on, I think there's another M35 in the far corner."

I listened until the sound of their boots striking the concrete floor faded. Then I let out the breath I'd been holding and relaxed, slumping to the floor of the truck.

I was stiff, sore, ravenously hungry, and to top it all off, I desperately needed to pee. I crept to the back of the truck, stuck my head through the flap, and looked around. This corner of the garage was dark and quiet, although I could hear the rough noises of men working and talking nearby.

I slipped out of the back of the truck and stood on the bumper, peering around. The garage doors were open, letting in the weak, postvolcanic morning light. The inside of the office was dark—its windows as opaque as sunglasses. At the far corner of the garage, a torch spread a separate pool of light, but the intervening trucks blocked my line of sight to whoever carried it.

It seemed safe enough where I was, at least for now. I turned my attention to more pressing problems—pressing on my bladder, that was. I could pee in the corner of the garage, just a few steps away. But if anyone came back here, the smell would be unmistakable. I spent a few minutes searching for a gas can, bottle, or some other container. I found nothing. Then the obvious solution to my problem hit me.

I found what I was looking for on the passenger's side of the truck I'd slept in. I unscrewed the gas cap, but I wasn't tall enough. I had to crouch on the running board to relieve myself into the tank. When I closed the tank, I couldn't smell anything except the grease and smoke odor of the garage and my own sweat. Problem solved—although the Peckerwoods were going to have a rude surprise if they ever tried to start that truck again.

For breakfast, I had three strips of beef jerky, a handful of wilted dandelion leaves, and a bottle of water. I had at least ten pounds of cornmeal in my pack but no good way to cook it.

After breakfast, I crept back out to explore. The rest and food had refreshed and revived me. I would discover a way out of this garage today. If Darla was alive, I would find her.

Two guys were working by torchlight in one corner, struggling to remove something they called an alternator bracket from a dilapidated truck. I hid behind a nearby pickup and listened to their conversation until I'd heard, "I cain't work in *zhees condishawns*" so often that I was tempted to stuff a sock down the guy's fake Cajun throat.

Instead, I watched the office from the safety of the shadows under a parked pickup. For a long time, everything was still. I wondered if I might simply be able to saunter out into the light.

Then I caught a flicker of movement from inside the guardroom. As I continued watching, I saw more motion—dark shadows of arms or heads floating, appearing disembodied within the darkness of the room. I thought about it a minute—the outside of the guardroom was brighter than the inside, so I couldn't see in, but the guards could see out, no problem. If I tried to waltz through the garage doors, I'd be painfully obvious, and probably painfully dead shortly thereafter.

I watched and waited, growing more and more anxious as the minutes ticked by, turning steadily to hours. When my stomach reminded me to eat, I retreated to the truck I'd slept in. As I ate a lunch of beef jerky, I thought about the situation. I couldn't keep waiting and watching. But getting killed wouldn't help, either. Maybe I could put a truck into neutral and push it into the guard shack? Or attack the two mechanics—they might be carrying keys.

The sputter of an engine growling to life interrupted my thoughts. I stuffed the remains of my lunch into my pack and slung it over my shoulders. I clambered out the back of the truck and onto the canvas roof to observe the center of the garage. Another cloth-topped deuce was pulled up alongside the stack of gas cans. One of the mechanics was gassing it up.

A hulking guy came around the corner of the truck. He might have been 6'4" if he had straightened up. But he walked with little mincing steps, hunched over as if he were cradling something to his chest. I couldn't see his face or clothing; he was silhouetted in the light of the open garage doors.

I saw a flash of brown hair around him. A girl was walking beside him, shielded by his rectangular bulk. I crawled closer, sliding across the truck roof, trying to get a better look.

A pair of wiry guys strutted around the corner behind the hulk. They talked to each other in voices loud enough to be audible over the idling truck.

"Iowa City is going to be off the hook."

"Them Dirty White Boys is scum, but they know how to party."

All four of them had gathered in a knot at the back of the truck. One of the wiry guys let down the tailgate.

"What you waiting for?" the other guy slapped the hulk alongside his head. "Get in."

The hulk hunched further over and moaned, an unnatural-sounding monotone noise that continued long past the point at which most people would have had to stop and breathe. The girl was saying something to him but too softly for me to hear her words.

Still moaning, the hulk took hold of the edge of the tailgate in both hands and hopped into the truck like a rabbit, both legs moving at once. There was a tinkling sound as he moved. Just before he vanished within the blackness of the truck, I saw why—his ankles and wrists were connected with lengths of heavy chain.

The girl heaved herself up onto the tailgate. I had a clear view of her back for a moment. My brain flooded with fierce light, and my heart leapt. Her height, her shape, the way her hair bunched around her shoulders—I'd recognize her anywhere. Darla.

Chapter 45

That truck wasn't going to leave the garage without me. Either I'd be on it, or I'd get killed trying to hitch a ride.

Darla disappeared into the blackness of the truck bed, following the hulking guy. One of the wiry guys closed the tailgate and tied down the flap. Then they strolled around the corner of the truck, heading toward the cab, out of my line of sight.

The only person I could see now was one of the mechanics. He was facing away from me, holding a five-gallon can above the truck's gas cap.

Only about two feet separated me from the roof of the nearest truck. I crawled to the gap and reached across, eyeing the mechanic the whole time. Once my hands touched the other truck, I swung my legs across. The mechanic didn't even glance up.

I scuttled over two more trucks in the same way until I was lined up roughly even with the one that held Darla, but three ranks back. The truck I was perched on had its hood open. The vehicles between me and the idling deuce were both pickups—there was no way I could keep hopping from roof to roof as I'd been doing.

I looked down the aisle on the left side of the truck. The two wiry guys were standing by the driver's door of the idling truck. If I tried to sneak down that aisle, they'd spot me. But from the aisle on my right, I'd be in plain view of the mechanic. I couldn't afford to wait—they were gassing up the truck for a reason. I had to get on it—and fast.

I slinked away from the aisle, stood, and jumped. I caught the metal girder overhead in both hands. My whole body screamed with pain—my tortured muscles being stretched by my weight. I gritted my teeth and started slowly working my way forward, hand over hand. Even with my taekwondo practice, I probably couldn't have traversed the beam that way ten months before, swinging from my arms. But there was one advantage to being blasted back into nineteenth-century farming by the volcano: I was at least as strong as anyone I knew, except maybe Darla.

I couldn't see the guys by the cab anymore, but I was in plain view of the mechanic. So long as he kept paying attention to the gas, I'd be okay.

I worked my way slowly along the beam. Twenty feet . . . ten . . . I hung over the bed of a pickup about ten feet below me. The mechanic pulled the spout of the gas can out of the truck and turned toward me. I froze, praying he wouldn't look up. If I moved, he'd spot me for sure. But maybe, just maybe, it was dark enough that if I just hung there, I'd be unnoticed.

A drop of sweat rolled along the bridge of my nose. The mechanic set the gas can on a pallet loaded with empties and hefted a full can from another pallet. My arms burned from the strain of holding myself perfectly motionless, and the drop of sweat tickled my nose, threatening a sneeze.

The mechanic opened the gas can, pulled out the spout, and thrust it into the truck, turning his back to me. I breathed a silent sigh of relief and started hand-over-handing it toward Darla's truck again.

How long would it take to empty the gas can? I didn't know, so I moved as fast as I could. I was steadily getting closer to the mechanic. If he turned around and looked up now, there'd be no way he could miss me.

This beam didn't pass directly over the truck. The closest I could get was about five feet from the back of it. I swung my legs, forward and back, gaining momentum and then letting go as I arced toward the truck.

I landed about in the center of the roof with a whump of compressing canvas. Instantly I fell flat, hoping the noise of the engine would cover the sound of my fall.

"What are you doing in there?" shouted one of the wiry guys.

The guy in the truck started moaning again. I heard Darla whisper, "Shh, shh."

"Freaks," another voice said, and they both laughed.

I pressed myself to the canvas. One of the struts supporting the roof dug into my belly.

To my right, the mechanic yelled, "Done! You only got a two-gallon reserve. You screw around at all, you won't make it back."

"Yeah, yeah," the reply came.

Two doors slammed in quick succession, and the truck rolled forward. Clinging to the roof, I rode from the blackness of the garage into the thin, yellow light outside.

Chapter 46

The truck picked up speed as we left the prison compound. It roared through a couple of turns, passing through the two-story brick buildings lining Main Street. Soon we were racing along a plowed road through the deserted and snow-smothered landscape outside of Anamosa. I figured we were going more or less south. The wind sliced viciously at my face, and I pulled my ski mask down over my eyes and mouth.

I watched as the collapsed strip mall and abandoned fast food restaurants outside Anamosa disappeared behind us. Then we passed an abandoned propane distributor, the tanks painted like giant ears of corn. I drew the knife from my belt and stabbed it into the canvas below me. The wind roared so loudly that I couldn't hear the noise of the canvas ripping.

"Darla," I hissed urgently through the slit in the canvas, "I'm here. Make some noise. Try to get the driver to stop."

"What? Who—"

"Just do it! Yell, bang on the cab, whatever." I removed my face from the slit in the canvas and crawled forward until I could see the top of the cab. I clung to the edge of the roof, poised, ready to attack when the truck stopped.

I heard some thumps below me and then Darla started to yell something. But her voice was barely loud enough to hear over the wind. I couldn't even make out the words. Come on, Darla, I thought. I know you've got better pipes than that. You never had any trouble making yourself heard over the noise of the grain grinder when you thought I wasn't pedaling fast enough.

The monotone moaning resumed. The moans were louder now—they threatened to drown out Darla's feeble shouts. A series of thuds and thumps started a counterpoint, as if someone were beating their fists and feet against the bed of the truck. The guy's voice broke, and the moaning was replaced by a frenzied, falsetto screaming. It was almost unbelievable that such a hulking guy could make noises like those—it sounded like a little girl throwing a full-throated temper tantrum.

That should work, I thought. It sounded like he was having a seizure. They'd have to stop and check on him.

But the truck didn't stop. The screaming fit went on and on. I heard a snatch of laughter coming from the cab. If anything, we were speeding up. The two guys riding in the cab obviously didn't care if one of their passengers was freaking out in back. I slumped to my belly on the roof of the truck, trying to figure out what to do. The noises from beneath me were just annoying now—it sounded more like an uncontrolled fit than an attempt to get the guards' attention.

I had to stop the truck. If I waited until we reached our destination, there were sure to be more than two guards to deal with. I could try crawling onto the roof of the cab. There were two antennae that would make decent handholds—if I could make it to them without sliding off. And even if I did make it, then what? Try to kick in the windshield?

Maybe I could throw something from my pack. I had the extra ammunition from my lost guns. Could I get it to fire by heating it or something? Make the guards think they were being shot at? Would that make them stop or drive faster? Perhaps I could soak my extra T-shirt in lamp oil, tie it around a fistful of bullets, and light it?

Lamp oil. That was it! The primitive oil was thick, completely opaque. I inched back to the slit in the canvas.

"Darla!" I yelled. "Can you give me a hand?"

No response. Maybe she couldn't hear me over the continued screams of the man-child with her.

I twisted my arms out of the straps of my backpack and unbuckled the hip belt. I took a firm grip on one of the straps and rolled over onto my back.

The truck bounced, and my heart lurched—for a moment I thought I was going to be bucked off. When my heart slowed a little, I scooted back, dragging my pack with me until I could jam one leg through the slit in the canvas roof. I got my leg in up to the knee and wedged my other foot against the curved rib supporting the canvas roof.

I slowly sat up. The wind ripped at my back, gusting so hard it lifted my butt off the roof now and then. I dragged my backpack onto my lap, where it was protected from the lash of the wind, and rummaged through it for the supplies I needed.

I had emptied more than half a dozen water bottles of various sizes in the two days since I'd left Worthington. The first bottles I found all had regular plastic caps. I pushed those aside, digging deeper. One of the empties got pushed out of the top of my pack, where the wind caught it. I grabbed for it, but the wind whipped it away— it spun drunkenly in the airy backwash of the truck and was gone.

Finally I found what I wanted: an Aquafina bottle with a sports cap—the kind you pop open with your teeth, squeezing liquid into your mouth. I unscrewed the cap and shoved it into my pocket, safe from the tearing wind.

The bottle of oil was all the way at the bottom of my pack, of course. I hadn't used my lamp or lamp oil in days—the risk of someone seeing the light had been too great. I finally dug it out; it was a plastic half-gallon bottle that had probably once held milk. The oil inside was polluted and black. Perfect.

I unscrewed the cap from the jug of oil and stowed that in another pocket. Then I lifted the jug and tried to pour oil into the Aquafina bottle. The truck jostled and my hands slipped. Oil went everywhere, coating my gloves. The wind whipped the oil away from my face, but it splattered all over my legs, backpack, and the roof of the truck.

I jammed the Aquafina bottle between my legs and cupped one hand around its neck. I upended the jug, using my hand to form a pipe connecting the two bottles. Oil splashed out, running through my hand, but some of it was flowing into the bottle. By the time I finished, more than half the oil was gone, and my glove and crotch were soaked, but I had a full squeeze-bottle of oil.

My left glove was slick. I wiped it off as best I could on the leg of my coverall, reaching below the knee to find a patch of cloth not already soaked in oil. I capped the bottle and the jug and stowed the half-empty jug in my backpack. Putting a backpack on while racing along in a fifty-plus mile-per-hour wind wasn't particularly easy, but I got it done. Clutching the squeeze bottle, I crawled back to the front of the truck.

The truck was approaching a broad S-curve in the highway. A farmstead was nestled on the inside of the curve—I could see two large concrete silos protruding above the massive snow berm that lined the road. It seemed like as good a place as any to try my crazy plan.

I clamped my left hand around the last bow supporting the front of the canvas roof, holding on in a death grip. The top of the bottle resisted my attempt to open it with one oily glove, so I pulled it open with my teeth, wincing at the acrid chemical taste. I thrust my right arm forward and squeezed on the bottle, aiming for the windshield.

A thin stream of oil flowed out about two feet, was caught by the wind, and flung back into my face. I ducked and squeezed my eyes shut, sputtering, and almost dropped the sports bottle. I rubbed my sleeve against my eyes and mouth, trying to clean them, but all I really accomplished was smearing the oil around. My eyes burned and my mouth tasted like the floor of a quick-lube joint.

Oil was splattered across the top of the truck's hood, but none had reached my target, the front windshield. I needed to either get closer or apply more force to the bottle. Plenty of oil remained—I'd only squirted out an inch or so. Crawling across the gap between the canvas roof of the load bed and the metal roof of the cab didn't seem like a good idea. I inched forward anyway until my head and shoulders were hanging over the gap. When I stretched out my arms now, they were above the cab, but if we hit a bump, I'd go flying. I clasped both hands around the Aquafina bottle, lacing my fingers together. Then I squeezed, groaning with the effort.

Oil shot out, coating the roof of the cab. I adjusted my aim. Now the stream arced down onto the windshield. I waved the bottle like a fire hose, still squeezing with all my might. The truck's windshield wipers squeaked, and its brakes squealed. It fishtailed sideways, tires grinding over the icy road.

We slammed into the mountain of snow alongside the road, and I was hurled into the air.

Chapter 47

The world spun around me, a jumble of yellow-gray sky, snow, and forest-green truck. Something slammed into my right shoulder, and I rolled down an icy hill. I plowed into fresh powder at the bottom, winding up splayed out and buried, with snow packed into my mouth and nose.

I rolled over. Spat snow from my mouth. Checked my shoulder. It felt like I'd slammed it in a car door six or eight times, but I could move it, so I figured it wasn't broken or dislocated. I felt a trickle of warm blood seeping along my arm—I must have split open my gunshot wound.

The twin grain silos towered over me. Beside them slumped a burned out farmhouse and mostly collapsed barn. I couldn't see the Peckerwood's truck—the snow berm beside the road was in the way. A long, chaotic trail left by my thrashing limbs marked where I'd rolled down the side of the berm. It seemed far too quiet for the aftermath of a crash. Shouldn't someone be screaming?

I tried to stand, but dizziness forced me back to my hands and knees. I slowly crawled up the snow berm, without using my bruised arm.

The truck had plowed into the berm and twisted so its back end was blocking the road. Its front wheels were stuck in the snow, raised three or four feet above the roadbed, so the entire truck was stuck at an angle. The front windshield was full of cracks, and a chunk about the size of a man's head had been punched out of the passenger's side. The windshield wipers had smeared the oil around, leaving long, half-moon streaks on what was left of the glass.

I crawled over the crest of the berm and slid down the far side. I grabbed the passenger door handle to pull myself upright, looked through the window, and recoiled in shock.

One of the guards was slumped against the passenger window, face pressed to the glass. Blood poured from his hairline, ran in rivers along his nose, sheeted over his sightless eyes, and dripped into his yawning mouth.

I took hold of the handle again. Turned it. The door opened easily. The guy fell out head first. The top of his skull was flattened and bloody.

Behind him, the driver held a pistol aimed at my head.

Chapter 48

The pistol wavered, dipping and bobbing as the driver struggled to hold it steady. His other hand was formed into a claw, clutching the center of his chest. His face twisted in agony. He squeezed the trigger. The shot whanged off the door trim a foot from my head.

I dropped flat, under his line of fire. If I crawled away from the truck, he might be able to get an angle on me. The blood-soaked face of the dead guard was inches from mine, contorted by a zombie grin. I had to move. I wormed around the guard's corpse and under the truck. Its front wheels had been lifted partly onto the snow berm by the crash, so I could rise to a high crawl, although my pack bumped against the undercarriage.

Now what? If the driver got out and poked his gun under the truck, I'd be as easy to kill as a pig in a slaughterhouse chute. I scuttled to the far side of the truck under the driver's door. I glanced around—the driver's legs weren't visible. Either he was still in the cab, or he was standing beside the tires.

I took a deep breath, trying to still my shaking arms. My hands were icy despite my gloves, either from the chill of the frozen road or fear—maybe both. I eased my head out from under the truck, hoping the last thing I saw wouldn't be the barrel of the pistol.

No flash or sudden retort of gunfire met me. Everything was silent, in limbo. I rolled out from under the truck and crouched to look into the cab. The driver was facing away from me—he had scooted across the bench seat to the passenger's side.

I turned and ran toward the back of the truck, avoiding the snow berm at the front. As I sprinted past the tailgate, I looked for Darla. I figured she'd be out by now, but the back flap of the truck was still tied shut. I couldn't see or hear her.

I skidded to a stop at the corner of the truck and peeked around. The driver's hand and gun protruded from the open passenger door, wavering above the guard's corpse. I broke into a flat-out sprint toward the door.

The driver was slowly emerging from the passenger door. He got his entire right arm and head out of the door. He looked over his shoulder, saw me, and started to bring his pistol around to shoot me. I jumped, launching myself in a flying front kick when I was still two steps away. My kick connected with his forearm, slamming it against the open passenger door with a sickening crunch. The pistol dropped from his suddenly limp hand. I fell, landing splayed across the corpse.

When I looked up, the driver was clutching his right arm. Either he'd magically grown a bonus elbow, or I'd broken his forearm.

I grabbed his pistol and stood. The driver had a hunting knife in a sheath on his belt. He didn't react when I took it from him—his breath rasped in his chest, and he was too busy hunching over in extreme pain. I glanced into the cab of the truck—a shotgun lay on the floorboards, so I picked up that, too.

"Darla!" I yelled. "I could use some help out here!"

"What's going on out there?" Her voice was faint, muffled by the canvas.

What did she think was going on? "Nothing much. I crashed the truck, subdued the guards, and got their weapons."

"Is it safe?"

That seemed like an even stranger question for her to ask. When had it ever been safe? Not since we had met. Not since the volcano had erupted. What was going on with her? "Yeah . . ." I said anyway.

"Coming."

I kept my gaze fixed on the driver. I needn't have bothered. His eyes were closed, and he rocked slightly back and forth, totally absorbed in his agony.

"What the hell is going on out here?"

I looked to my left at the girl who had just stepped out from behind the truck.

She wasn't Darla.

All the oxygen left my lungs, replaced by disbelief and pain. Like I'd taken a kick to the groin. "Who are you?"

"I'm Alyssa—I have no idea who this Darla you keep talking about is," she said.

"I thought you were Darla." She was the right height. Brown hair curled around her shoulders, exactly like Darla's. But Darla had a rectangular, Midwestern face—beautiful, but tough and solid. This girl was elfin by contrast—her face almost diamond shaped, her features delicate, her tiny nose slightly upturned. I guessed she might be a year or two younger than Darla.

"Who's Darla?" She hadn't moved from the back of the truck.

"Where's Darla?" I strode down the length of the truck toward her.

"How am I supposed to know? I just told you I don't know who she is!"

"She's a girl. Your height. Same hair. Peckerwoods took her to Anamosa."

"Shot in her right shoulder?"

"Yes! That's her. Where is she?"

"Clevis!" Her face twisted with rage, and she pointed behind me.

I spun. The driver had emerged from the truck and was scuttling down the road, hunched over and clutching his broken arm to his chest. As I stared, the girl grabbed the shotgun from under my arm. I turned back toward her, afraid she might try to shoot me, but she'd aimed it down the road at the driver. She tried to pull the trigger over and over again, but the gun was safetied.

"What's wrong with this thing?" she screeched, turning back toward me and leveling the barrel at my chest.

"Whoa!" I swept the barrel aside with an inner forearm block, wincing from the pain the move triggered in my shoulder. "Don't point that thing at me. You need to push the safety off. It's the button on the right side," I said automatically, instantly regretting my big mouth. Gunning down the driver as he fled seemed wrong, although letting him fetch his buddies in Anamosa wasn't such a bright idea, either. And what if Alyssa decided to use the shotgun on me?

She snicked off the safety and pulled the trigger. Her shot was high and wide, and she hadn't braced herself at all. The shotgun knocked her on her ass. "Piece of shit!" she screamed and threw the shotgun aside.

"Waste of a good shell," I said wryly.

She sprang back to her feet and reached for the knife on my belt.

I caught her wrist as her fingers wrapped over the hilt. "What are you doing?" I yelled.

"Let go!" she screamed back.

The driver had picked up his pace and was more than one hundred feet down the road now.

"What are you going to do with my knife?" I asked again.

"Fine," she said. "You win." She released her grip on the knife hilt, and I turned and crouched to retrieve the shotgun. Something tugged at my waist, and I spun back just in time to see Alyssa running down the road toward the driver with my knife raised above her head, ready to stab.

She'd only taken a few steps when an eerie, monotone moan emanated from the truck's load bed. She took one more step forward, then looked back, clearly undecided. Finally she pivoted and marched back to me.

"Now look what you've done. You've upset Ben."

"What are you talking about?"

She pointed the knife at me, waving it as she spoke. "Do. Not. Mess. With. My. Brother."

"Who do you think I am, other than the guy who just rescued both of you? Give me my knife back. Please."

She thrust the knife into her belt and turned away, marching toward the truck bed.

I looked down the road at the driver for a while. He was already out of the shotgun's range, but I wanted to make sure he didn't double back. I didn't relax until he was a solid quarter mile down the road.

I turned my attention to the corpse of the truck's passenger. A ring of keys dangled limply from his belt. I took the keys and started searching his pockets. As I searched, the moaning coming from inside the truck ended. I put the pistol in my belt, stowed the shotgun in the passenger-side footwell, and trudged to the back of the truck.

I pulled aside the canvas flap. Alyssa was crouched in the back of the truck beside the big guy I'd last seen in the Anamosa garage. They sat on a jumbled pile of wooden crates. She had a glove balled up in one hand, and she was rubbing the guy's back with it, running it repeatedly over his coat. He was blocky, but his flesh appeared to be hung on an oversized skeleton. Like he hadn't eaten well recently. He looked maybe nineteen or twenty years old.

I let down the tailgate and climbed into the load bed. "Is he okay?"

Alyssa looked at me over her shoulder. She didn't stop brushing the guy's back. "He'll be okay."

"You didn't get hurt during the crash?"

"Ben and I were thrown into the canvas wall. With the crates," she said. "I've got some ugly bruises."

"What about you?" I asked, addressing Ben. He was huge. Sitting with his ankles tucked under him, he was almost as tall as I was standing. He was shackled prison-style, wrists and ankles cuffed and linked with chains that severely restricted his movement.

He didn't respond. He was gently rocking forward and back, back and forward.

"Doesn't he talk?" I stretched, trying to work out the painful kinks in my side and shoulder.

"When he wants to."

"Why are you rubbing his back?"

"I'm brushing, not rubbing. It helps. Why'd you crash the truck?"

"I thought you were Darla. She fell onto a Peckerwood truck during an ambush. I've been trying to find her. You've seen her? Did you talk to her?"

"No, I never talked to her. The only time I saw her, she was asleep. They had her in the infirmary at Anamosa. She didn't look like she was hurt too bad."

"What'll they do to her?"

The girl shook her head slowly. "They won't flense her, probably. They're running out of girls. And we're valuable. I think they only decided to trade me away because I come with an extra mouth to feed." She glanced at Ben.

"I've got to get back to Anamosa."

"They'll kill you."

"Maybe. What do you want to do? If you stay here, the Peckerwoods might come back and pick you up."

"No!" She grabbed my arm and stared at me. A fierce light burned in her eyes. "Get us out of here. Anywhere. I don't care. Worthington, if they're still holding out."

"I can't waste that much time. I've got to find Darla. And if you don't want to wait for the Peckerwoods, we've got to get out of here."

"Why didn't you shoot Clevis? It might have been a

couple days before the Peckerwoods sent anyone out to check on him."

My face grew hot. "I don't know. I couldn't."

"He would have shot you without a second thought. Or done something even worse."

"I'm not like him."

The girl shook her head. "What planet are you from? And what's your name, anyway?"

"Alex." I wasn't sure what to say to the first question. I reached out to Ben, intending to check the lock on his wrist. The girl caught my hand and held it. "What?" I asked.

"Don't. He doesn't like to be touched."

"You're touching him."

"Brushing. I told you."

"I was just going to check the locks on his cuffs. I might have the key." I dangled the key ring I'd snatched from the corpse.

She took the ring from me and used a tiny silver key to unlock Ben's ankle and wrist cuffs. Then she tossed the chains away. "Thanks," she said, handing the keys back to me.

"Why doesn't he talk?"

"Like I said, he doesn't want to. If he decides to talk to you, you won't be able to shut him up."

"What's wrong with him?"

"Nothing!"

"Sorry. Look, we need to get out of here before Clevis gets back to the prison and sends out the cavalry. We can loop around, drop me near Anamosa, and then you can take the truck wherever you want to go." I started shuffling toward the tailgate. My body had stiffened as we talked—even walking hurt now.

"You should have shot him." Alyssa followed me, Ben trailing behind.

"He might not make it to Anamosa," I said as I climbed down from the tailgate. "I think he broke some ribs in the crash, and I shattered his right arm pretty good."

"You did that?" Alyssa hurried to get alongside me as I limped toward the driver's door.

"Yeah. He was trying to shoot me. Remember?"

"Hmm," she said, looking thoughtful.

I pulled open the driver's door, threw my pack on the bench seat, and climbed in after it. "I don't know if I can drive this thing. I've never driven anything but an automatic."

"Me, neither."

I dug a spare shirt out of my pack and handed it to Alyssa. "Clean off the front windshield, would you?"

"Sure." She took my shirt, climbed onto the front fender, and started wiping the oil off the windshield.

I took the keys out of my pocket and looked for the ignition. I couldn't find it. There was no keyhole anywhere.

"Won't it start?" Alyssa asked when she finished the windshield.

"I don't know," I said, staring at the gearshift. "The gears aren't even marked on here. And there's no place to put a key."

If Darla were in the driver's seat, we'd have been rolling down the road at top speed by now. The dashboard was confusing, covered in labels, symbols, signs, dials, and gauges. After a moment, a handle to the left of the steering wheel caught my eye—it was labeled Off and Ignition. I turned it, and the truck started making a low whine, but it didn't start.

"What's that?" Alyssa said.

"I don't know."

"It doesn't sound good. Turn it off."

I cranked the handle back to Off, and the whine died.

"Let Ben look at it. He's into military stuff."

Alyssa stepped off the running board and held the door open for Ben.

"What do you know about this truck?" Alyssa asked him.

"It's an M35A2," Ben replied. His voice was deep, which surprised me after his high-pitched moaning. But it still sounded odd, flat. "A multifuel model. That means you can drive it on gasoline, diesel, vegetable oil, heating oil, or jet—"

"Focus, Ben." Alyssa interrupted. "I don't need to know everything about it. How do you start it?"

"Turn on the ignition." Ben pointed to the same handle I'd turned. "Then push the starter button." He leaned into the cab, pointing at a button I'd missed to the right of the steering wheel.

I cranked the ignition handle over, starting the whine again. Then I mashed the starter button under my thumb. The truck roared to life.

Ben clapped his hands over his ears and stepped down from the running board.

I jammed the clutch to the floor under my left foot and

fiddled with the shifter. I wasn't sure if it was in gear, or if so, which gear it was in. There were no markings on the shifter. I started to ease up on the clutch, but realized I'd forgotten to buckle up.

I pulled over the lap belt and buckled it. I eased back on the clutch—my face felt hot, and I realized I was holding my breath. When my foot came clear off the clutch, nothing changed.

"I think it's still in neutral," Alyssa said.

"Yeah." I grabbed the gear shift and shoved it upward. The truck made a horrible metallic grinding sound.

"You've got to push in the clutch first," I muttered to myself.

I tried again, but the truck must have been in third. It lurched forward, buried its front wheels even deeper in the snowbank, and stalled.

"The New Guy should use the chart to the left of the steering wheel," Ben yelled.

"Chart?" I said. Then I noticed it, exactly where Ben said it would be. It showed all the gear positions.

Despite the chart, I stalled the truck twice more before I found reverse. And even then, the truck didn't pull free of the snowbank. The back wheels spun on the icy road, spitting snow and digging in a little. Ben showed me how to engage the all-wheel drive, but even that didn't help. The deuce was stuck. And thanks to my infinite genius, we had a limited amount of time to get it *unstuck* before Clevis returned. With all his buddies.

Chapter 50

Ben wandered around the truck, muttering.

"What?" I asked.

He didn't reply for a moment. "Was that intended to be a question?"

"Yes," I said. "What are you muttering about?"

"This truck has been badly maintained. There is no winch. The tires show excessive wear."

Lot of help that was. Alyssa and I traded places. As she got into the cab, she shuddered, staring at the blood smeared over the passenger side windshield and dash. I walked to the front of the truck and wedged myself against the bumper to push. The mountain of snow behind me reached above the cab of the truck. I heaved on the bumper with all my might while Alyssa spun the wheels. Nothing. I remembered how Darla had rocked the bulldozer free of the creek last year and tried pushing rhythmically to set up a rocking motion. That didn't work, either.

Now Ben was standing partway up the snow berm, a little ways off, watching the proceedings. "I could use a little help here, you know!" I yelled at him.

He turned his back on me and started trudging toward the top of the snow berm. "Where are you going?" I shouted. He didn't reply. Great. We didn't have time to mess around. By truck we were less than fifteen minutes from Anamosa. I wanted to be long gone before Clevis got back to the prison and informed the Peckerwoods that I'd stolen their truck.

Alyssa shut off the engine and climbed out of the cab. I chased after Ben, moving as quickly as I could on the slippery berm.

I caught up with him just as he started down the far side of the berm, heading toward the crushed barn. Alyssa was nowhere in sight.

"What are you doing?" I asked.

"I need a lever," he replied.

"What for?" I asked, but he talked over my question, ignoring it.

"Like Archimedes' lever, but it does not have to be that strong. I do not need to move the world; I only need to move a truck."

"Hey, that's a good—" I started, but Ben kept talking over me.

"Archimedes was killed by a Roman soldier. General Marcellus had ordered that Archimedes not be harmed, but Archimedes refused to accompany the soldier. He was working on a mathematical problem involving seven circles. His last words were, 'Do not disturb my circles.' Then the Roman soldier killed Archimedes with his sword."

"That's int—"

"The lever-action rifle was invented in 1849 by Walter Hunt. The first important model was the Spencer Repeating Rifle. It had a seven-shot magazine capacity. It was used during the U.S. Civil War by Union forces only after Abraham Lincoln test fired one in 1863. But it was too late for the rifle to make a significant difference in the war."

By this time we had reached the remnants of a crushed barn. Ben started rummaging through the rafters while he lectured me. I helped him shift the rubble, having some idea what he was looking for.

"The principle of the lever allowed E. M. Darque to invent a compact can opener used by American troops during World War II. The first military model was called the P-38, developed in 1942. Not long after, an additional model named the P-51 was introduced. Some people believe the can openers were named after the aircraft that share the same designation, but that is a coincidence. The can openers were named for their size; the P-38 was 38 millimeters in length, and the P-51 was 51 millimeters in length."

We'd found a suitable board—a broken two-by-eight. It was fourteen or fifteen feet long. Ben pried scraps of roof decking off it while he talked. He made it seem effortless—clearly, he was as strong as his size suggested.

Alyssa huffed up and more or less pushed her way between us. "What's wrong with him?" I whispered.

"Nothing!" she hissed back.

"Why's he going on and on about levers?" He'd continued talking—now he was giving a long dissertation on the importance of levers to the landing gear and ailerons on F-14 fighter jets. I was pretty much tuning him out.

"It's his special interest. Not levers, I mean. Anything to do with the military."

"So he's one of those, what do you call them? Idiot savants?"

"He's not an idiot," she whispered. "He's smarter than you are. Or me. And he's the kindest, most gentle—the best big brother anyone could have. Don't hurt. . . . Just get us somewhere safe. . . . Please?"

"I've got to get to Anamosa. But I'll give you the truck and all the supplies I can spare. You didn't answer my question, though—what's he got?"

"Dad called it Autism Spectrum Disorder," she whispered. "Mom said it was his special blessing, not a disorder. I used to think she was crazy. Before. When Mom and Dad were still alive."

We had the two-by-eight stripped of all the excess chunks of wood now. There were still about a zillion nails in it, but I didn't think they'd get in our way. I picked up one end of the rafter and Ben grabbed the other. He was still talking—now it was something about the use of levers in airplane launch-and-retrieval systems aboard aircraft carriers. We trudged back toward the truck. Alyssa walked beside me.

"He wasn't this bad before the volcano," she whispered. "Stress makes it harder for him to cope. And there's been tons."

"Yeah." I was quiet for a minute, paying attention to where I placed my feet as we crossed the snow berm. "How did you survive? With the Peckerwoods?"

Alyssa looked away. "I did what I had to. To keep us both safe."

How could this slight girl protect her overgrown big brother? It should have been the other way around. I didn't want to think too hard about it.

When we got back to the truck, Alyssa left me to get into the driver's seat. Ben fed one end of the rafter under the front bumper of the truck and joined me at the other. It would've been easier if we could have used the snow berm as a fulcrum, but it was too tall. Ben kept talking about aircraft carriers. He didn't seem to care or even realize that I wasn't listening.

Alyssa fired up the truck. The wheels spun in reverse. Ben and I pushed up on the rafter, trying to use the lever to force the truck up and off the snow berm.

We moved the truck an inch . . . then two. The board bowed as we heaved upward on it. Suddenly the rafter snapped. The truck rocked back into place and Ben and I fell, sliding down the snow berm and coming to rest against the front bumper.

The rafter was broken in a jagged line right where it had pushed against the bumper. "I should have placed the lever vertically," Ben said.

"Yeah," I replied. "It probably would have been stronger that way."

We tried using the longer of the two remaining pieces of rafter, but we couldn't get enough leverage to budge the truck at all. So we all trudged back to the wrecked barn.

We'd taken the easiest rafter the first time. It took twenty or thirty minutes to free another one of the right length and size from the tangled wreckage. I was starting to worry about how long we'd been there. Clevis had long since disappeared over the horizon.

Ben placed the rafter under the bumper—oriented correctly this time, and Alyssa got back in place behind the wheel. As soon as we pushed up on the rafter, we could feel the truck rolling backward. We started rocking it rhythmically. I slid up so my shoulder was jammed under the rafter, and I could use my legs to lift it. Ben and I heaved upward, Alyssa gunned the engine, and suddenly the truck was free. Ben and I fell forward, sliding down the snow berm again. The truck shot across the road, struck the snow berm on the opposite side, and stalled.

I sprinted across the road. "Don't get it stuck again!" I yelled.

"I wasn't trying to!" Alyssa retorted.

"I know. But let me drive, okay?"

"Gladly. Stupid truck." Alyssa unbuckled her seat belt and scooted to the middle of the bench seat, straddling the gearshift. Ben got in the passenger side, smearing the blood on the seat into his pants. I passed him my backpack to stow under the passenger seat. A bulging daypack already rested under there, but I didn't want to spend time investigating it at that moment. When I got in, Ben was pulling out the seat belt on his side. It stretched across both his lap and Alyssa's. I fastened my own seat belt.

Ben put the shotgun in his lap with the barrel pointed toward the passenger door. He bent over it, minutely inspecting some aspect of its workings.

"Will he be okay with that?" I asked Alyssa. What I really needed to know was whether he was likely to accidentally shoot me.

"Safer than you or me. Knows so much about firearms he used to get email from adult collectors who read his blog. Before."

"How many shells we got?" I said to Ben.

"This is a Remington 870 pump-action shotgun. It is the most popular shotgun ever made. Law enforcement and military all over the world use this gun." Ben tried to pump the shotgun, but the slide wouldn't operate. "It is loaded."

"So how many shots are in it?" I asked as I started the truck.

Ben clicked a lever on the side of the gun and started pumping the slide. Chunk-chunk. Chunk-chunk. Each time he pumped the gun a shell flew out, landing in the footwell. "None," Ben said when he finished.

"None? Those shells are duds?"

"No. There are no shells in the shotgun now. There were five."

I wanted to throttle him despite the fact that he was roughly twice my size. "Well, reload it, would you?"

"Yes, I would." Ben started picking up shells off the floorboard.

"You want to test fire one out the window?" I forced the shifter left and down for first gear, lifted off the clutch, and promptly stalled the truck again.

Ben ignored my question, continuing to reload the shotgun.

"He doesn't shoot guns," Alyssa said while I restarted the truck. "We took him to a rifle range for his tenth birthday. He was already into all things military then. He fired a .22, put it down, and left the range. He doesn't like the noise."

"That's . . . different." I stalled the truck once more before I got it in first. Then I pulled out too fast and nearly ran over the corpse we'd left lying in the road.

At last we were rolling down the road away from Anamosa—south, I thought. We'd made it away before Clevis could send a search party from the prison—though if the Peckerwoods sent anyone after us, it would be more like a search-and-destroy party. Ben put the shotgun back in the footwell. He rolled down his window and peered out, twisting his head to look behind us.

"Is that shotgun safetied?" I asked.

Ben didn't say anything. I glanced at Alyssa. "How should I know?" she said.

"Find out, would you?" I tried to shift into second gear and stalled the truck again. "God—"

"Don't cuss around Ben," Alyssa interrupted. "He doesn't like it." She turned back toward Ben while I restarted the truck. "You remember your social interactions class, Ben?"

He didn't respond.

"What are you supposed to do when someone asks you a question?"

"I am supposed to choose an appropriate response."

"And what did Alex just ask you?"

"Alex asked me whether I safetied the Remington 870 shotgun. I always check the safety before I handle any weapon. I always check the safety when I set a weapon down or pass it to someone else. I never disengage a weapon's safety."

"That's good." I'd gotten the truck restarted, even managed to put it into second gear. Ben was hanging his head out the window. "Would you close the window, please?" I asked. "I'm cold."

Ben pulled in his head and started rolling up his window. "The deuce-and-a-half behind us is an A3, remanufactured under the extended service program between 1994 and 1999."

"Wait, you mean our deuce-and-a-half, right?"

"No, the truck in which I am riding is an A2 with the multifuel feature and a manual transmission."

I cranked my window down and adjusted the mirror. A truck was racing toward us, gaining far too fast.

Chapter 51

"There's a truck behind us!" I yelled.

"I told you about the truck," Ben said.

"Is it the Peckerwoods?" Alyssa asked, craning her neck.

"Who else could it be?" I said.

"You should have killed Clevis."

She was probably right. I just grunted. The truck was whining loudly—I had crushed the pedal to the floor, but we weren't going very fast. I pushed in the clutch and tried to shift to third. My hands shook from the adrenaline, and I wasn't used to the shifter. I stalled the truck.

"What'd you do that for?" Alyssa yelled.

"I was trying to go faster!" I said, frantically groping at the starter button. Ben started a monotone moan. He was curled over, hugging his knees and rocking gently back and forth.

Just as I got the truck restarted, there was a colossal crash as our pursuers rammed us. I was thrown against the wheel. The truck lurched forward, and at the same moment I threw it into gear and jammed my foot down on the accelerator.

Alyssa started screaming, a high-pitched screech that was in no way helpful to our predicament. Ben's moan grew in volume until they were making a cacophonous tenor/soprano duet.

I glanced in the mirror just in time to brace myself as the deuce slammed into our rear end again. Instead of falling back to ram us again, they started to come around. I swerved, temporarily blocking them. But I couldn't block them forever, and I couldn't outrun them—I wasn't a good enough driver. They were like a cat playing with a particularly inept mouse. Unless something changed, things didn't look good for the mouse.

"Give me the shotgun!" I shouted.

Alyssa kept screaming, her hands up around her ears.

I couldn't see the truck in my mirrors, and the passenger-side mirror wasn't adjusted right. I figured it must be on our right. I cranked the wheel over hard and heard a satisfying crunch. But seconds later, they reappeared in my left-hand mirror, still coming on strong.

"Give me the shotgun!" I repeated. Alyssa didn't respond.

In desperation, I reached out and slapped her, hoping to shock her out of her hysteria. It was an awkward, back-handed slap since she was sitting right next to me and my right arm was stiff from the crash. I'd never laid a hand on a girl before—then again, I'd never been in a race to escape cannibals before, either.

The truck was almost alongside us now. "Shotgun!" I yelled.

Alyssa reached into the passenger footwell, pulled the shotgun out from under Ben's feet, and passed it to me. My hand had left a pink imprint on her cheek.

"Take the wheel!" I shouted. Alyssa gave me a blank look, so I grabbed her left hand and put it on the wheel. I flicked off the shotgun's safety and twisted to aim out my open window.

I was too short. My foot came off the gas pedal and our truck slowed. I squeezed the trigger as the Peckerwoods' truck rocketed past us. The shotgun boomed, kicking me backward, completely missing the tire I'd been aiming at. On the plus side, the guy shooting his pistol at me from the other truck missed just as badly.

My shoulder burned like it had been kicked by a billy goat. I could barely move my right arm. We were rolling ever slower, and the Peckerwoods' truck was at least one hundred feet ahead of us. I transferred the shotgun to my left shoulder, holding it awkwardly, and leaned out the window. Would a shotgun even work at this range? I wasn't sure. I lined it up on the back of the truck and squeezed the trigger left-handed.

The kick knocked the shotgun right out of my hand.

It clanged against the running board and fell to the icy road. I swiveled my head just in time to see it disappear behind us.

"Crap!" I yelled. The Peckerwoods' truck had come to a halt ahead of us. They were turning around, but the space between the snow berms was far too narrow for a U-turn. Instead, they'd started a laborious three- or four-point turn.

Instantly I knew what to do. I dropped back into the driver's seat and mashed the gas pedal under my boot. "Brace yourselves!" I yelled as I took the wheel from Alyssa.

I lined us up on the center of the Peckerwoods' truck, not that we could miss—they almost filled the road. It looked like I might be able to broadside them perfectly as they worked through their turn. It was just like a physics problem I'd had in high school—when two objects collide, the one going slower absorbs most of the acceleration and gets damaged the worst. I kept the pedal mashed to the floor.

The guy in the passenger seat of the Peckerwoods' truck had his pistol out, firing at me as we approached. I ducked under the dashboard. I couldn't see a thing, but all I had to do was keep our truck straight. I heard the pop-pop of his pistol twice more.

And then there was a tremendous crash.

Chapter 52

I was thrown against the steering wheel, but the lap belt kept me from flying farther. Our truck was at a dead stop. I slowly leaned back.

The Peckerwoods' truck was about forty feet ahead of us, upside down across the road. It was wrecked. The cover over the load bed was crushed so that the truck was tilted, its nose thrust into the air. Every window had shattered and the doors hung open. I couldn't see any movement inside.

Alyssa and Ben were curled over and squeezed together by their shared seat belt. "Are you okay?" I asked. Alyssa sat back. Ben's eyes were glassed over—he looked dazed. A cut on his forehead was bleeding heavily. A trickle of blood snaked into the corner of his eye. He blinked twice and started screaming—howling, really—in a way I hadn't heard since kindergarten.

"Is he hurt really bad?" I reached toward Ben.

Alyssa batted my hand away. "I got it. You touch him, you'll just make it worse." She turned back to Ben, talking to him in a calm, firm voice. "Ben, let me check your cut. I can fix it." She was bent low but not facing him, sort of talking in his ear. She pulled off one of her gloves, balled it up, and started brushing it down his arm. He kept screaming.

I saw movement in the Peckerwoods' truck. The driver was hanging upside down by his seat belt. He slid out of the belt and started dragging himself through the door. He was bleeding and didn't appear to be armed, but I didn't want to hang around and find out for sure.

I mashed in the clutch and pushed the starter button. The truck chugged for a moment and then roared to life.

My right arm had frozen up. I had to reach across my lap with my left arm to operate the gearshift. I was shaking so badly that I wasn't sure I could do it at all. Somehow I managed it without stalling the truck—maybe I was getting better at driving.

Ben was still screaming, and Alyssa was still brushing him. "You have any bandages?" Alyssa asked.

"There's a first-aid kit in my backpack," I said. She quit brushing Ben and pulled my backpack out from under the seat.

The Peckerwood's driver was now clear of their truck. I eased my foot onto the gas, and we slowly rolled forward. It didn't look like our truck would fit around the wreck, but I didn't want to turn around. For one thing, I was afraid more trucks might be headed our way from Anamosa. And for another, I didn't know if I could manage a three-point turn.

"Watch out," I said to Alyssa, who was still rummaging through my backpack.

"I found it." She twisted and sat, clutching the plastic case that held my first-aid supplies. Ben was still screaming.

I mashed the accelerator, racing toward the tiny gap between the wreck and the snow berm. The driver looked up in alarm and scrambled away on all fours. We struck the edge of the cab, barely registering the impact. The wrecked truck spun when we hit it, and we shot free, accelerating south away from the accident and the Peckerwoods.

Within minutes, Ben quieted down considerably. Alyssa had a gauze pad in one hand, mopping his forehead. With the other, she was brushing him continuously with her glove. She talked to him in a patient, straightforward voice. "It's okay. I'm going to put everything back the way it should be. You're going to be fine."

"Ben's blood belongs on the inside," he said.

"Yes, it does. I'm going to wrap your head up now to keep it there." Alyssa had wiped away enough blood to expose a long cut along his forehead. She started bandaging it, using strips of medical tape to hold the wound closed and covering it all with gauze.

We came to an intersection, and I turned left. I planned to drive east a ways then turn north, looping back to Anamosa by a different route. Once I got close, I'd head back to the prison on foot and give the truck to Alyssa and Ben. They could find their own way to Worthington. I had to keep searching for Darla.

I squeezed the steering wheel tighter, wondering if Worthington was still even standing. Maybe Alyssa and Ben would arrive to find a town burned out and looted by the Peckerwoods.

The truck was handling badly, pulling to the left. Or maybe I was doing it, trying to drive one-handed. I wasn't much of a driver even when both my arms worked. The pull got steadily worse. The truck started listing to the left and making a rhythmic whap-whap-whap sound.

"Something's wrong," I said. "I've got to stop."

"Okay." Alyssa didn't even look at me. "Does it hurt anywhere else?" she asked Ben.

"Ankle," he said.

"How did you hurt your ankle?"

"It got twisted in the straps of the backpack when we crashed," Ben said.

"I need to check it for you." Alyssa ducked down into the passenger-side footwell.

I let the truck coast to a stop and got out.

The front left wheel well was crushed. Its edge had carved a deep groove in the tire, shredding it. Now it looked like the whole tread might fall off.

The spare was obvious—it was attached horizontally just behind the driver's door. I'd clung to a spare tire on a deuce like this one during my wild ride from Cascade to Anamosa. What I didn't see was a jack.

I'd never changed a tire before, but I'd watched my mom do it once. She'd gotten a little plastic case that held the jack out from under the spare. I looked all around the spare, even wormed under the truck on my back, but I didn't see anything that looked like a jack. I went to look in the cab.

Ben was stretched out on the bench seat. Alyssa bent over his left ankle.

"How is he?" I asked.

"His ankle is hurt. It's swelling. I'm afraid if I take his boot off he won't be able to get it back on."

"Don't then. We might have to walk. And we're still way too close to the wreck."

"I don't know if he *can* walk."

"Wrap his ankle and foot in an Ace bandage. Over the boot. Try to immobilize it."

"Okay."

"Ben, do you know how to change the tire on this thing?"

"Which thing does Alex mean?"

"The truck we're sitting in."

"Yes. The operator must loosen each lug nut from the damaged wheel but not remove them. Then the operator must use the hydraulic jack to raise—"

"That's what I want to know. Where's the jack?"

"In the toolbox."

"Where's that?"

Ben swung his legs off the seat and started to slide out of the truck. Both Alyssa and I protested, telling him not to move, but neither of us was in position to stop him. When his feet hit the road, he screamed and crumpled to the ice.

I ran around the cab, ignoring the pain of my bruised right leg, but by the time I got there, Alyssa was already helping him up. Or rather, he was helping himself up, using Alyssa's shoulder for support. She barely touched him.

"Ben's ankle is not functioning properly," he said.

"No, it's not," Alyssa replied. "Lie down on the seat, and I'll wrap it up for you."

"Where's the toolbox?" I asked.

"Under the operator's door," Ben replied as Alyssa helped him back into the cab.

I went around to the driver's side. There was a metal compartment that I hadn't noticed before between the running board and the door. I twisted the handle and opened the toolbox. It was freaking empty.

Chapter 54

"There's no jack," I told Alyssa. "We have to walk."

"Ben can't walk," she whispered.

I'd sort of known that already. But we had to get away from here somehow. Maybe I could rig some kind of stretcher using the frame from my backpack and drag Ben along. But he was a big guy.

The engine was still running. I'd seen people driving along the shoulder of the interstate on flat tires before. They never went very fast, and Mom said it was a bad idea, but I couldn't remember why. Whatever—if it worked at all it would beat trying to drag a gigantic teenager down the road.

The passenger door was still open. Alyssa and Ben were busy wrapping his leg, so I limped around the cab and slammed their door myself.

I only stalled the truck once getting it in gear. It would move on a flat tire, but not fast. The speedometer never passed ten miles per hour. Still, it was far better time than we would have made walking.

I had to fight to keep the steering wheel straight, which was tiring using only one hand. The truck moved like it wanted to crash into the left-hand snow berm. After a while, keeping it on the road became a real test of my endurance and willpower.

At the first intersection, I turned right. I wanted to put several turns between us and the Peckerwoods to make us harder to follow. I planned to loop back to Anamosa and find a way to get inside the prison to look for Darla. A couple of miles down the new road, I spotted a narrow, plowed crossroad. When I let go of the wheel, the truck turned left all on its own—a brief moment of respite for my aching arm.

The numbness in my right arm started to wear off. Not a good thing—it was replaced with what felt like eight zillion angry bees swarming under my skin, stinging and chewing my muscles to hamburger. And to top it all off, I was exhausted. I tapped my left foot, bit my lip, and suppressed a few dozen yawns—all in a monumental struggle to stay awake.

"I can't do this much longer," I said.

"I'll watch for a place to stop," Alyssa said.

"I've got to get back to Anamosa. You drive for a while."

"I've got to take care of Ben." She turned away from me and resumed brushing Ben and talking to him in a low voice.

She'd already wrapped his ankle—it seemed to me that he'd be fine on his own for a while.

The first farmstead we passed was a burned-out husk. Few of the walls were standing, let alone any part of the roof that could shelter or hide us. A few minutes after we passed it, I heard a faint clang in the distance, like a bell ringing, but I couldn't figure out where the sound had come from.

The second place we found was different. The driveway wasn't plowed, but the snow had been deliberately packed down. I couldn't make out any footprints or tell what had packed the snow—there were no tire or snowmobile tracks.

It was a typical Iowa farm: two-story white clapboard house, red barn, three corrugated-steel grain silos, and a big metal garage that had been crushed by ash, snow, or both.

"Stop here?" Alyssa asked.

"We should keep going."

"Ben needs rest. You do, too."

"I don't like it. Looks occupied. But I can't keep driving." I thought about suggesting we camp in the truck. But we had no good way to heat it other than running the engine, and the gas gauge had already dipped under a quarter tank. I muscled the wheel into a turn at the driveway.

The truck lurched, sinking into the snow, but the four rear wheels of the deuce got enough traction to keep pushing us forward. I didn't have to use the brake to stop us—with the flat tire and packed snow, the truck simply coasted to a groaning stop after I let off the gas.

The farmstead was silent. I thought I smelled a faint whiff of smoke. There were no other signs of habitation.

I eased open my door. "Stay here," I said. "If you see anything, yell or come get me."

Alyssa nodded. I pulled the pistol off my belt, holding it in my left hand, and slipped out of the truck.

The flat tire had shredded, losing most of its tread. Some of the rubber had melted onto the wheel well. Maybe that accounted for the smoke I smelled.

I stalked to the back door. The snow on the walk was packed to icy solidity. My exhaustion vanished, replaced by another adrenaline-fueled buzz. I swiveled my head back and forth, totally alert—looking, listening, smelling, even tasting the air.

There was a lean-to addition on the back of the house. Only four inches or so of snow were on the roof; someone had cleared it off after last year's blizzards. A skylight, slightly off center, pierced the shingles. A round piece of metal covered the center of the skylight, as though someone had patched it. The snow had melted for a foot or so all around the skylight, which meant there was, or had been, a heat source inside.

The storm door was open and askew. Its top hinge had been ripped away. The entry door seemed solid, though. I took hold of the knob, slowly twisting it.

The door was unlocked. I pushed it open.

Inside there was a small mudroom. An ancient freezer sat in one corner, redundant because the room itself was below freezing, and useless because there was no hum of power. A pile of filthy, frozen clothing occupied another corner. Aside from that, the room was empty.

The next room was a large kitchen. I could tell it had been a kitchen by the pipes protruding from the walls and the outlines in the paint showing where cabinets had once hung. A thick three-foot-square chunk of foam-board insulation lay on the floor. Someone had laid a double stack of concrete patio pavers on it, and ashes from an old fire were clumped atop the pavers. A huge jumble of branches was heaped in one corner.

The patched skylight was directly above the makeshift fire pit. A long string with a loop tied in the end dangled from the metal patch. I tugged on the string experimentally—the patch proved to be a metal cover on a spring-loaded hinge. When I pulled it fully open, the loop in the string would just reach a nail jutting from the wall. It was an ingenious setup—you could open the hatch to let smoke out or close it to keep the heat in, all without having to reach the high, sloped ceiling. People had clearly been living here since the eruption. The only question: Were they still here?

I eased through the entire house, quietly checking every room. Some held furniture and belongings, but much of what I found was broken, ruined, or frozen. I saw lots of signs that people had lived here, but none that they'd been around recently. Where had they gone? And why? I even investigated the basement, returning to the truck to get a candle so I could peer into the dark corners around the dead furnace. This place was abandoned.

I went back outside to get the others. The truck was on the opposite side of the house from the road—not exactly hidden, but it was the best I could do. When I tried to help Ben out of the truck, Alyssa waved me away. It didn't seem like she helped him much, just offered a shoulder that he leaned on for support as they trudged inside.

I built a fire in the kitchen while Alyssa unwrapped Ben's ankle and struggled to take off his boot. His ankle was hugely swollen and red. We weren't sure how to tell if it was broken, so we decided to rewrap it for support but leave his boot off. We probably couldn't have gotten it back on him, anyway.

I searched Clevis's pack. He had a couple of two-liter plastic bottles full of water that had stayed liquid, warmed by the heater in the truck; a bundle of corn pone wrapped in paper; a plastic bag filled with dried meat; a few matches; and a small first-aid kit. I tossed the meat into the snow outside. No way would I eat any meat that came from a flenser's backpack.

Alyssa filled one of my pans with snow and put it on the fire to melt. Ben asked to use my hatchet. I handed it over, and he crawled to the woodpile and started breaking up the branches, sorting them by size.

I was starving, so I worked on lunch. Cornmeal mush with dandelion greens and bits of beef jerky—my gourmet specialty. While I worked, I tried to find out more about Alyssa.

"How long have you two been with the Peckerwoods?"

"Been slaves, you mean?" Alyssa said. "Almost four months."

"Why'd they keep you around?" I wanted to ask why the Peckerwoods hadn't killed and eaten them both, but that hardly seemed polite.

"I did stuff for them." Alyssa wrapped her arms around her chest, hugging herself.

"Stuff? Like what?"

Alyssa's face turned red, but judging from her expression, she was angry, not embarrassed. "Like—none of your business."

Oh. That kind of stuff. Suddenly I thought of Darla, held captive by the same men. I choked my words out through grinding teeth. "Sorry. And Ben . . . ?"

"I told Danny I'd kill myself if he hurt Ben. And I convinced him he didn't want me to kill myself." Alyssa's face was cold—hard and red as a brick.

"But he was sending you to Iowa City?"

"The Peckerwoods are running out of food and gas. I guess they got a good price for me." Alyssa shrugged. "And Danny has a new girl he got from the Peckerwoods in Cascade. He likes short brunettes. Guess she's that Darla you told me about."

My face grew hot, and I ground my teeth into fury. I thrust my hand into my pocket, gripping the chain 'til it cut my fingers. I had to get moving. Had to get back to Anamosa. Had to find Darla.

Chapter 55

Alyssa backed up a step, eyeing me warily. "I . . . I'm sorry. I didn't mean to . . . it didn't look like she was hurt too bad."

"What'll they do to her?" I wasn't sure I wanted to know.

Alyssa shied away from me. "Nothing good."

"I've *got* to get back to Anamosa." I started to push myself upright but made the mistake of trying to use my right arm. Pain reverberated through my arm and chest, and I crumpled, falling alongside the fire.

Alyssa knelt beside me and pulled off my right glove. "Why do you want to get killed over her? Who is she?"

"Darla. She's my . . ." Girlfriend didn't seem to cover it. I struggled to think of a word that did. "She's the reason I'm alive."

Alyssa nodded. "The only reason I'm alive is Ben. When I told Danny that I'd starve myself to death if he flensed Ben, I meant it. There's nothing in this shitpool life worth living for except him." She started to strip off my jacket, forcing me to sit up. I tried to protest, but she shushed me and kept going, taking off my clothing until I was bare-chested by the fire. I pushed a couple more sticks of wood into the fire. My back was freezing.

"Wow," Alyssa said, looking at my right arm. It was a swollen mass of purple-blue bruises. She gently lifted my arm. Even my armpit was bruised. Alyssa ran her fingers lightly over the horseshoe-shaped scar at the base of my ribcage. "What's that from?"

"A bandit—flenser, I guess, got me with a hatchet last year."

"And you survived."

"I killed him," I said flatly.

"And those?" She touched one of the round scabs on my belly.

"Shotgun pellets."

Her fingers wandered to my chest, tracing my pecs, which had gotten considerably larger over the months of nonstop farm work and physically challenging lifestyle, to put it mildly. "You're strong," she said.

I pulled away from her fingers and reached out to stir the corn porridge. "It's ready."

"I'm not sure what to do about your arm. It doesn't seem like anything's broken."

I shrugged my left shoulder.

"Maybe I should strap it to your side? Or make a sling? It might heal faster if you can't move it."

"No," I said. "I can move it a little. If anything happens, I might need it. Just help me put my clothes back on."

She didn't respond right away. She was staring at me—at the bruises on my arm, maybe, or maybe at my chest. Her eyes weren't on my face, that was for sure. I wasn't used to having a girl look at me that way—well, Darla had, sometimes.

I picked up my T-shirt and held it out toward her.

"If you go back to Anamosa, you're going to die. There's more than a hundred Peckerwoods there," she said as she helped me struggle into my T-shirt.

"Darla needs me."

"She'll be—well, they won't kill her. She's young and pretty. Valuable."

"They can't have her. I'm going to go get her. I'd leave now if I could."

Alyssa's eyes shone in the firelight.

"Hey. I'll just get close. Then you and Ben can have the truck—drive yourselves to Worthington. You'll be safe there." I sent up a silent prayer that Worthington hadn't been overrun, that Rita Mae and even Mayor Kenda were still okay.

"You're a tough guy, aren't you?" Alyssa said.

"Not really," I replied. "You're pretty tough. You survived being captured by the Peckerwoods. Kept your brother alive."

Alyssa started softly crying. I looked at Ben—he was immersed in systematically chopping and sorting wood, oblivious to his sister. I reached out and wrapped an arm around her, drawing her into an awkward, one-armed hug. "Hey, it's okay. You'll be all right now," I told her.

She clung to me. Her tears ran down my shoulder, and her arm hurt me where it pressed against my bruises. She smelled musky, salty—exciting, somehow. Her scent reminded me of Darla. Suddenly I was crying, too.

We held onto each other for a minute. Then I smelled something burning. I broke our hug and snatched the pot off the fire. Alyssa helped me get dressed while our lunch cooled.

We ate all the corn mush, even the burnt bits. I was utterly exhausted. I asked Alyssa to keep watch, tucked a pair of pants under my head, and fell asleep curled in front of the fire.

Chapter 56

When I awoke, Alyssa was up, cooking corn porridge for breakfast while Ben tended the fire. "Why didn't you wake me up to take a turn on watch?" I asked.

"There was no need," she said.

"You stayed up all night? You want to sleep now?"

"No. I couldn't stay up."

"Somebody should have kept watch."

"Nothing happened," she replied.

I grunted, mildly disgusted but unwilling to continue arguing.

After breakfast, I struggled to my feet. "I'm going to check the barn."

"You can barely move," Alyssa protested.

"There might be something useful out there. Maybe a jack." I took a faltering step toward the door.

Alyssa got up and tucked herself under my left shoulder. "I'll help."

"Shouldn't you stay with Ben?"

"He's fine."

We stumbled outside with my arm slung over her shoulders for support. A rusted tractor sat in the center of the barn. In one corner there was a huge pile of brown-and-yellow cornhusks, useless except to feed to goats or pigs.

On the way back, I looked into the bed of our truck. The wooden crates were a jumbled mess. "What's in the crates?" I asked.

"I don't know," Alyssa answered. "The Peckerwoods loaded them before they loaded us."

"Help me get up there."

Alyssa let down the tailgate and boosted me up. I hacked at the nearest crate with my hatchet. Opening it one-handed proved to be difficult—I struggled fruitlessly for fifteen or twenty minutes. Finally I got the blade of the hatchet jammed under the lid and used the handle as a lever.

Inside, it was full of steel chains. I picked one up—it was really four chains with manacles attached, identical to the set Ben had been wearing. The key was affixed to one of the manacles with a strip of duct tape.

I hacked open another box. It was packed with neat rows of identical brown paperboard boxes. I opened the flap of one at random. Gleaming rows of brass shotgun shells, stacked upright, filled the box. There must have been one hundred shells in that one box. Thousands in the whole crate.

"Too bad I lost the shotgun," I said. "Anyway, I guess we're rich."

"Those are worth a lot?" Alyssa asked.

"Yeah. A fortune—if we can find someone to trade with. I was hoping the barn would have something we could use as a jack and maybe a wrench."

"Can't we just drive real slow?"

"Yeah. But it would take all day to get to Worthington that way. You'd run out of gas."

"Oh."

"Maybe we can cut a beam out of the barn. Use it as a lever to lift one side of the truck and block it up."

"Will that work?"

"I don't know. I don't see any way to try it right now, as beat up as I am. I wish Darla were here. She'd know how to do it."

"She was good with trucks?"

"Yeah. She's a wizard with any kind of machine." I turned from Alyssa to hide the trembling in my lip.

"She'll be okay. The Peckerwoods . . . well, the crazy ones, the most brutal ones, they're already dead. The guys that are left . . . some of them are plenty nasty, but they're smart, too. They won't kill her. They won't destroy something that has value."

Something. That word sparked my fury. It filled me like the deep breath you take before a scream. But the Peckerwoods weren't Alyssa's fault. She hadn't created this ash-cursed world. I swallowed on my anger. "You're not really helping," I said as mildly as I could manage.

"Oh. Sorry."

• • •

We spent the rest of the day cooking, eating, and resting. Just the short walk out to the barn and truck had left me exhausted, and I couldn't do anything but sleep. The weakness in my body infuriated me. Darla might be suffering far worse than I, but there was nothing I could do about it. I'd abused my body so badly that I couldn't keep going, no matter how much I wanted to—I was completely out of gas.

After dinner, I offered to take the first watch while Alyssa and Ben slept. After waking up completely unguarded the night before, I didn't trust either of them to do it.

As they arranged themselves around the fire to sleep, I wondered how I was going to know when to wake Alyssa. In the past, sometimes I'd paced, counting steps and estimating time that way. Now, I was too weak to pace.

I started counting slowly on my fingers, trying to time a second per finger. As I tapped my pinky against the floor, a nursery rhyme came to mind, unbidden: "This little piggy went to market, this little piggy stayed home. . . ." I started muttering the rhyme instead of counting.

Reciting the nursery rhyme brought my mother to mind. She used to singsong it with my sister and me, grabbing our toes and wiggling them with each line of the poem. In my worry for Darla, I'd almost forgotten about Mom and Dad. They were the reason we'd left Warren, the reason Darla got shot. Just a week ago, I'd been determined to find them. Now, leaving Warren seemed like a stupid idea. The dumbest thing I'd ever done.

Maybe ten seconds passed each time I said the rhyme. Six rhymes a minute. Three hundred and sixty mind-numbing rhymes an hour. Fourteen hundred and forty before I could wake Alyssa. I'd probably have nightmares about stupid little piggies.

By the time I finished, I was speed-mumbling, saying the rhyme in seven or eight seconds instead of ten. My fingers hurt from tapping the floor, but if anything, I hit it even harder. The pain helped keep me awake.

I grabbed Alyssa's ankle and shook her. "Your turn to keep watch."

"Uh? 'kay." Alyssa slowly sat up. She'd taken off her coat to use as a pillow. The lavender sweater she wore underneath wasn't exactly form fitting, but it looked good on her.

I rummaged in my pack, looking for a pair of jeans to use as a pillow. "Good night," I said once I got settled. "And *please* don't fall asleep. We need to stay safe."

"You know, I never did thank you. For rescuing us." Alyssa squatted by my head, feeding the fire.

I would have shrugged, but I was resting on my left shoulder and my right hurt too badly. "I thought you were Darla."

"I think you would have helped us, anyway."

"Maybe so."

Alyssa put a hand on my shoulder, and I winced. "Oh. Sorry. I forgot." Her hand wandered up to my neck.

"It's okay. Goodnight."

"How did you beat Clevis? And learn to climb around on moving trucks like an action movie star?" Her hand caressed my cheek. I wasn't sure how to feel about her touch—my mind was annoyed and wanted to sleep, but at the same time, it felt somehow reassuring. And maybe something else, too.

"I've been training in taekwondo since I was five. Although we never practiced climbing around on a moving truck, that's true."

"You could, you know, come to Worthington with Ben and me." Alyssa was whispering, bent over me so our faces were close.

"I can't. I have—"

She kissed me. I knew it was wrong, was appalled with myself, but still I returned her kiss, my lips open, drinking in her hypnotic softness. I rolled away, onto my back, which Alyssa took as a sign of encouragement, kissing me more fiercely, her hands busy at my chest, spreading the warmth from my lips down toward my groin.

I pushed her away. "No."

"Why not? I could make you happy."

"No. You could make me feel good. Not happy. There's a difference."

"Most of the guys I've met don't think so."

I shrugged.

Her face scrunched, as if in pain. "You're just going to get yourself killed chasing after her."

"Probably."

I rolled back onto my side and stared into the fire, waiting for the tempestuous mix of desire, regret, and shame to subside. Alyssa was silent, staring at me. I closed my eyes and waited for sleep to take me.

• • •

I dreamed of pigs. A hog squealed as Darla slashed its throat. Blood fountained out as the pig cried, sounding exactly like my sister in the midst of a full-blown temper tantrum. Darla's arms and face were splashed, dripping red in my candlelit dream. She smiled then seemed to see me. Her head turned and her sanguinary visage shifted, mouth open in a little O, eyes wide with pain and betrayal.

Then the dream shifted and suddenly Darla was naked, suffocatingly beautiful. Her arms and face were still covered in blood. She drew a finger through the blood, painting herself, writhing suggestively, and whispering, "Alex . . . Alex . . ."

I woke up. Alyssa was spooned against my back, her arm resting on my shoulder, which hurt. On the other side of the fire, less than ten feet from me, a strange man stood, aiming a rifle at my chest.

Chapter 57

The man was lean and grizzled, his scraggly beard frosted white. His brown Carhartt coveralls were filthy, as if he'd been sleeping on dirt.

I pinched Alyssa's hand, and she startled awake. "Nice job keeping watch," I hissed.

"Sorry," she whispered back.

The man growled, "Don't move. Take that knife and gun off his belt, Brand."

I rotated my head to see who he was talking to. About five feet behind me stood a woman clutching a silver revolver in a two-handed grip, pointing it at Alyssa's back. A boy, maybe twelve or thirteen years old, stood next to her. He stepped over to where Alyssa and I lay and bent to take my knife and pistol. His hands were shaking so badly I was afraid he'd cut me with my own knife. He retreated to stand beside the woman.

Ben sat up. I hadn't even realized he was awake. The man swiveled, pointing his rifle at Ben. "I said, don't move!"

"Your tactical doctrine is flawed," Ben said.

The man gaped.

"In a three-person team, optimal tactical doctrine calls for enveloping the target in a triangular formation."

"Just don't move, okay?" the man said.

"If the Sister Unit or Her Attachment stood up, you'd be in each other's field of fire. If you missed or just grazed your target, you could easily wind up shooting one of your team members."

Her Attachment? Me? And what was he doing lecturing these people about infantry tactics? "Shut. Him. Up!" I hissed at Alyssa.

"Like I could," she whispered back.

Ben kept talking. "With a Winchester Model 70 at a range of twelve feet, even a hit might pass through the target and impact a team member."

The man looked down at his rifle, clearly surprised.

"Fixing your deployment would be easy. You, Short One," Ben said, addressing the kid. "Move over here, on the other side of me."

Great, I thought, now he's telling people how to kill us more effectively.

To my amazement, the boy did it, moving away from the woman.

"No. Farther away," Ben said, "so you can't be used as a shield or hostage easily."

The boy took two steps back.

"Now, you," Ben said to the woman. "Take three big steps to your right."

She started to turn.

"No," Ben said. "Sidestep. So your weapon stays on the target."

The woman sidestepped so that now the three of them formed a neat triangle around us.

"Good," Ben said. "Now if you discharge your weapons, each of you will have a clear field of fire. This formation is not recommended in situations where there is a risk of encountering flanking forces. In that situation, an enfilade deployment is preferable. . . ."

Ben kept talking about the benefits and drawbacks of an enfilade deployment, whatever that was. The man's mouth formed an O, probably because it couldn't very well form the letters WTF. The situation was so ridiculous and tense that I couldn't help myself. I started laughing.

Everyone looked at me as if I were crazy. Which was fair, I guessed. Then the man holding the rifle started laughing, too, and pretty soon everyone but Ben had joined in.

When the hilarity had died down, the man said, "You all are just crazy enough that I think I understand why you're still alive."

"Yeah," I said. I pushed myself slowly upright, keeping both hands in view. Maybe this guy was laughing, but he still had a rifle pointed my way. I took a step closer to him and stretched my left hand out as if to shake. My right arm still wasn't working too well.

He snicked on the safety and moved the rifle to his shoulder, pointed upward. His handshake was a little too vigorous for my liking—I could move my left arm, but it still hurt when he pumped it. "I'm Eli. My wife there's Mary Sue, and that's my son, Brand." He was so dirty he left a smudge on my hand. Not that my own hands were any too clean.

"What's wrong with him?" Brand said, looking at Ben.

"Nothing's wrong with him," Alyssa snapped as she stood up.

"He's autistic," I said.

"He doesn't seem artistic," Brand replied.

Alyssa wasn't smiling. "Autistic. And he's smarter than everyone *else* in this room put together."

"Sorry," Brand muttered.

Ben was ignoring us all, sketching something with his fingertip in the dust on the floor. More infantry tactics, maybe.

I still felt as if I were inching along the edge of a one-hundred-foot cliff. There were no guns pointed at us now, but they were still armed, and we weren't. "Can I have my stuff back?" I asked Brand.

He looked at his father, who shook his head.

"You all weren't planning on staying here, were ya?" Mary Sue said, the first words she'd uttered. Her voice brought to mind the sibilant whisper of a moving snake.

"We're headed to Worthington," Alyssa said.

"Huh, probably nothing there. Morley, Olin, and Mechanicsville's all been ransacked. Not a living soul in any of 'em. No dead people, either, 'less you count bones already cracked and sucked dry of their marrow. We visited, hopin' to trade." Mary Sue stepped closer to us as she talked. Her teeth shone yellow in the firelight. Each tooth was outlined in blood.

"Worthington was fine a week ago," I said. "Your gums are bleeding. You have scurvy?"

"Yeah. No fresh food. Girls got it worse."

"Girls?" Alyssa said.

"Alba and Joy," Mary Sue said. "They're hidden. Safe."

I rummaged through my pack. Eli readied his rifle, eyeing me suspiciously. I was running low on dandelion leaves, and the ones I had left were pretty badly wilted. As I pulled a bag out of my backpack, Eli aimed the rifle at me again and muttered, "Easy . . ."

"It's okay. I'm just getting dandelion leaves." I handed the bag to Mary Sue. "They're bitter, but they have vitamin C. That's all I have left."

She pulled a leaf out of the bag and bit it. "Fresh greens. Didn't think I'd live to taste them again. Where'd you get them?" She whispered the question, as if she were asking where I'd learned the secret nature of God, not where I'd picked up some weeds.

"Worthington. They grow 'em in cold frames."

"You got any seeds?" Eli lowered his rifle. "We could make cold frames out of some of our windows."

"Yeah, that's how they do it in Worthington. I don't

have any dandelion seeds, but I can do you one better. I've got kale seeds. Good winter variety. It can even come back from a freeze, if it isn't too hard or too long. Four times as much vitamin C as dandelion."

"And where'd that miracle come from?"

"Warren, Illinois. It's home now, I guess. We grow kale in greenhouses." I reached into my jacket and pulled open the bag in my pocket without taking it out. I didn't want them to see how many packets of kale seeds I had. I slid out one envelope.

Eli accepted the envelope I offered him. "You came all the way from Illinois?"

"Yeah. Now can I have my weapons back?"

Eli nodded slowly. "Brand, give the man his gun and knife, then fetch your sisters from the cellar." He set his rifle aside and fed the fire.

The girls were both younger than Brand. They reminded me of a bed of spring wildflowers I'd seen once after a flood. You could tell they were beautiful, even if they were beaten down and coated in filth.

Mary Sue carefully split the dandelion leaves into five portions. I noticed that Eli got less than the kids, and Mary Sue got barely any at all. While they ate, we traded stories. I told the saga of my trip from Illinois: how we'd found the shotgun, Blue Betsy, that had spurred this crazy trip to find my parents. Losing Bikezilla in the Mississippi. I choked on my words as I told them about Darla getting shot.

When I finished, Eli said, "Used to have a lot of trouble with the Peckerwoods ourselves. Had one visit from another gang, called 'emselves the Dirty White Boys.

Haven't seen either of them in almost two months—figured they'd run out of gas."

"How'd you survive a visit from the Peckerwoods?"

"Same way we did when you came. Hid in the root cellar. Could hear 'em shouting and carousing upstairs. We
keep everything important down there so we can hide at a
moment's notice. Speaking of which, we'd best post a
lookout again. Alba, it's your turn."

"Yes, Papi," she said in her little girl soprano as she
hurried away.

"You've been down there two days? I checked the
basement—I didn't see any root cellar."

"We moved the furnace to block the door. And yeah,
we would have stayed down there 'til you left, but one of
the dang pigs got out last night."

"You keep pigs down there?"

"Can't keep 'em up here, can we? Anyone comes, that'd
give us away fer sure—plus we'd lose valuable food.
Anyway, I figured the stupid thing would wake you up, so
we came up loaded for bear and found you all hibernatin'."

"How'd you keep the pigs quiet?"

"Well we didn't, did we? Used to feed 'em Nyquil, but
we're out."

I glared at Alyssa.

"I already said I was sorry."

I turned back to Eli. "You haven't slaughtered the pigs
for meat?"

"I'm saving a few. To breed. When things start to turn
around."

"What do you feed them?"

"Corn and soybeans. All the farms around here are abandoned—there's more crops left under the snow and ash than we can dig up."

I shook my head in amazement. Not only were they surviving, they were preparing for a posteruption future.

Eli was staring at me in a thoughtful way. He turned toward his wife, "Y'know, we could use more hands. 'Specially if we got to try farmin' kale."

"I'm not staying," I said. "I'm going after Darla."

"Going up against those gangs'll get you killed in a hurry."

I shrugged. Eli turned his gaze toward Alyssa.

"She can't stay. Not on her ownsome," Mary Sue hissed at him.

"I'm trying to get to Worthington," Alyssa said.

"We just need to get the tire on our truck changed, and we'll be on our way. You got a jack here?"

"Buried out in the shed, yeah. Might take days to dig it out, though."

"Crap. I need to get moving."

"Could probably rig something up, do the same work as a jack. Some levers and blocks, maybe."

"Sounds good."

"How're you payin' for the work?"

"Um, kale seeds?"

"That's your rent money for staying here. What else you got?"

I thought for a moment. "There're some crates in the back of the truck. We only opened two, but one of them had shotgun shells in it. You get the tire changed, and I'll split the truck's load fifty-fifty with you. Ammo's worth a fortune if you can find someone to trade with."

Mary Sue cupped her hands around Eli's ear, whispering something.

He recoiled from her, a growl rattling from his throat. "We do that, we ain't no better than the Peckerwoods."

I watched them carefully, looking away only when Mary Sue shot me a murderous glare. Why was she hating on me? I hadn't done anything.

Getting the truck jacked up and the tire changed took most of the day. First we had to bend the wheel well away from the tire using a wrecking bar Eli provided. We made a long, heavy lever out of a pair of two-by-ten rafters scavenged from the barn. Then we spent hours digging up patio pavers from the frozen ground at the back of the house to use as a fulcrum and blocks.

Improvising a makeshift tire iron was much easier— we used an adjustable wrench and a length of galvanized iron pipe cut from the basement.

We still had to actually jack up the truck. We wedged our lever under the truck just behind the blown wheel and stacked pavers under it to use as a fulcrum. More than twelve feet of the lever protruded from under the truck, angled upward so steeply that we had to reach above our heads to grab it. Using the lever, Eli, Ben, and I could raise the corner of the truck by ourselves, even though I was only using my left arm. We couldn't raise it very far, though. Brand rushed to stack pavers under the truck. Then we let

the truck back down and reset our fulcrum to lift it again. It
took seven or eight lifts to finally get the truck high enough
to swap the tires. Then we had to lift the truck again while
Brand cleared all the blocks out from under it.

"You ready to split up the load?" Eli said.

"Yeah." I helped him drag the wooden crates out of the
truck's load bed. We stacked the crates on the packed snow
outside. As I went to move one of the last crates out of
the back of the truck, something shifted, and I heard a
metallic clunk. Something had been buried under the pile
of crates. I couldn't see exactly what it was, so I grabbed
it and carried it out into the light.

"Son of a mangy coyote bitch," Eli said when he saw
what I was holding. Then we started laughing. I held the
truck's hydraulic jack and tire iron. Instead of stowing the
jack in the toolbox, the Peckerwoods had just tossed it in
the load bed.

Four of the crates held manacles; all the rest were
loaded with ammo. We split everything down the middle,
as agreed, although that probably made it the most fabu-
lously expensive tire change in history. Unfortunately it
was all rifle and shotgun loads, and all I had was a pistol.
That gave me an idea, "You have any long guns I could
trade for?"

"No way," Eli replied. "Just got the rifle and revolver
you already saw. Can't afford to give either of them up, not
for any price."

So much for that idea. We resealed all the crates—I
didn't want the ammo flying everywhere if we hit a pot-

hole or something. By that time the dim daylight was fading to night. We'd have to wait for morning to leave. Navigating unknown roads in a truck I could barely drive would be impossible in the pitch-black postvolcanic night. My anxiety increased with every day that passed—every day that Darla had to endure the Peckerwoods.

Chapter 58

I woke with a start. Something had touched my head. I slept using my backpack as a pillow; now, by the light cast by the embers of our fire, I saw the pale gleam of an arm being withdrawn from my pack.

I whipped out my left arm, caught the intruding arm, and twisted. I heard a high-pitched moan as I forced the intruder's arm behind her back, bringing her to the floor with a thump. I rolled over onto her, controlling her legs with mine. They weren't really taekwondo moves, but we had practiced ground fighting occasionally at my dojang.

I leaned down and whispered in her ear, lacing

my words with sarcasm, "You needed something from my pack?"

"I know you got more of them greens," Mary Sue replied.

"I don't, and if I catch you in my backpack again, I'll break your arm." I forced her wrist toward her neck, emphasizing just how easy it would be to break her arm in this position. Mary Sue whimpered quietly.

I let go of her wrist and rolled off her. Mary Sue crawled away. Ben and Alyssa hadn't even woken up. Mary Sue's enmity didn't make any sense to me—I'd given her dandelion greens, kale seeds, and ammo. Maybe it was a case of mama tiger gone rogue. I lay awake for an hour or more, wondering if she would return and force me to make good on my threat. To my relief, she never did.

• • •

I woke with the dawn. It took us less than ten minutes to get packed. Eli offered to make us breakfast, but I declined. I didn't want to spend any more time than I had to in close proximity to his wife. He and Brand said goodbye, clasping arms with me and Alyssa. Ben was already in the truck. Mary Sue wouldn't even meet my eyes, and the girls were too shy to shake our hands or offer hugs.

"Come back anytime," Eli said as I climbed into the truck.

"I will," I lied. The scowl on Mary Sue's face told me exactly how welcome I'd be if I ever showed up again.

I slammed the door, pushed the starter, and stalled the truck. Not my proudest moment. But on the second try I found first gear, and we rolled away from the farmstead, headed east. I planned to turn north at the first opportunity and loop back to Anamosa. Hopefully there'd be enough gas for Alyssa and Ben to get to Worthington after I left them. Less than a quarter tank remained. Maybe it would be enough.

I'd driven about a half hour when we approached a small town. A sign barely protruding from the snow bank read WELCOME TO OLIN. I drove down the abandoned and burned-out main street. The highway ended in a T on the far side of town, and a short knoll rose in the field to the left of the road.

I slowed as I neared the intersection, looking for street signs. Without warning, a telephone pole toppled in front of us. I stomped on the brakes, sliding to a stop well before the intersection. The pole had slammed into the snow berm just ahead of us, so it was perched about four feet above the road, completely blocking our passage. I struggled to throw the truck into reverse, but I was so freaked out that I stalled it again. It didn't matter. In the rearview mirror, I saw another telephone pole topple behind us, boxing us in.

The worst part: A line of nine or ten men appeared at the top of the knoll, bellies in the snow, aiming rifles right down at us.

Chapter 59

"Get down!" I yelled as I ducked below the driver's window.

I figured they'd start shooting. But instead I heard a voice amplified through a bullhorn, "Turn off your vehicle. Place your hands on the dashboard. Resistance will be met with deadly force."

Well, duh. I'd stalled "the vehicle" already. Alyssa crouched in the passenger footwell and Ben bent over so he was mostly behind the dash. Alyssa looked scared. Ben looked about the same as he always looked—a bit detached.

"You must comply or we will open fire!" the voice boomed. "Ten . . . nine . . ."

"Can we get out the passenger side?" I whispered.

"Their tactical position is excellent," Ben replied. "We could take cover on the opposite side of the truck, but if we climb the snow pile or move down the road in either direction, we'll enter their field of fire."

I thought about trying to restart the truck and using it to ram the telephone pole. But they were only thirty or forty feet away, and they were above us. Would the truck's roof stop a rifle shot from that close? I didn't think so. As the voice counted "three . . . two . . ." I got out of the footwell, leaned forward to lay my hands on the dashboard, and told Alyssa and Ben to do the same.

Four of them detached from the troop, sliding down the knoll toward us. They wore white and gray military camo—the first people I'd seen who had the perfect camouflage to hide in the volcanic winter. When they reached me, the nearest one wrenched open the driver's door while another guy trained his rifle on my head. One of them searched me, efficiently and none too gently, but he took only the knife and pistol off my belt. The patch on his chest read BLACK LAKE LLC. I stifled a groan. No way did I want to repeat my experience with Black Lake, locked in one of the camps they ran as a subcontractor for FEMA. But it wasn't like I had much choice.

On the other side of the truck, two guys were dealing with Alyssa and Ben the same way. Ben started moaning, and Alyssa tried to comfort him, but there wasn't much she could do.

"Hands behind your back," the guy ordered. When I complied, he slipped plastic ties around my wrists and cinched them tight. My right arm didn't like being held behind my back and wasn't shy about telling me so. I quickly had spasms of pain shooting toward my neck. I grunted as they pulled me out of the truck.

Alyssa, Ben, and I stood together, watching a short, pudgy Black Lake guy work his way around the edge of the knoll toward us. He was the only one not carrying an assault rifle, although he had a pistol on his belt. "What do we got? Flensers?" he asked as he approached. He unsnapped the leather strap that held his pistol in its holster, and the other four Black Lake guys took a step back, away from us.

"We're not flensers," I said.

"Looks like a flenser truck. One of the old-model deuces we were using 'til the flensers raided our Dubuque depot."

One of the guys with the assault rifles snorted, and Pudge silenced him with a glare.

"I took the truck from the Peckerwoods. Crashed it. See the windshield?" It would have been hard to miss, with the hole punched in the passenger side and long spiderweb cracks radiating out across the glass. I hadn't cleaned the blood off the inside of it, either.

"Yeah," Pudge turned to one of the grunts. "You search it yet? Any flesh on board?"

"No, sir."

"Do it now."

"Yes, sir." Two of the grunts trotted to the back of the truck. I stood with Alyssa and Ben, shifting my weight from foot to foot, waiting. Nails screeched from within the truck as they forced the wooden crates open. Pudge stared at me and fingered his pistol, a greedy look in his eye. The other Black Lake guys had left the crest of the knoll. They were using a hand winch to crank one of the telephone poles back into place. It was affixed to its base with a huge hinge and held up by guy wires. Obviously they'd prepared this spot as a trap long ago—and planned to use it again.

"Ammo and manacles," one of the grunts reported when they returned from inside our truck.

A disappointed look passed across Pudge's face. He snapped his holster strap shut. "Davis, Roberts: Follow us in the captured vehicle. Phelps, Miner: Load the prisoners."

I guessed that meant us. Two of the guys led us to the far side of the knoll where a cargo truck was parked. It was tall and armored, looking something like an oversized elephant with stubby legs. The Black Lake grunts lifted us into the enclosed cargo bed.

The door closed behind us with a resounding clang.

Chapter 60

A sparse light filtered through the small grate at the top of the cargo hold. When my eyes adjusted, I saw the area was bare except for a metal bench on either side. The truck roared to life, and I sat down with a lurch.

Ben was moaning, rocking back and forth. Alyssa talked to him, her voice inhumanly calm considering that we'd just been tossed into the back of a cargo truck. I wanted to yell in frustration, but I knew it wouldn't do any good.

After about ten minutes, Ben quieted. I tried to explain to Alyssa and Ben what I thought was happening. We were being taken to a camp, I figured, like the one Darla and I had done time in last year. Black Lake got paid by FEMA according to the number of "refugees" they housed, so they scoured the countryside looking for people to capture and move into their camps.

I wondered *how* Black Lake got paid. Dollars were worthless in Iowa and Illinois now—we had to trade for anything we needed. What would a big corporation want in trade? I couldn't guess.

Alyssa seemed to take it in stride. I suppose after you've been enslaved by a cannibal gang, anything seems okay by comparison. I roamed around the truck's cargo hold looking for a way out. The hold was solid and made of metal, and the doors were securely locked.

We were only on the road for half an hour. Then we were herded into a dingy makeshift room built inside an abandoned WalMart. A battered metal desk sat directly under a skylight, which let in what little light there was. Two guards lounged in cheap plastic lawn chairs, and a bored-looking guy—Captain Alverman, according to the cloth strip sewn on his fatigues—wrote on old sheets of copy paper.

One of the guards searched us. I had a brief moment of panic when he patted my chest, feeling the pockets that held my kale and wheat, but the packages must have been soft enough not to arouse suspicion—he didn't investigate further. Other than that, we had nothing to take. My backpack was still in the truck we'd taken from the Peckerwoods. As far as I knew, Alyssa and Ben had only the clothes on their backs.

Captain Alverman interviewed us in a bored monotone voice, jotting our names in tiny handwriting on a sheet of copy paper already packed with names. I remembered the printed list of refugees' names Rita Mae had shown me. Now there were no computers or printers visible. Evidently things were getting worse—even for Black Lake.

When Alverman finished, his guards escorted us out the front of the WalMart. On the far side of the road there was a huge enclosure built from chain-link fence—it stretched so far in either direction that I couldn't see the whole thing. It was easily as big as Camp Galena had been, and that place had held almost fifty thousand people. The fence was twelve feet high, not counting the coil of razor wire topping it. It looked identical to the fence Black Lake had built at Camp Galena—the one Darla had pretty much destroyed with a bulldozer as we escaped. I would never have escaped that camp by myself. But this time I was on my own.

As we got closer, I saw a pair of guards patrolling a well-worn path in the snow around the outside of the fence. Each of them carried an assault rifle.

We approached a tiny guard shack just outside a gate. One of our guards got a key from the guy in the shack and unlocked the gate. Another cut the plastic handcuffs off us and pushed us through. I rubbed my right arm, trying to work the painful kinks out of my shoulder.

Uneven rows of tents stretched out across the camp before us. Some were canvas tents like the ones in Camp Galena last year, but these seemed dirtier, more ragged. Many of them bore makeshift patches made with scraps of plastic. None of them rested on platforms—and I knew from experience how cold the frozen ground would be.

And not everyone had a real tent. Some of the shelters were just chunks of plastic propped up on sticks. I saw a few that weren't even plastic—instead made of old bedspreads. I guessed they'd at least keep the wind out. Hundreds of people were visible, talking in small groups or milling around. Thousands more must have been huddled in their tents, trying to escape the bitter wind.

Before we could figure out what to do, an Asian kid who looked to be about twelve broke away from a group nearby and strode up to us. Well, up to Alyssa. He raked his eyes up and down her. Not that there was much to see—she was bundled in winter clothes like everyone else. But the clothing and dirt somehow didn't dim her beauty, just cloaked it.

"Welcome to Camp Maquoketa," the kid said. The name of the camp rocketed through my mind. My parents might be here. How would I find them amid this multitude? "You need to go to The Principal's office, girlie."

"The principal?"

The kid gave me an annoyed look. "Not you, her. She's so hot I can warm my hands off her." He held out his gloved hands and rubbed them as if he were in front of a campfire.

I started to step between him and Alyssa, but she held me back with a hand on my arm.

"That's so sweet," Alyssa said in a syrupy voice. "What's your name?"

"Flash, The. Shaken *and* stirred. At your service, girlie."

Alyssa took one of his hands in hers. "Nice to meet you, Flash. My name's Alyssa. What do you mean, the principal's office?"

I eyed Flash. He didn't seem to be a threat, but maybe he was working with someone else. Ben was completely absorbed in watching the two guards as they patrolled outside the fence. He was mumbling something too quietly for me to understand.

Flash had a goofy grin on his face. The hand Alyssa held was visibly shaking with excitement. He still hadn't answered her question.

"Who's the principal?" she said.

"She looks after all the pretty girls. So they don't disappear. Well, mostly they don't."

"Disappear?" I asked.

"Come with me," Flash said, still addressing Alyssa. "I'll show you around. Make introductions, as they say." He was totally butchering a James Bond accent. He started pulling on her hand, leading her toward the center of the camp.

Alyssa and I followed him for about ten feet and then she stopped, pulling Flash to a halt as well. Ben hadn't moved. "Ben! Come on!" she yelled.

He didn't hear—or wouldn't respond—still absorbed in watching the guards.

"Will you get him, please?" she asked me.

I trotted back to him and reached out to touch him, pulling my hand back at the last moment. "Ben, Alyssa needs you."

"The Sister Unit needs me," he replied. "The rule is that when the Sister Unit needs help, Ben helps. I will observe the guards later." He turned to follow me.

Flash led Alyssa toward the middle of the camp. I hung back, watching, wary of an ambush. We crossed a wide cleared area, within which three rings of tents were pitched concentrically, like layers of an onion. At the center of these tents there was an open plaza, maybe sixty or seventy feet in diameter.

The center area was packed with girls. Some were as young as eight or nine. Some were older, women really, but none looked older than thirty. They gathered in clusters, talking through the tent flaps, some of them huddled together for warmth.

"What is—"

"Ask The Principal," Flash said.

He pointed to the back of a woman kneeling in the doorway of one of the tents. She was easily the oldest person in view—her black hair halfway to steely gray. She looked like . . . she couldn't be. Or could she?

"Principal," Flash said, "the guards caught some fresh fish."

The woman turned, "Welc—"

Her word died as her eyes locked on mine.

"Alex?" she breathed.

"Mom."

Chapter 61

My world lit up despite the dim light—fired into Technicolor brilliance by my joy. The last time I'd seen Mom, more than ten months ago, we'd had a terrible fight. Sometimes, in my old life, I used to hate her. Now I couldn't imagine anything better than the elation coursing through me. She was alive! And I'd found her!

Mom charged me, wrapping me in a hug so exuberant we were both knocked to our knees. The snow couldn't chill me—I was alight with the joy of seeing my mother again after ten long months. I cried as we embraced. Neither of us could get out any words.

Mom dragged her fingers across my face, like a blind woman might—trying to feel my features. Her fingertips slid easily on my teary skin. I clutched at her back, balling a fold of her coat up in my fist, holding on as if to prevent her from ever slipping away again.

"Principal?" Flash said. "You okay?"

Mom took a deep breath. "Yes, Lester, I'm better than okay."

"I told you, don't call me Lester. The name is Flash."

"This is Alex." She said my name as if it were an ineffable secret. "He's my son."

"Principal?" I asked her.

"That's just what they call me here," Mom hugged me even more tightly, hurting my injured shoulder. I must have let out a moan, because she said, "You okay, Alex?"

"Fine. It's just my shoulder."

She loosened her grip. "What happened?"

"A little truck accident. It's fine, really."

"Let me see."

I held her tightly as she tried to pull away. I never wanted to let go, despite the pain the embrace was causing me.

"Alex, I need to know you're all right."

"I'm fine," I said, but I loosened my grip on her, anyway. Now that she was worried, I knew she wouldn't relax until she'd seen the damage for herself. She started stripping off my jacket and shirts.

I thought about protesting but really couldn't summon the energy. I was still in a happy daze. And truth be told, I kind of liked the mothering attention.

"You look different. Thinner. And stronger."

I shrugged. "You, too." I realized she hadn't said anything about Dad. I was scared to ask—afraid of what the answer might be. But I had to know. "Um, Mom. Is Dad—?"

"Oh my gosh, I completely forgot. Lester, would you go get Doug?"

"It's Flash!" he yelled as he flitted away.

By then Mom had me stripped to the waist. The icy air made goose bumps rise all over my chest and arms. My right side was a beauty. Green, yellow, and purple bruises were splashed from my waist to neck, covering my side and arm.

"Good God . . ." Mom whispered.

"I'm okay."

"Who was driving?"

I couldn't think of an answer that would help. I just wanted to end the inquisition and get my clothing back on—I was freezing. "Um, I was on top of the truck the first time it crashed."

"You were—"

"The other two crashes, well, I was driving."

She was momentarily speechless. "You are *not* allowed to drive on a learner's permit without me or Dad in the car, Alex."

I gave her my best what-the-hell look. Like anyone cared about driver's licenses in the midst of all this chaos? "I think I lost my learner's permit when our house burned, Mom."

"Our house? Never mind, what're those?" She pointed at the spots on my arm and belly where I'd been shot. It looked like they were healing okay—a bit puffy and red, but scabbed over nicely.

"Oh. That's where I got shot."

"Shot? You got—?"

"Look, Mom. A lot of stuff has happened since Darla and I set out to find you. Don't stress about it. I'm okay. And I found you, thank God."

"Who's Darla?"

"My girlfriend."

"Ah." She nodded, accepting that bit of information way more easily than the three truck wrecks or the fact that I'd been shot. "Pleased to meet you." She held her hand out to Alyssa.

Alyssa took her hand. "Pleased to meet you, too. But I'm not—"

Dad rounded the corner of a nearby tent at a run, Flash trailing behind him. "Alex, you're—!" He crashed into me with a bear hug that forced tears from my eyes— both from my joy at seeing him and the pain of his embrace. Neither of us could speak.

"Doug," Mom said, "he's hurt."

Dad pulled back and looked at me. "Jesus. You look like you lost a fight with a grizzly."

"No, just a truck." I pulled him back into a hug with one arm, and drew my mother against us with the other. I wanted to stay there, to squeeze them both until they'd soaked into me and could never leave again. Even the stale scent of their sweat smelled heavenly.

"This is Darla," Mom said, "Alex's girlfriend." She freed one arm and gestured at Alyssa.

"My name's Alyssa. And this is my brother, Ben."

Mom looked at me. "But you said—"

"The Peckerwoods got Darla. Shot her." Something caught in my throat, making my eyes water. "I'm going back for her as soon as we get out of here."

"What?" Mom said. "You can't go charging into the middle of a gang. That's not safe."

Before I could even start to protest, Dad said, "She might not be alive. There're rumors all over camp about those gangs. Say they're eating human flesh."

I dropped my arms from behind their backs and leaned out of the embrace. "Yes, Dad. They are eating people. They deal in slaves, too. But Darla was alive three days ago. Alyssa saw her."

"It's too dangerous," Mom protested. Okay, maybe I didn't miss the *mothering* all that much.

"If the Peckerwoods had Mom, would you go after her?" I stared my father in the eye.

"I would."

I nodded and tried to fold my arms. Just the attempt hurt my right, so I picked up my shirt instead and started trying to struggle into it.

"I've known your mother twenty-six years. I owe her a different kind of loyalty than you owe a girlfriend."

I couldn't get my right arm jammed through the shirt-sleeve. "Piece of junk!" I tossed it aside.

"It's a hard world we live in now," Dad said mildly.

"It is the same," I said. "Exactly the same. If you knew what we'd been through, you'd understand."

"Guess you'd better tell us," Dad said.

"How's Rebecca?" Mom asked.

"She's okay. Darla and I left her at Uncle Paul's place.

That was, um, almost two weeks ago."

Alyssa plucked my shirt out of the snow and helped me get dressed. Ben wanted to watch the guards, and Alyssa didn't want Ben to be alone, so when she finished helping me, they left. Mom sent Flash with them, instructing him to return in time for dinner. The fact that she'd mentioned dinner was heartening. When Darla and I had been imprisoned in Camp Galena, we'd gotten only breakfast—and not much of that.

Mom, Dad, and I ducked into one of the tents out of the wind.

"My brother's still making out okay?" Dad asked.

"Yeah," I said. "Doing great. We grow and trade kale— it's worth a fortune. Get pork from Warren in return."

"Why did you leave?" Mom asked.

"We found Dad's shotgun. But I'd better start at the beginning." I told them about the house fire in Cedar Falls that had started my trek over ten months ago. About my thirsty trek across northeastern Iowa. About skiing into Darla's barn, and how we had come to depend on each other, to fight together for survival. About the times I'd saved her life. The times she'd saved mine. A year ago, death meant I'd have to get my armor repaired in *World of Warcraft*. Now it was an all-too-real shadow lurking behind the veneer of my daily life. I still wasn't entirely sure how I'd survived. My parents didn't interrupt much, but it still took hours to tell the whole story. I finished by telling them about Alyssa and explaining Ben's autism, which they seemed to take in stride.

"Ten months." Dad had clasped his hands together as if in prayer. "It seems like a miracle that you survived all that."

"I wouldn't have without Darla. I'm going to find her. Even if I get killed trying." I held his eye, making an effort not to blink.

Dad stared steadily back at me. His eyes were hollow, dark and gaunt, as if the father I'd known had been replaced by a shadowed replica chiseled from the same stone. "It's going to be hard just to get out of here. We've been here, what, four-and-a-half months?"

"Almost five," Mom said.

"Why haven't you left? Rebecca and I didn't know if you were even still alive." I ground my teeth—at Black Lake, at the volcano, at my parents. They clearly weren't getting enough to eat. Mostly I was angry at myself— why hadn't I come sooner?

"You didn't notice the fence? And guys with guns?" Mom said.

"We did try," Dad said. "Twice. Right after we got here. We got caught. Thrown into a punishment hut. I thought they'd let us starve to death in there, but Lester bugged the guards so much that they almost threw him into a hut of his own."

"Lester got us released," Mom said. "He's very persistent—and a little crazy."

"I noticed," I said.

"Four days without food and water when you're already weak is no picnic," Dad said. "I wasn't sure we'd survive much longer. So we didn't try again."

"We can't leave now," Mom said.

"Why not?" I asked.

"The girls need us. People started disappearing a few months ago. Not long after I organized the school. Mostly young girls. Every three or four days, we'd get up in the morning and discover more people missing. Whole families sometimes. Sometimes just the girls. I had to do something."

"Your mother created a camp organization, civil defense, I guess. They call her The Principal. Talked me into helping."

"People are still disappearing," Mom said. "But not as many as before. And we keep the girls safe."

"And the guards tolerate it? Your civil defense organization, I mean?"

"We're not sure why. Maybe there're two factions of guards. One taking girls, and one supposedly in charge. We keep a low profile, but they have to know what's going on."

It all fit. Alyssa being kept as a slave. Darla kept alive, instead of being flensed. The girls disappearing from the camp. I balled my left hand into a fist and punched the floor of the tent, getting nothing but bruised knuckles for the effort. I wanted to punch flesh, feel bones crack under my hands—preferably the bones of whoever was responsible for this whole cursed-to-ash situation. "I've got to go after Darla."

"I can't leave," Mom said. "These girls are depending on me."

"We patrol at night and guard the cleared zone around

the girls' tents," Dad said. "But we can't watch the whole camp."

"Who's we?" I asked.

"The prefects," Dad said. "That was your Mom's idea."

"And I convinced him to be Head Boy," Mom said.

Dad sighed heavily. "You're the only one who calls me that, Janice."

"You'll always be my head boy," Mom said with a coquettish smile.

Dad leaned over and smooched her.

"Um, gross. I'm thrilled to see you and all, but I do *not* want to watch you make out," I said. "Who's taking the girls?"

Dad broke their kiss. "We don't know."

"It's got to be the guards," Mom said.

"Probably. It's time for dinner, I think." Dad pushed himself up into a crouch and shuffled toward the tent flap. Mom got five worn Styrofoam bowls and plastic spoons from a stack in the corner of the tent.

"They feed you much?" I followed them out.

"Just enough food to keep us alive, not enough to give us the energy to fight." Dad kicked a clump of snow.

"They've passed out vitamin pills three times since we've been here," Mom said.

I shrugged.

We walked across the camp, rehashing the stories of our individual journeys as we went. A row of field kitchens was set up outside one of the fences. Black Lake mercenaries wearing winter camo were filling bowls and passing them through hatches in the fence in front of each kitchen. Unlike Camp Galena, the refugees here were organized in neat lines. Flash waved at us from one of the other lines, and Mom beckoned him to us.

Alyssa and Ben came over with Flash. Mom gave each of us bowls and spoons. "Be careful with these," she said. "It's hard to get more. I've got to go be The Principal." She walked off to talk to people in the other lines.

"I've got to get out of here," I muttered.

"Why?" Alyssa asked. "Flash said it's not too bad. They get enough to eat, sort of. Everyone has a tent— even if some of them suck."

"Are you crazy? Not too bad?"

"Anything's better than being chained to a bed in the Anamosa prison." She glared at me, and I had to look away.

"I guess it would be," I said softly. "I'm sorry."

"Why are you in such a hurry to get away from me, anyway?"

I didn't reply.

"Darla," she said, scowling.

"Yeah. I'm going to escape. I just don't know how yet."

"I can plan an escape," Ben said. "The guard pattern is suboptimal."

"You can?" I asked. "How?"

"I have several ideas. I need to observe the guard patterns for at least a week to confirm their effectiveness."

"A week? I'm leaving tonight."

"You just got to us!" Dad said.

I didn't reply. He was right. But finding my parents

hadn't fixed anything. It only made Darla's absence even more painful.

"If you attempt to leave without adequate preparation," Ben said, "you will likely be caught or killed, and your mission will fail."

He had a point. Getting myself killed wouldn't help Darla. But I couldn't sit around, either. Couldn't wait while she was . . . while the Peckerwoods—I didn't even want to think about what might be happening to Darla. Why they were keeping her alive. "I can't wait a week. She's in danger."

"Maybe I could devise a preliminary operational plan with two days' observation. More time would be necessary to confirm and optimize it. How many people would be escaping?"

"Shh," I said. We were approaching the front of the line, where a bored Black Lake guard slopped wheat gruel into my bowl. They didn't mark my hand. "How do they keep track of who's gotten food?" I asked Dad.

"They don't. We do," Dad said as we walked away, eating our gruel. "That's part of what your mom is off doing. They cook the same amount every meal. If someone takes seconds, someone else goes without."

"How many people must I plan for?" Ben asked me again.

"I don't think Mom and Dad want to leave," I said.

"No," Dad said, "not until I know the people we've promised to protect are safe."

I'd helped strangers on the road, helped Uncle Paul and Aunt Caroline on their farm, and saved Alyssa and

Ben. But now, when I needed help, everyone except Ben seemed to be allied against me. I wanted to punch something in frustration but knew it wouldn't do any good. Instead I said as flatly as I could manage, "I'm leaving. Darla needs me."

"Absolutely not," Dad said. "We just found each other. We're not splitting up now."

"Just a second," I said, glaring at my father. "I found you, not vice versa. And I owe Darla. My life, if it comes to that."

"If we could put a stop to the disappearances, be sure the people we promised to protect are safe, we could all try to break out together. But you're too young to—"

"I'm not some kid."

"Wait, what's this about people you promised to protect?" Alyssa asked.

Dad explained the girls' disappearances to Alyssa. He seemed relieved to change the subject.

"You need to catch whoever is kidnapping girls?" Ben asked.

Dad nodded.

"The goal of an additional operation is to catch the unknown people kidnapping girls?" Ben said.

"Yes," Alyssa said.

"That is an easy tactical problem," Ben said. "Prepare an ambush. Use whatever the unknown persons want as a lure. Would the Sister Unit suffice as a lure?"

"No!" Alyssa said. "No way. Forget it. I'm no one's bait. Not anymore."

Chapter 62

By that night, we'd worn down Alyssa's resistance. She wandered up and down a deserted corridor between two rows of tents. I listened carefully and caught fleeting glimpses of her through a peephole I'd cut in the back of one of the tents. Alyssa had dressed in the brightest clothing we could find. Dingy, cream-colored pants and a flaming-orange jacket.

She was a dim candle wrapped in oppressive darkness. Or maybe the night just seemed oppressive because I was so thoroughly trapped: first by the camp and second by Mom and Dad. They wouldn't leave without protecting the girls, and they forbade me from leaving without them. I didn't think they could stop me, but I wanted them to come, too. After all, Darla and I had returned to Iowa to find them. And I suspected I'd need all the help I could get to free her.

Ben was still out observing the guards, preparing an escape plan. If we could figure out who was kidnapping girls and put a stop to it, maybe we could all try to leave together. Dad even assigned two prefects to keep Ben out of trouble.

Dad and four other prefects were hidden in tents near me. I expected the prefects to be men, but most of them were women. They called Dad The Dean, which seemed weird, but I guessed it was better than Head Boy. Dad had offered me a knife—really a crude shank, made with a sharpened scrap of metal, but I'd turned him down. There weren't enough knives to go around, and I figured I'd rely on my hands and feet. I knew a bit about knife defense, but I'd never been trained to fight with a knife—that wasn't something we did at my dojang. My right arm was still sore, but I'd been stretching it—I would be able to use it if I had to.

Mom hadn't wanted me to help with the ambush. She'd fought with Dad at length over it. Alyssa finally announced that she wouldn't serve as bait unless I were there. I hadn't said anything at all. It didn't matter what Mom, Dad, or Alyssa said. I'd helped talk Alyssa into trying Ben's crazy plan, so I needed to be there to try to protect her, regardless of what my parents thought.

Alyssa paced slowly and endlessly back and forth. I'd tried to nap during the early evening but hadn't slept well, so I was tired. I started silently counting out the "This Little Piggy" nursery rhyme, tapping my fingers on my knee, both to keep myself awake and to keep track of time.

More than two hours had passed when Alyssa stopped near my tent. "This isn't working," she whispered. "How long do I have to keep doing this?"

"It won't work at all if you talk to me," I hissed back.

I heard my dad's voice from another tent. "We're staying out here until dawn. Now shut up." His tone shocked me—Alyssa was doing us a favor; she didn't have to spend her whole night trying to lure an attack.

Alyssa sighed and resumed pacing. As the night dragged on, her pace slowed. She dragged her feet, trudging as if she were more asleep than awake. I lost count of my This Little Piggies somewhere past two thousand. It had to be nearly dawn.

I caught myself nodding and bit my lower lip, hard. My knee was numb where I'd been tapping out the nursery rhyme. I returned my attention to the peephole in the tent just in time to see a dark shape collide with Alyssa's back. She fell into the packed snow and shrieked.

I lunged down, sliding under the back edge of the tent. I reached Alyssa in seconds. The guy who'd run into her was reaching down toward her. I caught his hand and cranked it into a wrist throw. He cried out, and I stepped forward, over Alyssa, hooking my leg behind his and tossing him to the ground. We were surrounded by my dad and the prefects now, but I didn't need any help. I allowed myself to fall on top of the guy, placing my elbow against his throat.

He made a hoarse, choking sound. Dad shook a little hand-powered flashlight—a rare luxury someone had smuggled into the camp and given to The Dean. He shined the beam on the guy's face. One of the prefects helped Alyssa stand.

"I think I recognize him," Dad said. "Let up a little, would you?"

I took some of the pressure off the guy's neck. He started coughing and shaking—I could feel his neck convulse against my forearm. When he finished coughing, he began cussing, running through pretty much every one of the words I'd looked up in *The American Heritage Dictionary* in third grade.

"Shut up!" Dad barked. I'd never heard him say "shut up" in my life, and now he'd said it twice in one night? "What are you doing out here?"

"That you, Doug?"

"Yeah, Deke, it's me. What're you doing out here?"

"Needed to piss something fierce. Ain't any camp rule against an old man going to the latrine, is there? Anyway, this kid scared it right out of me."

I felt dampness against my hip where I was lying on him and caught a whiff of urine. Great. I scrambled up.

Dad reached down to help him up. "Sorry, Deke," Dad said gruffly. "Thought you were trying to abduct this girl."

"Well. Sorry I ran her over. Too blasted dark to see anything at night."

"That's the truth. Look, Deke, don't tell anyone we're out here."

"You don't think it's one of us taking them girls, do you?"

"Don't know. Could be. There were psychos in the world before the volcano. Still are, I figure."

Deke's hands were pressed over his groin. "Okay. I'll keep it quiet."

"Pack it in for the night," Dad said to all of us. "It's almost dawn, anyway."

Alyssa stepped toward me, holding her side.

"You okay?" I asked.

"Yeah," she said. "Just sore from falling. Walk with me? At least as far as your tent?"

"Sure," I said.

Alyssa grabbed my arm for support, and we trudged away in silence. I was too tired to start a conversation, and maybe Alyssa was, too. It felt like a companionable silence with her leaning against my arm, both of us recovering from a long and tense night.

By the time we got to Dad's tent, the sky was starting to lighten. Alyssa turned to face me. I saw Dad following us. During the day, Dad used the tent; Mom and another woman slept there at night while Dad patrolled. I cracked open the flap and glanced in. It was empty—Dad told me that Mom often left before dawn to fulfill her duties as The Principal.

"I think I'll lie down," I said.

"Me, too," Dad said. "I'm beat."

"Um, can I talk to Alex? Alone?" Alyssa gestured at the tent.

Dad was quiet for a moment as he looked at her. "Yeah. I'll find somewhere else to nap."

"Thanks." Alyssa pulled the tent flap aside and crawled in.

It was more than a little annoying. Didn't *I* get any say over who got to share my tent? I turned to follow Alyssa.

Dad caught my arm. "Alex. You did good."

"Thanks." I started to turn away again, but he held on.

"What you do is your business, but, um . . . we lost one woman in childbirth already."

I had to suppress a groan. Uncle Paul had lectured me literally *ad nauseum* on this subject last year. "We're just going to talk. Besides, Darla and I—"

"I know—it's okay." Dad pulled me into a brief hug. "I'll come get you before they quit serving breakfast. You can *talk* for an hour and a half, maybe two."

I rolled my eyes at him and crawled into the tent.

Alyssa was sitting on a makeshift pile of rags and blankets. Her jacket was off. As I entered, she was pulling her sweater off. She stretched sinuously, thrusting her chest out. I couldn't help but stare.

When her head popped free of the sweater, Alyssa caught me staring and smiled. I moved my focus back to her face, but it nearly took more willpower than I had to succeed.

"What did you want to talk about?" I asked.

"When that guy, Deke, ran into me, you were the first one there." Under the sweater Alyssa had on a heavy, long-sleeved flannel shirt. Not in the least bit sexy—until she started slowly unbuttoning it.

"I was trying to stay alert—that's . . . that's really distracting."

As Alyssa unbuttoned the flannel shirt, its plackets fell open, revealing a form-fitting, lacy scarlet shirt beneath. "What? This?" She took a deep breath.

"Um, yeah." I reached one hand out to her collar and held her overshirt closed.

She placed a hand over mine. "That guy didn't stand a chance. He was a foot taller and probably fifty pounds heavier, and you took him down with one move."

I shrugged. I could pull my hand away from hers, but then her overshirt would fall open again. A growing part of me wanted to let go of her shirt and not pull away, let it fall open, and see what would happen next.

"You could have killed him."

"I wouldn't—"

She lifted my pointer finger and took it between her lips, biting gently. The supple warmth of her lips drove whatever I'd been about to say from my mind. She cupped her other hand behind my neck, pulling me closer. I was clay, moldable into whatever shape Alyssa wanted. She released my finger from between her teeth and moved my hand, sliding it beneath her overshirt until it rested on her left breast.

"Alyssa, I—"

She bent forward and kissed me. Suddenly I was kissing her back, and she moaned, and my hand clutched at her breast, far harder than Darla would have liked.

Darla.

I pushed Alyssa away, a little harder than I meant to. She rocked back on the bedding.

"What?" she said.

"I don't want—"

"I can clearly see that you *do* want." She reached, and I grabbed her wrist, stopping her hand inches from my groin.

"Yeah, look. He does what he wants to, not what I tell him to." I moved her hand farther from the, um, body part in question. "But I love Darla."

Her lips formed an insanely hot pout. "You can still love her. I wasn't proposing marriage, you know."

I shook my head sadly. "I can't."

"It's not like she'd ever know. Even if you do find her. Even if you don't get killed."

"I'd know."

Alyssa's face crumpled. "You could learn to love me," she whispered, her eyes brimming with sudden tears.

"Maybe I could have, if I'd met you first. But I didn't," I said more gently.

A tear left a glistening trail down her cheek.

What was going on? Her moods shifted gears faster than a NASCAR driver in traffic. I was a jumble. Horny, guilty for making her cry, and angry that she'd put me in this position—all at the same time. "It's okay," I said, hugging her in what I hoped was a brotherly fashion. "Don't cry." That made her start sobbing for real.

I held her and patted her back until her crying fit ran out. When she seemed calmer, I started buttoning her overshirt back up.

"I'm sorry," Alyssa said. "I'm not really a slut or anything."

"I never said you were."

"Ben and me, we've been on our own for five months, ever since Mom and Dad were killed, and it's, I don't know, I feel . . . maybe lonely sometimes. I mean, I love my brother, but it's just the two of us. And sometimes I could get the Peckerwoods to do stuff for me, if I did stuff for them, but that wasn't . . . I only got more lonely. And so I thought that you and me . . . it would be great to have something real."

"You do have something real." I clasped her hand in mine. "We're friends, okay?"

"Okay." Alyssa pulled her sweater back on. "Do you think maybe I could stay here while we nap? Just as friends?"

"Yeah. That'd be okay, I guess." I lay down on my back on Dad's bedroll. Alyssa snuggled against my side, one hand flung over my chest. In seconds, her breathing evened and slowed. I lay awake, staring at the canvas ceiling until Dad called us for breakfast.

Chapter 63

I finally got a few hours of fitful sleep after breakfast. A draft of frozen air woke me, and I peered out from under my bedding, bleary-eyed. My mother was holding the tent flap open and peeking in.

"Sorry," she said. "I didn't mean to wake you."

"It's okay. I wasn't sleeping that well, anyway."

"I just . . . I had to look at you. To make sure I didn't dream up yesterday."

"I'm too sore to be part of your dream, Mom." I pushed aside the layers of blankets and reached for my overcoat.

Mom brought me a pail of water so cold that a

rim of ice had already formed at its edges. I brushed my
teeth with Dad's toothbrush. Icy spikes of cold stabbed
my hands and face as I washed. When I finished, Mom
took me to see her school.

Several clear plastic tarps were hung from poles in the
center of the camp, forming a rough tent about fifteen feet
square. Mom pushed aside the corner of the plastic and
gestured for me to enter. Inside, about a dozen students,
mostly girls, sat in a circle around the perimeter of the
tent. A rangy, gray-haired woman stood in the center,
reading from a warped copy of *To Kill a Mockingbird*.

"Melba," Mom said, "this is my son, Alex."

The woman looked up. "Pleased to meet you. Will you
be joining our class?"

"I've already read that book," I said.

"If you don't mind," Mom said, addressing Melba,
"maybe Alex could teach this section? A self-defense
seminar? He's got a black belt in taekwondo."

"Certainly." Melba closed and pocketed her book.

"You could have given me a little warning," I whispered to Mom.

"You'll do fine."

I stepped into the center of the makeshift room.
"Saved by the sub, huh? There's nothing more boring than
English." I looked around. Nobody was smiling.

Melba stared daggers at me. "Let's welcome Mr.
Halprin properly," she said, extending her hand.

I reached to shake her hand, but she clasped my thumb
instead and did a little stutter step, moving closer to me

and bending my arm. Her other hand grabbed my elbow, her foot hooked mine, and suddenly I was flat on my back staring up at her.

"That," Melba said, "is what is colloquially referred to as a 'chicken wing.' My English classes are not *boring*, Mr. Halprin. And I also teach a judo seminar."

A chuckle passed around the room, and I felt my face flush. "Sorry, I should have warned you," Mom said. Melba held out her hand to help me up, but I rolled instead, coming up in a defensive stance.

"Good throw," I said. "You know the counter?"

Melba nodded.

"Let's demonstrate it," I held out my hand again, and we worked through the counter-move in slow motion. Taekwondo doesn't emphasize throws the way judo does, so Melba was better at them, but now that I was prepared, I mostly held my own. Soon I was into the rhythm of the class: demonstrating moves with Melba, coaching students, and pairing them off to practice.

I called a short break after about a half hour. "I've got to go check on the other classes," Mom said.

"There are more?"

"Dozens. We do martial arts in here since it's the biggest space we have. I call it the LGI."

"LGI?"

"Large Group Instruction," Mom snorted. "See you at dinner."

• • •

We repeated the ambush that night using Alyssa as bait
again. It was mind-numbingly boring; I had to fight to
stay alert all night, and absolutely nothing happened.

Ben had spent the night observing the guards. He
joined Dad, Alyssa, and me as we were getting ready for
breakfast.

"Did you figure out an escape plan?" I asked Ben.

"Yes. But I need more time to observe the guards and
confirm it will work flawlessly."

"I don't have more time." My brain was stuck in a loop,
thinking that Darla might not have more time, either.

"We've been over this," Dad said. "You might never
find her. You might get killed trying. Our family is going
to stick together."

"I know, but—"

"There's the minor problem of the fence, razor wire,
and guards, too," Alyssa said.

"It's not a significant problem," Ben said. "The guard
pattern has vulnerabilities, and with a simple weighted
canvas sling the razor wire can be defeated. There's a
device purpose-built for precisely that . . ."

Ben kept talking. I figured he might never shut up, so
I talked over him. "Dad, I'm going to leave. If you want us
to stay together, you're welcome to come along."

"That's not going to happen. Your mother and I have
a responsibility here. We're going to do whatever we can
to protect these people. Whatever that takes!" Dad was
practically yelling at me, talking far louder than needed to
be heard over Ben.

"It's useless, anyway," Alyssa said. "Walking around all night freezing my ass off. This is never going to work."

Ben interrupted his own discourse on methods for breaching fences. "It will work. Statistically, it's not likely to work on any given night, but with enough trial runs, it's virtually certain to succeed."

"Whatever, computer boy. I'm going to get a decent night's sleep tonight for once." She wheeled around and stomped toward the breakfast line.

Ben's hands were fluttering at his side. "No . . . no, no, no. The Sister Unit must complete Ben's plan."

"Jesus, Ben. It's not always about you!" she yelled over her shoulder. I'd never seen her dis her brother like that before.

Dad was staring, eyes moving from Alyssa to Ben as if he were watching a tennis match.

Ben started screaming in that high-pitched monotone of his. He lashed out, and his fist hit the side of his own head with a thud. I reached for his arm, trying to stop him from hurting himself. When I touched his arm, he punched wildly. I jumped back, and his forearm swished through the air where my head had been. His foot connected with a tent, tearing away one of its ropes from the canvas. People shouted from within, and Ben fell, tripped by his own kick, arms and legs still wildly flailing.

Dad grabbed Ben, trying to hold him down. But Dad had trouble even getting a firm grip—Ben thrashed with the insane violence of a fish just tossed in the bottom of a boat. Plus, he was bigger than Dad.

Ben wasn't exactly throwing a temper tantrum. It was too violent and uncontrolled for that. When he fell, he didn't throw out his arms or protect his head. He never looked to see if we were watching—I doubted he was even aware of us by that point. He seemed utterly out of control.

Suddenly Alyssa was back. She threw herself on top of Ben. She was like a cowboy on a bull at a rodeo—it'd be a miracle if she survived eight seconds. "Let go of him!" she screamed. "Don't touch him! It'll make it worse."

That seemed odd—she was lying on top of him. That didn't count as touching? But I figured she knew her brother better than any of us, so I pulled Dad off Ben.

Alyssa clung to Ben. Her voice dropped to a measured whisper. "It's okay, Ben. We'll keep trying your plan. You need to calm down."

Ben kept thrashing, almost throwing off Alyssa. I was afraid she'd get hurt. When my little sister had thrown temper tantrums, the moment she got what she wanted, the tantrum was over. This was different. Alyssa brushed her glove along Ben's side, whispering at him in an impossibly calm voice.

Gradually Ben quieted. It took fifteen or twenty minutes more, but eventually Alyssa got off him, he stood up and brushed the snow off his clothing, and we went on as if absolutely nothing had happened.

I turned to my father. "One more night. Then I'm leaving, with or without your help."

Dad's only reply was a scowl.

• • •

We moved our ambush spot that night. I was so sick of chanting "This Little Piggy" that I thought I might puke. I tried "Hickory Dickory Dock" for a while, then switched to counting one Mississippi, two Mississippi . . . five hundred Mississippi . . . one thousand Mississipi. I figured it was taking me a second just to say the numbers at that point, so I dropped the Mississippis, too.

Sometime after 4 A.M.—I'd just reached 21,300 in my count—everything changed. A group of shadows slipped out from between the tents behind Alyssa. Then a hand reached around her face, clamping over her mouth.

Chapter 64

I burst from under the tent in an explosive lunge, reaching the closest of the attackers in seconds. Four black-clad shapes had surrounded Alyssa. One of them was turning my way. I swept his legs from under him with a round kick and hit him in the side of the head with a right backfist as he fell. Even as my backfist connected, I was reaching toward the next one with a left uppercut to the stomach and launching a sidekick at a third attacker.

Suddenly it was all over. Dad and his four prefects swarmed over the attackers. There were six of us and four of them, and we'd taken them by sur-

prise from behind. They all went down. Someone produced a hank of rope and started tying their hands behind
their backs.

"You okay?" I asked Alyssa.

"Y-y-yeah." She was shaking.

I hugged her. "You did good," I whispered.

"You, too." Her cheeks were wet as she cried soundlessly.

The prefects had hauled all the bandits to their feet.
Everyone seemed to be okay, other than some bruises.

"What will you do with them?" Alyssa asked Dad.

"Find out who they are. How they got into the camp.
Figure out how to stop them—if we can." We'd started
walking back toward the center of camp, the tied bandits
in tow.

"You think it'd be okay if I went to lie down?" Alyssa
asked.

"Yeah, I think that'd be fine," Dad replied.

I caught her hand and squeezed it. "You did good. You
were brave."

"I don't feel brave. But thanks."

Dad directed that each of the bandits be held sepa-
rately. I followed him as he pushed one of the guys into a
tent big enough to stand up in. After a moment we were
joined by one of the prefects, Amy Jones, who took the
shake light from Dad.

Dad stood behind the bandit, holding his bound arms.
"Search him," Dad ordered. It was strange to hear him
giving orders—as if he'd been replaced by a different man

who looked like my father. Amy was holding the flashlight, so it fell to me to do the search. I started at his neck, working my way down. When I patted the guy's right ankle, I felt a long, slender shape under his pant leg.

He kicked without warning, aiming for my face. I got my hand between his foot and my head, but the force of the kick still knocked me backward. Dad hauled up on his arms so hard I heard his shoulders crack. The guy moaned, and Dad said, "Kick my son again, and I'll break your arms off and ram them down your throat."

The guy fell quiet, and I rolled back to my feet. "I'm fine, thanks for asking," I said.

"Get on with it," Dad snapped.

I pulled up the bandit's pant leg and extracted a wicked knife from its sheath. It was at least six inches long, with a blood gutter and evil-looking serrations along its spine.

Dad ripped off the bandit's black ski mask. He was dirtier than we were, his unkempt black beard caked with filth, and his face streaked with dirt and ash. Up until then, I'd thought maybe the bandits were guards, up to some kind of mischief in their off time, but all the guards I'd seen were far cleaner than he was.

"All you got is a knife?" Dad asked.

The guy was silent.

"Which one of you is in charge?"

"I ain't tellin' you shee-it," he replied with a cocky smile.

"Make sure he can't kick you again," Dad said to me.

I moved to the side, out of kicking range. Dad seized the guy's pinkie in his fist and bent it sharply upward. It

made a sickening snap as it broke, and the bandit
screamed. I turned away. This was my father, the same
guy who had never wanted to watch "CSI" on TV because
it was too gory?

I heard a slap and looked back in time to see Dad pull
his hand away from the side of the guy's head. "Now quit
screaming! What's your name?"

"Shawn," he gasped.

"You have any other weapons?"

"Ain't allowed to bring no others."

"Not allowed by who? Why? Who's in charge?"

"I can't—"

Dad grabbed his ring finger. This time he had to work
to peel it away from Shawn's fist. But it snapped as easily
as the pinkie. Shawn screamed again. My chest heaved,
and I tasted bile. "You've got eight more chances to tell
me," Dad stated. The calmness of his voice terrified me,
and I wasn't the one having my fingers broken.

"Cody . . . Cody's in charge." Shawn was panting.
"Can't bring guns in, case this happens and you get 'em."

"Where are you all from?"

"I was in Anamosa when the volcano blew."

"And now?"

Shawn hesitated, and Dad started peeling his middle
finger off his fist. "Quit!" he yelled. "Iowa City!"

"So you're in one of the prison gangs?"

"Yeah." Tears were streaking the dirt on Shawn's face.

"Which one?" There was a long pause.

"Ah, fu—" He screamed as Dad snapped his middle

finger, interrupting whatever he was going to say. "You could have just looked at my tats."

"Where?" Dad asked.

"Over my heart."

Dad looked at me, and I pulled the guy's coat and shirts up. Tattooed across his chest in an ugly blue color in fancy script were the letters DWB inside an outline of the state of Iowa.

"What's it mean?" Dad asked.

"Dirty White Boys," Shawn managed to say with a strut in his voice that was strange, given the tears streaking his face.

"You sure qualify on the dirty part," I said. He stunk.

"How'd you get into the camp?" Dad asked.

"Just kill me now. Cody'll flense me if he finds out I answered that."

Dad peeled his index finger back, and Shawn groaned. It snapped with a sound like a branch breaking, and Shawn's groan morphed into a scream. "Cody's not here. I am," Dad said. "You're going to tell me everything I want to know. Either now or after I've broken your other six fingers."

Shawn was sobbing now. "Just . . . break them all, then."

"Goddamn it, I'm not playing!" Dad yelled. "Give me that knife, Alex."

I couldn't believe what was happening. My teeth clicked as I closed my mouth. "W-why? What're you going to do with it?"

"Now!" Dad ordered, his rage barely contained.

I flipped the knife and handed it to him butt first. He grasped the hilt in his right hand and seized the tip of Shawn's pinkie in his left. The knife flashed as he lowered it, sawing into Shawn's finger. The icy ground under my feet reached up through my body, freezing me in place.

Dad was still sawing at the finger as Shawn screamed. The knife found the break in the pinkie and sliced through. Blood poured out the stump, splattering Dad's trousers. He stepped around Shawn, got right in his tear-stained face, and hollered, "You like that, you goddamn cannibal? You want to eat people, start with yourself." Dad jammed the bloody finger against Shawn's lips, trying to force it down his throat. "I'll feed you all ten of your bloody fingers—"

My icy immobility shattered, and I lashed out, striking Dad's wrist. The finger went flying, hitting the side of the tent with a thump. "What the hell!" I shouted. "This isn't us! This isn't you! Stop it!"

Dad's face was twisted by some kind of sick, almost gleeful rage. "Oh, we lost your finger," he cooed to Shawn. "I know where we can get nine more." He lifted the knife and stepped behind Shawn.

As he seized Shawn's broken ring finger, Shawn blubbered, "No. Stop. . . . The DWBs, we have a deal with some of the guards."

"A deal?" Dad asked.

"They let us in and out."

"In return for what?"

"We bring them supplies. Drugs, booze, food. Let them do the girls sometimes."

"What happens to the people you take?"

"Flense most of them. We keep some of the girls to trade."

I thought of Darla. If she was still alive, she was in the hands of a gang like this one. I stumbled out of the tent and vomited.

Through the wall of the tent, I heard Dad saying, "Which guards work with you?"

Shawn gave him about a dozen names. Then he asked in a tremulous voice, "You going to flense me now?"

"I haven't decided," Dad replied. The tent flap rustled, and he strode past me.

I hurried to catch up and grabbed his arm. "What the hell was that?"

"That's the world we live in now."

I swung him to face me. "No. You're blaming the world for choices you made."

Dad tried to pull away. "That's just the way things are now."

There was a wet, choking sound behind me and a thump. "What was that?"

"Jones. Taking care of the *flenser*." He said "flenser" like it was the vilest curse word ever invented.

Jones pushed through the tent flap, carrying the light in one hand and awkwardly dragging Shawn in the other. She was bent almost double, straining against his bulk. A trail of blood followed Shawn's head. His throat had been cut. "What . . .why?"

"They're flensers," Dad said flatly. "I'll do whatever it takes to protect those under my care from the likes of him. *Whatever.* I've got no apologies to make. Now let go of me, son."

"What're you going to do?" I asked.

"Take care of the rest of the flensers," Dad replied. "Go help Jones with that offal."

"So you kill the other three cannibals. What good does it do?"

"Three fewer flensers in the world."

"And they send four other guys. Or forty. It gets us nothing."

"So what? We let them go?"

Part of me wanted to say forget it, they deserved to die. To let Dad do whatever he wanted to the other three. I didn't really care what happened to them. But I did care about Dad, about what he was becoming. Or had already become. "What if we let one of them go? Would they trade something for the other two?"

"I don't know," Dad said. "What do they have that we'd even want?"

"An end to the raids on the camp would be a good start."

"We can't trust the DWBs. And some other gang might start raiding, instead."

"Yeah. You know, it's not the gangs. It's Black Lake. We need some way to stop them from letting gangs into the camp, period. Can we report them to someone? Call their HQ?"

"There's no cell network anymore. Maybe a shortwave radio. I've heard that's how Black Lake stays in touch with Washington."

"Can you keep two of them hidden while we work out a trade?"

"Maybe," Dad shrugged. "Worse comes to worst, we go with plan A and slit their filthy throats."

The three live flensers were called Trey, Darrell, and Cody, who was the boss. We released Trey with a message: Bring a shortwave radio transceiver and an extra set of batteries to camp, and we'll free Cody and Darrell. Continue raiding, or tell Black Lake we have captives, and we'll slit the two guys' throats without a second thought. For good measure, Dad retrieved the bloody, dirty pinkie stub and told Trey to take it along—to let his bosses know we were serious.

After releasing Trey, Dad went to help move our captives to new tents, and I returned to the tent I shared with Dad. I lay down but didn't sleep. It was after dawn by then, and the tent flap let in a sliver of light. It let in a frigid breeze, too, but I didn't have the energy to get up and tie it tighter. Instead I stared into the light while my thoughts churned my brain to mush.

I was still trying to sleep when Dad finally came in. "You're awake," he said.

"Yeah."

He started to take off his boots. "Look, I—"

"You don't owe me an explanation," I said, staring through him toward the sliver of light now blocked by his body.

"I was just doing what I had to."

"Bullshit. You cut off a guy's finger and tried to make him eat it, Dad."

He turned his back toward me. "Yeah," he said quietly.

I let out a breath I hadn't even realized I'd been holding.

"You remember what I did before the volcano," Dad said.

"CAD/CAM drafting. So what?"

"I didn't always do that. I've got a civil engineering degree. Got a great job right out of college. Just what I'd always wanted to do. Designing sewer systems might not sound like fun to most people, but I loved it. The flow dynamics, the treatment ponds—it all has to come together like the sections of symphony. Brown water comes in, and clean water comes out. There's a beauty to it if you can see it."

"You never talked about that."

"No. I designed a huge job in El Mirage, outside Phoenix. Made a mistake calculating the load on a wall. Dropped a zero. Maybe the contractor should have caught it, but they didn't. The cave-in buried three guys up to their necks. The other workers unburied them in less than an hour, but they still died. Crush syndrome."

"I didn't know."

"After that, I didn't have any passion for designing the systems anymore. The music of it was gone. I took a crappy job doing CAD/CAM renderings, and I've been doing that ever since."

"I always thought that was what you wanted to do."

"I guess it *was* what I wanted. After El Mirage, anyway." Dad paused for a long time. He was sitting hunched in the front of the tent, facing away from me. "Those three guys who died. They had families. Wives and children. I was responsible. I could have prevented it. . . ."

I didn't know what to say. I waited out the silence.

"If I made a mistake doing the CAD/CAM drawings, the architect was responsible for catching it. I wasn't in charge. But I didn't. Make mistakes. My drawings were perfect—the best. I've turned down three promotions in the last ten years. I didn't want the responsibility.

"When I got here, I helped your mom with the school. Taught math. But I wasn't really into it—it was just easier to do what Janice wanted instead of arguing with her. But there was one student—Karen. Sixteen. Energetic. Brilliant. I was teaching her what little integral calculus I could remember.

"She told me she was worried. She'd heard rumors about girls disappearing. I shrugged off her concerns." Dad lowered his head. "She hasn't been seen in four months.

"Responsibility's a cruel bitch. She comes for you whether you want it or not. And people are dying here, regardless of what I do, Alex." He swiveled at the hips toward me, his face silhouetted—all sharp black angles against the tent opening. "But it's still my job to protect them. If I had to cut off my own finger and eat it, I'd do that. Whatever it takes. Whatever."

"Some things are beyond our control," I said. "No matter what we do." I sat up and hugged him. I still couldn't reconcile the placid, benignly neglectful father I'd known with this mercurial maniac I had wrapped in my arms. The disaster had warped the landscape of our minds—perhaps even more than it had altered the physical landscape.

When, after a long while, we broke the embrace and laid down side-by-side on our bedrolls, neither of us slept.

Instead we stared silently at the tiny sliver of light still peeking from the outside world into the darkness within our tent.

Chapter 65

I found Ben in the breakfast line. "I need to talk to you," I whispered.

"You are talking to me," he replied in a normal voice.

"Talk about what?" Alyssa asked.

"Escaping," I whispered back.

"Escaping is not a difficult problem," Ben said. "There are vulnerabilities—"

"Ben," Alyssa whispered urgently. Our neighbors in the line had turned almost in unison to stare at us. "Later. After breakfast."

"The information is classified as need-to-know only?"

"Yes, only Alex needs to know."

After breakfast, the three of us huddled behind a tent, out of the wind, while Ben explained his plan. The guards changed twice each night around midnight and four A.M. Ben had observed them congregating at the guard hut during their shift change—the perfect opportunity to escape at the other side of the camp. The only problem: How would we cross the fence?

A bolt cutter would be the obvious solution, but none of us had any idea where we'd get one of those. Ben's other idea was to build a canvas sling about twenty feet long and two feet wide. The middle would be reinforced with a dozen layers of canvas. We'd toss it over the fence so that the reinforced part overlaid the razor wire. Then we'd tie both sides to the chain-link part of the fence and climb over via hand- and footholds sewn into the sling.

So we needed to dismantle a tent—one of the old types made of heavy-duty canvas. Dad was asleep so I went looking for Mom. I found her crouched in a tent feeding an older woman who was too sick to stand in the food line.

"You need any help?" I asked.

"Sure." She handed me a bowl of boiled wheat. "See if Jane wants to eat anything." She gestured at the other woman in the tent.

I took the bowl from her and crouched, shuffling deeper into the tent. "You think you can eat?" I said to Jane.

"Reckon' so," she replied in a low, rough voice. She started trying to push herself upright.

"Let me help you." I put my hand behind her shoulders and lifted, jamming the bedding in behind her to keep her partly upright. I took a spoonful of gruel and held it to her lips.

"Mom," I said, "I need a tent."

"Your father snoring or something?" she replied.

"No, it's not that. I need to . . ." How was I going to explain this? I didn't really want to lie to her, not that she'd believe me, anyway. "I need to make something out of one of the tents, a heavy canvas one."

"Make what?"

"A sling. To throw across the fence."

Mom swiveled toward me, slopping some of the gruel across the cheek of her patient. "You just got here! We're finally back together, and you—"

"So come with me," I said. "That's why Darla and I came back to Iowa in the first place. To find you and bring you home to Uncle Paul's. To Rebecca."

"We'll try to escape as soon as we know the girls here are safe, and we'll go back to Uncle Paul's together. Not gallivanting off after some—"

"Without Darla, I wouldn't be here. Wouldn't be alive. I'm going after her. With or without you."

"You're too young to—"

"I'm not a kid."

"It's hopeless—"

"It is *not* hopeless. I need a heavy canvas tent. And I'd like your help."

"There are some things we just can't do."

"We decide what we can do. That's the way it was before the volcano, and it's still true." I fought to keep my hand steady as I continued spooning gruel into Jane's mouth. "Things are just a lot harder."

"Things are different. We have to make hard choices now."

"Which is exactly what I'm asking you to do. Make a hard choice. Help me go after Darla."

"I . . . I can't."

"You done?" I asked Jane.

She nodded.

"Me, too." I left the tent without looking back.

Chapter 66

I napped uneasily the rest of the day. Every time I woke up, I looked to where Dad slept alongside me, thinking about waking him and asking him to help me get a tent. Every time I waited, figuring I'd be better off if I asked him after he woke up on his own. I hoped he'd be more likely to say yes.

But when I got up for dinner, he was gone. I looked for him all evening but didn't catch up to him until well after dark.

His answer was the same as my mother's. Maybe she'd gotten to him first. They didn't have any canvas tents to spare, didn't want to try to escape yet, and weren't going to go looking for Darla even if or when they did escape. We argued for what felt like at least an hour, but our positions were calcified. Any pair of statues facing off in a public park might have made more progress than we did.

Our argument ended suddenly when a distant scream pierced the air. No sooner had we started running toward it than two more screams, in different places, shattered the stillness of the night.

We glanced at each other. "Go wake up the day shift!" Dad ordered.

"Right." I reversed course, sprinting for the tents where the prefects slept. By the time I got back with rein-forcements, the whole camp was in an uproar. A flood of refugees was pouring into the center of the camp, fleeing the crescendoing screams and chaos. Dad was yelling to be heard over the noise, dispatching teams of prefects to search for whatever or whoever was causing the ruckus.

Dad grouped me with two others, Jones and Altemeier, and told us to sweep the perimeter of the camp along the fence. We set off at a run.

By the time we got to the fence, it seemed like the com-motion had mostly moved deeper inside the camp. I scanned constantly back and forth as we ran, hyperalert for any movement.

As we passed the gate, I saw four Black Lake guys, double the usual contingent, leaning against the guard shack outside the fence. "Why don't you do something?" I yelled. They laughed, and one of them pantomimed shoot-ing me. I turned away, and we ran on.

A few hundred yards farther on, we heard a child screaming. Following the noise, we found a little girl, maybe four or five years old, sitting in the snow between two of the tents, screaming, "Mommyyyyy! Mommyyyyy! Mommyyyyy!" She paused just long enough between each scream to breathe.

We quickly scouted the adjacent tents. Nobody was there. I scooped up the girl in my arms, which only made her scream louder. "I'll run her to the middle of camp, then catch up to you," I yelled. Jones nodded, and she and Altemeier took off along the fence line.

I headed toward the center of the camp, slowing to a jog to conserve my strength. I had to detour once, to avoid a chaotic melee between three black-clad biker-types and five or six prefects. I would have been worse than useless in the middle of a fight with a squirming little girl in my arms.

It took more than ten minutes to find Mom in the chaos at the center of camp. She was organizing refugees who weren't part of the prefect system into groups she designated runners or fighters. I guessed she was organizing for an attack, but I didn't stop to ask her. Instead I thrust the little girl into her startled arms and took off again.

I couldn't find Jones or Altemeier. I looked for a few minutes before I came across another fight. A group of three flensers armed with knives were fighting with a much larger cluster of refugees. I ran toward them, but by the time I arrived, the invaders had broken off, running toward the gate. Nobody chased them—two of the refugees involved in the fight had been stabbed and were bleeding badly. I stopped to help.

A few minutes later, it was over almost as suddenly as it had started. The cries of rage died, replaced by the wails of the wounded and moans of the dying.

It took more than twelve hours for Dad to get a clear picture of what had happened. We'd been attacked by members of the Dirty White Boys. Something between fifteen and thirty of them, working in groups of three or four, had swarmed through the camp searching tents and stabbing anything that moved.

We had eleven fresh corpses. Eight refugees and three Dirty White Boys. Dozens more were wounded, including a few that might soon join the dead. Dad decided to deliver all the corpses to the guard gate along with a protest— not that either of us really thought it would do any good. The guards had let the DWBs in. They knew what would happen.

The little girl I'd grabbed in the middle of the night turned out to be named Lisa. Her mother had gotten pulled away from her in the crush of fleeing people. The only good tears I saw that day were the ones when mother and daughter were reunited.

Hoping for Black Lake to take action seemed futile, so we spent an exhausting day preparing for the night to follow. We organized more fighters, distributed captured knives, and made plans for refugees to flee to the protected zone at the center of the camp if the DWBs came again. I had no time to do anything about my escape plan amid the rush to prepare for another attack.

Dad planned for everyone on defensive patrols to sleep in the late afternoon. We would need our sleep if the camp got attacked again. But organizing and getting cleaned up took far longer than it should have. By nightfall, neither Dad nor I had had so much as a nap. We were drunk with exhaustion. If the DWBs came again that night, we'd be useless.

So of course they did.

Chapter

67

One of the prefects Dad had assigned to watch the gate sprinted up to us. I was out of breath myself, having just returned from running orders to a patrol on the far side of the camp. What the scout said made further orders irrelevant.

"DWBs, sir." The woman was gasping, out of breath. "Just came through the main gate."

"How many?" Dad barked.

"Just two so far."

The three of us ran back toward the gate.

Trey was there, carrying one dirty plastic WalMart bag in his left hand and two in his right. A guy I didn't recognize was with him. They sauntered toward the center of the camp like they didn't have a care in the world, but I could see two separate groups of prefects shadowing them at a distance. I caught Trey's eyes darting sideways and realized the truth: That huge muscle-bound dude was scared out of his mind.

"Stop!" Dad ordered them.

They stopped.

"You brought our radio?"

Trey lifted one of the WalMart bags. "Shortwave transceiver." He hefted the other two. "Batteries."

Dad strode up to them, his eyes shifting warily from Trey to the other guy. I followed along. He took the bags from Trey.

"You going to flense us now?" Trey asked. His eyes darted from me to Dad.

"Why'd you decide to hand over a radio?" Dad asked.

"You kicked our asses yesterday. If it was up to me, we'd come back with shotguns and street sweepers and wipe this latrine pit off the map. But it's not up to me."

"You're not allowed to bring in guns, are you?"

"Nope. Some kind of candy-ass deal between the guards and Wolfe."

"Wolfe?"

"He's the captain. Guy who told me to bring you this here radio."

"I'm surprised the guards let the radio through."

"You bribe the right guard, you can get almost anything in. Except guns. So you going to skin us? Or keep your bargain?"

"What bargain?" I said. "By attacking us last night, you broke whatever bargain there was."

"Told Wolfe not to trust the cattle." Trey shrugged, making an effort at being nonchalant, but his shoulders were trembling.

Dad said, "Let's see if the radio works." Then he called out to the prefects, "Hold these two here for now."

I carried the radio to our tent. Dad got out the flashlight and started shaking it while I dumped the bags on my bedroll.

When the flashlight was charged, Dad held it on the radio. I grabbed the pair of wires coming out the back: one red, one black. They were greasy, as if they'd been installed in a car at some point. "Does it matter which one connects where?" I said, eyeing the terminals on the battery.

"It matters," Dad replied. "If it's like jumper cables, the red wire is positive and the black is negative. Hook up the positive side first."

"I can't tell which side of the battery is positive."

"Should be printed on the casing." Dad aimed the shake light at the battery.

The terminal labels were embossed into the plastic battery case. There was no obvious way to connect the wires to the battery. They terminated in a strip of bare copper wire—there were no alligator clips.

I held onto the insulated part of the red wire, pushing the copper lead against the positive battery terminal. When I pushed the black against the other terminal, sparks flew, searingly bright in the dim tent, and I dropped both wires.

"Least we know the battery's good," Dad said wryly.

"Is it *supposed* to do that?"

"Yeah, it's fine. Try the other battery. And just hold them there a minute so I can see if the radio works."

The black lead sparked again, but once I had it firmly against the terminal, it quit.

"Here goes nothing," Dad said, pushing the power button. Nothing happened.

"Bum radio?"

"Don't know." Dad pushed down the button again, holding it a couple of seconds this time. The radio crackled to life, and a staticky hiss filled our little tent. He dialed through the channels quickly but picked up nothing.

He pulled the mic off the side of the radio and depressed the lever. "Any idea how to check if this thing works?"

"Not a clue," I said. "Ben might know. It looks like some kind of military radio. He's gaga over anything military."

"That meltdown the other day didn't inspire my confidence."

"You got a better idea?"

Dad spoke into the mic, "Hello, hello, anyone there?" When he let up on the lever, the staticky hiss resumed. He shrugged. "Let's get some sleep. I'll take you off the patrol rotation tomorrow. You and Ben can try to raise someone on this thing. Might be more likely to reach someone during the day, anyway."

"Okay," I said.

"Jones!" Dad yelled. "Round up all the DWBs we've got and march them to the front gate. Let 'em go, and then keep a sharp watch to make sure nobody else comes in."

"Yes, sir!" Jones yelled from outside the tent.

Dad started pulling off his boots. "G'night, son."

"'Night, Dad."

• • •

The next morning, I searched out Ben and told him about the radio. He practically ran back to the tent Dad and I shared. Alyssa and I trailed along behind him.

When we caught up to him, Ben had folded his arms and was giving the radio a dubious stare. "That's not a military radio."

"It says Yaesu FT-897," I said, reading the label at the top of the transceiver.

"That is not a military designation."

"Okay, Ben, but can we contact someone on it?"

"Maybe. It looks a little bit like an AN/PRC-70."

"Can you run it?"

"Run it?"

"Operate it?" Alyssa said.

"Maybe. I read the operator's manual for the AN/PRC-70 once. But this doesn't look exactly the same."

"Can you try?" I asked.

"I do not think I should," Ben said.

"Why not?"

"An AN/PRC-70 will be damaged if the operator attempts to transmit without an antenna."

"We ran it briefly last night. Is it wrecked?"

"I do not know. But an AN/PRC-70 will not operate without an antenna. This radio probably will not operate without an antenna, either. Where is the antenna?"

Chapter 68

I had to ask three different prefects for directions, and even then wound up running halfway around the camp to find Dad.

"What's wrong?" he said as I huffed up.

"The DWBs," I replied. "They ripped us off. That transceiver is no good without an antenna."

Dad sighed heavily. "That's as much fun as a failed backflow preventer. Nothing to be done for it, I guess."

"Couldn't we make an antenna?"

"I don't know. Maybe. What does Ben say about it?"

"He doesn't know how. But I was thinking, there are what, twenty thousand people in this camp?"

"Almost thirty thousand."

"Someone's got to know something about radios."

"Yeah. A ham radio operator. Or electrical engineer. I'll organize the prefects to ask everyone."

I spent the rest of the morning going from tent to tent, asking everyone I could find if they knew anything about radios. All over camp, other prefects were doing the same thing. When we were asked why we wanted a radio expert, we told folks we were trying to turn some old cell phones into radios. We had two cell phones we could surrender to Black Lake if they got wind of the project. They were worthless—none of the cell transmission towers had worked since the first day of the eruption more than ten months ago.

Early in the afternoon, a prefect found me. "The Dean wants you. We found a ham radio guy."

When I got back to the tent, Dad was standing outside with Jones, talking to an older guy with a salt-and-pepper beard peeking from under his scarves. He stood out because his beard was neatly trimmed—most guys let them run wild since personal grooming was a lot more challenging without safety razors, hot water, or electricity. Not that I had to worry about it. I grew just enough wispy facial hair to look stupid, but not enough to bother shaving.

"Oh hey, Alex," Dad said. "This is Ken Bandy."

We shook hands as Dad continued, "Alex doesn't have a formal role in the prefects yet, so I'll assign him to help you." That "yet" was interesting. Not that I wanted a role. I wanted to get out of here already.

"Help me what?" Ken asked.

"I'll show you. But first I want it understood that you

can't reveal what's inside this tent to anyone, not even your wife."

"Got it. But how long are you going to need me for?"

"I don't know. A few days."

"I can't leave Carol alone that long."

"Jones," Dad said. "Organize a three-person, twenty-four-hour guard detail for Mr. Bandy's wife until he's done here."

"Roger," she replied and left.

Dad ushered Ken and me into the tent.

"Is that? It is!" Ken knelt by the transceiver. "A Yaesu. Nice model, too. Probably would have set you back $800 before the eruption. I can't imagine what it'd cost now. What kind of antenna do you have?"

"We don't," I replied.

"Nice boat anchor you've got, then."

"Couldn't we build an antenna?"

"You have an antenna tuner?"

"Um, no."

"You don't want much, do you?"

"Can you do it?"

Ken rubbed his fingers together. "Maybe. What frequency do you want to transmit on?"

I shrugged. "You tell me."

"Well, how far do you want to transmit?"

"Can we reach Washington?"

"With a good antenna, sure, no problem. Twenty meters would probably work best. I might be able to make a dipole antenna, but without a tuner . . . I don't know."

"What do you need?"

Ken was silent for a moment. "Forty or fifty feet of copper wire, any gauge will do. Co-ax cable. Fifty feet should do. Two six-foot copper grounding rods. Enough posts to suspend the whole antenna thirty feet off the ground."

I looked at Dad. "Where are we going to get all that stuff? And how are we going to put an antenna that high up without the guards noticing?"

He shook his head slowly. "I don't know."

Chapter 69

Getting the supplies turned out to be much easier than I'd anticipated. A lot of the refugees had been rounded up on the road while they tried to flee the disaster zone. They'd fashioned crude tents with whatever came to hand, and FEMA had allowed them to keep their improvised tents when they'd entered the camp. For some of them, the best raw materials available had been items ripped out of their homes. Wire torn out of walls—both electrical and co-ax—served as crude cordage for guy lines. Copper pipes substituted for tent poles. The prefects fanned out across the camp again, looking for the materials we needed and arranging replacements or tent upgrades for refugees who allowed us to take parts from their shelters.

While I searched for materials, I also kept an eye out for unused canvas. Unfortunately, tent materials were at a premium—all the canvas in camp appeared to be in use. I wasn't sure how I could manage to steal an occupied tent. Maybe Ben would have an idea.

We didn't find a forty-foot length of wire, of course. We had to splice it together from dozens of scraps, joining each chunk with its neighbor with the tightest twist we could manage. One of the prefects found a family using chunks of a tailor's cloth measuring tape as improvised belts—an invaluable find since Ken wanted the wire measured precisely. He did a bunch of calculations in the snow outside, muttering something about 468 megahertz to himself. When he finished, he told us to make each of the two legs of the antenna sixteen feet, ten inches long. With all the splices, Ken said he'd be shocked if it worked. The co-ax cable was even harder to splice than the copper without connectors or tape.

We used six-foot lengths of copper pipe as grounds, driving them into the earth by pounding on them with heavy rocks. The ends of the soft copper pipes belled out, and we couldn't get them driven more than a few feet into the frozen ground. It was as good as the rest of the haphazard setup, I guessed.

Raising a thirty-four-foot antenna thirty feet off the ground proved to be impossible. We simply didn't have any poles long enough. Plus, an antenna that tall would be visible from the guard shack—a risk we couldn't take. Instead we strung the antenna across the tops of the tallest tents. Ken wanted it thirty feet high—he got about eight.

By evening, we were ready to try it. Ken, Ben, and I crowded into the tent while Dad and some prefects kept watch outside. Ken slowly turned the dial on the transceiver, listening to static and squeals with the silent intensity of a priest at prayer.

He'd been at it fifteen or twenty minutes when something occurred to me. "Why don't you call out? Maybe someone's listening but not transmitting."

"Transmitting takes more than twenty times the juice as listening. We've only got the two batteries, right? Which do you want? Four hours of transmitting, or eighty of listening?"

"Oh." That made sense.

More than an hour passed before Ken gave up scanning. "I really can't tell if this is working without an antenna tuner or an SWR meter. Maybe the antenna is too long. Go trim an inch off each side. That'll change its harmonics, maybe even help."

Cutting the copper wire without proper tools was a pain. I had to get the end of the antenna down off a tent, lay the wire against a brick, score it with a knife, and then bend it back and forth until it broke. Ben came along to help, holding the shake light for me. Still, it seemed like it took a long time.

Ken spent another hour scanning channels, then sent me back out to trim the antenna again. Almost immediately upon my return, we heard a voice.

"Peace with the Lord, for the hour of judgment is upon you."

A huge grin cracked Ken's face wide open. "Damn, can't believe this spitwad setup actually works." He picked up the mic. "CQ, CQ this is station KJØB, Maquoketa."

"Welcome to our newest listeners!" the voice crackled back. "Sit back, relax, and hear the words of the Lord. Please keep the frequency clear of transmissions out of courtesy to our other listeners."

Ken started to lift the mic back to his mouth, but Ben took it from him and laid it on top of the radio. The voice continued, "Welcome, listeners, to our 127th broadcast of the Hour of Judgment, the radio program with all the answers you need for surviving purgatory, so you, too, can be called up to sit by His side when Jesus returns. I'm your host, Pastor Manny, coming to you from Crooked Lake, Florida. Our opening reading for today's show is from the Book of Matthew, chapter 24, verses 21 and 22: 'For then there will be great distress, unequaled from the beginning of the world until now—and never to be equaled again. If those days had not been cut short, no one would survive, but for the sake of the elect those days will be shortened.'"

"This guy's a lid," Ken said. "He hasn't even given his call sign."

I had no idea what he meant by a lid, but it didn't seem important. I picked up the mic.

"He said to keep the channel clear," Ben said.

"Whatever." I mashed down the push-to-talk switch on the mic and said, "Come in Pastor Manny, come in."

Pastor Manny kept right on reading from Matthew.

"He can't hear you when he's transmitting," Ken said.

"Oh." That presented a bit of a problem. Pastor Manny barely paused to take a breath, let alone long enough to let me talk. We listened to him talk about Matthew's end-of-times predictions for ten minutes or more. Then Pastor Manny announced a reading from Revelations, and our speakers filled with static. Maybe he was hunting for the right verse.

I pushed in the switch again. "Pastor Manny, come in, Pastor Manny."

"You're acting like a lid, too," Ken said. I ignored him.

The static ceased "Another new listener? How wonderful. Please keep the channel clear out of consideration for our listeners."

"This is urgent. I need to contact someone in the government. Maybe FEMA."

"Put not your trust in princes.'"

"This is urgent. People are disappearing."

"Son, I asked you nicely to keep the frequency clear."

"Do you even have any other listeners? Why aren't they transmitting?"

"Of course I do. They're far more courteous than you."

"How do you know? That anyone else is listening if they never talk?"

"I prayed on it, of course. Ah, here's the next reading, Revelations, chapter thirteen."

He read breathlessly for another ten minutes. He was an excellent reader—hollering and whispering, changing his voice to suit the words. I might have been impressed if I weren't so pissed off.

The next time he stopped, I broke in immediately. "Please, Pastor Manny, do you have any idea how we could get in touch with FEMA? Preferably someone high up?"

"'The worries of this life, the deceitfulness of wealth, and the desires for other things come in and choke the Word, making it unfruitful.'"

I slammed my free hand down on the tent floor. "I'm going to transmit right over your program unless you try to help me. People will hear a babble of both our voices and tune out." I wasn't sure it would really work that way, but when I looked at Ken, he was both nodding and glaring at me, so I figured my guess was right.

"You would dare thwart the will of the Lord?"

"I would and I will if you don't help us."

"Blasphemer!"

"Whatever. You want me off your frequency, I want some help."

The radio crackled with static for a moment. When Pastor Manny came back on, his voice was quieter, resigned. "Florida is in the green zone—it's one of the less-affected areas. There isn't much FEMA presence. The Florida National Guard is handling security here. I probably couldn't find anyone from FEMA even if I were inclined to abandon my calling to look. But the seventeen-meter band is usually full of transmissions in the late afternoon. Most of the signals are coded, but sometimes there's a clear transmission—I think some relief units are reporting in to Washington that way."

"Perfect. Thank you."

"Now will you keep my frequency clear?"

"Sure. Sorry," I said, although I felt anything but. Would it have killed him to tell me about the government transmissions right away?

Ken, Ben, and I fiddled with the radio for a few more hours that night. We found several other stations broadcasting. Most were in other languages: two that might have been Spanish, one that sounded vaguely Germanic, and another that Ken said was Russian. One station broadcast nothing but a woman reading numbers, which struck me as highly bizarre.

I talked to a guy for a while who called his station "Radio Free City." But when it became clear that we couldn't help him with food or "taking the fight to the fascist FEMA pigs," he lost interest and signed off.

I would have liked some news. I knew in Worthington they were monitoring their radios and posting anything they heard on the town's bulletin board. We tuned the radio to AM for a while but didn't pick up anything useful, so we shut down the transceiver to save the batteries and went to bed.

The next day, we trimmed the antenna to twelve feet, eleven inches on each side, which Ken said would help optimize reception on the seventeen-meter band. It didn't make sense to me—why wouldn't a longer antenna be better than a short one? But when Ben and I had messed around with the radio on our own, we'd reached no one, so we took Ken's word for it.

About the middle of the afternoon, the seventeen-meter band changed. Suddenly there were dozens of transmissions. Most of them were high-pitched static—I thought maybe someone was sending in code, but Ken said it was probably just data.

After skipping through five or six machine transmissions, Ken happened upon a person talking. ". . . bales of chain-link fencing, 850 pounds of coiled 8-gauge wire, 410 16-foot posts . . ."

When the guy took a short break from reading his list, Ken broke in. "KJØB."

The radio hissed. "QLR."

"That means he's busy," Ken explained. "QRA," he said into the mic.

"QLR."

"Rude bastard. I asked him for his call sign, and he basically told me to buzz off."

I took the mic from Ken and mashed the switch. "We have an emergency."

"I repeat, QLR. This block of frequencies is reserved for interagency coordination. Clear the frequency."

"Interagency—like, the government? That's great, I need to speak to someone high up in FEMA."

"Under the Federal Emergency Recovery and Restoration of Order Act, I am authorized to confiscate your radio and place you in summary detention if you do not clear this frequency immediately. QLR."

I shot a worried look at Ken. He shook his head. "They'd need a sophisticated triangulation setup to even find you."

"This is life and death," I said into the mic. "We're in a refugee camp. The DWBs are kidnapping people. The guards know, but they aren't doing anything—they're getting paid off by the DWBs. We need help."

"What sector?"

"Sector? We're in the refugee camp in Maquoketa, Iowa."

"Hold." I heard papers rustling for a moment. "Call 18,160 kilohertz in one hour. I'll notify the coordinator for your sector. QLR."

"Thank you," I said, but he was already reading another list.

We shut off the radio to save the batteries. Ben went to find Dad and tell him about our success. I started counting off an hour, one boring Mississippi at a time.

Dad joined us just as I hit 3,600 Mississippi. I turned on the radio and double-checked the frequency selector dial—it was still set to 18,160, where Ken had left it. I picked up the mic and offered it to Dad.

"You go ahead," he said. "I'll just listen in."

I mashed the push-to-talk switch under my sweaty palm. "Alex at Camp Maquoketa, calling the sector coordinator."

"Say 'CQ, CQ from KJØB,'" Ken said. "It's proper radio etiquette."

I was tempted to say "Thank You, Miss Manners." I mean, who cares about radio etiquette when people are getting killed? But it was easier just to do it his way. "CQ, CQ from KJØB." Nothing but static answered my call. I repeated it, over and over, at about one-minute intervals for what seemed like an hour. Had they forgotten? Or worse, was the guy I'd talked to just trying to get me off the frequency by lying about connecting me with the sector coordinator? Dad drummed his fingers on his knee and shifted his weight incessantly.

Finally someone responded. "KJØB here is N7ØVF. This is George Mason with the CBO's FERROA Oversight Committee."

"What's the CBO?" I said.

"Congressional Budget Office. I was told you wished to file a complaint?"

"I thought I'd be speaking to the sector coordinator?"

"She's busy. And anyway, we control their appropriations. What's your complaint?"

"So what does that mean? That you control their appropriations?"

"It means that if we don't give the say-so, they don't get paid. Well, next year, anyway."

Dad was making a rolling motion with his arm. "Get on with it," he mouthed. So I launched into the story—how people had been disappearing from the camp, especially young women. How we'd captured some of the Dirty White Boys. I glossed over the way Dad had gotten Shawn to talk and didn't explain what had ultimately happened to Shawn.

Talking on a shortwave radio had a huge advantage. The CBO guy couldn't interrupt me. So long as I kept the transmit lever depressed, there was no way he could break in.

Finally though, I'd said everything I needed to and lifted the transmit lever.

"Those are serious allegations. Can you substantiate them?"

"There are dozens of witnesses."

"Physical evidence?"

I looked at Dad, not sure what to say. "Blood stains," he whispered, "captured knives and other gear. Black Lake buried the people who died in the attacks. They could be dug up."

I passed on that information to the CBO guy. "Very serious allegations," he added. "Monitor this frequency for instructions. N7ØVF."

I wiped my forehead. I was sweating despite the cold. Dad clapped his hand against my shoulder. "You did good, son."

"Thanks. So that guy was from Washington?"

"The location code in his call sign was zero," Ken said. "That's the code for Iowa, Minnesota, and some of the states west of here. If he were out of Washington, his location code would be three."

"Hmm. Maybe he's a field agent or something?"

Ken shrugged.

We had a long wait by the radio. More than an hour, I guessed. The light was starting to dim when the radio crackled back to life, "CQ, CQ, this is N7ØVF to Maquoketa inmate station."

"This is Alex. Inmate?"

Ken was cringing, and I realized I'd messed up the radio etiquette again. But it didn't seem to matter.

"Sorry. Just jargon. Fortunately there's an inspector not far from you. Congressional Liaison Orley. He's in Rock Island. I've issued orders for him to move to Maquoketa tomorrow."

"Great. When will he be here?"

"When the other inmates, um, refugees gather for dinner, Orley will meet you at the gate. Be sure to bring absolutely everyone who can provide a statement related to Black Lake's corruption. We'll need all the corroborating evidence we can get. Okay?"

"Got it."

"Good. N7ØVF."

. . .

We spent much of the next day debating who should meet with Congressional Liaison Orley. If the corrupt Black Lake personnel discovered that we were reporting them, anyone who came along might be at risk. Mom was adamant that we all go despite the danger. Any chance to stop the kidnappings was worth it, she argued. In the end, we decided to keep the group to a minimum. Dad and I, because we'd heard Shawn confess; Ben and Alyssa, because they both had firsthand experience with the flensers' slave trade; and Mom, because she kept the lists and knew exactly who had disappeared.

At dinnertime we gathered in a knot near the gate. The two guards on duty glared at us. Usually this part of the camp was deserted at dinnertime—everyone was in the food lines.

We waited quietly for fifteen or twenty minutes. We were all tense—nobody seemed to feel like talking. A Black Lake guard in camo BDUs strode up to the gate guards and said something to them I couldn't hear. They stepped away from the gate. The new guard called out, "You here to see Orley? He's waiting for you in the vehicle depot."

I glanced at Mom and Dad. They were trying to keep their faces impassive, but I could tell they were worried. Maybe as worried as I was. But if there was any chance at all of keeping the DWBs out of the camp, we had to take it. If we solved that problem, maybe Mom and Dad would try to escape with me. I marched slowly through the gate with Alyssa, Ben, Mom, and Dad right behind me.

The guard led us to a huge tent directly adjacent to the highway. Inside, the front part of the tent was clear; the back was packed with vehicles: bulldozers, snowplows, Humvees, and modern military trucks Ben said were FMTVs.

As my eyes adjusted to the dim light coming through the open tent flaps behind us, a figure stepped out from among the parked trucks. "Orley?" I said.

Then I saw his face. It was the bastard who had run Camp Galena when Darla and I were imprisoned there last year: Colonel Levitov.

Chapter 70

I stepped back and shouted. But a dozen more guys in camo were already emerging from amid the trucks. They carried jagged-looking black assault rifles.

Dad sighed heavily, burying a word I'd never heard him use before under his breath. Five of the Black Lake guys detached from the rest, moving behind us. If we turned to run, they had clear shots. If we fought, some of us were going to get killed.

A guy about a foot taller than me forced my arms behind my back. I knew resisting would only make it worse. I felt thin plastic bands brush my wrists between my gloves and coat, and then the ties bit into my flesh. He kicked the back of my knee, and I fell to the ground, landing with a painful thud.

Within moments, all five of us were handcuffed and sitting on the unforgiving, frozen ground. Ben rocked back and forth, but he wasn't moaning. Maybe getting cuffed had become so common that it felt like part of his routine now.

"Now," Levitov said, "you'll tell me everything you were going to report to Orley."

"Does Orley even exist?" I doubted it—what a sucker I'd been.

"That's immaterial. Talk," Levitov ordered. An even worse thought occurred to me: What if Orley did exist and was working for Mason's FERROA oversight committee but had reported me to Levitov instead of investigating? Had the U.S. government been completely co-opted by Black Lake?

Dad shrugged, wincing as the cuffs cut into his wrists. "Might as well talk."

I was fuming. "This guy ran the camp outside Galena— the one where everyone was starving to death," I said to Dad. "How'd you wind up here, anyway?" I shot an impaler's glare at Levitov.

"Promotion. For exemplary performance at Camp Galena."

"Very funny. Mass starvation and a breakout won you a promotion? Right."

"No," Levitov replied, "after your stunt with the bulldozer, I convinced Washington to authorize us to reclaim the wheat you found on the stuck barges to feed the inmates. Conditions improved. I traded my leaf for a bird and was moved out here."

I wasn't sure how to take the fact that he actually remembered me from among the thousands of prisoners at Camp Galena.

"We're barely getting enough food here," Mom said.

I snorted. "More than we got at Camp Galena."

"Enough," Colonel Levitov said. "Talk."

I clamped my lips shut, but Dad started talking. Told Colonel Levitov the whole story: girls disappearing, his nighttime patrols, the battles with the DWBs.

When he finished, a long silence ensued. "Not acceptable," Levitov said finally.

"What's not acceptable?" I said. "That your guards are corrupt or that we had to do your job and protect the refugees ourselves!"

"Both. And you do not understand our mission here. If I could write my own orders, protecting refugees might be my first priority. But what the politicians care about is preventing a flood of refugees from entering the yellow and green zones. People in areas that were less badly affected by the eruption, at least initially, are afraid of being overrun by refugees."

"You can't keep people locked in camps forever," Mom said.

"True. Our strategic posture is unstable."

"Will civilian control order you to kill the refugees?" Ben asked.

Mom gasped, but Colonel Levitov didn't seem fazed. "A massacre? It could happen. I would not obey such an order."

"You would be within your rights under the Fourth Geneva Convention, which specifically protects—" Alyssa kicked Ben in the ankle, and surprisingly, he shut up.

"So what happens to the other refugees? To my girls?" Mom asked.

"I will see that those responsible for allowing the DWBs to enter the camp are reassigned."

"Reassigned?" I said. "They should be prosecuted."

Ben added, "Courts-martial would be the proper—"

"I don't have the manpower for that. But the kidnapping of inmates will end. You have my word on that."

I didn't believe him, but there wasn't much I could do about it.

"So what happens to us?" Alyssa asked, her voice low.

"You'll be transferred to Camp Aledo in Illinois tomorrow. I recommend you keep your heads down. If you continue to make trouble, things will not go well for you there."

"Better that than where I was," Alyssa whispered.

"Why not just let us go?" I asked. "Then we'd be out of your hair completely."

"My orders don't allow for that." Colonel Levitov strode past us, toward the exit.

"And the DWBs?" I yelled after him. "The ones who actually did the killing and kidnapping? What happens to them?"

"Not my concern," Levitov yelled back. "I've got bandit gangs coming out my ass. It's all I can do to hold off the Peckerwoods' raids." He left the tent.

I slumped. I was further than ever from finding Darla. Tomorrow I'd get shipped to some other godforsaken camp. Something was in my eyes, making them water, but I couldn't rub them with my hands cuffed behind my back.

Ben's voice cut through my morose thoughts. He yelled after Levitov, "I know how you can get rid of the Peckerwoods completely."

Chapter 71

Levitov reappeared in the doorway to the maintenance tent. "How? You've got thirty seconds."

Ben replied, "They're based in Anamosa—"

"I know that." Levitov sounded annoyed. I cranked
my head around, straining to see him standing
behind me.

Ben didn't pick up on it, just kept right on talking. "The Sister Unit and I were at the old prison."

"It's a limestone fortress."

"It is vulnerable because it is set up like a prison," Ben said. "The electronic systems are all off-
line, but the manual emergency lockdowns should
still work. There are fewer than 150 of the original

prisoners still there. The rest have left or been killed. A small force, attacking at the right time, could take control of the manual lockdowns. Then you could lock the Peckerwoods out of their own armory and split up the forces that bunk in each wing. Once they're isolated, you can clear the area via force or leave them there to starve."

"Not the most humane plan," Mom murmured.

Alyssa glared at Mom. "Not half as bad as they deserve!"

Colonel Levitov strode back into the tent and crouched in front of Ben, who was staring at his own shoes. "Do you know how to operate the emergency lockdowns? You know where they are? Can you draw us a map?"

"Yes, I can map most of the prison. I did not see it all."

"Cut him loose," Levitov ordered.

"Um, Ben?" Alyssa said.

"Cut the Sister Unit free, too," Ben said.

"Ben!" Alyssa whispered. "All of them."

"Yes," Ben said, "Ben will help you if you let all of Ben's friends go free."

"That's almost as good as transferring us to another camp," I said. "You can report that we escaped."

"I'm not allowing any of you to go anywhere until I've verified the intelligence you're supplying."

I had to go on the raid. Darla was in Anamosa. Or she had been a few days ago when Alyssa last saw her. "Fine. Take us all when you attack the Peckerwoods. That way if anything comes up, Ben'll be handy. When you're done kicking the Peckerwoods' butts, you let us go."

"Five noncombatants in the middle of a firefight? Forget it."

"Ben can't go by himself," Alyssa said.

"I could, in fact, go by myself, Sister Unit."

"Take us all. You can leave us outside or locked in a truck or something while you fight. We won't be in the way."

Colonel Levitov nodded slowly. "Deal. Captain Billson!" he yelled. "Escort these five to the infirmary. Put them in the empty bunks with a twenty-four-hour guard, three-man detail."

One of the camo-clad guards yelled "Sir!" as Colonel Levitov pivoted and disappeared. They cut the cuffs off our wrists and marched us into the abandoned WalMart. It was subdivided into hallways and rooms with canvas walls. After a couple of twists and turns, we arrived at a small room into which a dozen cots had been packed.

It was easily the most luxurious sleeping arrangement I'd seen since I left Worthington. One of the grunts even brought us two pails of water—one to wash up in and one to drink from. We huddled together and talked over what we'd learned from Colonel Levitov, trying to keep our voices low enough that the three guards just outside the doorway couldn't hear us.

We were stuck. We had to help Colonel Levitov no matter how much we distrusted him and hope he kept his promise to release us. Then maybe we could find Darla and hightail it back to Warren.

"I promised to let you take the truck so you could drive to Worthington," I said to Alyssa.

"Well, I . . . do you think your Uncle Paul would take in a couple more people?" she asked.

"I think he'd be glad of the extra help," I said.

"I don't know," Dad said. "They were running awfully low on food when your mom and I left."

"Things got better. We were doing okay when Darla and I left," I said. "And Alyssa and Ben would pull their weight."

"Yeah," Alyssa said, "I'd like to go to Warren with you . . . if that's okay." Her voice dropped to a whisper and she leaned closer to me. "You're the only decent guy I know in this shitball world."

"Alyssa, I'm not—"

She blushed. "I know you're not interested in me that way. But we're friends, right? I'd rather stay close to you. I don't know why, okay?"

"Okay." Alyssa had seemed different—less confident—since that morning in the tent. But I'd be glad to have both her and Ben around. I put my hand over hers and squeezed.

Mom and Dad were looking at me. "What?" I said as I released Alyssa's hand.

"Nothing." Mom shook her head.

"I'm going to try to get some sleep," I said.

I picked out a cot at random, lay down on my side, and rested my head on my forearm. We had missed dinner— my stomach was gnawing on a hard knot of nothing. I was exhausted and weak, but sleep refused to come.

My thoughts spun, revolving through the same worry over and over: Darla. I knew she was alive. She had to be.

I'd know it if she were dead, right? Or was that total crap made up by movie writers and believed by overly optimistic morons like me? Was she still in Anamosa? When Black Lake attacked the prison, how could I be sure she wouldn't be hurt?

Amid all these worries, a tiny but fierce flame burned: hope. Tomorrow I might find Darla. Finally.

Chapter 72

It didn't happen. The next day we were trapped in the infirmary. Black Lake employees came and went all day, setting up kerosene lanterns, bringing paper and pencils to Ben, and quizzing all of us about Anamosa and the Peckerwoods. They even brought food— some kind of wheat porridge—and more water.

Mostly they talked to Ben. I saw Colonel Levitov twice, but he didn't acknowledge anyone but Ben. We bugged our guards, but no one would give us any information. We passed a frustrating day of enforced rest and nervous chatter.

• • •

That night, I was startled out of a troubled sleep by the
light from a lantern. A Black Lake guard barked, "Get up.
We move out in fifteen minutes."

I rubbed the sleep from my eyes. Getting ready in fifteen
minutes was not a problem—I had nothing but the clothes
I was wearing and the seeds still secreted in my jacket. I
rolled out of bed, stretched, and waited for the guards.

When they returned, they hustled us to the vehicle
depot and loaded us into a big, boxy truck Ben called an
FMTV. Bench seats lined the back. We were packed in
with a dozen Black Lake guys in full gear. I eyed them
uneasily and got nothing but glares in return. The four of
us huddled at the end of one of the benches, and Dad
made a point of sitting between me and the first Blake
Lake guy. Our truck joined a convoy of four other vehicles
full of mercenaries and their weapons.

The ride to Anamosa took longer than I expected—
maybe two hours. From inside the truck, I couldn't tell
how fast we were traveling. I tried to peek out the back of
the truck once, but one of the Black Lake guys stopped me
before I could even reach the latch.

When we finally stopped, all but three Black Lake
guys vaulted out. They moved without speaking, weapons
cradled to their sides, in a deadly choreographed silence. I
started to ask, "What—" but one of the remaining guards
put his hand against my mouth.

When I tried to climb out of the truck, he stopped me
with a palm on my chest, but that didn't keep me from
looking out the back.

It was nearly pitch black. All the trucks were shut down, their running lights off. I heard a pop and hiss, and suddenly a flare of light appeared about twenty feet ahead of me—so bright it felt as if it were burning the backs of my eyes.

The limestone bulk of the Anamosa prison loomed above me. We had pulled up near a heavy steel side door. The light source was a welding torch that one of the mercenaries was using to slice through the lock.

Something metallic clanked, and the guy using the torch dialed it down from white-hot to orange. Another guy jammed an oversized pry-bar between the frame and door, wrenching it open. Then all the Black Lake mercenaries sprinted into action, charging into the prison in a double file.

I heard the muffled pop-pop of gunfire. The echoes of screams escaped the open door. None sounded feminine, but I still felt the cold hand of terror clenching my gut. Was it a massacre? If Darla was in there, would they shoot her? I tried to leave the truck again, but one of the mercenaries shoved me back so hard I fell, crashing down on a bench. I heard a distant clang, and all the sounds blended into a cacophony of death, pain, and clashing metal.

It was over inside of twenty minutes. Colonel Levitov emerged from the prison door, barked an order, and the headlights of the truck behind ours snapped on, bathing us in light. He stepped up to our tailgate and addressed Ben. "The prison is under control. The last of the Peckerwoods here will be dead or in our custody shortly. Your intelligence was nearly perfect. Well done." Levitov stuck out his hand.

Ben looked at his feet. Alyssa nudged him with her elbow, and he limply placed his hand in Levitov's, still staring downward. "You committed to releasing Ben and his friends," Ben said.

"I did." Levitov released Ben's hand and Ben balled it up, pulling it back against his chest. "You're free to go," Levitov continued. "Make trouble for my camp again, and I'll see that you regret it."

He didn't deserve a handshake, salute, or thank you from me. I couldn't give him what he did deserve, so I settled for glaring at him. Evidently Mom and Dad felt the same way—they didn't say anything to him, either.

I jogged toward the prison door. Levitov yelled, "We haven't finished mopping up in there."

Dad sprinted up to me, catching my arm just before I reached the door. "We need to clear out of here. They might still be fighting in there."

"Darla's in there," I said. "I'm going inside to look for her."

"We're going back to the farm," Mom said. "Back to Rebecca."

"After I find Darla." I twisted my arm free of Dad's grasp and ducked into the prison. Inside it was pitch black. It smelled terrible—filthy gas station bathroom blended with rank slaughterhouse. I heard Mom just outside the door, still arguing that we should return to the farm immediately.

Dad followed me into the prison, shake light in hand. He switched on the beam. And I ducked my head, fighting back vomit. Two corpses were sprawled inside the door. A dozen or more bullets had punctured their chests, and their blood had leaked in such prodigious quantity that it nearly covered the entry hall. I was standing in it.

I heard retching noises and looked back to see Alyssa vomiting in the corner. Ben was staring at the corpses, "These are 5.56 millimeter impact wounds," he said, "from an AR-15 rifle. The U.S. military designation is M16. Sloppy groupings—they should do much better at short range."

"Whatever," I said. "Where's the infirmary? Where they were keeping Darla."

Dad said, "Alex—"

"I'm going after her. Now."

"Third floor, toward the front. There is a staircase around the corner." Ben sloshed along the hallway.

"Won't it be locked down?" I asked as I hurried to catch up to Ben.

"Only the cellblocks will be locked down," Ben replied.

As we reached the staircase, Dad pushed past us both. I caught his arm and tried to pass him again, but he blocked me, stopped, and shook his head. He pointed me to the rear, but when he started up the staircase I crowded his heels. Darla might be at the top of these stairs. If I could, I'd be in the front, taking them at a run. Maybe that was why Dad had wanted me to take rear guard.

The distant boom of a shotgun echoed through the stairwell. The squelching sounds our boots made ended before we reached the third floor, but the coppery stink of blood followed us.

We emerged from the stairwell into a wide corridor. Ben led us right, and we passed through double doors set into a heavy steel gate. The flashlight's beam landed on a wide, hospital-style door. The doorplate read INMATE INFIRMARY.

Dad and I burst through the doorway side by side. An oil lamp at the far side of the room lit up rows of hospital beds. One held a large man with a wild, unkempt beard and mustache. He was asleep or unconscious, and despite the cold room, his skin gleamed with sweat.

A weathered woman in her fifties stood leaning against a Formica desk at the back. It took me less than a second to take in the entire room and focus on the single thing that really mattered: the muzzle of a rifle, pointing directly at us.

Chapter 73

The woman raised the rifle to her shoulder. I dove right and Dad dove left, seeking cover behind the beds. Mid-leap, I realized that I was leaving Ben, Alyssa, and Mom completely exposed.

The woman pivoted into a shooting stance, sighting down the barrel.

Alyssa shouted, "Elsa! Don't shoot! You owe me."

"Don't owe nobody nothing," she said.

I peeked over the top of the bed. Alyssa was striding down the aisle toward the woman. Ben and Mom had retreated into the hall outside.

"Those weren't your tears splashing on my stomach? The first time you stitched me up? And then you sent me back to them!"

"Weren't nothing I could do," Elsa replied, her voice still gruff but softer.

"Well, there is now." Alyssa was only ten feet from her.

"You stop there," Elsa ordered, gesturing with the rifle.

Alyssa stopped, her palms outstretched. "That girl they brought in here, with the wound on her shoulder. Darla. Where is she?"

"You mean Biter? Don't know nothing about no Darla."

I stood up. "Biter?"

"Yeah. Crazy girl. Had to strap her to the bed, she fought so hard. Beeyotch bit my thumb." Elsa took one hand off the rifle and waved her thumb. A crusty, dull-red scab encircled it.

"You tied Darla to a bed?" I was up and striding toward Elsa before I had time to think about it.

Elsa's hand slapped back into place on the rifle as she leveled it at my chest. "Had to gag her, too, so she wouldn't bite none of our fingers off."

"You . . . you gagged her? So help me God if she was raped. . . ." I passed Alyssa and kept walking.

"Alex . . ." Dad whispered.

I strode directly toward the gun until my chest was pressed against the barrel so hard I could feel the circle it made in my flesh. This was my fault. I should never have stood up on that overpass. Warning Earl and his guys about the ambush had been a horrible mistake. Darla had told me, over and over, that we had to look out for each other first. If I'd listened, if I hadn't screwed up, she wouldn't have been a prisoner. Wouldn't have been . . .

"Where is she?" I yelled.

"You back off or I'll pull this trigger," Elsa said. Her voice quavered, and her hands shook.

"You'd best not," Alyssa said, her voice soft and menacing.

Elsa took some of the slack off the trigger. I didn't care. I pressed my chest harder against the barrel, forcing Elsa to step back. Her legs were pushed against the desk now.

"Where's Darla!" I whipped my hand out, slapping the barrel of the rifle in an open-handed strike. It flew from Elsa's hands and clattered against the wall ten feet away. Pain flared in my hand. I didn't care. More fuel for my rage.

"Sh-she's not here." Elsa's hands were in front of her face, palms out, as if warding off an angry demon. She backed up farther, sitting on the desk now.

Out of the corner of my eye, I saw Dad pick up the rifle. I stepped forward. My thighs touched Elsa's knees. "I see that. Where. Is. She?"

"Danny had a deal with them DWBs. T-t-to get vitamin tablets and food." Elsa glanced at Alyssa. "She was part of the trade. When you all got away, Danny had to get more goods together. Had to include a girl. He sent Biter."

"Her name is Darla."

"O-kay. Darla."

I noticed my fists were balled and chambered to strike. It took a real effort of will to unclench them. "So you sent Darla to the DWBs. Where are they based?"

"When we Peckerwoods kicked them DWBs out of Anamosa, they went to Iowa City. Later we started trading with them."

"So Darla's in Iowa City?"

"Might be. I heard they trade stuff all over, though."

"Stuff?"

"Drugs, guns, girls . . ."

My fists had clenched again of their own accord. "Darla is *not* 'stuff.' No girl is."

"Ain't the same world now," Elsa whispered.

I brought my fist up. Elsa flinched. At that moment, hitting her would have brought me a vicious, unclean joy. But she wasn't worth bruising my knuckles over. She shrank into the corner near her unconscious patient, and I turned away.

Dad kept the rifle trained on Elsa. Ben had moved up beside him and was staring at the gun, muttering about Remington 700s, M24s, and M40s.

"See if you can find some ammo," Dad said.

"I'll look," Alyssa replied and started sifting through the desk drawers.

I heard a moan. Mom stood straight and stiff as a board in a corner of the room, clutching the rails of a bed. She looked white as snow. I stepped over to her. "You okay?"

She turned to face me, and her right hand shot out, slapping me so hard that my head rocked back and I saw colored lights. I was so shocked I almost didn't notice when she raised her left. I blocked her blow, catching her wrist and holding it. She drew her right back, and I caught that wrist, too.

"Do not *ever* do anything like that again!" she yelled. "Do you think I want to see my only son blown to bits? What were you thinking?" She pulled on her arms, trying to free her wrists.

Mom and I had fought often over the last three or four years, but verbally—she'd never struck me before. I easily held her wrists. It had never occurred to me that I was stronger than she was. "Are you done hitting me?"

"Yes." She didn't look the least bit apologetic.

I dropped her wrists. "I will do whatever it takes to find Darla. Take any risk. I don't expect you to understand."

"What I understand is that you're with me and you're alive. I want it to stay that way, Alex."

"Getting killed doesn't scare me half as much as returning to Warren and never finding out what happened to her. How would I live with myself if I abandoned Darla now? If I have to become as callous as the flensers, why would I want to survive?"

"You don't even know if Darla is still alive."

"No. But all the same, I'm going after her."

"Doug," Mom said, "talk some sense into your son."

"If it were you, Janice, I'd go," Dad replied calmly.

"That's different, and you know it," Mom said.

"Maybe not."

"We've got no food, no supplies—"

"Got extra rounds for the rifle." Alyssa lifted a box of ammo from the file cabinet she'd been searching.

"We need to get back to Warren. Rebecca's all by herself," Mom said.

"My brother and his family will keep watching over her," Dad said.

The argument was pointless. For me, there was no decision to be made. "I'm going to Iowa City."

"I'll help—if you want," Alyssa said softly. "Look for Darla, I mean."

I wasn't sure I'd heard her right. Why would Alyssa want to help me find Darla? But before I could ask her about it, Mom started up again.

"We're going back to Warren. All of us. That's final."

"I don't think Alex is going to Warren, honey," Dad said mildly.

"We could make him."

"I don't know that we could. Even if I were willing to."

Mom turned back to me. "Alex. I know you think—I know you love her, but you need to go back to Warren. With your family."

"Darla is my family."

Even by the lantern's weak light, I could see the fury reddening Mom's face, the tension in the cords on her neck. "We will *talk* about this later."

I shrugged. She could talk about it all she wanted to. I was done talking.

"That'd be fine," Dad said. "We're going to need supplies. Help me search."

We searched the room thoroughly. Under the desk, Alyssa found a whole stack of heavy canvas bags with Abilify and Bristol-Meyers Squibb logos on them. I stuffed one with medical supplies—bandages, a suture kit. I even found some antiseptic spray and a dozen aspirin.

We stuffed two bags with spare clothing we found in a closet. The men's clothing was all huge—sized to fit the still unconscious patient. The only person it would fit well was

Ben. The women's clothing was the nurse's and would fit the rest of us okay. I guessed cross-dressing beat freezing.

Mom found a lighter in a bedside table drawer. She flicked it and cracked a grim smile at the flame it produced.

Dad gave me the shake light. Then he grabbed the lantern off the desk and handed it to Alyssa. "Carry this. I want my hands free."

"I need that lamp," Elsa said.

"We need it more," Dad replied, and we left Elsa and her patient behind in the darkness.

Ben led us on a devious, twisty route through the back halls and stairs of the prison. On the main floor, we emerged into a huge, industrial kitchen.

Dad made a beeline for the walk-in freezer. I hung back, having some idea about what he might find. Dad cracked the heavy metal door while Alyssa held out the lantern. He turned back around almost immediately.

"Don't go in there," Dad said grimly. "There's nothing we can eat. Nothing you want to see."

It occurred to me then that Alyssa had been held captive here for months. What had the Peckerwoods fed her? I started to ask and then thought better of it. If I'd been forced to take up cannibalism, I wouldn't want to talk about it.

In one of the steel cabinets we found the motherlode: eight one-gallon Ziploc bags packed with coarsely ground cornmeal. We stashed them all, along with a frying pan and a pot we found hanging above the stove. We discovered three one-gallon jugs that would work to store water, once we'd melted some snow. A drawer next to the prep sink was full of butcher knives. We took one each. The knives were big and awkward—not made for fighting—but they might come in handy for chopping wood or something.

Next, Dad asked Ben to show us the way to the armory. We'd need something better than one rifle and an assortment of butcher knives to survive on the road. As he rounded the corner leading to the barracks and armory, Dad suddenly backed up, shuffling backward so fast he almost knocked Ben down. A loud pop-pop-pop echoed along the corridor.

Chapter 74

Shards of concrete flew off the corner. Dad had barely gotten clear in time.

"Peckerwoods?" I hissed.

"Black Lake," Dad replied.

"Quit shooting! We're the good guys," I hollered.

"Back up!" Dad ordered. "Now!"

We ran back down the corridor, Dad shuffling backward and pointing the rifle behind us. Maybe the gunfire had been a mistake, but none of us wanted to go back and find out.

We made our way out of the prison. The black night had been replaced by a greasy yellow light. A cluster of Black Lake mercenaries conferred by one of their trucks, but they paid no attention to us.

"Going to be a long walk to wherever we're going," Dad said.

"There's a vehicle depot at the back," I said. "We can try to liberate a truck."

"Gas?"

"Yeah, gas, too."

I led the way around to the back of the prison. The place was huge—just walking around it seemed like a half-mile hike.

Black Lake had beaten us to the vehicle depot. Three mercenaries were guarding it, and they flatly refused to let us "borrow" a truck or any gas. At least they didn't shoot at us.

"Maybe we can find a car in town?" I suggested.

"Any vehicle that was run during the ashfall will be damaged," Ben said.

"We might get lucky. Find one that was garaged. Or overhauled afterward."

Dad shrugged.

I noticed something weird as we kept walking: Although the snow and ash had buried most of each car we passed, all of them had a clear spot over their gas caps. It didn't matter whether the gas cap was on the left or right side of the car or which way the car was facing.

I stopped by one of the cars and pried open the gas hatch. The plastic cap unscrewed easily, and no air hissed out. I smelled only a faint odor of gas.

"Someone take the gas out of all these cars?" I asked.

"Looks that way," Dad said. "Why else would they just dig out the gas caps?"

"How would they do that?"

"A siphon would work," Ben said, "or a portable pump."

"We're not going to be able to find gas anywhere, are we?" I said.

"If the Peckerwoods drained all the cars, surely they hit the gas stations, too," Dad replied.

I nodded morosely.

It took only another five minutes to reach Anamosa's small downtown. Main Street was plowed. Towering piles of snow and ash lined both sides of the street, making the road a white-and-gray canyon. A few two-story buildings peeked above the snow, their brown bricks streaked with ash and ice. The five of us looked like refugees from a bombed out Bristol-Myers Squibb convention as we lugged our packed Abilify bags awkwardly on our shoulders.

A deeper brown caught my attention to the right. A UPS truck had hit the front of Anamosa Floral, shattering the plate-glass window. Someone had dug a narrow path in the snow pile to reach the open passenger-side door. A hillock of snow blocked the back of the truck, although one section had been dug away to reveal the deep blue gas cap of a very small car.

"What's that symbol?" Alyssa asked, pointing to a diamond-shaped red sticker on the truck that read LNG.

"Must be one of those new natural-gas-fueled trucks UPS has been testing. Lower emissions," Dad said.

"So the UPS truck crashed, and then that little blue car blocked it in?" I asked.

Dad shrugged. "Let's check it out."

I took the precious shake light out of my pocket. The path that had been dug to the truck was so narrow and its sides so high that it felt like a cave. Dad followed me in, but Mom, Ben, and Alyssa stayed in the street.

The inside of the truck looked as though a storm had swept through it. Scraps of cardboard and empty boxes were scattered everywhere, covered in an uneven layer of packing peanuts and bubble wrap. The keys were in the ignition, but the fuel gauge read empty. Which figured. We'd have better luck finding a scrap of paper in a blizzard than a working car in Anamosa.

"Check this out," Dad said, pointing at a row of four metal tanks strapped to one interior sidepanel. They were squat propane cylinders, like barbeque grills use. The tanks were linked with hoses, but the last hose in the row was disconnected, maybe knocked loose when looters rampaged through the truck. Dad grabbed the hose, slid the quick-connect sleeve back, and reattached it to the tank.

"Is propane the same thing as natural gas?" I asked.

"No," Dad said. "And they wouldn't put the tanks inside the truck, anyway. Somebody has converted this one."

"You think it'll run?" I asked.

"One way to find out." He sat in the driver's seat and turned the key.

The first time, the truck made a rusty cough and died. The second, it chugged for a moment, and I breathed a prayer, "You can do it, truck. Start . . . start." Darla would have laughed and informed me that machines run on gears and solvents, not hopes and prayers. But I knew nothing about natural gas-powered trucks; all I could offer was hope and a prayer.

The third time Dad cranked the key, the truck choked to life. The fuel gauge twitched, moving to just above empty. Dad shut down the truck right away—we couldn't go anywhere blocked in by the small blue car and snow. We trudged back down the narrow path and explained the situation to Mom, Alyssa, and Ben.

"Is it even worth digging out the truck?" Mom asked, "since we barely have any fuel, anyway?"

"I saw a propane distributor just south of Anamosa," I said. "They had tanks painted like ears of corn. Maybe there's still propane there."

"Good idea." Dad nodded, ruminating.

We spent the rest of the day digging out the truck. We scavenged some shelves from Anamosa Floral that we used as makeshift snow shovels and scrapers. A mountain of snow crowned the truck, entombing it completely. And we had to clear the snow from around the blue car—which turned out to be a VW Bug—not to mention figuring out some way to move it.

By nightfall, everyone was exhausted and cranky. We all had at least one nasty blister, and Ben had cut his hand on the sharp edge of one of the shelves. But the vehicles were clear of snow and ash. We built a small fire using cardboard from the back of the truck and wood scavenged from the flower shop's furniture. Dinner was cornmeal mush.

The temperature dropped more during dinner. We debated sleeping inside the floral shop, but if we built a fire inside, the wood floor might ignite. None of us wanted to risk a fire inside the UPS truck near those four propane tanks.

Instead we slept more or less on Main Street in the area we had cleared behind the truck. Each of us took a two-hour guard shift, feeding the fire and keeping a lookout. For once, Alyssa stayed awake during her watch. It figured that the one time she actually kept watch, the night would pass peacefully.

Chapter 75

In the morning, we had to face the problem of the VW Bug. "Maybe we could roll it," Dad said, "like L.A. rioters after a Lakers championship."

"Like what?" Alyssa asked.

"Whenever the Lakers won a basketball championship, people used to go out and roll cars over for fun."

"Destructive way to celebrate," Alyssa replied.

I bent my knees and hooked my gloved hands under the side of the car. By straightening my knees, I could rock the car, but I sure couldn't lift it by myself. "This is going to take all of us."

Everyone crowded in alongside the car. We

could only reach the front and the back, where the car was slightly longer than the back of the UPS truck.

"Three . . . two . . . one . . . lift!" I yelled.

We raised the tires a couple inches, and the car settled back to the ground.

"Harder this time. Lift with your legs," I said. "Three . . . two . . . one . . . heave!" We got the car about a foot off the ground before Ben's hands slipped and the Bug fell back.

"We can do this. Scream when you lift this time. Three . . . two . . . one . . . now!" I screamed. This time I was able to straighten my legs completely, and the car rocked past its center of balance and crashed onto its side.

We'd created about three feet of space between the car and truck. Now we had room to spread out. Each of us grabbed whatever was handy—the exhaust system, parts of the frame, or the tires. This time we rolled the car easily onto its back.

Now, though, there was nothing to grip. We couldn't generate enough force by pushing to roll the Bug again. And reaching down didn't help—we couldn't reach anything but the smooth, rounded body panels. And the car was still blocking the UPS truck.

"Everybody move down the street," Dad said. "I've got this."

As he climbed into the UPS truck, Dad yelled, "Move farther!"

We were half a block down the street when he started the truck. He revved the engine and threw the truck into reverse, crunching into the Bug. It slid easily on its roof, coasting five or six feet. Dad pulled the truck forward and backed into the Bug again. He had more space to gain speed this time, so he hit the Bug with a crash and screech of tortured metal. The car sailed across the road, spinning on its roof until it slammed into the snowbank on the opposite side and stuck.

Dad pulled out onto Main Street. "Hurry up, there's no fuel to waste!"

We sprinted to the truck and piled in. I took shotgun—maybe I should have offered the passenger seat to Mom or Alyssa, but I knew where the propane distributor was. I needed to be able to see and talk to Dad. Everyone else sat on the floor in back amid the remaining wrecked boxes.

The propane distributor was even closer than I remembered—just past the abandoned strip mall and collapsed fast food restaurants south of Anamosa on Highway 1. It was comprised of a low cinderblock building labeled TRI-COUNTY PROPANE, one tank about the size of a semitrailer, and a dozen smaller tanks, each fifteen or sixteen feet long and raised about four feet off the ground, so their bases were at the level of the snow around them. All the tanks were painted to mimic ears of corn—green leaves on one end peeled back partially to reveal yellow kernels on the other. Each tank sported a cap of deep snow. There was also a long row of lumps in the snow, probably marking smaller, buried tanks.

Dad stopped and cut the engine. "How in the world are we going to load one of those tanks onto this truck?"

"Dig out one of the smaller tanks and drag it out here?" I suggested.

"Yeah, maybe."

We struggled over the high snow berm. Flailing through chest-deep snow to reach the row of mounds was a huge chore, even though we had less than one hundred feet to cross. We dug through a mound, finding that there was indeed a smaller propane tank—an oval six or seven feet long—buried under all that snow. But the gauge on top of the tank read empty.

Mom and Dad started working on the next tank in the line, while Alyssa and I skipped down the row about twenty feet to work on a different tank. Working with our hands and arms, it seemed to take forever just to dig enough snow to read the gauges. Both tanks were empty.

In the meantime, Ben had wandered over to the big tanks. Their gauges were bottom-mounted and easier to clear. He'd checked half a dozen tanks in the time it took the four of us to check two.

"Any luck, Ben?" I yelled.

He stopped and looked down for a moment, as though thinking. "Yes," he yelled. "I am alive. I am free of the Peckerwoods and free of the Black Lake camp. That is very lucky."

"I guess. But I wanted to know if any of those tanks have propane in them."

"You did not ask that," Ben said.

Gah. What would it take to get a simple, straight answer? "So do they?" Ben looked again at his feet, and I realized what my mistake was. "Do any of the large tanks have propane?"

"I have only inspected six of them," Ben said. "The one on the end is full, and the rest are empty."

Dad looked up from digging in the snow. "Maybe we could clear a path and back the truck up to it. Run a hose or something to fill the tanks on the truck?"

"If we're going to do all that work," I said, "let's load the whole tank onto the truck."

"That thing's got to weigh a couple tons."

"So? I'm sure UPS builds these trucks to handle a lot of weight. And it looks like it'll fit."

Dad stood and eyed the tank speculatively. "How the heck would we load it on there?"

"It's at about the right height." I started pushing through the snow toward it. "If we back up the truck to it so that the end of the tank is already inside, maybe we can slide it the rest of the way on."

"Might work. I wonder what's holding up the tank?"

"One way to find out," I said as we both reached it. I started clearing the snow from its base.

The tank rested in a metal cradle. A crank on one side of the cradle would disengage a set of clamps that locked the tank in place, but the crank was padlocked to a flange on the side of the tank.

"Let's break the padlock," I said.

"I bet the key is in there." Alyssa gestured at the cinderblock office.

We went to check out the office. Two sides were solid cinderblock walls. The front and left side each had two glass-block windows. The only door—a heavy metal thing—was locked. I tried kicking it, using a simple front kick. I thrust my hips forward for extra power and landed my kick right alongside the knob, hoping to break the

lock. But the door barely shivered. I tried kicking it twice
more before I gave up.

"You need a battering ram," Ben said. "A Stinger has
the advantage of a one- or two-man operation and can
breach doors or masonry walls—but a tree trunk would
work almost as well."

That made sense. A narrow stand of trees remained
between two nearby fields. The ash and snow had stripped
them of their leaves and broken their branches, so they
looked like parallel cracks in the yellow-gray sky.

It took all morning to fight through the deep snow
and fell a tree with our butcher knives. We chose a pine
with a trunk five or six inches in diameter so we could
carry it without too much trouble. We left a dozen branches on the trunk, cut to about two feet each so they'd make
good handles.

By the time we got back to the building carrying our
tree, I was ready for lunch. Not looking forward to it
exactly—all we had to eat was cornmeal mush. But Ben
was so excited to try the battering ram that he harassed
the rest of us until we agreed to delay lunch.

We lined up in front of the door, each of us holding
one of the remaining branches. The rough bark bit into
my hands through my gloves, aggravating my blisters.
Our first swing was tentative but still made a solid thump
and dented the metal door. We swung the ram harder the
next time, and it hit with a resounding crash and left a
huge dent in the door. We swung it again and again, each
strike harder and louder than the previous one. The door

deformed, but the jamb didn't break. Finally, after a dozen or more hits, we bent the door so much that the deadbolt slipped out of the jamb and the door flew open.

Inside we found a small, utilitarian office with a metal desk and chairs. One wall was covered in pegboard. A dozen crescent wrenches hung from hooks. A set of keys hung beside the wrenches. Elsewhere there were bins holding a wide variety of brass hose fittings. In a back room that mostly held janitorial supplies, I found a snow shovel and a spade with a yellow fiberglass handle. The toilet in the tiny bathroom was cracked—all the water had frozen. In the medicine cabinet above the toilet, Dad struck gold: a bottle of Tylenol.

The office had a cement slab floor, so we chopped up our battering ram and built a fire right in the middle of the front office. It became a little smoky, but we got enough fresh air through the open door that it was tolerable. Not that we had a choice about leaving the door open—it had deformed so much that it wouldn't close.

After lunch, I took the keys outside and quickly found one that fit the padlock. But the lever that clamped the tank to its base still wouldn't turn. I tried banging on it with a wrench, kicking it, hanging off it awkwardly with my feet off the ground—nothing worked.

I slumped into the snow, defeated. Everyone else tried to move the lever, and each of them got the same results as I had: bupkis. If Darla were here, she would know exactly how to free up the lever. But we needed to free it to get fuel to go find Darla. I noticed that my fists were clenched, and I was grinding my teeth, so I tried to force myself to relax.

"The nut's frozen," Dad announced.

"You think?" I said.

"Yep," he replied. "You know how I'm going to unfreeze it?"

"No clue."

"I'm going to light a fire under that propane tank."

He wasn't kidding.

Chapter 76

"Are you insane?" I asked. "That would be like lighting a fire under a bomb!"

"Lighting a fire under a bomb usually will not detonate it," Ben said. "It depends on the intensity of the fire, the type of bomb, the age of the bomb, and its repair status. For example—"

"See, it'll work," Dad said. "The tank's in good repair. I don't smell propane around it. I'll build a fire just big enough to unfreeze the nut. It won't heat the propane enough for it to blow."

"Maybe." I still thought he was nuts. But on the other hand, I'd built a fire inside an SUV last year when we were escaping Iowa. Darla told me its gas tank wouldn't explode, and it hadn't. Would a propane tank work the same way as an SUV's gas tank?

"Everyone else go into the office," Dad ordered.

"If you're so confident it'll work, why are you sending us inside?"

"It'll work. But if I'm wrong, that office is built like a bunker."

"You sure about this, Doug?" Mom asked.

"Yeah." He kissed her. "Go on."

We all retreated to the cement-block office. Dad scooped some coals onto a log and grabbed a handful of kindling. Nobody else did anything. We stared at each other, dreading and half-expecting an explosion.

I leaned out the door to watch Dad work. He was silhouetted by the blaze he'd built under the propane tank. The idea seemed even dumber now as flames licked the underside of the tank, blackening it.

I felt a hand on my side. Looking over my shoulder, I saw Mom had joined me at the doorway. "Your Dad wouldn't want you out here," she said.

"I know. You either," I replied, but neither of us made any move to leave.

Dad took off his left glove and wadded it up in his right hand. He reached almost into the fire, grabbing the lever through the double layer of insulation. He turned it easily; I heard the clank of the catch releasing. Dad yelled "Yes!" and kicked his boot through the fire, scattering the burning sticks into the snow.

"Told you," he said as he passed us, returning to the office.

Mom and I ignored him.

We spent the rest of the afternoon digging a path from the truck to the tank. The only tools we had were the spade, snow shovel, and three sticks left over from our battering ram. The mountain of hard-packed snow and ice alongside the highway yielded slowly to our assault. Around midafternoon, the snow shovel broke. After that, working on our knees, we used the blade to scrape or push the snow.

The only tool left that worked well was the spade. Its sharp blade would cut into the packed snow, and the fiberglass handle was apparently unbreakable. Soon we settled into a rhythm—one person would always be on break, watching the road. When the person on the spade slowed, the rested person would take over. Everyone else used their hands to dig.

The highway was deserted all day. It made sense, I guessed—with the Peckerwoods wiped out, they wouldn't be using the road. And any Black Lake employees going back to their camp would head east toward Maquoketa, not south toward us.

By nightfall we'd cleared a hole in the snow berm barely large enough to pull the truck off the road. We still had almost one hundred feet of deep snow between the truck and tank.

We slept around the fire in the smoky office. Despite the draft from the open door, it was easily the warmest place I'd slept since I'd left Worthington.

It took us the entirety of the next day to excavate a path large enough for the truck. It was mind-numbing work that left me far too much time to imagine what Darla might be going through while we dug in the snow. By the time we had the truck backed up so that the open rear doors engulfed the end of the tank, the dim yellowish daytime light was being replaced by murky twilight.

The following morning, we faced the problem of how to get the tank loaded the rest of the way onto the truck. Dad tried backing the truck under it, but it just pushed the base of the tank along. And if the base collapsed, we'd have no good way to raise the tank back up to the right level.

We needed something to multiply our strength. We needed more of Ben's levers, although I could have done without his repeat disquisition on the role of the lever in military history. We cut three small trees and jammed them under the back end of the tank so we could slide it forward by pushing up on them. That was the theory, anyway. What actually happened was that one of the trees broke, and we didn't shift the tank one iota.

"Use these trees as a brace, maybe?" Alyssa asked.

"What do you mean?" I said.

"Brace the back end of the tank so it can't slide. Then back up the truck. The base will slide back, and the tank should be forced into the truck."

Her solution worked beautifully. In less than twenty minutes, we had a UPS truck-cum-propane tank setup that looked like the Jolly Green Giant had knocked over his brown lunch box, leaving an ear of corn sticking out the top.

It took an hour of fiddling with hoses and fittings to get the big propane tank connected to the smaller tanks inside the truck. When Dad cranked the truck, it started right up—and the fuel gauge shot to full.

"Now we're in business!" Dad yelled, a huge smile splitting his face. Alyssa, Dad, and I shared high fives. Ben did not like arbitrary touching, and Mom wasn't even smiling.

"What?" I asked her.

"Now that we've got a working vehicle and plenty of fuel, we should go straight to Warren," Mom said.

"We discussed this last night, Janice," Dad replied, his smile disappearing.

"I'm going with Alex," Alyssa said.

"Even if we did go to Iowa City and this Darla *is* alive, how are we going to find her?" Mom asked.

"Um," Alyssa said in a tremulous voice, "I have an idea."

Chapter 77

Dad and Ben thought Alyssa's idea was genius. I tried to talk her out of it, and Mom still wanted to return to Warren where Rebecca was. Ultimately I relented to Alyssa. I was outvoted, anyway.

We needed a button or switch—preferably something dangerous looking. Dad thought maybe the biggest propane tank would have some kind of control system, and sure enough, we found one buried in a hump of snow at one end of the tank. Under a label that read EMERGENCY SHUTOFF, there was a red thumb-sized button protected by a clear plastic cover. I hacked it out of the plastic control board with a butcher knife. It looked pretty crude with all the jagged, broken plastic hanging off it, but that would add to its menace—I hoped. I reached into the guts of the wrecked control panel and ripped out a pair of long wires, one black and one green. Perfect.

Dad made Alyssa practice her part over and over. He tied her hands behind her back with twine—we'd found a whole roll of the stuff in the UPS truck. Then he stuck a paring knife in her back pocket and made her cut herself free.

On her second practice run, she cut herself pretty badly, a deep slice in the web of her thumb. Alyssa let out a stream of curses while I worked on bandaging her hand. When we'd both finished, Dad said, "Again, preferably without the self-mutilation this time."

I saw Alyssa's throat work as she swallowed some retort. Instead she stood and turned, offering her hands to be tied. She was just as tough as Darla in her own way. She'd proposed this crazy plan, and now she meant to see it through, even if it cost her some pride and flesh.

• • •

By lunchtime, we were forty miles away, and I was wishing Alyssa hadn't been so steely. I was trying to shimmy up a downspout at the corner of the Bowman Chiropractic Clinic. It's not that I was having a hard time climbing the thing—I'm plenty strong. But a climb that looks easy from the ground doesn't feel easy when you're trying to reach up from the top of a downspout to get a grip on the gutter at the edge of a roof. In gloves. With a badly bruised right arm.

I had tried to talk Alyssa out of it again during the drive to Iowa City. Mom took shotgun this time, and Ben was behind Dad explaining the Great Turkish War in exhausting detail. Alyssa and I sat next to each other on the propane tank in the back of the truck. She started the conversation by whispering, "Alex, I need a favor."

"Sure. Anything," I said.

"If this . . . this thing goes badly—"

"You don't have to do it, you know."

"Yeah, I know. I want to do it. It was my idea, after all. But in case it doesn't go right, I need you to promise me something."

"What?"

"If I can't, well . . . I want you to look after Ben."

"Alyssa, you'll be okay. And Ben's a smart guy. He can look after himself."

"Just . . . make sure he gets to someplace safe. To your uncle's place in Warren, maybe. And keep an eye out for him, okay?"

I thought her request was a little ridiculous. If she got killed trying to rescue Darla, I'd almost certainly be dead, as well. But I said, "Okay."

"One other favor?"

"What?"

"You'll be up on the roof with the rifle. . . ."

"Yeah."

"Save a bullet for me."

"What!"

"If things go badly, if this doesn't work and I get captured, I want you to shoot me. I thought I'd do anything to survive, but I've gone that route before and it's not worth it. I survived for Ben. But I don't want to live that way again. I *won't* become a slave again!"

"No!" I was talking too loudly. Mom swiveled in the passenger seat to look at me. I dropped my voice. "Why would you even ask me that?" The answer came to me even as I asked the question. She was giving up. That's why she'd proposed this crazy plan and put herself in this position in the first place.

"Alex, please. I don't want to live that way again. I can't live that way again."

"There are *no* circumstances under which I would shoot you, Alyssa."

"You owe me," she hissed. "I'm risking my ass going after *your* girlfriend."

"Yeah. I do owe you. If the DWBs capture you and I'm alive, I will get you out. Or die trying."

"But—"

"But nothing."

She glared at me. "Then you don't care about me, do you?"

"And I retract my promise to look after Ben. If he needs looking after, then you're just going to have to stay alive to do it."

"You're no different than any other guy. You're all messed up!" Alyssa folded her arms and turned away from me.

I didn't know how to respond. I was trying to be nice. There was no use talking more and making things worse. Maybe she was the one who was messed up. Or maybe she was right.

I used the rest of the drive to unpack the ammo and first-aid kit we'd found in Anamosa. Even if we survived this, we might need those supplies in a hurry.

We reached the outskirts of Iowa City and almost immediately saw the glint of a campfire burning in the distance. Dad pulled the truck over, Mom got behind the wheel, and Dad, Alyssa, and I approached the fire on foot, walking in the deep snow on the far side of the berm.

When we got closer, we peeked over the embankment. A sentry was camped right atop the Highway 1 overpass over I-80, which sliced through the north side of Iowa City. He had a tent pitched near his campfire and a motorcycle next to it. It was a good spot: He'd be able to see anyone approaching from I-80 or Highway 1. But the campfire made him too obvious. I wasn't complaining, though—the fact that we'd seen him first made this whole crazy idea possible. My role in the plan was to shimmy up onto the roof of the chiropractic clinic and get a drop on him.

I pulled myself up with a gasp of relief, flopping in the deep snow. The roof was sloped so that I would be invisible from the far side until I reached the peak.

Pushing through the snow was hard. I worked my way up to the ridge on my stomach so that only my head and the barrel of the rifle I carried were visible. The sentry was still there, sitting atop the overpass, silhouetted by his fire. I'm not very good with a rifle, but even I could probably hit him. That wasn't our plan, though. We needed this guy alive.

We weren't even certain he was a member of the Dirty White Boys. But to survive this close to their base, he had to have some connection with them—a connection we planned to exploit.

I looked backward at Dad and Alyssa waiting below. I gave Dad a thumbs up and turned back toward the sentry. I still thought I should be the one down there with Alyssa. I'd argued with Dad about it to no avail.

I knelt and rested the rifle on the ridge, drawing a bead on the sentry. Out of the corner of my eye I saw Dad and Alyssa walk slowly into view. Dad had his hands up in a gesture of surrender. Alyssa's hands were bound behind her back, she was gagged with a strip of cloth, and a piece of shipping twine led like a leash from her neck to Dad's hand.

The sight made me queasy. I knew she had a paring knife in her back pocket. I knew the noose was tied loosely enough that she could duck out of it and the gag would slip over the top of her head once her hands were free. I didn't want to believe this was the world I lived in now— one where it wasn't shocking to see a girl treated like livestock. Before the volcano, Alyssa's biggest concerns might have been homework, swapping snark with friends on Facebook, or completing college applications. Now she was risking her life and freedom to help Darla, a girl she'd never met. Or maybe to help me. Either way, I didn't feel good about it.

It took a while for the sentry to notice Dad and Alyssa. He snatched a rifle from the ground and turned. I struggled to keep the rifle sighted on him as he moved. I kept moving the barrel too fast, getting the sighting U misaligned with the rifle's post and then overcorrecting.

The sentry stopped, aiming his rifle at Dad. I got the Remington lined up again—the U-shaped front sight, rear post, and the center of the sentry's body formed a neat line starting at my right eye. I was ready.

"Who are you?" the sentry yelled. Even from my post above him, I could hear the sneer in his voice.

"Just here to trade," Dad yelled back.

"Trade what?"

"Her." Dad yanked on the cord around Alyssa's neck, making her stumble.

A grin spread across the sentry's face, reminding me of a hyena looking up from his kill. He lowered his eye to the rifle, preparing to shoot my father and take the spoils for free.

"You shoot and you're dead." Incredibly, Dad was smiling, too.

"You're at the wrong end of my gun, bud," the sentry said.

"And you're at the wrong end of my son's." Dad gestured up at me, on the rooftop to his left.

The sentry swiveled, pointing his rifle my way.

I waved. Most of my head and shoulders were protected by the ridgeline. Unless he was exceptionally good with that rifle, I didn't think he could hit me.

"Boy can hit a squirrel in the eye at 300 yards!" Dad yelled, which was a total lie. "Lower your gun. We just want to trade."

"Why would I want to trade with you?" He lowered his gun slightly, but I couldn't relax.

"You're a Dirty White Boy, right?"

The guy pulled up his shirts. DWB was tattooed in ornate letters across his chest, arching over an outline of Illinois. "To the death."

"Heard you guys were pimping the hottest girls in Iowa."

"Yeah, not hags like that one you brought."

He was talking about Alyssa? Was he blind?

Dad unzipped her jacket and lifted her shirts, revealing a white bra that had been worn and washed so much it was starting to turn gray. He hooked his finger beneath the underwire and roughly lifted it, exposing one breast to the icy air.

I started to look away, realized I was putting us all in danger, and forced myself to look at the sentry again. I wanted to shoot the sentry to put an end to this farce. Even though Alyssa had hatched this lunatic plan herself, it was my fault she was in this position. I swallowed hard, struggling to concentrate.

Dad squeezed Alyssa's breast. "This isn't some hag. This is primo ass. Young and fresh."

Why did Dad have to be so damn crass? I was seized by an irrational desire to shoot *him*. But it was working. The sentry was chuckling. "Yeah. I'd hit that. But I can't negotiate. We gotta go see Wolfe."

"I'll give you a ride," Dad said. "We'll show up in style." He turned and waved his arms over his head, signaling to Mom to drive the truck up. She was watching with Ben from a spot about a mile down the road.

"I can't leave my sled." The sentry safetied his rifle and slung it over his shoulder. He walked up to Dad and Alyssa, and their conversation dropped in volume so that I couldn't make out what they were saying.

They shook hands. Then the sentry reached toward Alyssa's still-exposed breast. Dad slapped his hand away. They exchanged a few more words I couldn't make out as Dad pulled Alyssa's bra and shirts back into place and zipped her coat. I slid down the front side of the roof, trying to hold my rifle ready and keep one eye on the guard.

By the time I got down, Mom and Ben had pulled up in the UPS truck. The sentry was telling a string of crude jokes to Dad, who laughed and replied with a few of his own.

Dad introduced the sentry as Chad, talking like he was an old friend. Chad told us to follow him and started his motorcycle. Dad pushed Alyssa into the back of the truck with me, then walked around the front to the driver's side. Mom scooted over into the passenger seat.

I mouthed, "You okay?" at Alyssa.

She responded with the barest hint of a nod.

Chad led us through Iowa City on a winding series of plowed roads. We reached a rundown section of town full of auto repair shops and industrial sites. Suddenly the road ahead narrowed to one lane, partially blocked by snow and ash that had been bulldozed to form a huge wall. Two guys warmed themselves at a small fire just inside the wall. Chad pulled up next to them, his bike blocking the lane. He held out his palm, motioning for us to stop.

The two guys got up from the fire and turned toward our truck. They each wore an assault rifle slung over one shoulder. Dad cranked the truck through the fastest three-point turn I'd ever experienced, leaving it facing back the way we'd come.

One of the DWB guards left, jogging toward a nearby building. The other one was talking to Chad near the fire.

Dad turned around in his seat to offer Alyssa a hand climbing out of the truck. The gentlemanly gesture was completely spoiled when he grabbed the end of her noose with his other hand. He took a couple of steps from the truck and then stopped, one hand holding Alyssa's leash, the other jammed into his coat pocket.

I slid out of the passenger side and took a position alongside the truck. If things turned bad, I could take cover behind it. Or jump in the back if we had to make a quick getaway. I unslung the rifle from my back, making sure not to aim it at the DWBs. I snicked off the safety and held the rifle casually, pointed at the ground at my side.

Everything was still for a moment. Like that moment right before breaking a board, when you're totally focused and the world is calm around you. Preparing. Waiting for the violence of the break.

Four guys emerged from the building. The guy in the center had a huge chrome revolver on each hip. The others were armed with assault rifles. But the power resided in the guy with the revolvers; it was clear in the way every-one else circled around him, like planets turning in the warmth of their sun.

Six guys. Against me and my rifle. If this ended in a spray of bullets, none of us would survive. I wiped my damp trigger hand on my coveralls and swallowed my fear.

Chad yelled, "Heeeere's Wolfey!" in a demented, Jack Nicholson voice.

Someone else said, "That's Mr. Wolfe to you," and they all laughed.

Wolfe, the guy with the revolvers, strutted up to Alyssa. His gaze oozed down her body, lingering here and there. "Looks fresh." He grabbed a lock of her hair and yanked on it, pulling her close. He sniffed. "Smells fresh, too."

"There's another one in the truck," Chad said.

"Fresh?" Wolfe replied.

"No. But hey, if it was dark . . ."

They laughed. Dad's face had taken on a stony countenance. I adjusted my grip on the rifle. This didn't look good, but we were prepared for it. I hoped.

"You brought me two new back warmers? You're too kind."

Dad said, "I'm only trading—"

"And a truck? You shouldn't have."

"The truck's not—"

"Bring the chicks up to the club," Wolfe said. "Flense the rest." He turned his back to Dad as the other five DWBs raised their guns.

"You'd best not," Dad said quietly, withdrawing his hand from his pocket. I didn't think anyone else noticed that his voice wasn't as steady as usual. He held the red button from the propane distributor. His thumb was under the plastic cover. The two wires ran from the back of the button into his coat pocket. "I press this button, and the propane tank blows. Just like a bomb. Probably level three city blocks."

Wolfe turned around and stepped toward Dad. "Yeah?"

"That's right." Dad's hands were shaking.

"Bullshit!" Wolfe's hand whipped out, grabbing the two wires and pulling them free.

Chapter 79

"Waste him," Wolfe ordered.

"This isn't some game!" Mom screamed as she slid off the side of the propane tank and stood on the back bumper of the truck. She had an air hose in one hand and a burning torch made of rolled cardboard in the other. She was holding the valve open on the end of the air hose. "If I bring these together, we're all going to meet our maker. I'm ready to be judged, how about you?"

Mom let the valve snap shut, moved the hose out of the way, and thrust her torch into the space the hose had just occupied. There was a huge whoosh and a flash that left blue spots on my vision. "I'll blow us all to hell before I let you flense my family!" she yelled.

Wolfe was laughing. "Righteous! Do it again!"

"Screw you!" Mom spat.

"Maybe later." Wolfe turned to Dad. "I like that one. You want to sell her, too?"

"N-no." Dad's face was ashen.

"Woman like that, 'course you want to keep her." Wolfe stepped up beside Dad and laid a paw like a side of meat across his shoulder. "Y'all have balls. Maybe we can work together."

"Good," Dad said, visibly pulling himself together. "Let me show you around."

Dad gestured to me with the hand holding Alyssa's leash. "Give this to your mother and come with me."

As I did, Mom yelled, "If my men don't come back, I'll level this place."

Wolfe smiled up at her. "I believe you would." Then to Dad he said, "That woman's worth any three of mine."

"Like I said, she's not for sale."

"I know, I know." Wolfe led us into the walled area. To our left there was a brick building: GEOFF'S BIKE AND SKI. On our right stood a large metal shed marked SOUTH SIDE IMPORT AUTO SERVICES. About a hundred yards ahead there was a large, four-story brick building that appeared to have abandoned shops on the main floor and apartments above.

Chad and two of the guards returned to the fire. The remaining two guards came with us. One of them was built like a concrete mixer. The other was short and fat—totally different than the rest of the DWBs.

As we walked, Wolfe said, "So what are you looking to trade for? I got everything. Primo weapons and ammo out of D.C. Drugs out of the strategic reserve in St. Louis. Food out of Texas and Mexico. Got a truckload of flour and watermelon last week. Watermelon! Can you believe that shit? DWBs eat like kings!"

"I want another 30-30 hunting rifle," Dad said. "A thousand rounds of ammo. A hundred doses each of anti-biotic and acetaminophen. A gallon of hospital-grade antiseptic—"

"Whoa, whoa, she's a nice piece, but you're talking crazy—"

"And a party for me and my boy. Heard you got the best cathouse in Iowa."

"That I can do." Wolfe gestured at the four-story building ahead of us. "But that other stuff—"

"It'll be worth it. This girl is just a first taste. You don't want me dealing with your competition."

"What competition?"

"The Peckerwoods?" I said. "Black Lake?"

"Black Lake's a supplier—they're your competitor, not mine."

"I thought it was the Peckerwoods taking girls out of Maquoketa?" I asked as innocently as I could manage.

"Maquoketa's not the only camp Black Lake runs. And we ended the effin' Peckerwoods. You want to deal flesh in southeast Iowa, you're dealing with me."

"You ended . . .? Black Lake attacked Anamosa, not you. I was there."

"Nothing happens in southeast Iowa that I don't

approve. And that's all I'm going to say on the subject."

"Ask yourself who benefited," Dad said to me.

Wolfe grinned and said, "That's right."

We'd passed the bike and ski shop—it was closed up tight. Now we were walking past the auto shop. The big overhead door was wide open. A fire burned inside, throwing flickering orange light around a jumble of vehicles in various states of disassembly.

A girl was bent over, working on a pickup. She looked like—she couldn't be—I'd been wrong before . . . Darla.

Chapter 80

I had to know for sure. There was a bike just inside the garage doors, parts laid out around it on a tarp. "Is that a Harley?" I said as I peeled off from the group, walking toward the garage doors.

The girl looked up, her face illuminated first by the orange firelight, then by a flash of recognition and burst of emotion quickly suppressed. Darla. I'd found her. I had to fight down an urge to dash into her arms, to fall to my knees, to shout in pure joy.

"That's a Triumph," Wolfe said, trailing behind me. "Your boy don't know shit about sleds, do he?"

Dad spat on the ground. "Failed in my education of him, I guess."

The five of us were gathered around the motorcycle while I pretended to inspect it. Out of the corner of my eye I watched Darla. She moved over to a big tool cabinet. A chain clinked, dragging from her ankle. She pulled open the bottom drawer.

I moved around to the other side of the bike. "A Triumph? That's, like, way more rare than a Harley, right?"

The three DWBs looked at me like I was an idiot. But it worked—all of them were staring at me. Darla extracted a small, twisted piece of metal and a huge screwdriver from the tool cabinet. The tip of the screwdriver glinted in the firelight—it had been filed to a vicious point.

Dad glanced nervously from Wolfe to me and back again.

"He got that downer syndrome?" Wolfe asked.

"Can we buy it?" I said.

"No," Dad snapped. "Jesus, what's gotten into you, Alex?"

"Need to knock him around a bit. I could have Bull do it if you want to make a lasting impression." Wolfe gestured at the big guy and chuckled, a noise that made my skin crawl.

"He needs knocking around, I'll do it myself," Dad said. "But maybe the party will straighten him up. Everything ready for us?"

"It will be," Wolfe replied. "Slim, go make sure them whores are awake."

The pudgy guy trotted out of the garage, leaving Dad, Darla, and me with Wolfe and the big guy, Bull.

Darla reached down with the small piece of metal and did something to the cuff around her ankle. Her chain fell away.

"What's wrong with the Triumph? Can you fix it?" I asked, hoping to keep their attention away from Darla.

"No," Wolfe said, "we took it apart so we could bedazzle all the parts and hang them on the wall."

Darla stalked toward his back, her shank raised above her head in a two-handed grip. She was thinner, her face more angular, cut by tortured shadows. She was getting close—I had to keep Wolfe's attention on me.

I looked him in the eye and tried to control the trembling in my arms. "Figures that Dirty White Boys would use a Bedazzler. You're probably all too stupid to operate a needle and thread."

Wolfe roared and pulled one of the guns from his belt. He raised it over his shoulder, like he was preparing to pistol-whip me.

Darla plunged the shank into the back of his neck. The tip emerged from his throat, glistening red. She wrenched out the screwdriver, and blood fountained from Wolfe's neck as he collapsed.

Bull pulled up his gun. I kicked with my right foot—an inner crescent that caught his wrist and sent the gun flying against the wall with a clatter. I let the momentum of my kick carry me into a spinning left reverse kick. My foot slammed into Bull's groin hard enough to lift the huge man off his feet and drop him into a crumpled, moaning heap on the floor.

Dad grabbed Bull's assault rifle. Darla scooped up both of Wolfe's revolvers. "You got a way out of here?" she asked, her voice as sharp as the bloody screwdriver she'd just discarded.

"Truck. Just outside the wall. Three guards between us and it."

"Three? Usually only two."

"Yep. Three." I took the rifle off my back and readied it.

Bull groaned. I heard a wet crunch behind me and glanced over my shoulder. Dad had kicked him in the face. Blood was pouring from his nose and mouth, mixing with Wolfe's on the concrete floor. The sweet, coppery stink of it filled my nostrils, flooding me with an insane joy. I wanted more, wanted all the DWBs to bleed to death.

"There's more than a hundred of them in the apartments," Darla said. "We've got to go. Fast."

The three of us approached the open door of the garage. Chad and the two guards by the fire were on their feet, looking in our direction. Chad yelled, "Everything—" Then his eyes widened, and he reached for his gun. He was staring at me. I glanced down—my boots and coverall legs were soaked with Wolfe's blood.

All six of us raised our guns.

Chapter 81

The air burst with gunfire—the crazed sewing-machine rattle of the assault rifles and the metronomic boom, boom, boom of Darla's revolver. My rifle was snug against my shoulder, my eye on the sight, but I hadn't pulled the trigger. The three DWBs were down. We'd come out expecting a fight; they were only a second or two slower, but in the new world, the postvolcano world, that was all it took. The difference between life and death was measured in seconds and inches.

"Got to go. Now . . ." Darla said. Her voice wavered, and I glanced at her, alarmed, just in time to see her crumple. I caught her as she fell, easing her to the ground while I frantically checked for blood.

I heard a rattle of gunfire from our right. Slim was standing in the doorway of the apartment building, firing an assault rifle at us. "Go!" Dad screamed. He whirled to return fire. I slung Darla's limp body over my shoulder and ran for the truck.

I leaped into the truck, laying Darla out in the space behind the passenger seat. "Come on!" I screamed as I turned back toward Dad. Slim had ducked back into apartment building. Dad's rifle clicked empty. He turned and ran toward the truck, scooping up Chad's assault rifle as he passed the corpses. Slim stepped back into view in the doorway, firing his rifle. Dad stumbled, picked himself up, and kept running. I lifted my rifle, firing until the magazine was dry. Slim took cover again.

Mom was in the driver's seat. Alyssa and Ben huddled behind the driver's seat in the scant space beside the propane tank. Dad threw himself into the passenger seat. "Go! Go! Go!"

Mom floored the accelerator, and the truck leapt forward, racing north toward Warren and safety.

I checked on Darla. She was breathing and the pulse at her neck throbbed, hot under my fingers. I started stripping off her filthy coat, trying to figure out what was wrong. Had she been hit?

Dad groaned. My mind replayed the stumble he'd taken over and over, worrying at it.

"You're hurt!" Mom glanced at him, her face etched with a strange combination of fear and compassion.

"Yeah," Dad replied weakly. "But keep going. We've got to get out of here."

I looked from Darla to Dad, unsure what to do. "I'll check on him," Alyssa said, pushing past me.

Darla was wearing the same clothing she'd had on when she was shot on the overpass two weeks before. Her shirts were crusted with old blood. I tore her undershirt at the shoulder and pulled it away from the wound.

It was weeping greenish yellow pus and smelled utterly revolting. Her whole shoulder was swollen—red flames of infection licked out from the wound, reaching down her side and along her shoulder toward her neck. The reason for her collapse was obvious—what wasn't obvious was how she'd stayed on her feet, managed to stab Wolfe, and shot a revolver with a wound this badly infected. There was nothing I could do for her but give her Tylenol. We needed to get her to a doctor—and fast.

As I worked on Darla, Alyssa had stripped off Dad's coat and shirts. He was already sitting in a puddle of his own blood. It was everywhere, coating her hands in a nauseating crimson glaze. She pulled up his T-shirt, revealing the bloody hole a bullet had punched in the left side of his stomach. "Lean forward," she said.

Dad groaned as he bent away from the seat. Alyssa checked his back—low on his left side was a round, puffy entrance wound, welling blood. "I need some bandages!" she yelled.

"Janice," Dad began.

Mom didn't reply. She was staring at the blood welling from Dad's stomach. Her cheeks glistened, and she'd bitten her lower lip hard enough to draw blood.

"Watch the road!" Dad told her.

Ben had been moaning and rocking, but when Alyssa asked for bandages he stopped and looked directly at her for a second. Then he started rifling through the Abilify bags, tossing stuff everywhere as he searched for bandages. I was out of my mind with worry about Darla and Dad but still fiercely proud of Ben in that moment. He found several rolls of gauze and passed them up to Alyssa. She took the first roll and pressed the whole thing against the hole in Dad's belly. He moaned but then placed his bloody hand over hers and pushed harder. "Got to stop this bleeding," he gasped.

Darla stirred. "Cold," she moaned.

"Lieutenant!" Ben yelled. He yelled it again before I figured out he was talking to me. "We have a tactical problem." He pointed toward the open back of the truck.

Two pickups were racing on the road behind us, gaining fast.

Chapter 82

Both trucks had guns mounted on top of their cabs and a pair of guys standing in their beds. They were distant, but at the rate they were approaching, that wouldn't last. We were racing down a long, straight road lined with burned-out commercial buildings.

"Can you go any faster?" I yelled.

"It's floored!" Mom yelled back.

I heard a pop-pop-pop and the whang of a bullet ricocheting off metal as the gunner in the lead pickup started firing at us. The noise reminded me that we had a giant propane tank—aka bomb—sticking out the back of our truck.

"Tie a bandage around Dad's stomach as tight as you can," I told Alyssa.

I climbed up onto the propane tank. The first pickup was closer now, still firing steadily. Mom started weaving back and forth. The road was rough, bouncing us up and down. I didn't think the DWBs were likely to hit us until they got much closer.

I lifted my rifle, lined it up on the lead pickup, and pulled the trigger. Click. I'd forgotten I was out of bullets. "I need a gun!" I yelled. Ben grabbed the assault rifle Dad had taken from Chad and tossed it to me. As soon as I got it seated against my shoulder and roughly in line with the pickups, I pulled the trigger. And nothing. The trigger wouldn't even operate.

The safety, I'd forgotten the safety. I found it on the side of the gun and snicked it to full auto.

The gun still wouldn't fire.

"What's wrong with this piece of junk?" I yelled.

"The magazine is not seated," Ben said.

I lifted the gun and banged the base of the magazine against the propane tank. There was a dull clunk of metal on metal and a click as the magazine popped into place.

As I aimed the gun again, the tank shivered under me and rang with a series of colossal blows. A row of holes appeared across the tank. Bullets ricocheted and rattled around inside it. I caught a whiff of propane and wondered briefly why I was still alive. Why hadn't the tank exploded, instantly converting us into ash and charred meat?

"Don't shoot!" Ben screamed.

"What?"

"The muzzle flash of the AR-15 might ignite the aerated propane!"

"Stop! Now!" Dad yelled. "There!" He pointed left to a break in the embankment that allowed access to an alley. Mom slammed on the brakes, fishtailing to a stop. The trucks behind us raced closer, spraying bullets as they came. Mom dove out the driver's door, taking shelter in the alley. Alyssa followed, chivvying Ben along with her. Darla crawled out on her own, and I helped Dad out of the passenger seat to the driver's side and tried to slide him out the driver's door. He stopped and sat down.

"Come on!" I screamed. The trucks were almost on us.

Dad screwed his face up in agony, planted his left foot on my chest, and shoved. I fell backward onto the icy road. Gears ground as Dad shifted into reverse. "Goodbye," he said calmly. "Tell everyone I love them."

The truck shot backward. "Dad!" I screamed. The propane tank slammed into the lead pickup. I rolled, scrambling toward the shelter of the alley.

The explosion plucked me off the road and hurled me into the air. I flew for a few seconds before gravity caught me again and dashed me to earth. My back burned, as if I'd been stung by a thousand angry hornets. I smelled smoke, twisted, and realized my back was literally burning. I rolled on the icy road to put it out. The world around me had gone silent, and my ears had become hot knives stabbing into my brain. I touched an earlobe, and my hand came back covered with fresh blood.

Dad.

I looked back down the road. I had to squint against the inferno engulfing the conjoined wreckage of the trucks. The buildings on either side of the road had been flattened. One corner of a brick building was still standing, a rough masonry triangle that had sheltered Darla, Alyssa, Ben and Mom. Ben's hands were clasped around his ears, and he was rocking again. Otherwise they all looked dazed but unhurt.

I stumbled to my feet and staggered toward the wreck. "Dad," I breathed, releasing the word like a prayer or kiss goodbye. A secondary detonation—the pickup's gas tank, perhaps—knocked me flat again.

A few moments later, I felt hands under my arms, lifting me up. Alyssa was there, dusting the ash and grit from my singed clothing, checking me for punctures. She said something to me, and I shook my head, pointing to my ears.

Darla was still sitting against the ruined brick wall, doubled over, maybe unconscious again. Mom stood nearby, staring at my father's fiercely burning pyre. Her eyes were vacant and dry, but her mouth was twisted into an expression of such horror that I had to look away. Ben's mouth was open now—maybe he was moaning, but I couldn't hear. Anything.

I put my arm across Alyssa's shoulders for support. "Come on," I said, hobbling around the fire. Alyssa replied— I saw her lips move, but no sound reached my brain.

Alyssa and I gave the wreck a wide berth. Even so, the heat was intense. The snow berms on both sides of the road had started to melt. Water trickled off them to join the ashy pool forming around the entire mess.

About fifty feet farther on, I saw the rear-most pickup. It was slewed across the road, hood half-buried in a snowbank. It was huge for a pickup—both a king cab and a dually. On the left side of the truck, the windows had blown inward, and its body was the color of charred steak. The door was open, and the driver had slumped out. The left side of his face was a horrifying patchwork of blackened skin and blood-covered glass fragments.

A plume of steam rose from the back end of the truck. I thought about it a moment and realized that the truck was idling, although I couldn't hear the engine. Despite the pounding it had taken, the truck still worked.

I grabbed the least charred part of the driver's collar and dragged him the rest of the way out of the truck. He didn't move at all. Maybe he was dead, but I didn't care enough to spend the energy to check.

It occurred to me that there had been two guys in the bed of the truck manning the roof-mounted gun. There was no sign of them now. The truck's airbags had deployed. I shoved the deflated airbag out of the way.

By the time I finished, the driver was awake, reaching up to me with one trembling arm. The horror of the situation seized me suddenly, squeezing the air from my lungs, the life from my heart. Dad, dead. Darla, hurt. Why had the DWBs followed me? Why couldn't they have let me slip away, let me take my family back to Warren to struggle together to survive—or at least to die united?

I had no answers, just pure rage. I knelt before the bandit, pulled the butcher knife off my belt, and lifted it high over my head. Someone caught my arm from behind. I turned—Alyssa was there, shouting something at me—I saw her mouth working soundlessly. I twisted my knife hand free and brought the blade slashing down toward the driver's throat.

Alyssa caught my arm again. She put her face inches from mine and shook her head. The rage washed out of me as quickly as it had come. I again twisted free of her grasp and threw the knife. Powered by my disgust and grief, it flew clear across the snow bank on the far side of the road.

Alyssa wrapped her arms around me, and suddenly I was sobbing. I clung to her and cried until the back of her coat was wet with my tears.

The sewer stench of death brought me back to my senses. The bandit's arm was down, and the unburnt right side of his face had relaxed into a facsimile of peace.

I lifted my eyes past him. Tears still clouded my vision. All I could see was a blurry gray—the ashen smear of my father's remains upon the eternal snow.

Chapter 83

"Let's get out of here," I said. It was weird, not being able to hear myself. I could tell I was talking only by the vibrations in my mouth and nose. Alyssa nodded.

She started to turn away. I caught her arm and gestured at the truck. "You drive?" I asked.

She shook her head and said something I couldn't understand.

I sagged against her. I could barely walk, and now I'd have to drive.

Alyssa slid into the truck and I followed, stopping behind the wheel. The truck was an automatic. The keys were dangling from the ignition, and the

fuel gauge read just shy of full. I slid the gear selector into
reverse and eased my foot onto the gas. We lurched free of
the snowbank with a bounce.

I backed the truck around the body of its former
driver. The fire amid the wreck had died down to a dull,
angry glow. I cranked the wheel over and inched past,
staying as close to the berm as I could. I pulled up beside
Mom and Ben. Neither of them made any move to get in.
Darla was still curled against the ragged brick wall.

Alyssa and I got out. I ran to Darla. She was conscious
but dazed. I helped her into the front seat of the truck,
buckling her into the middle, where she'd be next to me.

I turned back toward Mom. "Can you drive?" I asked.

Her eyes were focused on a world apart from this one.
Maybe her hearing was damaged, too.

"Mom!" I shouted.

Her lips were still. She stared past the dying glow of
the wreck.

I took Mom's hand. I led her like a child into the passenger seat of the pickup and buckled the seat belt around
her. When I slipped back out of the truck, I saw Alyssa
brushing Ben, trying to coax him into motion.

"We've got to go," I told Alyssa.

She nodded at me and led Ben toward the truck. They
slid into the back seat. I put the truck in drive and headed
north, away from Iowa City and the DWB slavers, toward
Warren and the safety of Uncle Paul's farm.

The windshield was cracked so badly, it was tough to
see through it. I had to bend my body and crane my neck
to peer through a patch of clear glass.

I found a map in the glove compartment and handed it to Alyssa. Darla had passed out again, and Mom was awake but in another world. Alyssa charted a course that skirted around Anamosa and its prison. Each time we reached an intersection, she would point the right direction and yell. I still couldn't make out words, but at least I could hear that she was saying something now.

My ears started buzzing with a high-pitched whine. I took that as a good sign, even though it was incredibly annoying. I was constantly dizzy—I worried I'd accidentally drive into a snow berm. About twenty miles out of Iowa City, I got so nauseated I had to pull over and vomit on the icy road.

My eyelids were drooping. Mom, Darla, and Ben were completely zoned out. I fought to stay awake, biting my lip, slapping my face, and pinching my legs. The cold air rushing through the broken side windows helped some, but I didn't think I could keep going long enough to get us to Warren. And Darla needed help—soon.

I wanted nothing more than to stop, curl up, and cry. To mourn my father. To try to help Darla with her infection and my mother with her grief. But I had to go on. The frozen roads of Iowa were no safe place for funerals or remembrances. I pointed to Worthington on Alyssa's map. "Go there."

She nodded.

"I don't know if it'll still be there, because the Peckerwoods in Cascade were planning to attack. Hope the walls held."

Alyssa nodded and said something I couldn't hear.

By the time we reached Worthington, it was late afternoon. We approached from the west on 272nd Street.
There was no gate on this side, just a sheer ice wall towering above the road, blocking it completely.

I could make out figures running atop the wall, so I
stopped the truck well out of rifle range.

I looked over my shoulder. Mom and Ben were awake
but dazed. "I can't go talk to them," I said to Alyssa.

She shrugged.

"My ears. They're still not working. You'll have to go
do it. If they look like Peckerwoods, run. If they're farmers, tell them you're with Alex Halprin, and we've got
Darla Edmunds with us and she's hurt. Tell them I've still
got kale seeds to trade. Ask for the librarian, Rita Mae.
She'll help."

"Okay," Alyssa yelled into my ear. I was amazed I could
sort of hear her in an echoey way.

Alyssa tumbled out the rear door. She trudged toward
Worthington, her hands up and palms out. There were
nine or ten people on the wall now. I hoped they were
farmers, citizens of Worthington, but I couldn't tell from
this distance. All of them aimed guns at her.

A lump of guilt lodged in my throat. I should be the
one walking out there alone. But since I couldn't hear any
commands, I might get myself shot. And surely Alyssa
would seem to be less of a threat by herself.

There was one thing I could do: If something went
wrong, I could drive up and get her. I put my hands back
on the steering wheel, put the truck in gear, and rested my
foot on the brake. Then there was nothing to do but wait.

Alyssa stopped a few hundred feet from the wall and stood there for a long time. When she finally started back, she moved at a far brisker pace than she had on the way in. When she reached us, I couldn't contain my impatience. "Did Worthington hold out? Did you talk to Rita Mae? Will they let us in?"

With a combination of shouted words and gestures, Alyssa told me that, yes, Worthington had beaten back the Peckerwoods' attack, and they would let us in. Apparently there was a road around Worthington adjacent to the wall that we could follow to reach the town's only gate.

I inched forward under the guns of Worthington's defenders. The road along the wall turned out to be more of a track of packed snow than an actual road. Still, the four-wheel drive dually handled it with ease. The DWBs were murderous cannibals, but they sure had good taste in pickups.

At the gate we had to surrender our guns. I still had the assault rifle Dad had taken from Chad, and the gun mounted on the roof turned out to be another assault rifle. I hadn't thought to check earlier.

I pulled the truck up in front of the low metal building that housed the fire station, city hall, and library. Mayor Kenda came out to meet us before I'd even stepped from the truck.

She yelled something at me, but I couldn't make out the words. I pointed at my ears. She said something else, and Alyssa shot me a worried look.

"Is Rita Mae around?" I asked.

Mayor Kenda said something else, and Alyssa answered her.

I'd had enough of being outside the loop of this conversation. I knew Mayor Kenda meant well, but she might decide that the best thing for us would be to take our truck and keep us here in Worthington, where we'd be "safe." I strode directly to the library door and jerked it open.

Rita Mae was at her desk, reading by the light of an oil lamp. She had one hand on the shotgun propped against a bookcase, but when she saw me her face broke into a huge grin. She let go of the shotgun and darted around her desk. She hugged me surprisingly hard for such a tiny old lady, and I struggled not to collapse and pull us both off our feet.

When Rita Mae broke the embrace, she started talking to me. I could make out a word here or there, but not enough to follow what she was saying. I pointed to my ears and pantomimed an explosion.

Rita Mae got it right away. She took a stubby library pencil and a sheet of paper that looked like it was the flyleaf from a book off her desk. "I was afraid I wouldn't see you again," she wrote.

"Darla's gunshot wound is bad," I said. "We need help." I swayed on my feet and grabbed the edge of the desk for support.

"Paramedic's in the fire station," Rita Mae wrote. She tucked the paper and pencil into her pocket, grabbed my arm, and led me out of the library.

I tried to veer toward the pickup where Darla was, but Rita Mae pulled me to the pedestrian door of the fire station. Inside, the station was sparsely illuminated by a small fire smoldering on the concrete floor. A man in a worn paramedic uniform sat on a metal folding chair beside the fire. Rita Mae said something, and he sprang to his feet, rushing past us toward the pickup.

A small hole had been cut high up on a nearby wall to let out the smoke. A row of cots lay to the left of the fire. On the right, there was another room created with make-shift curtains. More metal folding chairs were scattered randomly throughout both rooms. There wasn't a fire truck in the station. When I'd been here last year, it had been stuck in the ash outside—obviously it had been moved, but not back into its garage.

The paramedic returned, carrying Darla in his arms. He ushered me into the curtained area, and Rita Mae followed us. Inside, there was a vinyl exam couch, two rolling chairs, and a stainless-steel table with cabinets under it.

The paramedic examined Darla efficiently, inspecting the wound in her shoulder and taking her temperature, blood pressure, and pulse.

"Can you treat the infection?" I asked.

The paramedic said something I couldn't make out. Rita Mae whipped out her paper and pencil and wrote out his words for me. "I'm not supposed to have to treat everything. I just stabilize them and drive them to the Mercy Medical in Dyersville. That's the way it's supposed to work."

"She needs antibiotics, right?"

"Yes. And a doctor to clean and debride that wound."

"So what do we do?" I asked.

"Nothing," the paramedic replied. His voice was so loud and anguished that I could understand it even without Rita Mae's written translation.

"Nothing?" I yelled. "At least give her some antibiotics!"

"Can't. They're rationed. Mayor Kenda keeps them locked up."

"They're—" I stepped away from the paramedic and slammed my palm into the corrugated metal wall. The pain got me thinking again.

I dug around in my jacket and pulled out the last eleven packets of kale seeds. "I want a ten-day course of antibiotics and a week's worth of food for five people." It suddenly occurred to me that kale seeds might not be as valuable now. Presumably Worthington would be growing the ones I'd traded to them right after Darla was shot. I dug deeper in my pocket, pulled out one of my carefully hoarded bags of wheat, and handed it to Rita Mae with all the kale seeds.

"I can get a lot more than that if you give me time to negotiate," Rita Mae wrote.

"I don't care. We're leaving Worthington in fifteen minutes. I'm taking Darla to Dr. McCarthy in Warren."

"You're falling down on your feet. You leave now you'll wreck your truck."

I started to yell that I didn't care but bit back my words. She had a point. Crashing on the way to Warren wouldn't get Darla the help she needed. "You're right," I said quietly. "We should get Darla started on her antibiotics, get something to eat, and sleep a few hours."

The paramedic said something to Rita Mae. "Floyd says he's got extra blankets," Rita Mae wrote. "You can all stay here if you like. I'll be back with the medicine and food."

Floyd had laid a heavy blanket over Darla. As I turned to help get everyone else settled, I saw Darla staring at me from the exam table. Her eyes reflected the light, shining like distant campfires on an icy winter night. I stepped toward her. I wanted, needed, to talk to her about what had happened, to learn how she'd survived. But by the time I reached her side, she was asleep again. I pulled up a chair to sit in vigil over her—as if my will alone could keep her alive.

Chapter 84

Rita Mae returned in less than an hour, carrying a backpack stuffed with food and drugs. Floyd woke Darla up and gave her a glass of water, two Tylenol, and a Cipro tablet. I held her hand for no more than a minute before she fell back asleep.

Everyone else bedded down on the cots, close to the small fire. I dragged my blankets into Darla's room and wrapped them around myself, sitting on the chair by her bed. Soon I was asleep.

Darla haunted my dreams. She was naked and curled into a ball, alone in a vast white space. She curled up tighter and tighter, and her skin turned red and blistered, as if from sunburn. I screamed, "Darla!" but she couldn't hear me. I ran toward her, but she receded faster than I could run. Purple and green and yellow blotches crawled across her skin, and she hunkered down even further, into an impossibly small ball. Suddenly her skin was black and charring, and then there were flames. Darla was burning before my eyes. The flames jumped and lit Mom, who was somehow beside her, and they jumped again and burned Dad. Everything charred to ash.

Alyssa crawled toward me, blocking the cinders of my family from view. She was naked and above me, her breasts swaying pendulously, hypnotically. I was excited and ashamed. She called to me seductively, "Alex . . . ," and I lifted my head toward her.

I woke up. "Alex! Alex!" Alyssa was above me, fully clothed. And she was shaking my shoulder and yelling my name, although it was in no way seductive. And I could hear! Not well, maybe, but well enough to understand her.

"Yeah?" I mumbled.

"You said you wanted to leave in four hours," she said. "It's time."

"Thanks," I said. Alyssa left, and I stood, turning toward Darla. "You okay?" I asked as her eyes opened.

"Shoulder hurts," she said. "I'll live. How about you?"

"I'm okay. Now that I found you." Suddenly I recalled what finding her had cost. My dad slamming the shifter into reverse. I choked back a sob.

Darla reached out with her good hand, drawing me down into an embrace, and I bawled into the comforting semi-circle of her arm. "Shh," she said.

When my tears subsided, I whispered, "Things are never going to be the same again, are they?"

"What do you mean?"

"I thought that finding my parents would change things. Would . . . well, I knew things wouldn't go back to the way they were before the volcano, but I thought they'd get better."

"Get better how?"

"I guess I thought I wouldn't have to carry everything on my own shoulders, every decision. It's—I don't always know what's right. Sometimes I think it'd be nice to be a little kid again, to leave the weightiest decisions to my parents."

"Alex," Darla said, her face serious, "you haven't been a kid for a long time now."

"And now I never will be again."

"No."

I was afraid I'd start bawling again, so I changed the subject. "You, how did you—I was afraid they'd flense you or . . ."

"Danny didn't want to flense me. He thought I was cute." Darla's face twisted with disgust. "He was going to let me heal and then make me . . . take me to bed."

"Rape you." I held the rail of her cot in one hand, gripping it so hard I wondered if it might crumple in my fist.

"Yeah. But Alyssa went missing, and he had to send a girl to the Dirty White Boys as a replacement. I was handy."

I sat down, rested my head against her shoulder, and listened.

"The truck broke down on the way. Radiator problem. I told them how to fix it. So when I got to Iowa City, I wound up repairing stuff for them instead of filling a bed in their whorehouse, thank God."

"Yeah," I replied, as gently as I could manage. "You had a lockpick and a weapon—why were you still there?"

"Look at me. I'm weak. And sick. I wouldn't eat the meat the DWBs offered me, so I never got enough food to get stronger. And I never found the right moment to use my lockpick and shank until you showed up."

"The important thing is that you survived," I said. "Nothing else matters to me."

"Well it matters to me!" Darla snapped.

An overwhelming gratitude flooded me. I'd been insanely lucky to find her amid the chaos of Iowa. Words failed me, and I hugged her gently instead.

Then she pushed me back out to arm's length. "I've seen the way Alyssa looks at you."

"I rescued her and Ben. At first I thought she was you."

"There's more than gratitude in her eyes."

"Yeah. She tried to—"

"I knew it! I swear to God, I'll shank that bitch."

"Darla, no, it's okay. She found a way to protect herself and her brother when she was with the Peckerwoods, and she's still falling back on that—on using sex to survive."

"It's wrong."

"Give her a break. What's wrong is that she felt she had to—that she had no other options."

"I don't trust her."

"You don't have to trust her. You can trust me."

Darla stared into my eyes for a pregnant moment, then pulled me back into a hug.

"I saved this for you," I said, pulling away from her embrace. I extracted the broken chain from my pocket.

Darla's eyes shone as she fished the 15/16ths nut I'd given her out of her own pocket. "It was stuck in the layers of my shirts. I fiddled with it when things were bad. It helped."

I threaded the nut onto my broken chain and knotted it behind Darla's neck. "We should get moving."

Fifteen minutes later, we were rolling away from Worthington. Rita Mae had gotten everything I wanted, although she scolded me about not giving her enough time to negotiate properly. She'd also spent part of the night taping plastic over the broken windows of our truck. I hoped I'd see her again—she was one of the few people I trusted.

Mom offered to drive, which I took as a good sign that she might be emerging from her daze. But her hands trembled and her voice quavered, so I told her no. She didn't argue, which struck me as a strange role reversal.

The black night faded to gray and then to a suppurated yellow as we drove. With the increased visibility, I punched our speed up to about forty. The roads were too uneven and slick to go any faster.

The fuel gauge read three-quarters. I thought that would be enough to reach Warren. Maybe. If we didn't wreck or have to take a massive detour on the way.

Alyssa navigated. We avoided all the big towns and as many of the small burgs as we could. The few we did pass through were burned and abandoned.

When she wasn't busy plotting our route, Alyssa brushed Ben. He didn't seem to need it—given everything we'd been through, he was holding up remarkably well. Maybe she was brushing him to comfort herself.

I didn't want to cross the Mississippi on any bridge. I assumed they'd all be watched, either by Black Lake or one of the gangs. Nor did I want to get anywhere near Lock #12 and the barges of wheat Black Lake defended. Instead, we found a boat ramp between the lock and Sabula, Iowa, and used it to drive out onto the frozen expanse of the Mississippi.

On the far side of the river, I pulled the truck into a cove where we were sheltered by trees. We ate a breakfast of cold cornmeal mush, beef jerky, and dandelion leaves. I didn't leave the truck running, but the warmth from the heater lingered long enough to keep us fairly comfortable during breakfast.

As we ate, I sat sideways in my seat, watching Darla. Her face was more angular, her cheeks concave with hunger and illness. But she was here, beside me. The miracle of it left me breathless. I stretched out a hand to hold hers.

After breakfast I asked, "Can I check your fever?" I placed the back of my hand against Darla's forehead.

"I'm okay," she said. "I think the Tylenol is working."

I thought her forehead still felt hot, and she was slumped against the seat. "We should go."

I started the truck and pulled out of the cove. It took more than an hour to find a way off the ice of the Mississippi. We moved slowly in Illinois, picking our way through the back roads, trying to avoid both Galena, where there was a Black Lake camp, and Stockton, where all the roads were blocked by their crazy wall of cars. It took us almost two hours to travel the last thirty miles to Warren.

We approached my uncle's farm from the north—the same way Darla and I had arrived last year. I let my speed pick up a little in anticipation. Evidently there'd been a lot of traffic recently—when we left, there had been a few inches of unplowed snow on Canyon Park Road. Now it was packed solid.

I cruised up the last rise before the farm. But when I saw it, I slammed on the brakes, fishtailing to a shivering stop. The farm was gone. In its place there was an enormous, ramshackle tent city, swarming with people.

Chapter 85

I slammed the shifter into reverse and backed down the hill, out of sight from the farm.

"What are you doing?" Mom yelled.

"Getting out of here!" I cranked the wheel over so fast the truck slid into a 180.

"That's your uncle's farm! Rebecca's down there."

"We don't know who all those people are." I shifted into drive and accelerated down the road, away from the farm. "What if they're another flenser gang?"

"Then we need to get in there right now!" Mom screeched. "To check on Rebecca."

"We'll figure out what's going on. And find Rebecca. But I'm not going to rush in there and risk getting us killed."

"You have another route in mind, Lieutenant?" Ben asked.

"Park in Apple River Canyon and come in on foot through the forest. Scout it and see what's going on," I said. "What do you think?"

"That is a sound plan."

Fifteen minutes later, we were inside Apple River Canyon State Park, which backed directly against Uncle Paul's farm. I pulled the truck to the side of the road. "I'll hike to the back side of the farm, see what's going on, and come right back. Two hours, tops."

"I'm going with you," Darla said. She struggled to lift herself out of the seat.

"No. You need to rest."

"Somebody needs to go with you. What if you run into trouble?"

"I'm going," Mom said.

I leaned over to kiss Darla, and Alyssa suddenly became fascinated with something in the back-seat foot-well. I opened my door, and Mom and I left. Slogging through the deep snow was hard work. I broke the trail, working my way through the leafless forest to approach the farm from the west. Before we were close enough to see anything, I heard the rhythmic thwacks of several axes in use. We slowed our pace, moving from tree to tree until we were close enough to see.

A party of about a dozen men and women were felling and stripping trees. Most of them had rifles slung across their backs. Five logs were laid out in the snow already. "Isn't that Stu, from Warren?" I whispered to Mom.

"I don't recognize him," she whispered back.

Just then, one of the men lowered his ax and turned our way.

"Paul!" Mom yelled. She started pushing through the snow toward him.

Still, I hesitated a second, trying to make sure.

"Janice!" Uncle Paul dropped his axe and rushed toward us. The rest of the woodcutting party put aside their axes and unslung their rifles, eyeing me and Mom warily.

Mom embraced Uncle Paul, and for a while there were just joyful tears of reunion. "You found them!" Uncle Paul said to me at last. "And my brother? Did he . . ."

"Dad," I said. "He . . . he didn't make it."

Uncle Paul's face passed through two quick transformations. His Adam's apple bobbed twice, and his face broke and sagged. Then he bit his lower lip, and his face reformed as if he were delaying his grief through pure force of will. He turned to the rest of the group of woodcutters and shouted, "It's okay! My nephew and sister-in-law are home." They slung their guns and picked up their axes again.

"You have any food?" Uncle Paul asked.

"Yeah," I said. "Enough for the five of us for a week or so."

"Five of you?"

"Darla and two people I met on the road. Alyssa and Ben. I promised they could stay with us."

"Huh. Might not want to. Never mind. Keep the food a secret."

"Okay. That reminds me . . ." I reached into my jacket pocket and pulled out my last, carefully hoarded bag and passed it to Uncle Paul. "Wheat."

Uncle Paul stowed the bag under his coat, shaking his head in admiration. "Bag could save all our lives."

"Our truck's in the park. I've got to get back—take Darla to Dr. McCarthy in Warren. She's hurt."

"Warren?" Uncle Paul said. "Dr. McCarthy is here. All of Warren is. Everybody who's left, anyway."

"What?"

"Slimeballs running Stockton attacked Warren a few days after you left. Took it over. Threw everybody out of town. That's why they're all here."

"Why?"

"Out of food. Wanted Warren's store of pork and kale, I guess."

"Bastards!" I said. "Like we don't have enough to deal with?"

Uncle Paul nodded grimly. "I'll take your mother up to the house and let everyone know you're coming."

I hugged him and turned away, trudging back through the dead forest.

I returned to the truck, filled everyone else in, and drove back to the front side of the farm on Canyon Park Road.

When I got closer to it, I could see that tent city was too generous a description of the chaotic settlement that had engulfed Uncle Paul's farm. Sure, there were tents. There were also crude wooden shacks, igloos, lean-tos crafted from tree branches, and structures that appeared to be made of plastic scraps and twigs. People were moving everywhere, and hundreds of small fires burned within the camp.

Thirty or forty people were working to build something new. They'd erected a wall—about a dozen stout logs lashed together with their bases buried and tops sharpened. If they planned to encircle the whole camp, they had a lot of work ahead of them.

We couldn't get very close to the house—all the makeshift shelters blocked the driveway. I parked at the edge of the road and grabbed the backpack with the food, slinging it over my shoulder. I carried one of the assault rifles and handed the other one to Darla.

As we set out for the house, Darla stumbled. She handed her rifle to Alyssa.

"I don't know how to use one of these," Alyssa protested.

"Just carry it!" Darla snapped. "And fake it."

Instead Alyssa handed the assault rifle to Ben and helped Darla thread her way through the camp, supporting her with a hand under her shoulder.

The house still stank of goat, which surprised me. Surely if there wasn't enough food, they would have slaughtered all the goats. But then I heard a bleat from the direction of the guest room and realized that Uncle Paul was protecting a few. Maybe he was planning to breed them. There was also an unclean stink, like rotting flesh and feces. When I stepped through the small entryway to the living room, I saw why.

All the living room furniture was gone, replaced with a dozen crude pallets packed into the limited floor space. A fire roared in the hearth. The room was crowded with the sick and the dying. Some had bloodstained bandages on their torsos. One was missing most of his arm. Others just looked sweaty and feverish. It was horrible—I couldn't bring Darla in here.

Dr. McCarthy and Belinda were both there, working together to roll a patient over.

"Dr. McCarthy," I said.

"Good to see you, Alex! Give me a sec." Dr. McCarthy finished rolling the patient, and Belinda started cleaning his backside with a sponge.

Dr. McCarthy stood. "You look like hell."

"I'm okay. Darla's sick," I said.

"What's wrong?"

"Bullet wound in my shoulder," Darla said. "It's infected."

"Come into the kitchen," Dr. McCarthy replied.

The kitchen table had been draped with a sheet and pressed into service as an exam table. Alyssa tried to help Darla onto the table, but Darla pushed her hand away and levered herself up. Alyssa shrugged it off.

"All the rest of you, clear out," Dr. McCarthy said.

Darla seized my hand, holding me there as Alyssa and Ben left. "He stays," she said.

Dr. McCarthy shrugged. "You can help hold her. I've got to clean and debride that wound and check to see if the bullet is still in there. You remember what that's like."

I nodded, my thoughts as grim as the look on Darla's face. Dr. McCarthy passed Darla the familiar leather-wrapped stick.

When he started working on Darla's shoulder, her face turned vivid red, and she started sweating despite the cold air. She gripped my hand so hard I could feel my bones grinding together. When he started cutting away the dead flesh around her wound, she screamed around the stick and tried to launch herself off the table. I fell across her, pinning her arms down.

Finally, mercifully, Darla passed out. I collapsed into a chair as Dr. McCarthy finished treating her shoulder. He didn't sew up the wound—just painted it with antiseptic and affixed a bandage over it. I was relieved not to have to help: My head swam in a way that suggested I might be following Darla to la-la land shortly. I stumbled to my feet and stepped out the back door in search of fresh air.

Chapter 86

Dr. McCarthy followed me outside. "You okay?"

I was kneeling in the snow, head in my hands. "I should never have stood up on that overpass. Should never have gone looking for my parents. None of this would have happened if we'd just stayed put."

He placed his hand on my shoulder. "Terrible things happen to good people, Alex. They did before Yellowstone blew, and it's even more true now. Hiding out on the farm wouldn't have protected you or Darla from that."

I shook my head, and Dr. McCarthy extended a hand to help me up.

"You going to the meeting?"

"Meeting?"

"Mayor's addressing all the able-bodied adults in camp tonight."

"Guess I'm going, then."

"You should."

When Darla woke up, Alyssa and I helped her upstairs and got her settled in one of the bedrooms. It was bitterly cold up there, but at least Darla wouldn't have to sleep with the crowded stench in the living room. As we came out, Mom and Uncle Paul came up the stairs with Rebecca, cousin Max, and cousin Anna in tow.

We had a little party of hugs and smiles right there in the hallway. For a moment, I was able to forget the horrors of Iowa. The moment passed quickly. They looked tired and wan. After the joy of our reunion had passed, I saw something else in their faces. Fear.

"Rebecca. I'm sorry," I whispered, "about Dad."

She scowled at me for a moment before her face melted, and she started sobbing. I pulled her into a hug.

I started trying to explain. "I, he—"

"I know," she choked out the words between her sobs. "Mom told me. How he saved your lives."

We held each other like that for a bit, while everyone else shuffled uncomfortably around us. Eventually I tried changing the subject. "You going to the meeting tonight?"

"No." She broke the hug, folded her arms, and scowled. "They say I'm not an adult."

"That's crazy! At fourteen you're old enough to walk

and chew bubble gum at the same time—of course you're an adult!"

Rebecca punched my arm, hard enough to hurt. She'd gotten a *lot* stronger.

"Seriously, would you do me a huge favor? Keep an eye on Darla while I'm gone at the meeting—"

"You get to go? That's so not fair."

"I know. Look, Darla's sick. Just make sure she stays in bed and rests and get her water and food if she'll eat."

"There *isn't* any food, Alex."

How could I explain to my little sister that I'd brought food and fully intended to make sure Darla ate even if everyone else in the camp starved? "Never mind the food."

"What's wrong with her?"

"She got shot. The wound is infected."

"Got plenty of that around here. Yeah, I'll watch her."

"Thanks. Love you, sis." I kissed her on the forehead and left.

Uncle Paul, Aunt Caroline, Mom, Alyssa, Ben, and I went to the meeting together. A huge bonfire had been lit between the edge of the camp and the woods. Everyone crowded in close enough to absorb the heat radiating from the fire.

The mayor of Warren, Bob Petty, stepped even closer, so that the fire illuminated his face as he spoke. Soon he was sweating, and the orange light glinting from his wet face gave him a demonic look.

His speech was long and convoluted, but basically it boiled down to this: Since Stockton invaded Warren, the

mayor had assigned scouts to keep watch and look for an
opportunity to fight back. Stockton had only moved a
small amount of pork and kale out of Warren in the week
they'd held it. But earlier today, eleven trucks had pulled
into Warren. They were being loaded with pork, kale, and
cornmeal, the food the people of Warren needed to survive. The mayor had decided that instead of waiting to
starve on the farm, every able-bodied person with a weapon would try to retake Warren. He ended his speech with
a bunch of meaningless rah-rah stuff and instructions to
be ready at dawn.

When the applause and scattered cheers died down,
Ben spoke into the silence. "That is a stupid plan," he said
in a loud voice. A few people booed, but Ben went on, "It
does not make sense to attack where the enemy is expecting it or when he expects it. A better alternative—"

Ben kept talking, but the mayor shouted over him.
"You're not from Warren, son, and I don't recall asking for
your opinion. It's decided."

The crowd broke out into a babble of conversation. I
sucked in a deep breath and bellowed, "He's right! It's like
sparring. You never strike where your opponent expects
you to."

The mayor glared at me. "And what would you sug-
gest?" His voice practically dripped with derision.

"Attack Stockton," I said. "All their fighters will be in
Warren. They won't be expecting it."

"Our food is in Warren, not Stockton!" someone yelled.

"Their homes, wives, and children are in Stockton," I
replied. "Once we control it, we can negotiate."

"We're not going to negotiate with the aggressors," the mayor yelled. "Tomorrow we're going to Warren to get our food back! This meeting is adjourned. Get a good night's sleep—we leave at dawn."

Dispirited, I turned away from the fire. We trudged back to the house in silence, except for Ben, who talked nonstop about famous military attacks that had failed because they were too predictable. Uncle Paul got an oil lamp off a hook in the entryway and lit it using a stick from the hearth in the living-room-cum-hospital.

Upstairs I paused at the door to the girls' room. I wanted to talk to Darla but didn't want to wake her. I heard voices through the door and knocked. "Come in," Rebecca called.

It was pitch black inside. The light from Uncle Paul's lamp receded down the hall. "You guys make a place for Alyssa to sleep?" I asked.

"Yeah," Rebecca said. "Let me get some light." I heard a thump, thump and then Rebecca pushed past me carrying a tiny oil lamp, like they used to put on tables at fancy restaurants. She lit it from Uncle Paul's lamp and returned to the bedroom. Since when had she gotten so efficient? Amazing what a volcanic eruption can do to change a pesky little sister into an ally.

There were two beds in the small bedroom and two places to sleep on the floor, made up with extra blankets and pillows. Darla was snuggled into the far bed. Her face looked wan but more peaceful than I'd seen it since we'd rescued her.

"You okay?" I asked her.

She shrugged at me and told Rebecca and Anna, "I want to talk to Alex for a minute. Alone, okay?"

"Sure," Rebecca said. "Yell when you're done." Anna got out of her bed. She was fully clothed—they all were. It was freezing in that room. They went into the hall, and I closed the door and sat beside Darla's bed.

"You seem better," I said.

"Maybe a little."

"That's good."

We lapsed into silence for a moment.

"Can I get you anything?" I asked.

She reached out and grabbed my hand. "Dr. McCarthy says you might blame yourself for what happened to me."

"I should never have stood up on that overpass. Never have dragged you back to Iowa with me."

"You didn't drag anyone. I insisted on going."

"But I—"

"But nothing, Alex. Maybe standing up on that overpass was a mistake. Maybe not. But you came for me. You found me and saved me." She crushed my hand in hers.

"I always will," I whispered.

"I know."

"Tomorrow I'm going to help with the attack on Warren. It's a stupid attack, at least that's what Ben thinks, and he's probably the smartest guy here. But whatever happens, I'm going to find a way to survive and come back to you. Because I love you. And I always will."

"I . . . " Darla's eyes brimmed with tears, "I love you, too, Alex."

Her words fell on me like rain in a desert, bringing the promise of a glorious field of new blossoms. "We'll make a place for ourselves in this shitty world somehow. We'll find a way to make the life we want, to get married and have a family. I swear we will."

Darla reached out, pulling me down onto the bed alongside her. My father was dead, my mother crushed with grief. I couldn't surrender my burdens—the life-and-death decisions we had to make on an almost daily basis in this new world. But together, Darla and I would carry them.

As we embraced, my spirit soared. I was seized by a fierce joy. I would survive. I would survive and do battle at Darla's side. We would fight together to make a place in this disaster-hewn world—a place where we could live in peace.

Or die trying.

Author's Note

The severity of the volcanic winter that would follow a supervolcano eruption is the subject of considerable debate in the scientific community. The most commonly held view is that a volcanic winter would lower the average global temperature by 5 – 9° F for a period of 6 to 10 years. Other scientists believe the temperature change would be much less drastic, on the order of 2° F. Yet another hypothesis, the controversial Toba Catastrophe Theory, holds that a such an eruption could trigger a volcanic winter so severe that it would lead to an ice age. As a novelist, I've chosen to depict the most severe—and dramatic—possibility.

Acknowledgments

The process of creating *Ashen Winter* led me to a host of subjects that I knew nothing about. I'm indebted to the following people for their technical help. Any errors that remain are probably the result of my bullheaded refusal to take their good advice:

- Carol Oates, Linda Poitevin, Nick Liwosz, Jill Robinson, and Zack Robinson for patiently answering my questions about autism and for suggesting numerous changes to *Ashen Winter*—I couldn't have brought Ben to life without you.
- Joseph E. Boling for training with his extensive collection of pistols and shotguns.

- Terry Farley for teaching me the rudiments of operating an M4 carbine, Uzi submachine gun, and Remington 300 sniper rifle.
- Fred Ropkey of the Ropkey Armor Museum for allowing me to crawl all over and under his beautifully restored M35A2 and for loaning me its operation and repair manuals.
- Helen-Louise Boling and Josh Mugele for their help on medical questions.
- Ray Liwosz for his pharmaceutical expertise.
- Ken Bandy for training on shortwave radio operation and his wife Carol for putting up with me while I kept asking "just one more question" an hour after dinner was on the table.
- Aubrey Wesson for advice on the properties of propane, natural gas, and BLEVE explosions.

Thanks to my critique group, the YA Cannibals (Shannon Alexander, Lisa Fipps, Robert Kent, Jody Sparks, and Virginia Vought), for making *Ashen Winter* take months longer to write than I anticipated. The extra time was worth it.

Thanks to Karen Brissette and Kathrina Senft for their cheerleading of *Ashfall* and helpful comments on the *Ashen Winter* manuscript.

Thanks to everyone associated with Tanglewood Press and Publisher's Group West for making my first publishing experience a wonderful one. I particularly appreciate Rebecca Grose for her superbly well-organized book tours and Erin Blacketer for making my life easier.

Above all, thank you to Peggy Tierney. She never loses sight of why we do this—for our readers.

On that note, thanks to all my readers. Your enthusiasm buoys me when I begin to sink into the dark water of self-doubt.

Thank you to all the booksellers, librarians, and teachers who've helped *Ashfall* connect with its readership. I dedicated *Ashen Winter* to my mother partly in your honor: she was a teacher before I was born, a librarian while I grew up, and is now a bookseller.

Thank you to the people of Iowa and Northwest Illinois who have been so welcoming during my three research trips to the area. I'll be back soon.

And most of all, as always, thank you Margaret: my wife, first reader, best friend, and true love.

A
b
o
u
t

t
h
e

A
u
t
h
o
r

Photo by Larry Endircott

Mike Mullin's first job was scraping the gum off the undersides of desks at his high school. From there, things went steadily downhill. He almost got fired by the owner of a bookstore due to his poor taste in earrings. He worked at a place that showed slides of poopy diapers during lunch (it did cut down on the cafeteria budget). The hazing process at the next company included eating live termites raised by the resident entomologist, so that didn't last long either. For a while Mike juggled bottles at a wine shop, sometimes to disastrous effect. Oh, and then there was the job where swarms of wasps occasionally tried to chase him off ladders. So he's really glad this writing thing seems to be working out.

Mike holds a black belt in Songahm Taekwondo. He lives in Indianapolis with his wife and her three cats. *Ashen Winter* is his second novel. His debut, *Ashfall*, was named one of the top five young adult novels of 2011 by National Public Radio, a Best Teen Book of 2011 by Kirkus Reviews, and a New Voices selection by the American Booksellers Association.

Connect with Mike at www.mikemullinauthor.com.